MOTOR CITY SHAKEDOWN

Also by D. E. Johnson

The Detroit Electric Scheme

MOTOR CITY SHAKEDOWN

D. E. Johnson

Minotaur Books ✖ New York

MOTOR CITY SHAKEDOWN. Copyright © 2011 by D. E. Johnson. All rights reserved. Printed in the United States of America. For information, address St. Martin's Press, 175 Fifth Avenue, New York, N.Y. 10010.

www.minotaurbooks.com

Library of Congress Cataloging-in-Publication Data

Johnson, D. E. (Dan E.)
    Motor City shakedown / D. E. Johnson.—1st ed.
        p. cm.
    ISBN 978-0-312-64457-4 (hardback)
    1. Murder—Investigation—Fiction.   2. Automobile industry and trade—Fiction.   3. Organized crime—Fiction.   4. Detroit (Mich.)—Fiction.   I. Title.
    PS3610.O328M68 2011
    813'.6—dc22
                                                                            2011018770

First Edition: September 2011

10 9 8 7 6 5 4 3 2 1

For Mom and Dad

MOTOR CITY SHAKEDOWN

CHAPTER ONE

Sunday, August 6, 1911

My left index finger traced the shape of the little morphine bottle through the outside of my trouser pocket. Nearly two hours had passed since my last dose. Even though the pain in my right hand was tolerable and my mind was still enveloped in the delicious fuzziness of the opiate, I'd been fighting with myself for the last fifteen minutes—one more taste before Moretti showed? I might not get another chance for a while. But I couldn't take too much. I had to be sharp.

Movement on the sidewalk down the block caught my attention, and my hand went to the .32 tucked into my belt. I pressed farther back into the shadows of the alley, squinting at the couple who had just turned the corner. The few streetlamps that worked were dim and widely spaced, doing little to add to the meager glow spilling from the windows of the crumbling redbrick buildings.

They strolled underneath the cone of light from a streetlamp. Both were men, one of average height, the other six inches shorter, perhaps a little over five feet tall—about Moretti's height. I studied them. Both wore white shirts, dark trousers with suspenders, and black derbies, but no—Moretti was stocky, built like a fireplug. The smaller man was wiry and moved more gracefully than Vito Adamo's muscular driver. I relaxed as they walked into Moretti's building.

I couldn't get worked up over every man who passed by. This was a busy area—a run-down, though typical, slice of Detroit's Little Italy.

I was plenty familiar with the scenery here, after investigating Vito Adamo's Black Hand gang for the last few months. Even though Adamo hadn't been directly responsible for the death of my friend, Wesley McRae, he had helped. That was enough. I pulled out my watch and angled it toward a streetlamp—twelve thirty. Moretti should be here.

Every night I'd watched, he had gotten home between 12:15 and 12:30, always with a different woman—prostitutes, I assumed. The women left within thirty minutes, and Moretti exited the building at 1:45 sharp to go back to Adamo's saloon, the Bucket. This was the third straight night I had planned to jump him. On both previous occasions I'd chickened out. But not tonight. Tonight Carlo Moretti and I would talk.

I pulled off my derby and the handkerchief I'd tied around my head and I wiped the sweat from my face. Past midnight and still somewhere near ninety degrees. For the tenth time tonight, I slipped the handkerchief back over my head and spun it around to cover my face below my eyes—to be sure it would stay in place. If Moretti recognized me, I'd have to kill him. I didn't want to do that. After shifting the mask around to the back again, I returned my derby to my head and settled in to wait. I needed a cigarette but restrained myself—it would give away my position.

Another couple turned the corner and ambled up the street. It was him. Carlo Moretti sauntered down the sidewalk with a slender woman on his arm. He wore a dark suit and a straw boater, she a green satin evening dress with a matching wide-brimmed hat. Moretti stood half a head shorter than she, but I wouldn't let his diminutive stature fool me. He was one of Vito Adamo's most accomplished killers.

They entered his building, and I glanced at my watch: 12:40. She'd be here until 1:10. I wanted to burst in the room while they were in *fla-grante delicto*, while Moretti's hands were occupied. But I didn't want any witnesses. I'd been waiting a long time. A few more minutes wouldn't matter.

My right hand throbbed, and I brought it up near my face. In the darkness of the alley, my black glove was nearly invisible, but I could see the silhouettes of my fingers contracted over my palm. I tried straightening them. They moved perhaps an inch, and a searing wave burned its way up my arm.

I grimaced and pulled the little bottle of morphine from my pocket. A taste—just a taste—would be enough to keep me from thinking too much about the pain. Trapping the bottle against my chest with my right arm, I twisted off the cap with my left, raised the bottle to my mouth, and tipped it back for a second, just long enough to taste the bitter brown fluid. The numbing warmth began to trickle down my throat. This was the time to which I so looked forward. I took a deep breath, and another, and then leaned against the wall to enjoy the peace that was beginning to cradle my mind.

The front door of the building opened, and the prostitute burst out, hat in hand. She hurried away, shoes clacking against the sidewalk, her stride somewhere between a walk and a run. When she passed under the streetlamp, she glanced behind her, as if to see if someone followed. I saw hints of red in her dark hair.

Odd. She'd been inside for perhaps ten minutes. But Moretti was a son of a bitch. Who knew what he did to these women?

I pulled the Colt pistol from my belt and checked the load—seven bullets I hoped I wouldn't need tonight. I cocked it, flicked on the safety, and stuffed it back into my belt. At one thirty I crossed the street and entered the dark stairwell. The mews of kittens came from a crate in the corner. Trickles of light filtered in from the hallway, illuminating the steps to vague dark shapes. The stair rail was sticky, the air wet, smelling of mold and sewage. Muffled voices rose and fell as I crept up to the second-floor landing. I leaned out over the rail and looked above me. No one stood guard. Moretti didn't rate his boss's protection.

Something touched my ankle. I jerked the gun from my belt before I saw it was only a cat. Breathing a sigh of relief, I shooed it away and continued up the stairs. When I reached the top, I peered out at the hallway, lit to dusk by sputtering gas lamps. A dozen doors stood at fifteen-foot intervals, all but the third one on the right blanketed with Italian graffiti, as were the walls between. I kept my eye on the clean door. In roughly ten minutes that door would open, and a well-armed Moretti would head for the stairs, on his way back to the Bucket.

But tonight he wasn't going to make it to the Bucket.

From below, a man and woman started up the stairs, their slurred words and drunken laughter filtering up the stairwell ahead of them.

Though they didn't sound like they'd be a threat, I had nowhere to hide, and certainly no explanation for lurking on the steps. Hoping they'd stop on the second floor, I sprawled out on the stairs and feigned sleep. In this building, drunks sleeping one off in the stairwell couldn't be that unusual.

They continued up from the second floor, pausing when they stepped onto the landing below me. After only a brief hesitation, they climbed the stairs, laughing still, more intent on their own plans than on me. They skirted me and turned down the hallway, a door opened and closed, and their voices blended into the quiet murmur of the building's other residents.

I spun the handkerchief around so it covered my face and stood, flattened against the wall, looking around the corner at Moretti's door. The building creaked and groaned around me. Any minute now.

I waited. The door didn't open. I pulled my watch from my waistcoat. Six minutes of two. He was already nine minutes late. I put my watch away. Footsteps clattered up the stairwell from the first floor.

Where was he? Had he left and I'd somehow missed him? Perhaps he'd gone out the back door tonight. Perhaps he'd spotted me. The footsteps headed off down the second-floor hallway, and it was quiet again.

I couldn't wait all night. I had to do something before I lost my nerve. Pulling my .32, I crept down the hall to Moretti's door. Light leaked out through the crack underneath. I put my ear against the flaking paint on the door and listened. The apartment was silent. I slipped the gun into my belt and tried the knob. It turned. I pushed against the door, just the slightest pressure. It began to open. Once the latch cleared the doorjamb, I pulled out the pistol again and used my worthless right hand to open the door. It swung inward, creaking, and I tensed, preparing for Moretti's attack.

But the apartment was still—no sound, no movement other than the curtains of the only window riffling in the hot wind. I stepped inside and pushed the door shut behind me, eyes scanning the room. The apartment was about fifteen feet square with little more than the bare essentials— a box stove, two chairs and a rickety table with a straw boater atop it, a bureau holding a dozen liquor bottles, and a single bed near the wall on the right, covered by a threadbare blue blanket.

I tiptoed to the window and slipped my head outside. A fire escape snaked up the building only a foot away. I cursed. He must have seen me and left through the window.

I turned to leave and saw a spray of red on the dingy ivory wall at the side of the bed. I took a step toward it, and another. Near the wall, the blanket was spattered with dark stains. Now I saw a form—a naked man lying facedown, jammed between the bed and the wall. I pulled the handkerchief down around my neck and leaned in.

It looked like Moretti. I reached over the bed, took hold of his pomaded hair, and pulled up. His body didn't move, but his head fell back in my hand. His throat was a yawning wound, puckered tubes and bloody tissue. I stared in horror. Moretti's dark eyes were half open, dull. His tongue looked out of place, a sea slug—blue, slimy, hanging out of his gaping mouth. The floor beneath him was covered by a dark pool. I let go of the greasy hair, and his head dropped like a lead weight, thumping against the floor.

My gut churned. Trying not to vomit, I took a step back. The bitter taste of the morphine syrup gave me my first realization I'd even taken the bottle from my pocket.

I had to get out of here. Now. But not like before. Not like an idiot. I needed to be sure I left no clues.

I thought I had touched the window frame, so I used my glove to wipe it down, and did the same with the doorknob on the inside. After a quick look around, I peeked out into the hall. No one was in sight. I slipped out and ran my gloved hand over the knob on the outside. The morphine was keeping the burn to a tolerable level.

A door creaked. A young woman in a faded blue nightgown, her dark curls bound up in a white kerchief, leaned out the next door, a saucer of milk in her hand. Our eyes met before I was able to turn away, waiting for her door to close again. The only exit was the stairway, and I had to pass her to get there.

She asked me something in Italian. Her voice was soft.

I shrugged and said, "No," trying to disguise my voice.

She said something else.

Son of a bitch. Still keeping my face angled away from her, I shook my head.

She asked me something again, her voice more insistent now.

She hadn't seen my face for long. Hoping she hadn't seen it well, I pulled the handkerchief up over my face and bolted past her, down the hall to the stairway.

A few hours later, I lay awake in a small stand of maple trees along the edge of one of Belle Isle's grassy fields, smoking a cigarette and staring up at the stars through silhouettes of leaves. I'd found myself wandering in this direction when I stopped running, but I wasn't sure why. The cooler air off the river provided some relief from the heat, but I thought it more likely I had come here because it was a comforting place for me, filled with warm memories of time spent with Elizabeth. We'd stood on the bridge for hours talking about our future, had walked the paths, boated in the pond, watched the buffalo graze peacefully in their pasture. Nothing bad had happened to me here, something that was getting difficult to say about most parts of Detroit.

Thousands of sleeping people dotted the small island, driven out of their homes in the city by the relentless heat. With my sleeve I wiped a warm film of sweat from my face. Four in the morning in the middle of the river, and I was still sweating. A streetcar rattled past over on Jefferson Avenue. The rhythmic drone of cicadas pulsed around me, rising and falling. A chorus of frogs sang across the island—delicate chirrups and clicks from tree frogs, the rumbling croaks and snores of their larger cousins. But they didn't lull me to sleep as they might have done on a normal night, even though I had finished off the last of the morphine.

Could the prostitute have killed Moretti? The wound was so deep, the cut so sure, it was hard to imagine his death being at the hand of a woman. I struggled to recall her appearance. Tall—or at least in comparison to Moretti—slender, a reddish tint to her hair. My impression of her clothing, green satin dress and matching hat, was of expensive fabric and a fashionable cut. She didn't necessarily have to be the killer. She could have merely let him in from the fire escape or distracted Moretti while the killer entered the apartment.

If the police came after me, I was sunk. I would have to find the prostitute, get the truth out of her before they caught up to me. The one thing

I didn't doubt is that they *would* come after me—if not now, then soon. The police knew I hated Vito Adamo. The woman in the apartment next to Moretti's had seen my face. The hallway was dim, and she saw me only for a second, but we had locked eyes. Though it had been at least six months since I was last featured in the local papers, my face was one familiar to many Detroiters. Still, at the rate new immigrants were arriving, it was anyone's guess whether she recognized me. That she lived in Moretti's building was in my favor. She had probably been brought into the country illegally by Vito Adamo, and would therefore be unlikely to involve herself in a police matter.

It also occurred to me that my appearance had changed drastically since my picture was in the papers. I'd lost twenty pounds from my already-thin five-foot-ten-inch frame, and my face was drawn, with hollow cheeks and sunken eyes. I couldn't remember the last time I'd gotten a haircut. I kept my shaggy brown mop at bay with a handful of pomade every morning, but my hair hung over my ears and down my collar. Perhaps if I got it cut, it might help keep the woman from identifying me.

As I thought, I massaged my dead right hand with my left, an unconscious habit I'd picked up shortly after I left the hospital. I wasn't sure if it was just a nervous tic or if, somewhere deep down, I thought if I massaged it enough, the pain would stop. I watched the fingers spread apart and then close halfway into a fist. A new wave of pain shot like lightning up my arm.

Shit. I shook my head. I'd planned it all out. I would surprise Moretti and get him back in his apartment. He would tell me where I could find Vito Adamo, Big Boy, and Sapphira Xanakis—the people who helped John Cooper murder Wesley McRae. They had all disappeared without a trace. I would hunt them down and kill them, or at least bring them to justice.

Seven months had passed since Wesley was murdered, and I'd gotten nowhere. Seven months of stumbling around, trying to put my life back together—all the while trying to find Vito Adamo and his accomplices. And now my only lead had been murdered, and I was certain to be a suspect.

I looked up at the sky and mouthed, *I'm sorry, Wes.* He was the best friend I could have ever had, repeatedly risking his life and finally giving it—for me, a man who had disdained him for his homosexuality. I shook my head. I never deserved a friend like Wes, and now I despaired that I would ever be able to pay back even a fraction of what he had given me.

The stars were beginning to fade, the black sky graying as dawn approached. I needed to be home before sunrise. I stood, brushed myself off, and headed back across the bridge to the city. Half an hour later I crept up the fire escape at the back of my apartment building in my stockings, just as I had exited the previous evening. I'd had my new neighbors, Mr. and Mrs. Preston, over for dinner. When they were leaving, I'd made a big show of going to bed early. I had thought I was being clever to set up an alibi I'd never need.

Now I hoped it held.

CHAPTER TWO

The newsboy on the corner bawled out the day's headline: "Six dead from heat—Factories close!"

Ninety-five yesterday and the day before, after the hottest July ever. Yet I, and every other man standing on the corner waiting for a street-car, wore a dark wool suit. Most wore black or gray derbies, while a few older men stood out with fedoras or porkpies, and the less serious among us wore straw boaters. I'd gone with a summer-weight gray sack suit, *sans* waistcoat, with a matching derby and a white shirt that would partially hide being sweat-soaked before I even reached the office. The heat was less bothersome to me than to many, given the capful of morphine I'd swallowed.

I'd decided to go to work this morning as I would on any normal Monday and get a haircut at lunch. Today was not the day to break my routine, to do anything that might be suspicious. I'd wait until tonight to begin my search for the prostitute. Somehow I doubted she was an early riser anyway.

I squeezed myself onto a trolley, every surface sticky from the humidity, and headed for Clay Street and what was now called the Anderson Electric Car Company. Carriage sales were decreasing, and it had been time for a change. The "Anderson Carriage Company" sounded like it belonged in the last century.

When I arrived at work I saw that my father had closed down the foundry operations for the day, though the rest of the men were heading for their positions as usual. I climbed the stairs of the main building to the third floor and the engineering department, my current stay on the whirlwind tour of learning the business—and truthfully, the only one to which I had any claim of belonging, with my degree from the University of Michigan.

Before I stepped into the office, I blew my nose so as to keep my sniffling to a minimum. When necessary, I'd been telling people I had a cold, and I was trying to keep the side effects from my medication as low key as possible.

When I opened the door, I stopped in my tracks. Sitting in my chair, feet up on the desk, was Patrolman Dennis Murphy, looking miserable. His face was red, his bottlebrush mustache beaded with sweat. Dark rings stained his uniform under the arms. His neck and chins bulged over his collar like he was an overstuffed muffin.

"About time, Anderson." Murphy swung his legs off my desk and raised his bulk from my chair.

"Murphy. What do you need?" I hoped he was here with information for me, but somehow I doubted it.

"Not happy to see me, boyo?"

I glanced around the office, where six men were studiously ignoring us, every one with an ear straining in our direction. I nodded toward the door and walked out. His black boots slapped against the tile floor. I closed the office door behind him and then leaned in close. I'd bluff it out. "Did you find any of them?"

"Nah." He shook his head. "I wouldn't come all the way down here for that, not even for your dough. You come to me, remember?"

"Yeah. Then what?" I met Murphy's beady blue eyes.

"Riordan wants to see ya."

My guts clenched. "What about?"

"I expect he'll tell ya that himself."

Detective Riordan leaned against the grungy plaster wall of one of the Bethune Street station's interrogation rooms, his ice blue eyes nearly invisible in the shadow of his fedora. He wore a heavy gray wool suit even though it was ninety and humid. And he wasn't sweating. "So, Will, what have you been up to lately?"

I stood across from him. Sitting somehow felt like capitulation. "Still recuperating," I said. Rather than illustrate the point, I kept my right hand behind my back. The ragged purple scar angling from the left side of Riordan's mouth to his ear looked fuzzy, smeared. This bottle seemed a bit more potent than usual. I was going to have to think through my answers.

He pulled a cigar from his waistcoat and patted himself down before glancing back at me. "Lighter? Must a left my matches in the office."

I pulled my lighter from my coat pocket and handed it to him. He looked at it. "Nice. Gold?"

I nodded. He lit the cigar, puffing away until the tip glowed orange. Finally he lowered the cigar and held the lighter out to me. "How's the hand?"

I took the lighter and tucked it into my pocket. "The same."

"Hmm." He cocked his head at me. "Why only one glove? Two wouldn't be so noticeable."

"Try putting on a glove when your other hand can't grip anything, Detective."

He nodded again and looked at me a moment longer. "How are you doing with the left?"

"So-so." I rocked my hand in front of me. "My writing looks like an imbecilic five-year-old's. But I can at least make myself understood."

"How about shooting? Knife work?" He took another casual puff from the cigar.

Ah. So here's where we're going. I folded my arms over my chest, right arm underneath, careful to keep pressure off my hand. "Don't have the time. Or the inclination."

"You're right-handed, aren't you?"

"Was."

"So you can't do anything the way you used to."

I shrugged.

"That still has to make you angry. If it weren't for Adamo and his men helping Cooper, you wouldn't be crippled."

"I'm trying to get on with my life, Detective. I don't have time for grudges, if that's what you were alluding to."

He drew in deeply on his cigar, tobacco seeds snapping, then pursed his lips and breathed the smoke out to the side. It was a delicate action that seemed almost sexual. "Where were you last night?"

"Why?" I tried to sound casual.

Riordan's mouth tightened. "Humor me."

"I spent the evening with my neighbors."

He tilted his head back and looked at me through slits. "Are you sure about that?"

"Of course I am."

Riordan stared into my eyes while taking a pull on the cigar. When he spoke, the smoke spilled out with his words. "Can they vouch for your whereabouts?"

"I'm sure Mr. and Mrs. Preston would be happy to do so."

He nodded and stared at the lit end of his cigar. "Does the name Carlo Moretti mean anything to you?"

My stomach lurched, but I pretended to think about it before I shrugged. "Tenor with the Detroit Opera?"

He puffed on the cigar, building a hazy gray cloud between us, while he seemed to consider my answer. Finally he said, "Moretti was your old friend Vito Adamo's chauffeur when he wasn't breaking kneecaps for the Employers Association. I was sure you'd have run into him somewhere along the line."

It hit me then that the witness hadn't come forward. Riordan was fishing. I shrugged again. "Maybe if I saw him . . ."

Riordan studied me, his head turned a bit to the side, the cigar crammed into the left corner of his mouth, hiding the scar. He had been handsome before the union man slashed him. "The only place you could see him now is in the morgue," he said.

"Oh. I'm sorry to hear that."

"Is that so?"

"That's all behind me, Detective. I'm getting on with my life now."

He shook his head. "I wish I could believe that. You weren't too happy they got away."

"Well, of course I'd like to see them brought to justice, but that's your job, not mine."

Riordan put a hand on my shoulder and pulled me in close. "I gave you one break—'cause I thought you were innocent. I won't give you another."

"I don't need a break. I haven't done anything."

He squeezed my shoulder and leaned in closer. The lit end of his cigar smoldered an inch from my cheek. "Don't leave town. I've a feeling we're going to need to talk about this some more."

I stared into his cold eyes. "Can I go back to work?"

Riordan sighed and walked past me to the door, then hesitated and turned around. "Will, can I give you a piece of advice?"

I shrugged.

"Your world is money and parties and pretty women. This world"—he gestured around us—"is dirty and violent and ugly. You're going to get yourself killed. Go back to your world."

I agreed with him and must have said the right things. He told Murphy to take me back to the factory in one of the "flying squadron's" black Chalmers 30 police cars. It wasn't two years old, but the upholstery was in shreds, bare springs sticking up, and it reeked of the sour body odor brought on by fear. I knew the smell.

Murphy cut down to Grand Boulevard and headed east, back toward the factory.

"Hey, take me downtown, near the opera house. I've got some business to attend to."

He threw me an annoyed glance over his shoulder. "What am I, your fuckin' chauffeur?" When he turned right to head downtown, he said, "Gimme a smoke."

"Sure." I pulled a cigarette out of my case and handed it to him.

"Got a light?"

"Of course." I shook my head. Riordan was the only cop I'd ever met that I thought might actually pay for things himself. The rest bummed, stole, or blackmailed their way to financial independence.

Not slowing a bit, Murphy craned his neck back toward me, cigarette poking from between his lips. I lit it and another for me. "Murphy? You didn't tell Riordan about our . . . arrangement, did you?"

He laughed, and little bursts of smoke shot from his mouth. "Like I'd tell anybody. Most of the bosses would want a cut. Riordan, though." Murphy shook his head. "That son of a bitch'd bring me up on charges. There's only one thing more dangerous than a cop like me, boyo." He waited for me to take the bait, but I didn't accommodate him. After a moment, he gave me the punch line anyway. "And that's an honest one." He roared with laughter.

"And you're going to let me know when you hear something?"

"Did you kill the wop?"

"Of course not."

"Too bad. Information's more expensive for murderers." He laughed. "I'll keep me ears open, so long's you keep me in pin money."

I leaned forward and slipped a twenty-dollar bill into one of his chest pockets. "Good," I said. "Keep your eyes open too. I want Adamo."

I sat back and looked out the window for the rest of the trip, thinking about my conversation with Detective Riordan. He'd given me some fatherly advice that, a year ago, would have made perfect sense to me—*Go back to your world.*

But it wasn't my world anymore. There was no going back.

Murphy dropped me off in front of the Detroit Opera House, and I began my short trek east. I studied all the women, thinking about the auburn-haired prostitute. The odds of finding her lounging around on the street were minuscule, but my mind was attuned to the search. An alarming number of women had auburn hair. When Elizabeth and I started seeing each other, her hair color was unusual. I couldn't believe I hadn't noticed this before, though, to be fair, I hadn't noticed much of anything for the past three years.

I put my head down and continued on my journey. Only a few blocks from Woodward, gaping holes pocked the street, the loose cobbles stolen for other uses. An odor of rot joined the oily stink of coal smoke. As I walked, the buildings became more and more squat, down to the single-story clapboard shop that was my destination—the Empire Pharmacy. It had taken me a number of months to find a pharmacy to my liking, that is, a pharmacy that would sell me morphine over an extended period of time without making an issue of it. Practically the only one I hadn't tried was Adamo's pharmacy next to the Bucket. I wasn't going there.

A bell tinkled when I opened the door. The pharmacist, an old, stooped man I knew only as Mick, nodded when he saw me. "How many today, sir?"

"I'd like a sixteen-ounce bottle."

"Well," he said, a glint in his eye. "I'm not supposed to sell those except to doctors, sir."

"What's the difference, Mick? You don't want to fill all those little bottles anyway, do you?"

"I don't know." He rubbed the back of his neck and made a point of looking around furtively. "You'd have to make it worth my while. I could get in a lot of trouble."

He normally charged me two dollars per one-ounce bottle, twice the amount charged by a respectable pharmacy. But a respectable pharmacy wouldn't sell morphine to the likes of me. At least, not without a prescription. "I'll give you forty bucks."

Shaking his head, he looked down at the floor. "Sir, I don't think I can do this."

"Fifty." It was at least two weeks' pay for him.

His eyes cut to mine. "I could do that."

I pulled my wallet from inside my coat, took out a brand new fifty-dollar bill, and placed it on the counter.

He grabbed the bill and stuck it into his trouser pocket. "Right away." While he rooted around behind the counter, I wiped my nose.

He put the bottle in a paper bag and handed it to me. I turned to leave. As I did, I glanced up at his face and saw an expression that made me turn away even faster. His eyes were narrowed and his mouth set into a tight frown. It was a look you might give to a man who'd stolen money from his children.

Disgust.

CHAPTER THREE

A top my walnut bar, Sophie Tucker's voice warbled out of the horn of Wesley's Victrola—*Some of these days you're gonna miss me, honey / Some of these days, you're gonna be so lonely. . . .*

I cherished this Victrola and its records far more than the two thousand dollars Wesley had left me. Music was what his life had been about—writing, playing, singing. I missed him almost as much as I missed Elizabeth. The only postcard she'd sent me, with a picture of Alexandre-Gustave Eiffel's tower on the front, had arrived three months earlier. It was still on the end table next to the sofa. I sat down and flipped it over, reading her message for the hundredth time:

> *Dearest Will,*
>
>   *I hope this note finds you well. I am feeling better since my last letter, though I must admit the thought of returning home someday still fills me with dread. Of small comfort is the fact that we won't be doing so any time soon. My mother is nearly as overcome with melancholia as when we arrived in Europe. I'll write again soon. I miss you.*
>
>   *Yours,*
>   *Elizabeth*

I'd had no word from her since.

I noticed again that I was rubbing my hand. I tugged off the black kid glove a quarter-inch at a time. First to appear was the scar from the gouge on the inside of my wrist that I'd dug trying to cut the rope tied around it. Next, on my palm, a knotted mass of scar tissue, then the collection of mottled scars on all sides of my forefinger and middle finger, and the gnarled stumps of my fourth and fifth fingers, all burgundy, all disfigured—all courtesy of sulfuric acid. I didn't bother to look at the back of the hand; it was simply more of the same. I tugged the glove on again, until my fourth and fifth fingers reached the cotton I'd stuffed inside to hide their deformity.

Since it was only six o'clock, I thought I'd kill a little time before I began the hunt for the prostitute. Riordan's question about gun and knife skills had got me thinking. I'd been shooting fairly regularly with Edsel Ford on Sunday afternoons, but I hadn't even thought about knives. I was again going to have to drag the city's cesspool, and I had to be prepared.

I hung my dartboard on the parlor wall and stepped back behind the sofa. Holding my switchblade in my left hand, I took careful aim and hurled it at the wall. The knife bounced off the plaster a foot to the left of the board and clattered to the floor. Walking over to pick it up, I shook my head to clear it. I wasn't sure I could have hit the board even if my right hand was still functional.

I'd never taken an opiate for an extended period. All that came to mind was a couple of days of morphine for a broken wrist when I was twelve. The emotion associated with that memory was fear, though I didn't remember why. Perhaps I was afraid I wouldn't change back, regain my mental equilibrium. These days, it was a wish rather than a fear.

Alcohol had been a poor substitute. It left me depressed, volatile, and sick, and served only to dull my pain, rather than assuage it. Morphine had its own set of side effects, but it brought me the peace I'd always craved.

I walked behind the sofa to throw the knife again but stopped and closed my eyes, just listening to Sophie's voice. Music had become a welcome accompaniment to the relaxed feeling morphine gave me. I'd found I could sit for hours with my eyes closed and just enjoy music.

Earlier in my life, music had seemed somehow trivial in comparison to the serious considerations of commerce and manly endeavor. Now it seemed so much more valuable. Millions of men in this country hurried through their lives, believing the lessons hammered into them. From the tiny classroom of the most humble one-room schoolhouse to the ivy-covered walls of Detroit University School, we take to heart the most important lesson they can teach us—fit in, do what you're told, don't make waves. The nonconformist is vilified, singled out, and shunned. The rest of us learn well and perpetuate the lesson.

I'd learned as well as anyone. But something in me had changed. The men with whom I'd been so impressed were nothing but puffed-up roosters strutting down the sidewalk pretending to be important—trying to fool themselves more than anyone else. Those breast-beaters were just as unhappy as the rest of us.

Manly endeavor. Teddy Roosevelt's "strenuous life." Prove you're a man by killing things, by besting others, by cutting a wide swath through life, regardless of whom you hurt.

These are the things in which I used to believe.

I spun and threw the knife again. This time it stuck, quivering, in the wall—over the Victrola. A shower of plaster fell onto the record, and the needle bounced back and forth. I walked to the bar, wiped off the record, and replaced the needle at the beginning before wrenching the knife out of the wall and returning to the sofa.

How would these things I'd found important help me live my life? The "successful" men seemed to have found the trick to living. Was it as simple as staying so busy you don't realize how miserable you are?

I took another drink from the little brown bottle, closed my eyes, and let Sophie's deep voice wash over me.

The doorbell rang twice before I realized what it was. Scott Joplin's "Maple Leaf Rag" had ended—half an hour ago? Clicks and pops came from the Victrola as the needle bounced back and forth at the end of the record. It wasn't dark out yet, but everything seemed gray, out of focus. I looked at my watch—eight o'clock.

The bell rang again. I pocketed the bottle and hurried to the foyer, wobbling as I did. I flipped on the light and opened the door. Elizabeth Hume stood before me with a grin on her face. My breath caught in my throat. She was magnificent—high cheekbones, plump lips, those alluring green eyes. With her auburn hair piled under a sky blue narrow-brimmed hat and a matching silk dress with lace at the throat and sleeves, she was the first day of spring, Christmas morning, a cool breeze on a hot summer day.

"My God, Elizabeth, you're back. You're . . . stunning." I was mortified to hear a slur in my words.

"Hello, Will. It's so nice to see you."

"Please, Elizabeth. Come in." Trying to look alert, I opened my eyes wide and stepped to the side of the door, my right hand behind my back.

Her head tilted a bit, and she studied me for a second. Her face froze. "Mother and I got home yesterday. I thought we could catch up tonight, but I see this is not a good time." Her voice trembled. I met her eyes and was surprised to see them welling with tears. She turned to leave.

I laid my good hand on her arm. "No. Please, Elizabeth, stay."

She stopped and looked at my hand until I removed it. "I thought you had quit drinking, that you were trying to make something of yourself, but you're obviously drunk out of your mind. Damn you!" A tear slipped down her cheek. "I thought you were past this, that we—" She shook her head and, without another word, strode down the hall.

It took a moment for my brain to kick into gear. I ran into the hallway and saw the back of her dress as she disappeared down the steps. "Elizabeth! Wait!" I caught up with her just before the first-floor landing. "Please, come back." She kept walking. "Let me explain." Even as I said it, I wasn't sure how I could. *No, I'm not drunk. I'm just high on morphine.* Really? Would that really be my defense?

She spun around. I was only just able to stop without running her over. I took a quick step back and tripped over the landing, falling onto my backside.

Looking away, she said, "Please, Will." Her voice was quiet. "Stay away from me." She opened the door and hurried out, leaving me behind.

———

I awoke on the couch with the sun already high in the sky. I sat up and put my head in my hands, ignoring the pain in the right one. I'd taken another swig of morphine after Elizabeth left and had never gotten out of my apartment, never made it out to look for the prostitute.

I shook my head and took a deep breath. Is this what I've come to? I can't even mount a search for the one woman who could keep me out of the state prison?

An odd thought struck me. Elizabeth was back. She was tall and slender and had auburn hair. She had even more motive to kill Moretti than I did. Moretti had done a lot of Vito Adamo's dirty work, and there was certainly a good possibility that Moretti had assisted in Judge Hume's murder.

She said she'd just gotten back from Paris, but how did I know that was true? Could she have pretended to be a prostitute to lure Moretti to his death? I considered the idea for half a second before rejecting it out of hand. It was stupid. Elizabeth was no killer. I put the thought out of my mind.

After two cups of coffee to pry my eyes open and a capful of morphine to take the edge off the pain, I dressed and took a trolley to the factory. I detoured to my father's office in the administration building. His secretary, Mr. Wilkinson, a neat, fastidious man with a thick brown beard that hung to the perfect knot of his cravat, told me I could go right in.

My father stood at the window, hands clasped behind his back, peering through the blinds at the men striding down the cobblestone road toward the factory. He turned and waved me in. "Will, my boy, how are you this morning?" He wore a warm smile on his fleshy face. He'd become much more demonstrative with his affection since my stay in the hospital, and I knew he was very concerned about my state of mind. I'd politely refused his entreaties to see Dr. Miller and tried to act happy when I was in his presence.

"I'm fine, Father. And you?"

"I'm fine." He appraised me for a moment. "What can I do for you this morning?"

"I'm going to need to take some time off—perhaps a few weeks."

His eyes searched my face for some hidden meaning. "Why?"

"Just a little vacation."

"This seems rather sudden." He walked around his desk and stopped a foot away from me. "You've just been getting settled in engineering."

I maintained eye contact. "I just need a week or two."

"Dr. Miller said you need normalcy, a regimen."

"I know."

He placed a hand on my shoulder and gave it a squeeze. "Keep working. In fact, come back and live with your mother and me. Just for a while, until you feel better."

"Thank you, Father, no. We've been over this." I stepped back, and his hand slipped off my shoulder. "I appreciate your concern. I do. But I have to do this."

"You *have* to take a vacation?" He sighed and sat on the edge of his desk. "This is about Wesley, isn't it? You're going after them."

I looked away and then met his gaze again. "No. It has nothing to do with Wesley."

He stared into my eyes. "Will. You can't bring him back. Let the police do their job." His tone turned to pleading. "You have important duties here. The engineering department needs you."

Even he had to know what a stretch that was. The engineering department hadn't been impacted in the least by my presence. "I'm sorry, Father."

He looked down at the wooden floor. When he met my eyes again he looked older than his fifty-nine years. "All right, son. But take care of yourself."

I thanked him and left his office with a feeling of regret. I'd been a disappointment to my father since I'd come to work for the company two years earlier, due to my drinking and the personal problems I'd allowed to interfere with my work. I had no doubt he'd already given a great deal of consideration to who would take his place as president of the company when he retired. There were many candidates more qualified—and infinitely more reliable—than I.

I got my hair cut and then rode down to the towering Penobscot Building and the Peoples State Bank, where I withdrew a hundred dollars in cash. Assuming I could find the prostitute, it was unlikely I'd be able to get any of her time without paying for it. If I couldn't find her, I'd have to spread some money around, bribe some people.

When I returned home, I thought about my next move. It seemed all I could do was find the prostitute and get the truth out of her, a task I viewed with a great deal of trepidation. Finding this woman among the denizens of Detroit's "Paradise Valley" would be both difficult and dangerous.

At five o'clock I stuck the .32 into my belt at the small of my back and squeezed onto a trolley. I got off at Grand Circus Park and worked my way over to the unsavory climes of Detroit's three-block run of brothels, dives, after-hours clubs, and sex show establishments. Thousands of prostitutes called Detroit home, and most of them could be found here in Paradise Valley.

Every address in this section of Hastings Street was a likely spot to have your pocket picked or your throat cut, none of them more so than the Bucket, Vito Adamo's saloon that slouched on the corner of Hastings and Clinton. There was no reason for me to go there. Anyone who had participated in killing one of Adamo's men would be insane to walk into the Bucket—and it wasn't safe for me either.

I figured I'd start at the obvious spots—the brothels. First up was Fanny's Men's Club, a narrow redbrick three-story with large wooden doors at the top of a brick staircase. Stained glass windows on either side of the entryway depicted winged nymphs feeding grapes to a young man whose robe had been thrown casually (and strategically) across his lap. Subtle, it wasn't.

I climbed the steps and rang the bell. A large black man with a completely bald scalp answered the door, took my derby, and ushered me down a dusty hallway. Laughter and the murmur of conversation became louder as I walked farther inside. Turning the corner into the parlor, I came upon half a dozen men—all of whom looked well-to-do—lounging around the room. Seven or eight young women, wearing low-cut evening dresses, circulated among them. I looked them over. Three of the girls had auburn hair. One was plump, the other two of a slender build. I saw nothing that gave me a hint that they were—or were not—the prostitute I'd seen.

A woman of about fifty in a red evening gown stood at the base of the stairway, speaking quietly with a pair of men. When she noticed me, she excused herself and sashayed in my direction. "May I help ya?"

Her face was heart shaped with sharp lines, and her voice carried a strong Irish lilt.

"Yes, I'm . . ." It was hard to get out. "I'm looking for some entertainment. With a woman."

She chuckled at my naïveté. "We do provide that service."

"But I have strict requirements," I said. "I'd like to see all of your taller, slender women with auburn hair." I took my wallet from my inside coat pocket, clutched it against my chest with my right hand, and pulled out a ten. "I'm sure this will cover your trouble."

She eyed my gloved right hand before slipping the bill into the top of her corset. "Would you like a drink?"

"Ah, no, thank you." My palms were sweating. I wiped the left one on my trousers. I'd had no idea I would be so uncomfortable in this setting.

"Please take a seat in the next room," she said, pointing toward another doorway. "I'll have the girls come in, see if one of them tickles your fancy." She looked me up and down. "Or anything else."

I headed for the doorway toward which she'd directed me and stepped into a smaller room, where I sat on a yellow velvet settee. A few minutes later, a young auburn-haired woman slipped through the door, followed by another, and another, all wearing revealing dresses and high-heeled shoes. I watched their movements, hoping to see something that would trigger recognition. The madam followed the seventh auburn-haired, slender, relatively tall woman.

Seven—at one house.

CHAPTER FOUR

I studied each of them. Though I had nothing more to go by than the recollection of my impression of a woman, nothing distinguished any of them as being the one who was with Moretti.

"A friend of mine recommended one of you," I said, "though I can't remember your name. Maybe you know him. Carlo Moretti."

The girls looked at one another. None of them showed any sign of recognition or alarm. After a few seconds, a voluptuous girl with acne said, "Carlo? Maybe. I don't remember his last name."

"What did he look like?"

"I'da know. Regular."

That's not how anyone would describe Moretti. "Anyone else?"

The only answers were a few shrugs. I stood and looked back at the madam. "These are all your girls who fit the description?"

She nodded.

"I'm sorry, but I don't think I'll be needing their services after all." I pulled another ten from my wallet and handed it to her. "Thank you, though. They're all quite lovely."

"The mister wouldn't want a taste of these?" The well-endowed prostitute grabbed her breasts and thrust them upward, licking the top of each lasciviously while staring into my eyes.

"I'm sure they're quite . . . delicious," I said, feeling even more stupid. "But you're just not exactly what I'm looking for."

She scrunched up her face and said, "Come on, then, girls." The young women turned on their heels and marched out of the room.

I turned to the madam. "Could I ask you a question?"

She raised her eyebrows. It looked like my twenty dollars had bought me an answer.

"To be completely honest with you, I'm not looking for sex. A friend I went to school with is trying to find his sister. He thinks she's a"—it was uncomfortable to say, even to a madam—"a prostitute. He got word she was with this Moretti character Sunday night, and I'm trying to help him track her down. There's fifty bucks in it for anyone who locates her."

"What's her name?"

"He's sure she's changed it."

With a frown, she said, "You've never seen her?"

"No."

"So all you know is she's tall and skinny and has auburn hair."

I nodded.

"Honey, take my advice and tell your friend not to waste your time. Most girls in the life are skinnier than normal, and if you haven't noticed, about half the women in Detroit have auburn hair. You don't know what house she works in?"

"No. I'm not even sure she works in one. She apparently went to Moretti's apartment Sunday."

She laughed. "Oh, good luck with that. You're lookin' for a streetwalker. Ye'll not find her in a house." She began ushering me out of the room. "Now, I've answered your questions, and I have to get back to work." We walked through the parlor and down the hallway to the front door. The black man took my hat from the stand and handed it to me.

I looked at the madam again. "One more thing, a curiosity: I don't remember so many women having auburn hair, but it seems to be all I see now."

"Ye've not been payin' attention for a while, eh? Henna rinse, young man. European fashion. You picked a bad time to look for a pa'ticular auburn-haired lady."

I thanked her and wandered down the steps to the street. At the bottom of the stairs I took a deep breath and moved along to the next brothel. I thought I'd get another opinion before giving up on the houses. I had a similar experience, though only five women who fit the description were paraded in front of me. I was again told that I would not find this woman in a house of ill fame.

After a drink from my bottle to strengthen my resolve, I continued the search at the other businesses along the street, the saloons first and then the clubs, which had shows that turned my stomach.

Even though my mission was a serious one, in the back of my mind I had thought this would be a titillating evening. Instead I was deeply troubled. These women were used and degraded with no more regard than throwaway dolls. They weren't human beings; they were receptacles. The women who "performed" in the sex shows were the saddest of all. As they aged, became more desperate, their choices became more and more limited. And what became of them when they were no longer able to earn a buck that way?

By the time I'd spent my last dollar and caught a trolley home, it was almost three in the morning. I'd been forced to pull my gun twice, both times to discourage thieves. I was filled with the blackest of melancholies, and not only because I'd come up empty-handed. I stared out at the buildings alongside Woodward as we rattled away from downtown.

The lives of these women. How could the city turn a blind eye to this? I'd heard plenty of arguments for the policy of "containment"—allowing these types of businesses in one small area while keeping the rest of the city clean, or at least relatively so. The cry against "white slavery," however, had been rising, and most cities, even Chicago, were taking a stand against vice in any and all locations.

But Detroit . . . How could anyone reconcile themselves with this?

The next morning, after barely a capful of morphine, I bought a dozen white roses from a street vendor and carried them to Elizabeth's house. I needed to make peace with her. Even so, my steps slowed as I got closer to the huge yellow and white Queen Anne, all gables and turrets and spindles and bay windows, gingerbread trim under the eaves and around every squared corner. I steeled myself and strode up the sidewalk, through the gate, and up the steps to the Humes' door. Both hoping and fearing she would be home, I knocked.

Alberts, the butler and sometime chauffeur, answered the door. He was a gaunt and trim man, getting elderly now. "Mr. Anderson," he said with a smile. He'd had no affection for me while Elizabeth and I were courting, but I knew he felt deeply indebted to me for saving her life.

I smiled back at him. "May I speak with Elizabeth, please?"

"I'll see if she is available, sir. Would you care to wait in the living room?"

"That would be fine, Alberts. Thank you."

"My pleasure, sir." He held the door open for me.

I walked inside, and he closed the door. Before he could leave, I patted him on the back. A sharp pain made me realize I was touching him with my disfigured hand, the first time I'd touched anyone with it since it had been burned. I could only imagine how horrified he was. I pulled away and coughed, embarrassed. "It's very nice to see you again, Alberts."

"You as well, sir. Good luck."

"Good luck?"

"With . . ." He cut his eyes up the staircase toward Elizabeth's room.

I thanked him. He headed up the stairs, and I wandered into their living room. I was last in this room when they still called it a parlor, for Judge Hume's funeral, but prior to that, Elizabeth and I had spent many happy hours here. Even though I'd been careful with the morphine dosage, the green stripes on the white wallpaper pulsed with intensity, and the white silk sofa and chairs were blinding where the sun cut across them.

I had decided to just apologize and not correct Elizabeth on her assumption that I'd been drinking. Telling her I'd taken too much morphine would open a door I needed to remain shut.

"Will?"

I turned to see Elizabeth, wearing a loose pink skirt and white shirtwaist, standing in the doorway. One of her hands was braced against the doorjamb, as if she were ready for a hasty retreat. My gloved right hand behind my back, I said, "Hello, Lizzie. I want to apologize for the other night." I handed her the roses. "I'm sorry. I'm not drinking. It was a onetime slip, and it won't happen again. Can we start over?"

Her beautiful green eyes searched my face as she stepped into the room. "All right, Will. Perhaps we could talk." She looked toward the doorway. "Alberts?"

He turned the corner into the room. "Miss?" He'd been waiting just outside.

"Would you be a dear and put these in water, please?"

His eyebrows rose a quarter of an inch. "Certainly, miss." He gave a little half bow and retreated from the room with the roses.

She turned back to me. "Thank you for the flowers, Will."

"I swear I'm finished with drinking."

She put a smile on her face, but it didn't look genuine to me. She wasn't convinced, but at least she was trying. "I'm glad," she said. "Would you like a cup of tea?"

"Please."

"Would you like to help?"

"I would."

We walked to the kitchen, a large room with a white tile floor and a big maple table in the center. Alberts was filling a vase with water at the sink.

Elizabeth set a kettle to boiling and busied herself preparing a teapot and bringing out a pair of china cups and saucers. I stood back near the table, giving them space.

"How've you been?" she asked, her eyes still on the china.

"Fine, good." I stopped. "No, not so well, really, as you might have guessed."

Alberts gave me a sympathetic grimace before placing the roses in the vase and setting it on the center of the table. While he exited into the hallway, Elizabeth walked around to the other side of the table and said, "How is your hand?"

"It's all right," I said, slipping it behind my back. "I can't do much with it, and it's no joy to look at, but I manage." Time to change the subject. "How have you been doing? And your mother?"

She placed both hands on the back of a chair. "I'm fine. I'm keeping busy with the Michigan Equal Suffrage Association and the McGregor Mission."

"Oh. I thought you just got back to town."

She laughed, and it sounded a bit nervous. "Well, yes, I just started. But I can see how they're going to keep me busy."

"Good." I tried to read her eyes. "We all need goals to achieve."

She cocked her head and her eyes narrowed, but the next second she smiled at me. "I'll tell you what's exciting. This morning my mother had Mrs. Bell from next door over for coffee."

I waited for the exciting part.

"No, you don't understand," she said. "My mother hasn't so much as initiated a conversation with anyone since we left for Europe. She's been so buried in melancholia she hasn't been able to find her way out." Elizabeth gestured around us. "I think coming home is what did the trick. She might snap out of this after all. I was beginning to give up hope."

"That's great. I'm glad for her."

"It was a last-ditch effort. Frankly, it's the only reason I decided to come back. Paris is such a beautiful city, and Detroit, well . . ."

"Isn't the Paris of the West anymore?"

She turned and glanced out the window. "It's not so much the city," she murmured, "as it is the memories."

I understood. Much better than I wished I did.

The kettle began whistling, a slow and wavering note that built toward a scream. I walked to the stove, took the kettle off the burner, and turned back to her. "Did you hear? One of Adamo's men was murdered Sunday night."

Her eyes locked on me.

"Here, let me. . . ." I gestured in the direction of the teapot. "You sit. I'll get it."

She sat at the kitchen table while I prepared the tea. With one hand, it was awkward, but I used my body to shield Elizabeth from my fumbling. I brought the pot to the table, and then the cream, and finally, our cups. Elizabeth didn't speak, just looked at me, expressionless.

I sat across from her and tipped some tea into her cup. "It was Adamo's driver—Carlo Moretti. I'd actually been watching him, though I didn't see who killed him." I clenched my teeth, seeing his corpse in my mind. "His throat was cut. He went into his apartment building with a prostitute who ran out a few minutes later. She might have killed him, though I think it was a man because . . . well, let's just say I think it was a man."

"So you were there?"

Pouring my own tea, I nodded and leaned in toward her. "Yes. And a woman saw me."

"The prostitute?"

"No. Moretti's neighbor."

"Were you in his apartment?"

"Outside it. But close enough."

"Do you think she could identify you?"

"Probably," I said. "But I think she's an illegal, so it's not likely she'll go to the police. I know she didn't tell them anything initially, because Detective Riordan didn't lock me up."

"Well, let's hope that's the end of it."

"Somehow I doubt it will be."

She was quiet for a moment. "Did you get a good look at the prostitute?"

I thought that a curious question. "No." I took a sip of my tea.

"So, you don't think you could identify her?"

"No. I've tried to find her. It's hopeless."

Elizabeth looked down at the table and nodded. "You know, I don't think I've ever properly thanked you for what you did. I guess . . . I guess the pain is still there from that, from everything." She reached out, took hold of my left hand, and met my eyes. "But you saved my life. Thank you."

"You're welcome. I wish I could have done more. For you. And for Wes."

We talked for a few more minutes, and I left while I was ahead, catching a Jefferson Line streetcar downtown. I was happy she was home and that if I played my cards right, I'd get to see her, but I considered her comment about keeping busy. By her count, she'd been home for only three days, which after seven months overseas was barely enough to unpack, much less have a need to keep busy.

I hopped off at Woodward. After I withdrew another hundred dollars from the bank I caught another trolley home. I decided to get off a stop early, at Temple, and bought a few apples and peaches from the fruit market before cutting through the alley that led to the back of my apartment house.

I was strolling through the shadows of the dusty alleyway, wiping peach juice off my chin with my handkerchief, when I caught a fleeting movement in my peripheral vision. Someone stepped into the doorway at the back of my building. Though I had no more than a glimpse, I was certain it was a man wearing navy blue—a uniform, perhaps—and I had the impression that he'd stepped backwards in one quick motion.

He was hiding, not entering the building.

Without pausing long enough to think, I turned and ran.

CHAPTER FIVE

I sneaked to the side of the house on the corner of Second Street and Peterboro, catty-corner to my building, and crouched behind a shrub. It had been dark for two hours. No light or movement showed through the windows of my apartment. No police cars, wagons, or motorcycles were in sight.

Had I imagined it? Two days ago the police, having no evidence of my involvement in the murder of Carlo Moretti, had done nothing more than question me. But of course the woman could have come forward. If that was the case I'd never get Adamo, much less Big Boy or Sapphira.

A gray Model T touring car crawled by in front of me, passing through the light from the electric streetlamps. When the *putt-putt-putt* of the motor faded off into the distance, the cicadas' drone drowned out the murmur of late-night traffic. The night smelled of peat and dried horse manure.

Though I had no good reason for it, I never considered crossing the street. The whole situation felt wrong. My body was taut, my gut said stay away, yet going on the run seemed premature. I'd run before, and what had that gotten me? Arrested, beaten, nearly killed. That, and the fifteen ounces of morphine hidden in the back of my wardrobe contributed to the feeling that I should be sure before I ran.

A man walked, a bit unsteadily, up the sidewalk on the other side of the street. When he passed under a streetlamp I saw it was my new neighbor, Arthur Preston, his face shining with sweat. He was a puffy though not corpulent thirty-year-old, the *head* accountant (his emphasis) for the Detroit Salt Mining Company, and an exceedingly dull dinner guest. His collar was sprung on one side, his tie askew, his derby pulled down around his eyes.

When he reached the sidewalk in front of our building, he turned and looked up at the miniature towers and turrets that festooned the roof of the three-story toy castle in which we lived. He was also interested in the level of activity on the top floor, although his concern would be different from mine—was his teetotaling wife awake? He was probably more relieved than I had been to see no lights on in his apartment. Straightening his waistcoat, he marched up to the door, unlocked it, and stepped inside.

He stopped. It appeared he was talking to someone, though I couldn't see the other party. After a minute or so, he walked out of sight, and another man stepped forward and peered out the door. This man wore the navy blue wool of the Detroit Police Department, complete with brass buttons and a badge.

I cursed and fingered the little morphine bottle in my pocket. I would have to say good-bye to that sixteen-ounce bottle. At least I had plenty of money to replace it. As soon as the cop moved from the door I slipped away and circled around to the south, toward Jefferson Avenue.

She must have come forward. It was time to leave town and work up a plan.

I crept down the shoreline, heading for the downtown Michigan Central Depot. I entered from the track side, hidden by the rows of empty boxcars on the auxiliary tracks. The moon had disappeared. Behind me it was black, the gurgling of water against the bank the only evidence of the Detroit River. The platform lights reached out far enough that I could see the cars' black shapes.

I crept forward, careful to make as little noise as possible. This was the main hub of the Michigan Central line. Hundreds of trains left this station every day. If the police wanted me, they might expect to find me here, particularly as it was the only place to catch a train in the middle of the night. Even if they weren't after me, the railroad cops would be out looking for hoboes. Unfortunately, I felt I had to take the chance. My face was too well known in Detroit for me to hide for long.

When I reached the set of cars closest to the station, I peeked around the edge of one in the middle. The platform, only fifty feet away, was nearly empty. A man lay on a bench, and a handsome young couple sat slumped against each other, staring straight ahead.

To my right, a ringing of metal on metal caught my attention. It sounded like a muffled bell clanging violently. It stopped as quickly as it had begun. I crouched and looked to where the sound had come from. A few tracks over, the light from a swinging lantern moved toward me, careening back and forth through the boxcars. Now the sound of boots crunching against stone began to filter to my ears. The ringing sound started and stopped, started and stopped. This time of night it could only be a policeman of some sort. If I were caught here, it didn't much matter whether he was specifically looking for me or not. At best I'd be arrested for trespassing. It would be only a matter of time until my identity was discovered.

I took one step away from the light and froze. Another light moved toward me from the other direction. The first light was close enough now that the man would surely see me if I made a break toward the river. I'd have to go through the station.

I glanced around the side of the boxcar toward the platform again. A Detroit policeman stood on the edge staring directly at me. I froze, my heart hammering in my ears. He seemed to hold my gaze for a few seconds before his eyes swept away, down the train of cars. I breathed a sigh of relief. I was hidden by the darkness. He hadn't seen me, but he had me hemmed in. I slipped under the car and hid behind a wheel.

The first light stopped two tracks over, almost directly behind my position. The metal bottom of the lantern clanked against wood, and I heard a grunt of exertion followed a few seconds later by the striking of a match. Inwardly I cursed the Detroit Police. Leave it to one of those lazy bastards to take a break in a boxcar at the worst possible time and place.

The other light moved away from me down the tracks but soon turned again and headed toward me, up the last set of cars. The light got brighter. I gauged my position by the light, staying in the shadow of the wheel. The sounds got louder, the intermittent ringing, the boots like teeth chomping on gravel.

A voice bawled out, "Mueller!"

"Yes, Sergeant?" the man near me replied in a clipped German accent.

"Seen him?"

Mueller let out a quiet sigh and, under his breath, said, *"Dummkopf."* He raised his voice and said, "No. I have not seen anyone."

I didn't have to wonder any longer if this was a routine patrol.

"Carry on," the sergeant called.

"Jawoll," Mueller muttered. I almost felt sorry for him. He stopped just in front of the wheel behind which I was hiding, thrust a thin metal rod under the car, and whipped it back and forth. The rod whistled past my face, just missing me, and clanged off the metal pieces on the underside of the car like he was ringing a gong.

He walked past me and repeated the action, then moved to the next car. Once he finished with that, I began crawling under the train in the other direction, moving slowly in the darkness. When I'd gotten a few cars between us, I pushed myself to my feet, peering behind me at Mueller slowly moving away. Near as I could tell, the sergeant was still sitting two rows back, smoking. I took a cautious step, heel to toe, trying to muffle the sound of the rocks, and another, and another.

Three cars ahead of me a bright light flared. "Here!" a voice shouted. "Here he is!" It was the policeman from the platform. He blew his whistle and began running toward me, gun in hand. "Freeze, Anderson!"

I ducked under the train and rolled to the platform side of the last set of cars, visible in the station lights, and ran for the edge of the platform amid shrieking whistles. Another policeman ran from inside the station onto the platform. I veered off and ran west along the tracks with at least two of them on my tail. As soon as I was in the darkness again, I turned south, heading for the river. In the dark, I tripped but scrambled to my feet and ran with all I had, vaulting a track and another before the ground gave way under me and I flew, arms flailing, into the water.

I shrugged off my coat and swam with the current, putting distance between them and me as quickly as I could. Shouts and whistles rang out behind me. When I'd gotten a few hundred yards downstream, I changed direction, pulling across the current for the other side of the river and Canada, almost a half mile away.

After five minutes or so, my left calf began cramping. I stopped and treaded water as best I could while massaging the muscle, and looked across the river again. I was downstream now from Windsor, but the shoreline looked as far away as it had before.

The sound of a large motor rumbled over the water behind me. I looked back. A searchlight cut across the river, methodically working back and forth. It was upstream but not far. I dug into the water again, pulling hard for the shore, but the knot in my calf made that leg nearly useless, and I was exhausted.

The light passed over me, then quickly reversed direction and locked onto the back of my head. I dived again, again swimming downstream. This time when I came up, the light found me almost immediately, and the boat sounded like it was very close.

"Freeze, Anderson," a voice called. "You go down again, you ain't coming up."

A pair of policemen dragged me out of the wagon and pulled me up the broad concrete stairs toward the maw of the Bethune Street police station. My shoes made a squishing sound with each step. A man stood in the doorway, hands on hips, silhouetted by the light behind him. Detective Riordan. His six-foot frame, fedora, and the curl of smoke rising from his ever-present cigar made him immediately recognizable. We stopped two steps below him.

"God damn it, Anderson," Riordan growled.

I looked up, startled. It wasn't that long ago he'd punched me in the mouth for taking the Lord's name in vain. In the near dark, the scar that curled from his mouth toward his ear looked like the lopsided grin of a jack-o'-lantern.

Riordan shook his head. "You are one dumb son of a bitch. She saw your face. How could you have thought you'd get off this time?"

I shrugged. What was I going to say?

Riordan pulled the cigar from his mouth and looked at it, a disgusted scowl on his face. He hurled the cigar onto the steps, spun around, and walked into the station. Without looking back, he said, "Lock him up."

I sat awake all night in a cell with three other prisoners, all drunks sleeping one off. Shortly after a pinkish light began to show through the small barred window at the back of the cell, I started sweating and sniffling, and silently lamented the loss of my morphine. The guards were probably enjoying it by now.

The sun was full up when a guard slid four bowls of gruel and cups of coffee under the bars. I ignored them, keeping my arms wrapped around me to try to stay warm. One of the drunks, a husky German who stank of stale beer, grabbed two bowls of oatmeal, if that's what it was, so it didn't go to waste.

Shortly after lunch, which I also ignored, a guard brought me to a telephone, and I called my attorney, Mr. Sutton. I spoke with a secretary, who told me to keep my mouth shut (advice I already took as gospel) and wait for Mr. Sutton, who would be there as soon as possible. Then it was back to the cell. The drunks were gone now, replaced by a small man with long greasy hair and the sunken mouth of the toothless. Even though he was sitting on the bench at the back of the cell, I could hardly stand being pushed inside. A stench poured from the man, some combination of shit and rot.

I sat at the end of one of the side benches, as far away from him as I could, and leaned back against the bars. My stomach was cramping, and sweat ran down my face. I closed my eyes, hugged myself, and shrank into the corner of the cell.

"Hurts, don't it?"

I opened my eyes. The stench-ridden man was now sitting five feet away from me on the bench. He looked closer to death than he did a threat, so I closed my eyes again and ignored him.

"Opium?"

That opened my eyes. "What?"

"Is it opium?" His mouth was a black hole, framed by pink gums. "That's mine. Looks like it's yours too." His jaws worked back and forth, and I couldn't take my eyes off the wrinkled, puckered skin around his lips.

"No," I said. "I'm no addict."

He cackled. "So you say, so you say. Bet if I had some you'd change your tune, eh?"

I sat up and gave him the "dead eyes" look Wesley had taught me. With a look of alarm, he slid back a few feet. "Man! No offense, I just know what you're feelin'."

"If you don't shut your mouth," I said, "I'm going to shut it for you."

Looking hurt, he shuffled to the back of the cell and sat where he had previously. I had to resist the urge to get up and beat the hell out of him. He and I shared nothing.

Shortly thereafter, a guard pulled me out of the cell, clapped handcuffs and leg chains on me, and brought me to an interrogation room.

Mr. Sutton was already pacing the wooden floor. He looked up when the door opened. "Hello, Will."

The guard stepped out of the room and closed the door. Sutton walked up close to me. He was a handsome man, trim and energetic, and looked younger than I remembered. Then I saw why. He'd trimmed back his side whiskers from the muttonchops to a pair of brown slashes in front of his ears. That alone probably took five years off him.

"Another murder arrest?" he said. "Is this harassment?"

I walked over to the small wooden table and sat. A few moments later, I muttered, "Yes, well . . . no, not exactly."

"What?" He hurried around the table and looked down into my face. "Did you do this?"

I shook my head. "No. And I have an alibi."

"I'm listening."

I told him about my dinner with the Prestons.

"What time did they leave?"

"I don't know—around ten, I think."

"And then what did you do?"

"I . . . I went out." I looked up at him sheepishly. "I went to Moretti's. But he was already dead."

"Oh, yes, that *is* a clever alibi."

"Well, I wouldn't say the last part."

"You won't need to. The prosecutor will explain that you set up an alibi before going out to kill Moretti."

I shrugged.

"You were in his apartment?"

"Yes."

"And an eyewitness saw you run down the hall after the incident?"

I nodded.

He sighed and sank into the seat opposite me. "Why were you there in the middle of the night? No, don't tell me. This has something to do with Vito Adamo, doesn't it?"

I nodded. "Moretti worked for him."

"Do you know who killed him?"

"No." And I wasn't going to bring up the prostitute I'd seen. My association with Elizabeth was too well known to raise the possibility that Moretti had been killed by a tall, slender, auburn-haired woman. I raised my hands and awkwardly wiped my nose on my sleeve.

Sutton took a deep breath, placed his hands on the table, and stood. "Okay, well, you know the drill. You'll be formally charged, followed by the bail hearing and the preliminary hearing a couple of weeks later."

"What do you think about bail this time?"

He rubbed his chin. "I don't know. The judges could still be holding you at least partially responsible for Judge Hume's death, which would be a problem. But you never know what's going to happen."

"Don't tell my parents I'm in here."

"If I don't, they're going to find out from the newspapers. You know—'Return of the Electric Executioner,' or some such thing."

"Yeah. All right. But tell them to stay away." I thought about Elizabeth. "I don't want *any* visitors."

"Are you all right?" Sutton was looking down at me with a great deal of concern in his eyes. "I have to tell you—you look terrible."

"Just not feeling well. Influenza or something."

"Can I get you anything?"

I thought about it for a split second before rejecting the idea. "No."

"You don't need anything?"

Oh, yes. There was something I needed. But nothing I would ask him for.

CHAPTER SIX

I vomited again, now only a weak stream of stomach acid burning my throat. I spit and curled up on the cold concrete floor, hands clutching my stomach. It was dark, just the dim glow of a light at the end of the corridor illuminating the cot and bucket in the tiny cell.

My heart raced. My guts felt like they had been torn to ribbons. I groaned. Voices shouted out around me, some making fun, others telling me in no uncertain terms to shut up so they could sleep. I cursed them, their mothers, God, morphine, myself, before finally passing out.

I woke sometime the next day and wished I hadn't. I hurt like I never had before. My hand was nothing more than a passing interest. My stomach was filled with shards of glass. My head throbbed and pounded, ice picks stabbing behind my eyes. I couldn't sleep. I couldn't think. I didn't want morphine any longer. I only wanted death.

I begged the guards to either get me a doctor or kill me and be done with it, but they ignored me. Eventually the men in the other cells shut up. I may have been reading too much into their reaction, but I think they actually sympathized.

I didn't eat, drank little, and fouled myself frequently. By the end of the third day in the cell, I could only lie on the floor, drifting in and out of consciousness, nightmares blending with reality. My pain began to fade. I was just alert enough to know it wasn't because I was healing.

I embraced the thought of death, welcomed it, wished for nothing else. My lucid moments disappeared.

Dr. Miller leaned down close to me, his kind face crinkled with concern. Lights reflected off his pince-nez glasses, making his eyes invisible. His fluffy white hair and beard made me think of clouds. He smiled. "Nice to see you're back with us, my boy."

"Thanks," I whispered. Looking past him, I saw I was in a hospital room. "Where am I?"

"The state hospital. You nearly died."

I took a quick inventory of my pains. My hand had its normal burn, but the agony in my stomach and head was gone. "What happened?" I whispered.

"Dehydration. If you'll think back a bit, you'll recall my instructions to keep Elizabeth hydrated. You were dying for lack of water." He sighed. "Will, I told you to be careful with the morphine. You saw what heroin did to Elizabeth. How could you expect it to go better for you?"

I looked away from him. "I needed medicine."

"You should be dead now. You've been given a reprieve. Use your second chance." He gripped my forearm. "Change your life."

"As if it matters now. I'm never getting out of jail."

"Why, I'm sure Sutton will be able to convince the jury of the truth, Will. You'll be out before you know it."

I shook my head. I wasn't going into it with him. "My parents haven't seen me like this, have they?"

"Yes. I wasn't sure if you were going to make it. The State had to let them in."

"Shit." It was hard to imagine how I could hurt them any worse, but given my recent history, it seemed to be only a matter of time.

A week later, the police brought me to a cell at their Detroit headquarters. Physically I was weak but was feeling better than I had any right to be. My mental state was something else altogether. I had a niggling itch twenty-four hours a day. Whenever I thought of morphine my mouth turned dry, and I felt a craving digging at me that was impossible to ignore.

They'd taken away my glove, so I had a front-row seat to watch my fingers curl inward, the muscles tightening as they had done after I'd been burned by the acid. I didn't bother with my stretching exercises. It hurt too much, and the hand was useless anyway. No matter what I did, I'd never regain the ability to hold a pen or caress a woman's body, not that, with the likelihood of a life sentence, the latter would ever again be a possibility.

My parents and sisters, Elizabeth, and Edsel Ford came to the jail, asking to see me. The only person I agreed to speak with was Elizabeth.

It was early afternoon about a week after I'd been returned to the jail. A guard chained my arms and legs before pushing me along to a small interrogation room, where Elizabeth stood near the window, wearing a yellow day dress with a matching small-brimmed hat. My heart ached. Worry lines creased her forehead. Her eyes were red and puffy. But still and all, she was the most beautiful thing I'd ever seen.

The guard closed the door behind us. Eyeing Elizabeth with a leering smile, he said, "You got five minutes."

I turned back to him. "Could we have some privacy, please?"

"No. And don't touch her either. You stay on this side. She stays on that one."

I realized my mutilated hand was on display, and, as it was chained in front of me to my left hand, I had no way to hide it. I slid into the closest chair, and Elizabeth sat opposite me, her hands out on the table in front of her. I kept mine out of sight.

"How are you, Will?" Her eyes were pooled with tears.

I was determined to show her a brave face. "I'm fine. I have a cell to myself. It's boring, but I'm okay. Getting better."

"I didn't know about the morphine."

"No." I looked away. "It was just medicine." I glanced at her again. "My hand hurts all the time. It just got away from me a little bit."

"Yes."

I ducked my shoulders and tried to talk casually, to keep the guard from discerning any importance to my question. "Have the police been to see you?"

"Yes," she said. "But of course I couldn't tell them anything, other than I didn't believe you would kill anyone. Well . . . anyone else."

"Right. Were they fishing to find accomplices or anything?"

"No."

"Good." No one but me had seen the auburn-haired woman with Moretti. Or at least no one had come forward.

She asked if I needed anything, and we chatted for a few minutes before the guard told us our time was up. I stood and put a smile on my face. "Thanks for coming, Lizzie. But I'd appreciate it if you would stay away for now. I'll be out of here soon. I don't want you to see me like this. And I don't want you ogled by these degenerates." I glanced back at the guard. "The inmates, I mean." I turned back and winked at Elizabeth. That got a real smile out of her.

I think the guard knew what I did, because he hauled me out of the room, shoved me down the corridor, and threw me into my cell without removing the chains. They weren't taken off until the next day. But that was all right.

Whether she was involved in Moretti's death or not, Elizabeth wasn't a suspect.

Now I told Mr. Sutton again to keep everyone away. It would be humiliating enough to see them in court. We went through the preliminary hearing and bail hearing with no surprises—the prosecution had more than enough evidence to bring the case to trial, including an eyewitness who could put me at Carlo Moretti's door at his approximate time of death. Judge Morton denied me bail even when Mayor Thompson and Governor Osborne pressured him. The judge told Mr. Sutton he wouldn't grant bail even if he got President Taft and Pope Pius to vouch for me. Word had it that Morton had been a friend and confidant of Elizabeth's father—Judge Hume.

The next month dragged by. Most days I did nothing but sit on the floor of a windowless six-by-eight cell, my back propped against the redbrick wall, no one but the guards for company. My father's position in the community kept me out of the general population, for which I was grateful, but after my previous experience I wasn't as afraid of spending time in jail as I'd been.

I was simply miserable, plagued with as bad a melancholy as I've ever had. Every night I dreamed about morphine. Most of the dreams had me taking a dose, only to panic, remembering after the fact—and before the morphine took effect—that I had quit. That realization woke me, robbing me of what I was sure would be the dream equivalent of a morphine high. I tried to negotiate with the guards for drugs or alcohol, for anything that would bring me the peace I needed, but Riordan had sent out the word—if anyone brought me *anything*, they'd be out on the streets. I wondered if he thought he was doing me a favor. I smoked—a lot—but it did nothing to assuage my cravings.

I thought about the morphine in the back of my wardrobe. My father said he'd pay my rent until I was freed, however long that took. Assuming no one cleaned out my apartment too thoroughly, fifteen ounces of morphine awaited my return, which in my weak moments was enough to keep me going. But the longer I thought about it, the more often I thought of the opium addict who had seen through me. He had taken on some sort of otherworldly presence in my mind. I wasn't even completely sure he had been real. Was he a vision of a future me—a hideous, toothless monster, frightening children and eliciting pity from the charitable?

I had to free myself from the drug.

Mr. Sutton petitioned the court for a change of venue, arguing that it would be impossible to find twelve men in Detroit capable of trying my case without prejudice either for or against me. He argued that any man who was unaware of my fame had to be illiterate and deaf, and one who hadn't formed an opinion regarding my innocence or guilt had to be an imbecile.

Judge Morton rejected the petition out of hand. Sutton filed motion after motion with no result. It was clear to me that without some breakthrough, I had no chance whatsoever.

A guard wearing a filthy blue wool uniform with no top button shoved me to a small interrogation room—four plaster walls that at some point long ago had been white, with a heavy oak table and a pair of chairs on the scuffed plank floor.

Sutton was pacing the back of the room. His briefcase lay open on the table. "Ah, Will." Sutton, a human perpetual motion machine, crossed the floor to me in an instant and shook my left hand. He closed the door behind me and gestured toward a chair.

I shook my head. Standing gave me a better view out the window of a Detroit street scene—cars, trucks, and people racing by, some glancing nervously toward the police station. Life. As opposed to whatever this was.

Sutton resumed his pacing. "We need to make this a case of mistaken identity. No one is going to believe that you just happened upon the body. The papers have already raised too many questions about that mess with John Cooper. We have to convince the jury you weren't there."

"What about the truth?"

"My Lord, Will." He stopped abruptly and pointed at me. "You were seen running from Moretti's apartment. Shortly thereafter his body was discovered. Any extenuating circumstances will be thrown out the window."

"But no one saw me with a knife. The man who killed Moretti would have been soaked in blood. I didn't have any on me."

"Perhaps that would be enough if your name were Sister Mary Theresa of the Blessed Sacrament. But your name is Will Anderson, the Electric Executioner, a man who has admitted to killing once already."

"In self-defense."

"Yes, in self-defense against a man who was allegedly being helped by this man—a man whose head was nearly cut off. For all anyone knows—hell, for all I know—you went there with the intent of killing Moretti, but someone beat you to the punch."

I started to protest, but he held up his hands. "It doesn't matter. At least you were smart enough this time to keep your mouth shut, so we can present our case any way we want. We have no choice but to go with a flat-out denial. You weren't there. Only one witness can identify you—Maria Cansalvo, a nineteen-year-old illegal immigrant who lives alone and works as a housekeeper. She doesn't speak English, and she didn't get past primary school. I can destroy her credibility."

"How are you going to do that?" I thought of the girl.

"It's common knowledge that organized gangs are bringing in the illegals. We can't prove it was Adamo, but we can certainly establish it as a possibility. Given that a single phone call could get her deported, the people who brought her in have a great deal of control over her actions. She could very well be doing the bidding of Vito Adamo in identifying you as the man who killed Moretti."

"But . . . it's not right."

Sutton stopped pacing. "Listen, Will. After the trial, she's going back to Sicily whether you go to prison or not. What do you say to being a free man when she leaves?"

A blue Newcomb-Endicott delivery truck, a Detroit Electric, passed through my view of the street. "What do you think my chances are?"

He smiled. "Good. You just need to relax and let me do the work."

"All right." I was glad he was confident, but I was still concerned about the girl.

Sutton clapped me on the back. "Look at the bright side. If all else fails, we have excellent grounds for appeal based on Morton denying the change of venue."

"That's the bright side?" I said. "To have to go through this twice?"

CHAPTER SEVEN

One morning, while lying on my cot, I realized that once I went to prison I would be in with the general population, and it would likely be at the state prison in Jackson—the worst prison in the state, with the most heinous criminals the Michigan state justice system could cull from the public. My safety would be entirely up to me. In my condition I'd be somebody's rag doll, barely worth a cigarette. My hand would make it difficult for me to defend myself if I was completely fit, and I was far from fit.

I dropped to the floor and did a hundred sit-ups. It took me all morning, but what else did I have to do? After lunch I started on squat thrusts and running in place, before starting again on my hand-stretching exercises. The next morning I woke almost unable to move, but I did another hundred sit-ups. This time my sore stomach muscles stabbed me with every one, but I gritted my teeth and took it. By the end of the month I was up to two hundred sit-ups, one hundred squat thrusts, and an hour (approximately, since I had no watch) of running in place. I was also able to almost completely straighten the fingers of my right hand.

Now I needed upper body strength. I started working on push-ups. Using my right hand to support myself was incredibly painful, but I worked through it. At first I struggled through ten, then twenty, then fifty, then a hundred, then two hundred. About two months in I realized I was no longer exercising out of fear, but because it made me feel good, physically, mentally, and spiritually.

My mind became alert, and I stopped constantly thinking about morphine. I started taking visitors, and spent time with my family and friends. I began reading again. Elizabeth and my parents brought me books and magazines—Elizabeth leaned toward Upton Sinclair, Jane Addams, and Mother Jones; my mother to Mary Johnston and Booth Tarkington. My father brought me trade magazines—*The Automobile* and *Horseless Age*.

I pressed Sutton to let the State get on with the trial. But now it was their turn to stall. The trial was to begin in December, and then January, and they actually seated a jury in March before discovering that one of the alternates had moved from the area, and another did business with my father's company and was therefore disqualified.

Elizabeth came to visit me for an hour every week. It wasn't like old times—that would have been difficult through iron bars—but we enjoyed our time together. She *was* keeping herself busy, and her mother was doing better day by day. As I spent more time with her, my suspicions that she was involved in Moretti's murder faded and then disappeared. She was simply too comfortable around me, which would have been impossible for her had she felt guilty.

I actually felt less imprisoned than I had before I was arrested. The morphine and melancholy shackled me more surely than bars ever could. I redoubled my resolve to stay away from morphine if I was ever released.

The newspaper articles had slowed, but it seemed that at least once a week one of the papers resurrected my old appellation—the Electric Executioner. Most now were editorials demanding the police reopen the case of Wesley McRae's death, given that the evidence was sketchy once one eliminated my testimony and that of my "gun moll," Elizabeth Hume. It would have made for great comedy had the stories been about someone else.

After nine long months in jail, my trial finally came.

The trial dragged through its early stages, as District Attorney Higgins laid out his case piece by piece. Witnesses, including Detective Riordan, described the death of Wesley McRae and my belief that alleged crime boss Vito Adamo had been involved.

My mother and Elizabeth sat behind me nearly every moment of the trial. My father came when he could. It was a relief to see them, to have someone believe in me, support me.

Sutton did a good job on cross-examination, poking holes in the testimony where he could, but the faces of the men on the jury just kept getting grimmer and grimmer. By Friday, the few who had met my eyes on Monday and Tuesday quickly turned their heads whenever they saw me looking at them. I was glad they'd let me wear a glove, as I found myself rubbing my hand during most of the testimony. It would have been a bloody mess otherwise.

When we returned from the lunch recess on Friday, the court was buzzing with murmured conversation. I looked out into the gallery and immediately saw what had caused the commotion. An albino man in a heavy tan overcoat was standing in the aisle in the back of the courtroom. He wore a tan fedora pulled low onto his forehead, a pair of small dark-tinted wire-rimmed glasses, and black gloves. He was speaking quietly to a young woman who stood next to him, taking notes.

Something about her caught my eye. She stood a few inches taller than the man, was perhaps twenty-five years old, and was slim and well turned out in a white shirtwaist and a light green skirt and jacket. She was attractive, though handsome rather than pretty, with a slash of a mouth, small dark eyes, and auburn hair pinned up under a green hat.

The bailiff called the court to order, and I turned my attention to the front of the room.

When the judge returned, Higgins, a portly man with a red face and thin blond hair, waddled toward the bench gripping the lapels of his brown suit coat. "If it please the court, the State would like to call Maria Cansalvo to the stand."

Judge Morton, a stern man with waxed gray mustaches, nodded and moved his hand in a circular *get on with it* motion. The bailiff called for the girl.

Sutton nudged my arm and leaned in toward me. "Keep a sympathetic and concerned look on your face the entire time she's up there. No frowns, no scowls, no smiles."

Staring straight ahead, I nodded. When I heard the wooden gate creak, I turned and saw Maria Cansalvo for the first time since the night her neighbor was murdered. She was a slight but pretty young woman in a faded yellow day dress and a plain, small-brimmed white hat, with dark curly hair and large brown eyes that I still remembered intimately. She slipped past our table and walked to the front of the courtroom.

Higgins, sweat beaded on his forehead, adjusted his wire-rimmed eyeglasses and turned to the judge. "Miss Cansalvo cannot speak English. I would like to call Ferdinand Palma to serve as an interpreter."

Judge Morton looked at our table. "Do you have any objection, Mr. Sutton?"

Sutton stood and allowed that he didn't. When he sat, he looked at me, shrugged, and whispered, "Palma used to be a Detroit city detective. He's interpreted in other cases I've had. I think he's all right."

I nodded and pulled on my collar. The air in the courthouse was stale, and it was hot. I wished someone would open a window.

The judge nodded to the bailiff, who called Ferdinand Palma to the stand. Palma, a stocky man in his midthirties, strolled up to the bailiff like he was taking a walk through the park. He wore an impeccable white summer suit—Brooks Brothers, I thought—with a crimson handkerchief in his breast pocket and a matching carnation on his lapel. His hair was so soaked with pomade it looked like he combed it with a pork chop. Palma wasn't a handsome man, but his self-assurance made him almost seem so.

The bailiff swore in Miss Cansalvo, who took her seat in the witness box, and then Palma, who stood nearby on the jury side of her.

Higgins waited until everyone was comfortable. "Miss Cansalvo, you live at 2400 Rivard in apartment 304, do you not?"

She looked at Palma, who asked her the question in Italian. "*Sì,*" she answered in a quiet voice.

He asked her if anything unusual happened the night of August 6. Palma interpreted, and her answer took about a minute. When she finished, Palma turned to the judge. "Miss Cansalvo was awakened by a shout in the apartment next to hers. She couldn't fall asleep again. While she was lying awake, she remembered she didn't leave any milk out for her cat. She was setting it outside when she saw a man lurking in the hallway, wiping off the doorknob of her neighbor's apartment."

"And approximately what time was this?"

Palma asked Miss Cansalvo. Her reply was, "Two in the morning."

"What did the man do?"

She said he'd wiped off the doorknob and tried to hide his face, even covering it with a handkerchief like the Old West bank robbers she saw in flickers at the nickelodeon.

Higgins harrumphed and gripped his lapels again. "Is that man in this courtroom today?"

When she said he was, Higgins asked her to point him out.

Palma translated. Miss Cansalvo looked at me for the briefest moment before raising her hand and pointing at me. *"Lo,"* she whispered. "Will Anderson."

Sutton walked around our table and slowly approached Miss Cansalvo. He was impeccable in a dark gray suit with matching waistcoat, an ivory and gray ascot, and a pair of black oxfords shined to a high gloss.

He paused for a moment, looking into her eyes, then began. "Miss Cansalvo, I commend you for coming forward even though you must have known this testimony would lead to your deportation. That had to be a difficult decision." He looked at Palma, who translated.

Her eyes narrowed a bit, but she said, *"Sì. Grazie."*

Sutton nodded and cupped his chin in his hand. "And it must have been a difficult decision to leave Sicily in the first place, to travel alone to a new country. Not many people would do that, unless of course they had good reason to leave. Why did *you* leave your homeland?"

Palma translated. Miss Cansalvo's response was that she left because she was poor and couldn't find a job. She had heard that America was the land of opportunity.

With a sympathetic smile, Sutton nodded. He looked every bit the doting grandfather. "And how did you get here?"

Palma repeated the question in Italian and listened to her response. She started and stopped several times, clearly unsure what she should say. When she finished, Palma said, "There is a man in Palermo who arranges such things. She paid him and traveled to Canada by ship, then by train to Windsor, and another boat to Detroit."

Sutton nodded again. "Who brought you across the river from Windsor?"

She said it was a fellow Sicilian, though she did not know his name.

"Whom did he work for?"

She didn't know.

"Do you know the name Vito Adamo?"

When Palma translated, she said, "No."

"What business was Carlo Moretti engaged in?"

She didn't know.

Sutton sighed and gave her an admonishing glance. "Miss Cansalvo, you can be honest with us. You lived next door to Moretti for almost a year."

"Objection!" Higgins barked. "Asked and answered."

"Sustained," Judge Morton said. "Move on, Mr. Sutton."

"I apologize, Your Honor. But you have to admit, it's difficult to believe—"

"I said, move on," the judge said, this time louder.

"Yes, Your Honor." Sutton turned back to Miss Cansalvo. "Just so I'm clear, you came to this country illegally, secreted across the border by Sicilian men engaged in illegal activity, just as Mr. Moretti was—"

"Objection!" Higgins shouted again. "It has not been established that Mr. Moretti was involved in anything illegal."

"Sustained."

Sutton shot an annoyed look at the judge before turning again to Miss Cansalvo. With a casual air, he said, "Knowing you would be deported, you must have had a very compelling reason to come forward. Why did you?"

Palma translated. Miss Cansalvo said, *"Giustizia."*

"Justice," Sutton said. "I admire you, Miss Cansalvo. Risking so much for 'justice.' And for a man you didn't even know well enough to know what he did for a living. Admirable." After a moment passed, he said, "No other reason?"

She said no.

"Hmm." Sutton spoke slowly, almost to himself. "You are willing to be deported, to go back to the country from which you fled, a country with no jobs and no prospects, for no reason other than justice." He moved closer to her, leaned in, and quietly said, "We would all understand if you were, let's say, forced into this testimony by members of the Sicilian underworld. It would be terrifying for one such as you, alone in a strange country. So please tell us the truth, Miss Cansalvo. Who forced you to identify my client as the man outside Carlo Moretti's apartment?"

As Palma translated, Miss Cansalvo's eyes grew wide. She glared at Sutton. "*Nessuno.*" She jabbed her finger at me and said in heavily accented English, "It was him."

I shot a glance at the jury. Most of them were tight mouthed, staring at Mr. Sutton. He was dancing on the edge. Now he went on the attack, firing questions at her, trying to poke holes in her testimony. She held up well, responding calmly and assuredly. Although she hadn't seen a knife or any blood on me, she had no doubt whatever about whom she saw. My face was burned into her memory.

When Maria Cansalvo left the witness box, I looked at District Attorney Higgins. He was sitting back in his seat, smirking. His fingers were interlaced over his bulging brown waistcoat. To all appearances he was the cat that swallowed the canary. I thought he was smiling because his witness had held up under questioning from the most respected defense attorney in town.

Unfortunately for me, he was smiling for an entirely different reason.

Higgins stood and said, "Just one more witness, Your Honor. The State calls Arthur Preston to the stand."

Preston had been on our witness list, simply to establish that I had an alibi for part of the evening. I couldn't think of any reason Higgins would call him other than to clarify when he and his wife left my apartment. It seemed odd that the district attorney would end his case with a small detail, rather than with the eyewitness.

Preston scurried up the aisle, nervously smoothing his pencil-thin mustache and his greased-back ginger-colored hair. He wore a tight black suit, a little too tight, with a white shirt, a winged collar, and a black tie. His puffy face was a little puffier than usual. That, and the dark rings under his eyes, indicated another night of hard drinking.

The bailiff swore him in, and Higgins got right down to business. "Mr. Preston, how do you know the defendant?"

Preston brushed something off the front of his jacket and looked up at Higgins. "We—my wife and I, that is—moved into the apartment across the hall from Mr. Anderson in June 1911. We saw him a few times in the hall, and he invited us over for dinner on August sixth of last year."

"When, that night, did you last see Mr. Anderson?"

"We had dinner and a couple of drinks. We left at nine thirty-two." He turned to the judge. "I looked at the clock when we went back to our apartment. We have a large wall clock in the foyer. It was my grand-mother's. She—"

"Thank you, Mr. Preston," Higgins said. "When did you next see Mr. Anderson?"

"The next morning. I was going to work early."

The next morning? I sat up, startled. I hadn't seen Preston again until the night the police caught me. How could he have seen me?

Preston looked at Judge Morton again. "I'm the Detroit Salt Mining Company's *head* accountant. My department is busiest at the beginning of the month, so I make sure everyone is in the office by six A.M. I get there earlier, being the boss and all. Have to set the example, you know."

My heart was pounding so hard I thought it would explode.

Higgins leaned against the rail, took a deep breath, and let it out while looking toward the window, seeming to savor the moment. After a few seconds, he turned to Preston again. "What time did you see him?"

"It was five thirteen A.M. I had just looked at my watch."

Higgins nodded and smiled. "And where did you see him?"

"He was entering his apartment via the fire escape."

CHAPTER EIGHT

We resumed on Monday, this time with Mr. Sutton taking the offensive. For more than two weeks, he hammered away at the prosecution's case. The albino man and the auburn-haired woman sat in the back of the gallery every day. I asked Mr. Sutton if he had any idea who the albino was. He didn't, and I didn't bother him about it given that he had a larger concern, namely keeping me out of prison. He worked methodically, recalling all the prosecution's witnesses, including Maria Cansalvo. By the time he finished with her, I don't think even she was sure she had seen me.

Arthur Preston was another matter. His time fixation and the certainty with which he spoke made his testimony unshakable. The net impact was to verify every bit of the State's evidence, because if Preston was right, the testimony of every other State's witness made perfect sense.

Sutton's badgering had no effect on the jury other than to make them angry. They were clearly convinced I had murdered Moretti. By the time Sutton rested his case, I was as certain as I could be that I would spend the rest of my life in prison.

Judge Morton pulled out his pocket watch and glanced at it. "Gentlemen, I think we've had enough for today. We'll listen to closing statements tomorrow morning." He banged his gavel. "Court is adjourned."

When the judge left through a door in the front of the courtroom,

I turned to speak with my father, but my eyes first rested on the albino, who was standing by the door, staring at me behind his little dark glasses. A broad grin was plastered across his face, teeth yellow against the pallor of his skin.

The judge asked Higgins to give his closing statement. He ran his fingers over his head, making sure his thin blond hair was still pomaded in place; then he shuffled the papers on the table in front of him before ponderously rising to his feet. I think he was being dramatic, but it looked like he had difficulty lifting his bulk from the chair. He plodded around the table and approached the jury, all of whom were following his every movement. Thunder rumbled in the distance. I looked out the window. Raindrops began to slap against the glass.

Higgins took a deep breath, sighed, and began. "Gentlemen of the jury, the decision you have before you is a simple one."

Four of the men in the jury box nodded in agreement.

"We have proved beyond a reasonable doubt that Mr. William C. Anderson, Jr., did with malice and forethought brutally murder Carlo Moretti early in the morning of August seventh, 1911. We have established that Mr. Anderson had motive—revenge. We have proved that Mr. Anderson believes Mr. Moretti's *alleged* employer was a direct cause for the death of Wesley McRae, his"—Higgins paused and turned to me—"homosexual friend." Pointing back at me, he again turned to the jury. "Will Anderson needed someone—anyone—to pay for the death of this *friend*. It was Carlo Moretti's bad luck that Anderson turned his rage onto him.

"We have heard from the coroner that Mr. Moretti was killed sometime between midnight and four A.M., and an eyewitness puts Anderson at Moretti's apartment at two o'clock.

"Further, we have proved that Mr. Anderson had opportunity. Trying to establish an alibi, he invited his new neighbors, the Prestons, over for dinner. However, they left his apartment more than four hours before Anderson brutally murdered Carlo Moretti by slitting his throat—in his own home.

"Picture that, if you will—Anderson's cold eyes burning with rage as he ripped a dagger through poor Carlo Moretti's neck with such strength that he nearly took off his head. Think of the gouts of blood spasming out of Carlo's jugular vein, splashing off the wall, ending the all-too-short life of a twenty-four-year-old man."

He shook his head mournfully. "For revenge. Misguided revenge. Revenge against another man. Should Carlo Moretti have been punished? Nay, should Carlo Moretti have paid with his life, for . . ."

The door at the back of the courtroom banged open. Higgins looked, and his voice trailed off.

Detective Riordan marched down the aisle, his eyes locked on Judge Morton. Rain dripped off the brim of his fedora. A woman in the gallery gasped, I suppose at Riordan's scar, though I'm not sure. He stopped at the gate and said to the judge, "May I approach, Your Honor?"

Morton nodded, and Riordan marched across the room to him. He was tall enough that his chin was nearly as high as the bench. He spoke quietly but urgently. The judge seemed to be asking him questions, to which he responded.

After a couple of minutes, Judge Morton nodded and announced, "I want to see counsel in my chambers. Now. You too, Detective." The judge strode to a door in the front of the courtroom, threw it open, and rushed inside.

I shared a mystified glance with Mr. Sutton. He patted my arm. "Look at the bright side. It's unlikely to make things worse." He hurried around the table and followed Higgins out of the courtroom.

I sat at the table squirming for fifteen minutes, until Mr. Sutton, District Attorney Higgins, and Detective Riordan returned. Higgins looked deflated. Mr. Sutton was beaming. When he sat down, he even tousled my hair.

"What?" I said.

He just sat back and said, "Listen to this."

The bailiff called the court to order, and we all rose for the return of the judge. He came in, sat at the bench, and said, "Mr. Higgins, you have something to say?"

Higgins tugged at his collar, stood, and said, "Yes, Your Honor. The prosecution would like to enter a motion of *nolle prosequi*."

The judge banged his gavel and said, "This case is dismissed." He turned to me. "Mr. Anderson, you may go. Please accept the court's apologies for the inconvenience."

I sat stock-still, not believing what I had just heard.

Sutton stood and pounded me on the back. "Can you believe it?"

I looked up at his grinning face. "No, I can't. What's *nolle prosequi?*"

"The State dropped its case against you."

"Why?"

He laughed. "Another man confessed."

With newspapers over our heads to protect us from the steady rain, we shoved our way through two dozen reporters to Sutton's Pierce-Arrow touring car, a light blue, long-bodied giant with shining chrome fixtures. The din was incredible—shouted questions, scuffling men pushing to get a better position, the *whump* of camera flashes, rumbling thunder. I splashed down the steps and the front walk onto the street, where Sutton's chauffeur waited.

Sutton wouldn't answer my questions in the courthouse, instead telling me to wait until we got to his car. As soon as we piled in, I said, "Who confessed?"

He leaned forward in the blue leather seat and pulled the tail of his coat down behind him as the driver pulled onto the road. "A man named Giovanni Esposito. According to Detective Riordan, Esposito is about your size and looks somewhat similar. He's an illegal who's been in Detroit about two years. No fixed address, no occupation. He's from the same part of Sicily as Moretti. The police confirmed that their families have feuded for centuries. He said he saw Moretti by chance and lay in wait for him inside his apartment. When Moretti came home again Esposito cut his throat."

"Why would they believe him when a witness identified me, and all the evidence points to me?" I shook my head.

"He brought in the knife when he confessed. His story works as well as yours, and he says he did it. I don't think Riordan is convinced, but I say don't look a gift horse up the patoot."

I nodded and looked out the side of the car, watching the city go by. We rolled past businesses, houses, and apartment buildings I didn't remember. After three-quarters of a year in jail, the blocks were unfamiliar, foreign. I sat back and listened to the water thrum off the leather roof of the touring car, and the tires of passing automobiles whiz by on the wet cobbles.

My mouth suddenly went dry. Was the morphine still there? I remembered the soothing relief, the soaring happiness. I could almost feel the warmth, the well-being. But . . . I knew what I should do. I had gotten through the withdrawals, had gotten the poison out of my system. I needed to dump it the minute I got home.

Sutton's driver dropped me off at my building, and I slogged through the rain to the door and then climbed the two flights of stairs to my apartment. Margaret Preston was locking her door as I turned the corner at the top of the stairway. She glanced at me and looked away, and then her head spun back. She stared for a few seconds before remembering her manners. Bustling past me with her head down, she mumbled, "Good afternoon," and bolted down the steps.

I unlocked my door, walked into the foyer, and shut and locked the door again. My first stop was the bedroom. I opened the doors of my wardrobe and stood there a minute, afraid to look. I was afraid it would be gone, but I was more afraid it would be there. Finally I swept aside my clothing and looked behind my shoes. A large brown bottle—exactly where I had left it—stood in the back of the wardrobe. I grabbed it, took it to the bathroom, and turned it over the sink. The bitter smell of the morphine wafted to my nose as the syrup disappeared down the drain. I found myself inhaling deeply, but I finished dumping the bottle with a grim smile on my face.

I won.

I headed into the parlor to the shelf that held Wesley's Victrola. The dartboard still hung to the right of it, surrounded by chipped plaster, though someone had removed the knife I'd left buried in the wall. The Sophie Tucker record was on the Victrola. I picked it up, blew off the dust, and put it on again.

As the music poured out from the horn, I thought about the albino and Giovanni Esposito. The albino was involved in this somehow. The way he smiled at me showed something—could it have been knowledge of Esposito's confession? Perhaps he was the one who had gotten Esposito to confess.

But it didn't really matter. Sutton was right: I was a free man.

I went to my parents' house for dinner. They had invited Elizabeth too, and she sat next to me. The mood was celebratory. We all acted almost manic, with unrestrained bursts of laughter, loud conversation, wild gesticulations. Anyone watching us would have assumed we were all drunk, though not a drop was served. We were four people who had been certain I would never return home and weren't entirely sure how to react to my being released.

I saw Elizabeth home on a streetcar, and we fell into a gay conversation about our mutual friends, who in reality were her friends. I walked her the last two blocks on the wet sidewalk, her arm in mine. In front of her next-door neighbors' house, I had a childish impulse. I nudged her with my hip so that she stumbled into a puddle on the walk.

She laughed and kicked water at me. I ran ahead. She chased me, finally catching up at the white gate in front of her house. We grabbed each other and spun halfway around before we stopped, finding ourselves looking into the other's eyes.

"Lizzie," I said. "This is like a dream. No matter what happens with us, this is all I could want. Thank you for believing in me."

She leaned in and gave me a kiss on the cheek. "It's good to have you back, Will."

"Could I phone you?" I asked.

She smiled and nodded. I watched as she walked up the sidewalk. She climbed the steps and turned back to me with a little wave. I stood there for a few minutes, inhaling the cool clean air coming off the river, looking up at the stars peeking through the clouds.

None of this seemed real. Earlier today, there was no doubt I'd be sentenced to life in prison. Now I was free. Elizabeth had kissed me. She wanted to see me again.

I had my life back. This time I wouldn't waste it.

When I woke the next morning, my apartment was warm, the air stale. I opened the windows. The ground was still wet from yesterday's rain, and the grass and trees shone the brilliant green of late spring. Over a cup of coffee, I thought about what to do. I hadn't been in the position to decide much of anything for the better part of a year, and it was disconcerting. It seemed to me that another attempt at normalcy made sense. Go to work; go see Elizabeth afterwards. Perhaps this could be my new normal.

I dressed in one of my work suits, and found the trousers baggy at the waist and the coat so tight in the shoulders I could barely get it on. I dug into the back of my wardrobe and found the gray sack suit I'd worn at my college graduation. It was also snug in the shoulders but a much better fit overall.

When I walked out the front door of my building, I took a deep breath, enjoying the wonderful springtime scent. The sky was a brilliant cornflower blue; birds sang in the trees around me. I walked down the sidewalk whistling.

Two men—one a hulking six-plus feet, the other a short, slight man—both dark complexioned and wearing black suits and derbies, climbed out of a black Hupmobile roadster in front of the building. I eyed them as they walked up the sidewalk, The big man had huge hands and a large head with a heavy brow. The small man was at least two days between shaves. His big dark eyes were wide-set, and his suit was worn at the knees. They didn't look like they belonged in this part of town.

When I got inside ten feet of them, both men stopped, blocking me, and opened their coats with their left hands. Both had very large pistols stuck into shoulder holsters. The big man spoke. "You come wit' us." He had a heavy Italian accent.

Oh, shit. I held my hands up in front of me. "There must be some mistake."

The big man pulled his pistol and held it at his waist, pointed at my chest. "Get in car. Now."

"Wait just a minute." I looked around for witnesses and saw no one. My guts clenched. "What's the meaning of this?"

He stepped closer and growled into my ear, "Get in car or I kill you."

I had no choice. Heart hammering in my chest, I began walking to the car.

The small man moved around to the driving seat. The big one used his gun barrel to direct me into the back. He joined me, the gun leveled at my midsection.

My pulse raced. "Listen," I said. "Adamo's got this all—"

"Shut up."

"But you don't understand. I—"

He jammed the gun barrel into my ribs. "If you don' shut you mouth I put bullet in you."

I shut up. Adrenaline pumped through my veins, but I couldn't move. I'd have to be alert for any chance to turn the tables. If they brought me to Adamo, I was dead.

The big man kept his eyes and the gun pointed at me, while the driver drove fast, staying on side streets. He stopped perhaps ten minutes later next to a forest just west of town. The big man used the gun barrel to push me out of the car and said, "Aroun' back."

I figured this was it. Adamo would be showing his face any second. He'd want to see the coup de grâce. "Where is he?"

The big man stuck to his standard line. "Shut up."

I walked to the back of the car. The big man said something in Italian to the driver and then held his gun on me while the other man searched me.

"Now, get in trunk," the big man said. He pointed to the steamer trunk lashed to the Hupmobile's bumper.

"What? You must be kidding. I'll never fit in there."

The big man looked at the driver and motioned toward the trunk. The driver fumbled with the latch for a moment before throwing back the lid. I saw what the problem was. His right hand had only three fingers. "Inside," he said.

It was a reprieve from being killed, assuming I didn't suffocate in the trunk, but it seemed to be only delaying the inevitable. I folded my arms over my chest. "If you're going to kill me, do it here. There's no one around."

The driver shoved me, slamming me against the trunk. "Get in." He pulled a dagger with an eight-inch blade from a scabbard on his belt. It glinted into my eyes. "Or we put you in—in pieces."

Son of a bitch. I put one foot, and then the other, inside the trunk, and tried to fit myself in. Folding my knees against my chest, I bent my neck forward and crammed my head inside. The lid slammed on my right shoulder. One of them put his weight behind it and clasped it shut. A few seconds later, the car pulled onto the road. I could barely move. My arms were pinned to my sides, my knees crammed against my chest, and my neck bent forward as far as it would go.

I pushed against the lid with my shoulder and cracked it open just enough to let in some fresh air. Slowing my breathing, I tried to think, but I had no ideas—other than that I was probably going to disappear without a trace, unless Adamo left my body somewhere as a message to his enemies. After half an hour or so, the car stopped. The springs squeaked as the car rocked toward the passenger side and back again. The car pulled ahead slowly a few feet and then stopped. The engine shut off. Doors slammed. The trunk lid opened, and the two men loomed over me.

"Out," the big man said. I levered myself out of the trunk like a vaudeville contortionist and clambered down to the dirt floor. We were in a small stable, lit only by thin shafts of light poking through cracks in the wood. I couldn't hear any traffic noise, or anything else for that matter.

The big man muscled me to a chair, shoved me down into it, and tied my hands behind me while the driver held a gun on me. The smaller man then hurried to a side door and disappeared outside. Before the door closed I caught a glimpse of a white clapboard house and a small fruit tree. I sat back and tried to slow my heart. I'd wait for my chance.

If they gave me one.

CHAPTER NINE

A pair of big men walked through the door, followed by the driver. I expected Vito Adamo to walk in behind them, but he didn't. The driver closed the door and stood next to it. The new men were clearly brothers, stocky and big shouldered with pudgy faces and thick black hair. They wore white shirts and dark trousers. The shorter man had a knife scabbard on his belt, the thick handle of a Buck knife rising from it.

They stopped in front of my chair. The first man crossed his arms and stared down at me under heavy eyelids. He had thick black eyebrows, a broad, flat nose, and thick, liver-colored lips. "You Will Anderson?" His accent was three-quarters Italian, one-quarter lower-class Detroit.

I stared back at him. "Who wants to know?"

With a smile he glanced at his brother. The shorter man backhanded me across the face, and I crashed to the floor along with the chair. He was incredibly powerful. I shook my head to clear it. The big kidnapper grabbed my arms and jerked me upright.

"Let's try again," the man said. "You Will Anderson?"

I spat blood and saliva at him. It was a strange moment. I felt as if I were watching myself from the outside. I'd never done anything like this, but I wasn't going to give in to Adamo. I pictured him standing in the darkness of the stable, laughing at me.

The man wiped off his face and bent over with his hands on his knees. "You do that again, I'm gonna give ya to Sammy here." He gestured toward the shorter man, who was horse-faced with wide-open, almost bulging eyes. "He's been wonderin' how long he could keep a man alive while he's skinnin' him." He stayed there, his face six inches from mine, looking at me with those half-open eyes, like he was begging me to do it.

I glanced at his brother, who pulled the knife from his belt and tested the edge with a fingertip. I looked again at the first man, but I didn't spit.

"Awright." He straightened. "Why don' I start. My name is Tony Gianolla, and this"—he used his thumb to point at the shorter man next to him—"is my brother Sam."

"Why would I care?"

"Listen, *stronzo*," Tony Gianolla said to me, visibly fighting his temper. "Vito Adamo is your enemy, yes?"

"Like you don't know that?"

His mouth turned up in an amused smile. A tiny ball of white saliva perched at the center of his lower lip. "Just didn' pitcher you this way. Tough guy." He shook his head. "We need to get Adamo off our asses. And you're helpin' us."

"You're not with Adamo?"

He laughed. "Not hardly."

That explained why I was still alive. "Why would I help you?"

"'Cause I'm the only reason you not behind bars."

I stared into Tony Gianolla's hooded eyes. "What are you talking about?"

"Giovanni Esposito owed me a favor. He paid it back. Now *you* owe me."

"I didn't kill anybody. I don't owe you anything."

Tony smiled. "Don' matter if you killed Adamo's boy or not. You were goin' down for it. I got you sprung."

"So are you saying Esposito was the killer?"

"No, what I'm sayin' is you owe me. Big."

A cold dread filled me. "What do you want?"

"A lot less than I wanted from Esposito." The brothers laughed and then Tony got serious again. "Vito Adamo killed a friend of mine a couple days ago. He won't let us alone. You gonna bring him a gift from us. We need peace with him."

"The minute he sees me, he'll shoot me down. Get someone else."

"No. We can give him somethin' he can' get from anybody else. He'll be grateful, an' it'll make sense comin' from you."

I clenched my fists behind me to keep my hands from trembling. "What are you talking about?"

"Me and my brother got a little arrangement with the Teamsters Union. You gonna offer Adamo our cut of a car company."

"Why me?" I was afraid I knew the answer.

"'Cause it's your company."

Of course it is. "I can't do that. Look, I don't even know where Adamo is. And I don't have any control over what they do at the company. I don't even think I still have a job there."

He reached down and patted my cheek with a very large hand. "We give you a couple addresses. You gonna figure out where he's hidin'. Otherwise"—he hooked a thumb toward his brother—"Sam here's gonna pay you a visit. You won' like that. And if you still think you're a tough guy, maybe he'll go see your mama and papa. Or your girl."

I looked into Tony's eyes and then Sam's. "You stay away from my family. If you do anything to them, I'll kill you. And I don't have a girl."

"Why am I not surprised?" Tony gave me a smile that reached nowhere near his eyes. "We ain't gonna have to see your family, 'cause you gonna want this as much as we do."

"Why's that?"

He tilted his head at me. "'Cause I'm gonna help you kill Adamo."

He went on to explain that the Teamsters had deals with the employees of a number of delivery and moving companies, as well as drivers in the ice, coal, and milk industries.

They had yet to get their claws into the automobile business.

"That's where the money is," Tony said. "Adamo knows that. He'll understan' you bringin' him the offer. You want him to call off the dogs, we want him to call off the dogs—he wins. Then he can start musclin' us out of our own thing." Tony Gianolla smiled for real, and his upper canines dented his lower lip. It transformed him from a pudgy, overgrown boy into a dangerous carnivore. "But that ain't what's gonna happen. Once't he settles in a bit, you gonna off him."

"Listen," I said. "As much as I want Adamo dead, I can't do this. It's my father's company, and he reports to a board of directors. When I worked there, I was an assistant in the engineering department. I have no say in running the business. And why the hell would they let a union in anyway? The Employers Association will just run them out. This won't work."

Tony shook his head, all the while looking amused. "Not my problem." He gave the big man an order, and he bent down and untied my hands. Tony motioned for me to stand. When I did, he put his arm around me and walked me back to the car. "Giovanni Esposito gave his life for your sins. There's no getting it back. To you I am God." He stopped and looked me full in the face. "If you run, I'll kill your family. If you fail, I'll kill your family. If you go to the cops, I'll kill your family. And I'll kill you too. You want ev'body healthy when this is over, you do your job."

He patted my cheek and then cupped my chin in his meaty hand. "We got all kinds a cops on the payroll—city, sheriffs, state." He gave my head a shake. "Get this inta that thick skull a yours. You talk to anybody—anybody—and ev'body dies. You and me is partners. My partners make me happy. You don't"—he shook his head and smiled at his brother—"Sam's gonna pay you a visit. Right after he sees your ma."

"Who are you guys?" I said.

"Hey." He spread his hands in front of him. "We just poor immigrants tryin' to make our way in America, huh, Sam?"

His brother grunted out a laugh. "*Sì*, just tryin' to make our way."

I folded my arms over my chest. Another Black Hand gang. "So this is just a shakedown?"

" '*Shakedown*' is a ugly word," Tony said. "We did you a favor, now it's your turn. So get to work." He handed me a folded piece of paper and pushed me toward the car. "Be lookin' for a visit from the Teamsters."

The side door opened, and a woman walked in. At first she was silhouetted against the sunlight, and I couldn't make out her features. She walked over to Sam Gianolla and nuzzled him, and I saw her clearly.

It was the auburn-haired woman from the trial.

She wore a low-cut red silk dress that stopped above her ankles, with white button-top boots and a white, wide-brimmed hat. She kissed Sam on the cheek and took his arm. It was like watching a butterfly light on a piece of shit.

"Who's that?" I said to Tony, gesturing toward the woman.

Tony glanced behind him. "Sammy's girl. Why do you care?"

"Just curious."

He turned to the driver and rattled off some quick Italian. The other man eyed me.

"What was that about?" I asked.

"I was just tellin' him what to do wit' you," Tony said.

I stared at him.

He laughed. "Don' worry." He held my eyes. "At least not yet."

The kidnappers forced me to climb into the trunk again. In the dark of the trunk, knees against my chest and head bent forward, I considered what I knew. The Gianollas, assisted by the albino and Sam's girlfriend, had orchestrated Esposito's confession. Was it simply so they could blackmail me?

Tony Gianolla must have ordered Carlo Moretti's death. If I were a betting man, I'd say Sam Gianolla killed Moretti, though I supposed either one of the thugs driving me could have done it as well. Or perhaps Giovanni Esposito was actually in jail for a crime he committed. Sam's girlfriend could very well have been the prostitute—or at least played the role. It didn't really matter. The Gianollas had me over a barrel.

So what alternatives did I have?

Somehow finagle my father into accepting a union? It was laughable, unprecedented, not to mention impossible. Not only had no Detroit automobile company ever allowed a union through its doors, the Employers Association of Detroit existed for no purpose other than to keep the unions out. Anderson Electric Car Company wrote a big check every month to pay the EAD's thugs and strikebreakers for protection—not so different from the Black Hand, now that I thought about it.

What else could I do? Go after the Gianollas?

My family would be dead before I could kill the second brother.

Go to the police?

Hah. Other than Detective Riordan, every cop I'd met in this town was a crook. I'd bet dollars to buttons that Tony was telling the truth—they had cops on their payroll. I'd have better luck bringing in the Boy Scouts. But . . . Detective Riordan. It might be worth talking to him. If worse came to worst, I'd have to go along with the Gianollas' scheme until I could turn the tables on them. If it got me Vito Adamo, so much the better.

Finally the car stopped, and the trunk opened. The kidnappers pulled me out feetfirst and dumped me into the dirt. Sharing a grin, they climbed back into the roadster and drove away.

I lay on the ground with my hands over my face. My head pounded; sharp pains pulsated behind my eyes. I massaged the tight muscles in my forehead and felt deep wrinkles between my eyebrows. When I climbed to my feet, I saw I was in an alley between a pair of redbrick three-story houses. I worked the kinks out of various parts of my body and walked out to the road. I was on Second Street, only a few blocks from home.

I hurried to my apartment, locked myself in, and ran a bath—as hot as I could stand. When I lay back in the steaming water, I took a deep breath and exhaled slowly. I would see if Detective Riordan could pull any miracles from his sleeve. Then I'd speak with my father about getting my job back. Assuming Riordan wasn't a miracle worker, the Gianollas would have to be convinced that I really was going to help them.

And what of Elizabeth? I couldn't put her in the crosshairs.

I couldn't see her.

The next morning I emptied the pockets of my trousers and found the piece of paper Tony Gianolla had given me. Unfolding it, I saw two addresses—one in Ford City, down by Wyandotte, the second an address on Hastings, which I was certain was Adamo's saloon, the Bucket.

I was plenty familiar with that location. It seemed likely that the first was a home address.

They wanted Adamo dead. I shared their desire. Perhaps if I killed him, I could hold the Gianollas and the Teamsters at bay. It would at least lessen the urgency of their request. But I'd try Riordan first.

I walked down Peterboro toward Woodward. The morning was warm, with only a few clouds to mar a brilliant blue sky. As I approached the streetcar stop, the dozen people already standing there started shouting. When I got closer, I saw a pair of newsboys scuffling on the sidewalk, while the men in the crowd rooted them on. The boys looked to be about ten years old. One of them, a freckled redhead, was a foot taller than the little dark-haired boy he was fighting, but he was stymied by jabs and kicks that kept him from getting inside.

Everything turned quickly when the smaller boy wound up and missed a kick to the redhead's groin, and in return received a haymaker that knocked him straight over backwards. The redhead dived on top of him and began throwing punch after punch into the smaller boy's face, which was quickly spattered with blood. The adults just kept cheering.

Adrenaline pumped through me. I ran the last thirty feet, pulled the redhead off, and shoved him away. He snarled and tried to jump back on the other kid, but I held on to him. He fought me, but finally spat at the boy and stomped away. I wheeled on the crowd. "What the hell is wrong with you people? These are kids."

A distinguished-looking man of about sixty gave me a disgusted wave with his shiny black cane and turned his back. Another man jutted out his jaw and said, "You just cost me two bits. That Mick was gonna kill the Jew."

I shook my head and turned to the boy on the ground. Through the blood I could make out a long narrow face, large hooked nose, dark eyes, and thick black hair. He pushed himself up to a seated position, his face contorted as he tried not to cry. Blood and mucus ran from his nose. He had a cut over one eye that bled down his face, but it didn't look too serious. His white shirt was dirty and torn at the collar.

Looking at him made me want to cry, which surprised me. I'd seen my share of fights. At times I'd been exhilarated, other times horrified. But this boy filled me with sadness. Maybe it was too close—a smaller person brutalized by a larger one. Regardless, I really felt for the boy. I gave him my handkerchief and helped him to his feet. "You all right?" I asked quietly.

He shoved away from me. "I'm okay. But he's not gonna be."

"Forget about it," I said. "That kid is half again your size."

The boy glared at me. "This is *my* corner." He picked up a white bag with perhaps half a dozen *Detroit Herald* newspapers inside. "Sonuvabitch!" He spun around toward the crowd. "Who stole'd my goddamn papers?"

A couple of people turned around, but no one said anything.

"I gotta pay for those fuckin' papers, you cocksuckers."

The distinguished-looking man waved his cane at the boy. "You watch your mouth, you young whelp, or I'll give you a good caning."

The boy's mouth puckered like he was eating a lemon. He stared back at the man for a moment before saying, "Just like I gave your ol' lady this mornin' after she sucked my dick?"

The man raised his cane and advanced on the boy, but I stepped between them. "Get out of here," I said over my shoulder.

The man poked his cane into my chest. "Mind your own business, sir, or I'll turn my cane on you."

I grabbed the cane, twisted it out of his hand, and gave him a shove. He fell to the sidewalk. I jabbed the cane toward him and was only just able to stop short of his face. I wanted to run him through or pound him into mush. My face must have shown it, because he didn't move.

The trolley rattled up the street, almost at the stop. I threw the cane to the ground and shoved my way onto the car, which already had people hanging off the sides. After I dropped my nickel into the coin box, I remembered the boy. I looked out at the sidewalk again. He was gone. Good. I hoped he wouldn't reappear until the older man had left.

The trolley started up again, and I took a few deep breaths to calm myself. The closer I got to the police station, the more I filled with doubt. How did I know Riordan wasn't on the Gianollas' payroll or would say something to a cop who was? Murphy saying Riordan was honest didn't make it so. Even if he was as honest as I thought he was, this path was still fraught with danger. He knew how much I wanted Adamo. I would need to be careful with him.

I hopped off the car at Bethune Street and walked the remaining four blocks to the police station. As soon as I walked in the door, the smell hit me—a vague odor of bleach that failed to cover the sour stench of vomit and sweat.

The desk sergeant, a gray-haired Irishman with a florid face, bellowed, "Oh, the prodigal son has returned, now, has he? We've missed you terribly. What would you like to confess to today?"

I swallowed the response that came to mind and said, "I'd like to see Detective Riordan."

"You would, now, would'ja?"

I nodded.

"Well, the detective isn't in just now, laddie." He smirked. "But I think we've got an available guest room where you could wait."

"If it's all the same to you, I'll wait out here."

I sat in one of the old wooden chairs in the lobby, working the problem with the Gianollas in my mind. If I could get Riordan to go after them, they might forget about me—and my family. If not, I couldn't risk talking to any other policeman. Riordan had to believe me.

After about an hour, he walked in along with another man. Both wore dark wool suits with waistcoats and ties. I jumped up and called out, "Detective Riordan? Could I speak with you, please?"

He turned toward me, his face registering surprise. "'Please,' Will? I don't think I've heard you use that word before." He nodded for the other man to leave. As I walked up to Riordan, his lip curled. The burgundy slash on his face shone in the electric lights.

I looked away from his scar and lowered my voice. "Privately?"

He pursed his lips and nodded. "All right." Without another word, he turned and walked toward an interior door. I followed him into a hallway with dirty white plaster walls and a scuffed plank floor. Finally he ducked—literally—into an office near the end of the hall. The doorway was barely six feet high. A small oak desk filled a quarter of the tiny room. A line of beat-up file cabinets filled half. The remaining few feet created a narrow walkway to his desk and left just enough room for his chair on one side and another small chair to be wedged in sideways against the opposite wall.

"I pictured you with a little more finery than this," I said as Riordan squeezed himself behind his desk.

"Reward of my investigation into the Electric Executioner. When it turned out it wasn't you, the mayor and commissioner tried to get me to resign. When I wouldn't—" He spread his hands in front of him. "Now, what can I do for you?"

I sat in the other chair. "Do you know Tony and Sam Gianolla?"

He pulled a cigar from his coat pocket, bit off the end, and spit it into a small wastebasket next to him. "Can't say I do." Lighting the cigar, he puffed cloud after cloud of rotting leaf stink into the room.

I waved my left hand in front of me, which did nothing more than rearrange the smoke. "Tony Gianolla is the leader of a Black Hand gang. Sam is his muscle."

Riordan leaned forward, looking interested. "Where do they work out of?"

"I don't know. They kidnapped me, threatened to kill my family. They dumped me into a trunk and drove for half an hour. I don't know if they drove around in circles or took me straight to wherever I was."

"Why are they after you?"

"They have some sort of stake in the Teamsters Union and want me to get them into Detroit Electric."

He opened a desk drawer and pulled out a form. "What did you say their names were?"

"No paperwork."

He looked up at me.

"The Gianollas have cops on their payroll. If they find out I came here they'll kill my family. They're already into it with the Adamo gang. Tony Gianolla said Adamo killed one of his men a few days ago."

Riordan rubbed the stubble on his chin. "Seems quite a coincidence, doesn't it?"

"What? That Adamo is a player in this?"

One corner of his mouth slowly turned upward. "Yes, that's exactly what I meant."

"Two Black Hand gangs fighting each other? Judging from the newspapers, that's just about all they do. Please, Detective Riordan, I need your help. Off the books."

He shook his head slowly. "I don't do business that way, Will. Especially with a murderer. You know, for some reason I never doubted you killed Moretti."

That stopped me. "My Lord, I didn't kill him. If you were so sure of that, why'd you bring Esposito's confession to court?"

He flung an arm over the back of the chair and blew a big cloud of smoke toward the ceiling before he looked at me again. "I've been asking myself the same question."

CHAPTER TEN

My father's secretary, Mr. Wilkinson, looked up when I entered the office. He was sitting at his small walnut desk, atop of which were only a blotter with green leather trim, a black telephone—the finish of its candlestick polished to a high gloss—and a single stack of paper. All were neatly squared to the lines of the desk.

"Will." He smiled. "You look good." He stood and walked around his desk, holding out his left hand. "Congratulations. I was so happy to hear the news." He ducked his head. "Of course I knew you didn't do it."

I tried to smile while I was thanking him, though I'm sure it was more a grimace.

"What brings you in today?" he asked. "Your father didn't say anything about it."

"No. I didn't expect to be in. I'd just like a minute with him."

"Certainly. Let me see if he has a moment." He stepped to my father's office door and knocked twice.

My father's muffled voice carried through the door. Wilkinson opened it and stepped just inside. "Have you a moment to see an innocent man?" I could hear the smile in his voice.

"What?" my father said. "Oh, Will's here?"

Wilkinson nodded and stepped aside as my father hurried out of his office. "Good, good. There's something I'd like to speak with you about."

"All right. I'd like to speak with you as well." My voice was weak, pathetic. I tried to build some enthusiasm.

"Certainly. Come in." He put his hand on my arm and escorted me into his office. He'd gotten new chairs since the last time I was here. I sat in one of them. The chair bulged in odd places that stuck into my back, and I shifted in my seat in a fruitless effort to get comfortable. "What's wrong with this chair?"

My father grinned. "I'm tired of people wasting my time. I've been on the lookout for the least comfortable chairs in the country."

I stood. "I think you've found them."

"All right." He sat in his gray leather swivel chair. "What can I do for you?"

"I'd like to come back to work—but not in engineering. I'd like to work with you."

"Mmm." He chewed on the inside of his cheek. Finally he said, "We might be able to arrange that. But first I need *you* to do something."

"What?"

"See Dr. Miller for a complete examination."

"Why?"

"Humor me. I want to be sure you're healthy before you come back to work."

I shrugged. "Fine. But what sort of work might I do?"

"Let me ponder that. There are a few special projects I haven't been able to get to."

"I was thinking of a front office job. Administration. Something like that."

"We'll discuss it after you see Dr. Miller," he said. "And you must promise to follow Dr. Miller's instructions . . . should he have any."

Again, I shrugged. "Fine."

He picked up the receiver of his telephone. "Wilkinson? Call Dr. Miller. Tell him Will and I will be in this afternoon." He listened for a moment. "Yes. He said whenever I could get him there." He hung up.

"Today?" I said.

"Well, yes. He told me he'd fit you in any time."

"All right." My father and Dr. Miller had obviously planned this out, but I didn't anticipate any difficulty. I'd known Dr. Miller since I was a child, and he'd helped me immeasurably in my trials with Elizabeth. I had nothing to worry about. Once I finished with Dr. Miller, I'd begin to work on my father again. He *had* to give me a good job.

"Neurasthenia," Dr. Miller said, turning to my father. "Or 'Americanitis,' if you prefer. There's no doubt."

"Oh, please." I shook my head and jumped off the examination table. "There's nothing wrong with me that a week out of jail won't cure."

"I'm afraid not, Will." The doctor flipped through the pages of his notebook, peering over his pince-nez glasses. "Dispepsia, melancholia, a tendency to addiction—I could go on." He spread his hands in front of him. "It's simply your body's response to the speed of life in this country. I believe your dependence on morphine came from a subconscious desire to slow down your life and to escape from the pressure exerted on you. The human body and mind weren't designed for this kind of strain. You need the rest cure."

"I can't do that."

"Will, listen to reason," my father said. "There are any number of nice sanitariums—Dr. Kellogg's in Battle Creek, for instance."

"He's right, Will," Dr. Miller said. "Though I'd recommend traveling a bit farther. The Glen Springs Hotel in New York has been getting wonderful results with their radioactive mineral springs. A month or two there will give your body time to heal itself."

"All I've been doing is resting. I need to get back to work."

My father shook his head. "You promised to follow Dr. Miller's instructions."

"Father, I'll go crazy there. The best thing for me is to work. If we work together you'll be able to keep your eye on me. You'll know if I'm getting better or worse. Please." I reached out to him with my left hand. "I need to work."

He sighed and turned to Dr. Miller. "Are there any other treatments?"

"Well, there's one possibility." He looked thoughtful.

"Will I be able to work right away?" I asked.

"Shouldn't be a problem."

I looked at my father. "And you'll let me work with you?"

He rubbed his chin with a forefinger before nodding.

Then it didn't matter what it was. "I'll do it." I looked out the window at Dr. Miller's vegetable garden and was brought back to the day I discovered Elizabeth was addicted to heroin.

"All right," Dr. Miller said. "We can start immediately."

"Fine." I turned to my father. "I'll be in bright and early tomorrow morning."

"I'll need a few minutes," Dr. Miller said. "I have to warm up the machine."

"What machine?"

"Oh, I'm sorry," Dr. Miller said. "Electrotherapy is what I was talking about."

"That's putting my feet in electrified water?"

Dr. Miller chuckled. "No, of course not. Studies have proved that to be completely ineffective."

"Oh." I felt a little relief. "Well then, what are you going to do?"

"We connect a pair of electrodes to a machine." He stepped up to me. "And we affix one here"—he touched one of my temples—"and the other to the inner angle of the eye, about here." He pointed to my eye, just to the side of my nose.

"No." It came out automatically.

Dr. Miller glanced at my father, who said, "There's always Glen Springs, Will."

Shit. "No . . . no, I'll do this—the electrotherapy." I had to protect my family.

"I've done this hundreds of times, Will," Dr. Miller said. "The charge is relatively mild. You've nothing to worry about." He looked at my father and then again at me. "Okay?"

The thought of shooting an electrical charge into my head scared me to death, not to mention that it brought back frightful memories. But what choice did I have? "Fine."

Dr. Miller left the room. I waited with my father until the doctor came back and escorted me into a small room with no windows. It contained a hospital bed, a small white table, a cabinet with medical supplies, and a single wooden chair. On the table was a wooden box with a pair of wires sticking out of it. It was plugged into a light socket.

Dr. Miller asked me to sit on the bed before taking two small white disks out of the cabinet. He applied a bit of glue to the back of the disks and stuck one on my left temple and the other at the edge of my right eye. While he did, he said, "Electrotherapy is a tried-and-true technique. I prefer the rest cure because it's less intrusive, but this is as likely to cure you. Now, lie down."

I lay back, and he hooked the wires to the disks glued to my head. My fingers were trembling.

Stroking his long white beard, he said, "When we start, you will feel a tingling sensation first, and then a mild jolt that may disorient you a bit. I'll want to watch you for a few hours and then your father can take you home." He reached over to the box. "All right, here we go."

Little fingers tickled my skull and danced down my arms and legs. A second later, a bomb went off in my head.

I remember bits and pieces of the rest of that day—a nurse, mashed potatoes (though I don't recall any other component of a meal), and someone tucking me into an unfamiliar bed. The next morning I got dressed and came back to my apartment. While I was standing in the hallway in front of my door, a vague memory appeared—I had tried to open a locked door and then climbed out a window. I didn't remember how I got home.

After unlocking my door, I walked into the foyer. The telephone in my den was ringing. I strolled in and picked up the phone. A man was on the other end, and he sounded angry, but I couldn't make out what he was talking about. Eventually I hung up and wandered into the parlor, where I sat on the sofa and stared out the window. Throughout the day people knocked on my door, and the telephone rang numerous times, but I was content to just sit. Twice that I recall, a man twisted the knob and pounded on the door with his fist, rattling the dishes in my china cabinet, before stomping down the hall, cursing.

I noted this somewhere in the interior of my brain, but didn't examine it at the time and had forgotten all about it when I decided to get something to eat. My mind had cleared to the extent that I felt like I had just awakened from a night with too little sleep—dull, head heavy, my vision surrounded with darkness.

I dressed and headed out the door, down the stairs, and out of the building. It was dark, which surprised me. I had no idea what time it was but didn't think to look at my watch.

A dark figure appeared in front of me. The next thing I knew, I was lying on my back, writhing in pain. My stomach felt like it had been torn apart, but the attack was so sudden, so violent, that I didn't know if I had been shot or hit with something.

The man grabbed my collar and dragged me into the alley between my building and the house next door. With one hand, he lifted me to my feet and pinned me against the wall. I gasped from the pain as my stomach muscles stretched out.

The light of the electric streetlamp cut across his forehead at an angle. One eye was in the light, the other in shadow. Even in my state, that one eye—brown, wide, bulging was all I needed to see—Sam Gianolla. He tapped me under the chin with a baseball bat. My teeth clicked together. I clenched my jaw.

"My friend say you don' take him serious."

"I—I don't know what you're talking about."

"Fuck you don't." He brought the bat up under my chin and popped me again, this time a little harder. "Joe from the Teamsters called ya this morning. Ya hung up on him."

"No. I don't know what you're talking about."

"Listen to me, *stronzo*. This ain't no game." He let go of my collar and pushed his forearm hard against my windpipe. "You got one more chance. I liked Esposito. He wasn' a piece a shit like you."

"All right." I still didn't know what he was talking about, but denying him would only get me hurt worse. "It was a mistake. I'll do what you want."

Gianolla stepped back and dropped the bat to his side. "Adamo got a warrant out on him. Your job right now is to get the Teamsters in. If this work out, we won't have to cut him in at all." He smiled a cold, dark smile. "Makes your job easy." He wound up and rammed the end of the bat into my stomach.

I fell to the ground and curled up in the fetal position, gasping for breath. Gianolla used the bat to turn my head toward him. "Only reason you not dead is my brother. Next time I gotta come here it gonna hurt a lot worse. And next time gonna be *permanente*."

Sam Gianolla stalked off, and I picked myself up from the alleyway and stumbled, doubled over, toward the front of my building. I was nearly to the door when a pair of voices called out, "Will!"

In the dim light of the streetlamps, I saw my mother and father hurrying up the walk. "Oh, thank God," my mother said. "Will, dear, are you all right?"

"Yes." I straightened, my stomach muscles stabbing at me. "Just a little sick to my stomach."

They stopped in front of me. "Well, you don't look all right," my mother said, putting her arm around me and steering me to the door. Now seeing me in the light, she gasped. "What happened to you?"

I pushed my hair back from my forehead and straightened my coat. "Nothing. I took a tumble."

"Let's get you into bed." She turned to my father. "William, you need to phone Dr. Miller and let him know Will's here."

They fussed over me and got me back into my apartment. My mother put me to bed while my father went into my den to use the telephone. When I was situated, she left to make me a cup of tea, and my father sat in my rocking chair. "Why did you leave Dr. Miller's?"

I shook my head. "I don't know. I don't remember."

"His contraption malfunctioned. I don't know how many watts you had shot through your head, but it was probably enough to power the Victoria through the entire thousand-mile endurance run."

I nodded. "Sounds about right."

"You scared Dr. Miller and your mother to death. After you disappeared, they came here to find you, but you weren't home. She phoned me, and we both came over this afternoon and then contacted everyone we could think of, including all the hospitals."

"I'm sorry. I'm pretty sure I was here all day. I don't think I got into any trouble."

"You should go to a sanitarium, Will."

"No." I thought about it. "I'll keep getting the treatment."

My father's eyes grew wide. "You're not serious."

"I'm not leaving town."

"See Dr. Miller again. He'll figure something out."

"Fine." I nodded back. I couldn't go to a sanitarium. "But I'll be in to work Monday."

"No. I don't want to see you in the office next week."

"Be reasonable, Father."

He was having none of it. My mother bustled into the room with a cup of tea and shooed my father out. She plumped the pillows and took my temperature and generally did all the things mothers seem to be under contract to do. When she ran out of maternal duties, she sat on the edge of my bed and took hold of my hand. I had always borne a close resemblance to her, but she had changed. Her brunette hair was now shot with steel gray, and her long face seemed even longer, with more prominent cheekbones. Crow's-feet were etched into the skin at the sides of her eyes, deep wrinkles cut into her forehead, and sharp semicircles curved around the edges of her mouth.

"What happened to you, Will?"

"Nothing, Mother. I'm fine."

"You know, we didn't stop being your parents when you turned eighteen. We still love you. Let us help you." She squeezed my hand. "We're not stupid, Will. You're obviously in trouble again."

"I'll be fine."

"You need to get out of Detroit—just get away from everything. It's no wonder you have neurasthenia. With Wesley's death and your trial and your . . . situation with Elizabeth, how could you not be plagued with melancholy?" She patted my hand. "Go to a sanitarium."

"No, Mother." I pushed myself up on the bed. "That would make me worse. I need to work." If I didn't deliver, the Gianolla brothers would kill her, I had no doubt of that. Anger flared inside me. They threatened my mother and father. Though I said nothing, I could feel my jaw tighten. Those sons of bitches were not going to harm my family.

I touched my mother's hand. "Trust me. I'll stay at your house after the treatments until I'm back in my right mind." I was going to have to figure out how to fake having the treatment. I couldn't keep this up, what with the problems I was facing.

She just looked at me for a moment. It was then I noticed that, with all the deep lines on her face, there were no laugh lines. She had taken a few trips to the Battle Creek San over the years. She knew what I was going through. "What about all those holes in your wall?"

"Oh, that's nothing. I just throw knives sometimes. It's helping my coordination."

She looked at me a while longer, biting her lip. I wondered what she was thinking. Finally she nodded. "I'm spending the night."

"Mother, really, it's not necessary. I'm perfectly—"

"That's enough of that nonsense, Will. I'm your mother." Her tone softened. "You need someone to take care of you. You've been through so much. If you don't work it out of your system, you're going to do something you'll regret."

I couldn't help but laugh. Do something I'll regret? I was looking forward to the day I would do something—anything—I *wouldn't* regret.

CHAPTER ELEVEN

Dr. Miller came over a little while later and examined me. After apologizing a few dozen times, he declared me fit enough for home bed rest. By Sunday morning, I felt like I was back to normal. My mother stayed all day, watching over me like a hen. I had things to do, but there was no shaking her, so I exercised and stretched my hand when she let me out of bed. It also gave me time to think.

According to Sam Gianolla, the police were after Vito Adamo. The Gianollas wanted me to concentrate on getting the Teamsters into Detroit Electric. That wasn't going to happen, no matter what I did. If I could find Adamo, I would have options. One would be to do what the Gianollas wanted—set up Vito Adamo to be murdered. But that looked like a short-term solution. Once Adamo was out of the way, I would still have the Teamsters problem.

I had to rid myself of the Gianollas, and I could think of only one way to do that. But it would require working with a man I'd sworn to kill, or at the very least, bring to justice. I wondered if I could do that. The very thought of Vito Adamo made me smolder with anger. I doubted he felt any more congeniality for me. If I could get past my feelings to make the attempt, would Adamo do the same? Perhaps, if the Gianollas presented as big a problem for him as they did for me.

In the late afternoon I was lying on the sofa reading when the telephone rang. My mother answered it. She talked for a few minutes, and I assumed it was one of her friends. But then she called, "Will? It's Elizabeth."

I felt a moment of panic. This conversation was inevitable, but I so wanted to avoid it. I went to the den, took the phone from my mother, and waited until she retreated from the room. "Hello?"

"Hello, Will," Elizabeth said. "How are you?"

It wasn't the standard reflexive "How are you?" Her voice was full of concern. My mother must have told her about the electrotherapy mishap. "I'm doing fine," I said. "And you?"

"Fine. There's a new Impressionist exhibition at the art museum, and I thought, if you weren't too busy, you might like to see it with me."

"No. I can't. Between work and this treatment I'm getting, I really have to put my social life on hold for a while. I'm sorry. Maybe things will settle down in a few weeks." I hoped we'd be able to resume our relationship when I finished with the Gianollas. I didn't want to shut her out forever.

"Oh. All right. I understand."

We talked a few minutes more before we hung up with no plans for getting together or even phoning. I was watching my chances for a happy life slip between my fingers.

The next morning I was able to convince my mother that I was in my right mind, or at least as near as I was going to get, and she agreed to leave me to my own devices. I tried to hide from her the sharp pains that stabbed me in the gut every time I bent over or twisted my torso, courtesy of Sam Gianolla and his baseball bat.

At ten o'clock I left my apartment. It was cool but sunny, a perfect morning of the type that helped me forget the dark cold months of winter. My first stop was a sporting goods store, where I bought a switchblade and two .32-caliber seven-shot Colts with two boxes of bullets. I stuck the knife in my pocket, one of the guns into my belt, and when I got home, the other gun into my nightstand. Things were getting uglier, and the path I was being forced to take would be dangerous.

While I was deciding what to do next, a thought struck me: The Employers Association of Detroit used Vito Adamo's men on occasion to do their dirty work. I didn't know who had taken John Cooper's place as the Labor Bureau's security head, but he would know how to get hold of Adamo.

I hurried to my den and phoned the EAD. A secretary answered and, after I explained whom I was looking for, told me the head of security was now a man named James Finnegan. I vaguely remembered him as a member of John Cooper's union busters. He was a good-sized man, though not huge, with acne scars pitting his cheeks. I couldn't recall ever speaking with him. When he came on the line, his voice was serious and gravelly. He said he was busy, but I persisted and he finally made an appointment with me for an hour later.

I took a Woodward Line trolley to Grand River Avenue and then walked the last two blocks to the EAD office in the Stevens Building. The walls of the foyer and lobby had been covered with rich mahogany paneling since I'd last been here, and a new oriental rug graced the hardwood floor. The office smelled of money.

The receptionist showed me to Finnegan's dark-paneled office, a large room with dozens of wooden filing cabinets and a pair of upholstered chairs in front of the desk. Finnegan was sitting behind the desk and stood when I came in.

"Mr. Anderson." He held his right hand out to me and looked surprised when I shook it with my left. "Please." He gestured toward one of the chairs in front of his desk and waited until I sat to sink back into his chair. "I've got a meeting in a few minutes, so perhaps we should get right to it. What can I do for you?"

"Your predecessor worked with certain . . . criminal elements when he needed men to do dirty work. I need to get in touch with one of those men—Vito Adamo. I know John Cooper would have left information on how to contact him. I need that information."

He sat back, and his chair gave out a long shrill creak. "No. I'm sure you're mistaken. Believe me, I'd know."

"You are aware that Cooper used criminals?"

Finnegan eyed me from across the desk. Finally he said, "Mr.

Anderson, we do not employ criminals for any reason. I've been through every file in the place. There's nothing about any Adamo."

He didn't know Cooper used Adamo's men? It wasn't outside the realm of possibility, but still . . . "Perhaps you could check again."

"Tell you what, Mr. Anderson." He stood and walked out from behind his desk. When I stood, he took my arm and led me toward the door. "I'll look through everything again. If I find anything about Adamo I'll give you a call."

I thanked him, though I'm not sure why, and left the office. Walking back to the trolley stop, I shook my head. Finnegan wasn't going to be any help.

I was going to have to hunt down Adamo on my own.

I returned home and ate lunch. It was only one o'clock. I decided to go to work, whether my father wanted me there or not. I dressed and headed down to the streetcar stop. Curious if the newsboy had made good on his promise, I looked for the foulmouthed whelp.

Sure enough, he stood on the corner with his white bag slung over his shoulder, holding up a *Detroit Herald* and bawling out, "Shoot-out in Little Italy! Two dead!"

I stopped and stared at him with my mouth hanging open. I flashed back to the boy who had taken the blackmail money from me a year and a half earlier.

"Man says you got a envelope for him. Says I'm s'posed to get it."

I glanced around. "Where is this man?"

"Says that's none a your business." He dug through his thick black hair and scratched the top of his head.

I squatted down, holding tightly to the envelope in my pocket. "You tell him I need my package before he gets this envelope."

The urchin was still grinning. "Says you'd say that. Money first or no clothes. Says the coppers wants 'em."

I was sure it was him—heavy-lidded eyes, recessed chin, a thatch of black hair. The blood must have obscured his appearance when I'd seen him before. I stood off to the side and studied him carefully.

No. This boy looked the same age, and the better part of two years had passed. A younger brother, perhaps? This was worth investigating. I sauntered up to him and handed him a nickel for a paper. "You got the corner, huh?"

He handed me a paper and three cents change. "Yeah. So?"

"So nothing. Good for you. What happened to the other kid?"

The barest trace of a smile crossed his lips. "He ain't a problem no more."

"What's your name?"

"What's it to ya?"

I grinned at him. "You're a friendly one, aren't you?"

"Lemme alone." He turned away and called out, "Coppers nab fifteen illegals! Read it here! Getcher paper!"

I figured he must like me—he hadn't called me a name. I took a few steps away and thought. It would be worth my while to find out something about this kid. If his brother had taken the blackmail money, he might be able to lead me to Vito Adamo. My father didn't want to see me today anyway. I crossed the street and sat in the window of a café, nursing a cup of coffee and watching the boy.

Every time a streetcar rattled up to the stop, a herd of people tried to cram themselves on board. Most were turned away, the trolleys already packed to their roofs. A few cars didn't even stop. The waiting customers shouted and cursed, but the motormen stayed on the throttle. It was a daily occurrence all over Detroit, and unless the city finally broke through the Detroit United Railway trust, the situation would just keep getting worse. More and more immigrants flooded into town every day, yet the streetcar company—which had a stranglehold on the business in the city—refused to add more trolleys to meet the demand. Nor would they lower the price from a nickel a ride to an amount the average person could afford. It only made good business sense to solve the problem of too few cars, but the DUR had drawn a line in the sand, and they weren't going to budge.

I was going to have to get myself an automobile. First chance I got, I'd talk to Edsel about buying a Model T. I certainly couldn't afford a Detroit Electric.

I sat back, picked up the newspaper, and looked for the story about the shoot-out. The headline read: GUN BATTLE IN LITTLE ITALY—TWO

DEAD. The dead men were unidentified, but this had the Adamos and Gianollas written all over it. I read and watched the newsboy. On page eight, I found a short article headlined, SUSPECTS GONE TO GROUND, POLICE SAY. Vito Adamo and a man named Filipo Busolato, who were wanted for the shotgun murder of Carlo Callego, had disappeared. The police speculated they'd fled to Canada. But Adamo didn't strike me as the kind of man who would run from anything. He was probably somewhere in Detroit. I just had to find him.

I pushed the paper aside and went back to watching the boy.

It was nearly three o'clock when he finally exhausted his supply of newspapers and began walking south on Woodward. I threw a dime on the table and followed him from across the street. He dodged and weaved through the crowds on the sidewalk. With all the wagons, carriages, trucks, automobiles, and bicycles hurtling down both sides of the road, I lost sight of him a few times, but I managed to shadow him to Winder Street. There he crossed the road and headed east. He threaded through the business district to the Bishop Ungraded School, a three-story redbrick building that served two distinct purposes. Half the building was a regular school for kindergarten through eighth-grade students. The other half served as a trade school for delinquents. I was fairly certain on which side this boy belonged.

He cut around back to the school yard and hopped the short picket fence. I followed him at a distance and stopped just outside the yard behind a tree at the edge of the building. He had joined a group of perhaps ten boys who stood or knelt by the rear entrance. They looked to range in age from ten to fourteen or fifteen. The blackmail boy would be right in the middle.

They all looked poor—tufts of hair standing out from their heads, wool trousers held up by suspenders, cotton shirts shiny from wear, scuffed and dirty lace-up shoes, a few with heels flapping behind them. One of the kneeling boys flung something against the wall with a sidearm delivery—dice. The boys shouted, some excitedly, others in despair. The kneeling boy gathered up the dice, while others picked up or threw down coins.

Two boys stood, facing each other. I tried to get a look at them but couldn't see either clearly. They were talking, and their voices rose, though I was too far away to hear what they were saying. One of them dropped the other with a straight right to the chin. When the kid fell, the first one followed up with a kick to the side of his head. The rest of the boys laughed and pulled him away. He turned, and in that moment I saw him clearly.

It was the blackmail boy.

Everyone went back to their craps game. The boy who'd been beaten picked himself up from the ground, brushed off his trousers, and tentatively rejoined the game—at the opposite side of the semicircle from the blackmail boy. About fifteen minutes later, a man called out from the other side of the school yard and began walking over to the boys. He wore a black suit and derby, and his face looked dark—Italian? He was well over a hundred yards from me, too far away to make out features. The clothing was no help, since 90 percent of the men in town wore the same things.

One of the boys, a thin lad in a black derby, met him halfway down the wall and handed over a fistful of change. The man counted the money, said something, and shoved the boy, who spread his hands in front of him. *That's all,* the gesture said. The man grabbed his collar and gave him a shake before pushing him away and heading back toward the side of the building. He flipped something over his shoulder. The sun sparkled off it—one of the coins. The boy picked it up out of the dirt and stood with his hands on his hips, staring at the man's back. Finally sticking the coin in his pocket, the boy returned to the rest of the gang, and they all left together, cutting across the school yard and hopping the fence in the back. I followed at a distance.

The blackmail boy seemed to be second in the pecking order. The boy in the black derby, perhaps fourteen or fifteen years old, looked like he could be another of the newsboy's brothers. They all hooted and laughed, and pushed one another around as they turned down Saint Antoine. I followed them from a block behind, staying to the other side of the street and using whatever cover I could. We were in the Russian ghetto now, actually only a few blocks from Paradise Valley. The business's signs were in Hebrew or Cyrillic lettering, and only a few feet separated the four- and five-story tenement buildings, built of crumbling brownstone and brick. Clotheslines hung diagonally across the alleys, weaving a spider's web trapping hundreds of pairs of dull brown and gray trousers, and a greater number of white shirts and underwear. Men sat on stoops, passing the time.

The boys suddenly split up and raced to the steps where the men sat. Each of them pulled the hat from a man's head and tore down the street. I broke into a run to stay with them. The men ran after them, shouting, *"Mamzers!" "Trombeniks!"* and other words I presumed to be even worse. A second later, the boys threw the hats into the air and bolted down an alley behind Gratiot.

The men retrieved their hats, dusted them off, and shouted a few more halfhearted curses at the boys before heading back to their perches. *"Feh!* Like the butcher says," one of the men said to me. "Those boys are rotten, purple—like spoiled meat."

I slowed and then stopped across the street from the alley. A few rickety wooden privies stood at the side of the alleyway, and dozens of garbage cans and their contents were strewn across the dirt. The boys were gone.

I hesitated. These boys were clearly capable of doing damage. They would be on the alert for the men whose hats they'd stolen. To go down that alley was a big risk. I had a gun, but I wasn't going to shoot a child. No. I'd wait. I knew where to find the blackmail boy now.

CHAPTER TWELVE

The next morning, I took a streetcar to the factory to speak with my father. Wilkinson directed me to the carriage building. It was the largest in the complex, three stories with almost a quarter million square feet of floor space. My father was in the body department that took up most of the first floor. I was surprised to see it half-empty, with dozens of Detroit Electric coupé and brougham bodies strewn in among the carriages and coaches. He and William P. MacFarlane, the general manager of the factory, stood off to the side, deep in discussion, while electric sanders buzzed and saws ripped. They both wore dark gray suits with waistcoats and ties. The workmen around them wore their ties tucked into their trousers. Their jackets were hung on pegs on the exterior walls of the building, away from the sawdust.

A pair of men rolled the shiny maroon body of one of the "clear vision" brougham models—rounded glass at the corners gave the driver nearly 360-degree visibility—out from paint finishing to the overhead door at the shipping dock. They parked it behind a dozen other automobile bodies of various models in maroon, brewster green, or blue, all sitting on the wheeled dollies that carried our vehicles, motorized or otherwise, from department to department.

Mr. MacFarlane saw me first. He was a bony Scotsman with huge drooping mustaches, now more gray than red. "Will, why, hello!" He held out his right hand before he remembered, and then awkwardly patted my arm. "It's great to see you. Congratulations on the, ah . . . Are you coming back?"

I looked at my father. "I hope to."

My father held my gaze. "How are you feeling today?"

"Good." I had to sell him. "Wonderful, in fact."

"Well . . ." My father turned to Mr. MacFarlane. "What would you think of Will looking into this for us?"

"Don't see why not." MacFarlane leaned in close to me and said in a serious tone, "You're not an imbecile, are ye, lad?" His grin gave him away.

"Depends on whom you ask," I said. "What do you think, Father?"

His head tilted a bit to the side, and he studied me with mock seriousness. "Imbecile?" He thought for a moment and shook his head. "No." He thought some more. "Moron, perhaps." Another pause. "Idiot." He began nodding. "Yes, that's it, idiot."

I bowed. "Much thanks to my trusted supporters."

They laughed. My father put his arm around me and steered me away from the noise. The three of us walked out onto the macadam, which was radiating heat from the sunshine. It had warmed into the mid-seventies and was an absolutely beautiful day. We stopped on the test track near one of the small hills.

"Let's talk turkey," my father said. "We're leading the electric market, but we're heading for serious trouble."

"Trouble?" I said. "Why?"

"Well, it doesn't take a genius to see that the carriage, wagon, and coach business is going to all but disappear over the next ten years."

Mr. MacFarlane stuck his hands into his back pockets. He never looked at home in a suit. "After growing every year for more than a decade, our horse-drawn business was down twenty-three percent last year and is going to be off double that this year. And I need not remind you that's a bigger part of our business than automobiles. The market is a disaster."

I shook my head. "But automobile business is making up for it, right?"

"That was the plan," my father said. "But our production isn't growing fast enough, and our costs are stratospheric. Gasoline automobiles are dropping in price every day, and their growth is off the charts.

Worse, Kettering's self-starter has those cars taking away a significant amount of our customers. Turns out the noise and smoke are much less a factor than easy starting when it comes to ladies driving automobiles. We've made no progress whatever in getting men to accept our 'sedate' vehicles." He glanced away and folded his arms across his chest before looking back at me. "We're stuck. Our automobile business is showing solid growth, but our overall volume is falling off the table. Because of that we're paying more for materials, but the squeeze from the other automobile manufacturers keeps us from raising prices."

"What exactly do you want me to do?"

"Help us improve our efficiency."

"So you're thinking of Taylorism?"

He sighed. "I'd go with voodooism right now if I thought it would work. Virtually all of our manufacturing employees are craftsmen. We're paying them as much as six dollars a day when the market for unskilled labor is a quarter of that. If we could get more work out of the craftsmen we need, and turn over some of the tasks to unskilled laborers, we could significantly raise our margins."

"Don't you think that might provoke some labor problems?"

My father squinted at me. "Perhaps, but I don't see a choice. If we can't keep our margins up, nobody's going to have a job."

I examined the macadam in front of me. "I think we need to keep the men happy. We don't want union organizers getting a toehold."

"Who's unhappy?" my father demanded.

"No one I know of," I said. "It's just . . . I think it's a bad time to stir up the men." If the Teamsters Union got a foot in, the Gianollas would pry the door open any way they could. The Anderson Electric Car Company employees had to be satisfied with their lot.

He turned to Mr. MacFarlane. "What do you think?"

"*Ach,* we've got the happiest men in the business. And if we do lose some, there's another hundred coming to town every day. They'd be crazy to cause trouble."

My father turned back to me. "You don't sound like you're interested in the project."

"No, I am. I want to help."

"You're one of the few people in the company with a college degree.

Mechanical engineering ought to put you in mind of how things fit together."

I shuffled from foot to foot. "I really would like to help you in the front office . . . if I could."

Mr. MacFarlane's eyes narrowed, and he gave me a bit of a scowl. "Do ye suppose, lad, that pushing papers around is going to help as much?"

"No, I suppose not. I'll help out, of course." The project would still allow me to spend time with my father, which might slow down the Gianollas enough to let me figure a way out of this. But I had to talk with someone about my problems.

The secretary walked me down the hallway past dozens of doors. I peeked in and saw men hunched over their desks, pens scratching furiously.

As I got closer, I heard Mr. Ford's voice rising over the quiet office. "You said Tuesday! Listen to me, Dodge. If I don't see those chassis by Tuesday, I'm going to find someone else! You hear me?" The receiver banged against the candlestick, and the shouting was replaced by low muttering.

We had just reached Edsel's door when his father came storming out of his office. I'd never seen him smile, and this was not going to be the first time. He was a small man who looked more a Kansas dirt farmer or New England minister than a tycoon, but he carried the unmistakable aura of power.

And he didn't like me.

He stopped abruptly. "Anderson." His voice carried a note of derision. "They let you out. Haven't killed anyone lately, have you?"

I nodded a tentative greeting. "Mr. Ford. How are you today?"

"How am I today?" He barked out a laugh. "Suppliers that fail me, employees that loaf, banks that all want a piece of me. How do you think I'm doing?"

My hand burned, and I realized I was rubbing it. I stopped. "I'm sorry, sir. If there's anything I can do . . ." Edsel was standing in his doorway. I hadn't noticed him before.

"Yes, there's something you can do. Let my son get his work done."

"I only need a minute of his time."

Ford turned to the secretary, said, "Time him," and stomped off down the hall.

The secretary looked at me, shrugged, and pulled his watch from his waistcoat. "Proceed."

Edsel grimaced an apology. I could see his embarrassment in his big dark eyes. "I'm done in half an hour. Why don't you grab a cup of coffee across the street."

I nodded. "Thanks." The secretary escorted me out of the building, making uncomfortable small talk until he was finally able to leave me at the door.

I ran across Woodward, dodging traffic, and ducked inside the huge automat. Men, women, and children bustled back and forth. Plates, cups, and silverware clanked and pinged, conversation so ubiquitous as to be nothing more than a loud hum. It had been less than two years since the first Detroit automat opened, and they were now the rage. In front of me were hundreds of little windows, filled with coffee cups and a variety of foods. A few distorted figures were visible behind the glass—a section of face here, the white of a cook's hat there—but only one restaurant employee was out with the customers, and all she did was ladle out nickels for change. In another wave of "progress," our eating experience had become impersonal and sterile, yet another factory setting, this time a food factory built to feed people in as little time as possible.

I looked around at the patrons. Most were hunched over their plates, shoveling food into their mouths, as if fearful someone would steal their hamburgers or wilted vegetables or gluey apple pie.

Studying faces, I saw one thing in common—tension. Worry lines, rapid movement, loud bursts of conversation before diving back into the food. Was this what my father saw in me? This nervousness, almost a fever, that held people in its sway? It was no wonder so many Americans were suffering from neurasthenia, and no wonder it was called American-itis. We seemed to be perfecting the art of nervousness.

We were all in such a hurry—rushing from home to work to a game to a recital to home to work and so on—that this type of restaurant was a revelation to many. But this was exactly what was wrong with this country. People hurrying through their lives, rats scurrying from one place to another as quickly as they could without half a thought as to why.

I joined the rats. I stuck nickels into a pair of slots and grabbed a hamburger and a cup, which I filled from the nearby coffee urn. Dodging other customers, I picked my way to a window seat and looked out at the frantic scene in front of me. The area was so busy you'd have thought Highland Park was just more of Detroit. Ford employed thousands, adding more workers all the time, and smaller buildings radiated around the factory like supplicants bowing to their master.

I ate the sandwich and gazed at the factory while I thought. The building, more windows than walls, was bright on the inside, saving Mr. Ford a fortune in electricity bills. On this day, the windows sparkled like a wall of light. The only evidence of industry was the filth spewing from the five huge smokestacks standing guard over the building.

Murmured conversation behind me suddenly coalesced, as it does when a familiar word or phrase cuts through the wall of noise surrounding us. A man said, "Will Anderson." I turned around in my seat. Half a dozen young men in wool trousers and dirty white cotton shirts, with caps on the table in front of them, looked away quickly. I caught an eye or two. They were . . . afraid of me?

I turned back to the window and lit a cigarette. Six men in the prime of life, yet my celebrity caused them to fear me. Will Anderson—the killer, the Electric Executioner. Though I had been exonerated both times I'd been brought to trial, the people of Detroit would forever know me as a murderer, guilty in the court of public opinion. Maybe I'd have to consider a change of scenery. Once I got rid of the Gianollas.

A hand clapped me on the shoulder. I jumped.

"Will, my lad. It's so good to see you again." Edsel grinned down at me and set a coffee cup on the table.

As he slid his slender frame into a seat, I said, "Got an office by the old man now, huh?"

"Yes, he wants me nearby. Can't do too much damage that way, you know?"

I pulled my cigarette case from my pocket and offered him one.

"No," he said, glancing out the window. "Not so close to the factory.

Have to set an example." He smiled, but I knew him well enough to see he wasn't happy about it. "Is this a social call, or is there something you wanted to speak with me about?"

"I've got a few problems, and I need some ideas."

"I'm happy to try."

I leaned in and told him about the Gianollas and the Teamsters and the Adamos, and, finally, about my project at the Anderson Electric Car Company. He sipped his coffee and listened, missing nothing, asking questions and clarifying, until I had finished.

He wrapped both hands around his now empty cup and leaned in toward me. "Your father will never let the Teamsters in. Even if he wanted to, the Employers Association wouldn't let him. Heck, the other car companies would string him up."

"You tell that to the Gianolla brothers."

"Go to the police."

"I did. Riordan wouldn't give me the time of day."

"What about the state police?"

I thought for a moment, biting the inside of my lip. "Gianolla said he had men in the city police, the sheriffs, and the staties. If he was telling the truth, my family'd be dead."

"Well, that doesn't leave many options. The only way you're going to get out of this is to get the Gianollas arrested—or killed."

"I do have one idea—if I can find Vito Adamo."

Edsel arched his eyebrows.

I took a deep breath and articulated my idea for the first time. "The Adamos obviously hate the Gianollas as much as the Gianollas hate them. If I could arrange a meeting between the two factions and make sure the Adamos have the upper hand, they might be able to eliminate my problem."

Edsel leaned in still closer and spoke quietly. "But you'd be helping your enemy."

"I can put aside my desire for revenge to save my family, and I bet he'd do the same to win this war with the Gianollas."

"He might think you killed Moretti. You'd be taking quite a chance."

"Give me another solution."

He pursed his lips and shook his head slowly. "No great ideas come to mind. But I'll think on it. As to your other problem, I'll do your efficiency homework for you. That's practically all *my* father's working on. I'll show you some of the things he's trying, and it'll look like you're burning the midnight oil." He reached over the table and clasped the back of my neck. "You take care of the big problem, and I'll take care of the small one."

"Thank you, Edsel. You're not half as big an ass as everyone says you are."

"Ah." He waved a hand in front of him. "It's not like we're competitors. Much as he'd like to, my father's never going to come out with an electric. He and Mr. Edison talk about it all the time, but unless there's a dramatic breakthrough in price it'll never happen. So drink up. We'll go look at a few things. You just have to keep this between us boys."

I nodded and took a last gulp of coffee, and we left the restaurant, heading back across the street to the factory. Bypassing the office entrance, we walked in a side door and climbed the steps to the second floor.

Edsel held the door open to a room perhaps three hundred feet long, with partially assembled Model T's and a huge variety of parts scattered around. Draftsmen's tables nearly filled the window wall. A long conveyor belt, like you might see in a production bakery, ran down the center of the room with smaller belts feeding into it from the sides. Car chassis in various states of completion sat atop it. The long belt went into, and out of, a pair of enclosed rooms.

As we walked over to the tables, Edsel asked, "How many man-hours do you have in an automobile's production?"

"I have no idea," I admitted.

He frowned at me. "If you don't know where you're starting from, how are you going to know if you've made any improvement?"

I held my hands up in front of me, a gesture of surrender. "Point taken."

"In 1910 it took us twelve and a half man-hours to build a flivver. Two years later we're tracking at eight. And my father wants to improve *that* fourfold."

"Two hours per car? That's not possible."

"You tell him that. Anyway, here's what we're working on. The first thing is interchangeable parts. We've got that down now, though Mr. Olds certainly beat us to it. You wouldn't believe what a difference it makes. Just having every part fit without adjustment takes a load of hours off the build process." He picked up a brake assembly and inspected it. "One one-hundredth of an inch tolerance. Every part fits."

"Well, sure," I said. "Common knowledge. We can't do it at this point, but we certainly understand interchangeable parts."

He smiled. "Here's the difference." He turned and walked back to the beginning of the big conveyor belt. "We could use almost any factory as an example, but let's use yours. You have a number of departments, body and paint and chassis and so on, and every car is carted from one of those to the next. You have dozens of workmen doing nothing more than moving cars around the floor." He looked at me for confirmation.

I nodded. "So you're working on an assembly line. The Olds plant had those, what, ten years ago? Hardly a revolution."

He gave me a sly grin. "Well, this one's a little different. One of our men," he said, and paused. "Do you know Pa Klann?"

I shook my head.

"Well, no matter. Pa toured one of the big Chicago slaughterhouses last year. He said it was fascinating, though I think it would make me vomit. Apparently they hook the pigs to an overhead conveyor, and every man has a single part to cut off from every pig. The chain delivers the pig to the man, and he hacks off a bit while it's moving past him. At the end of the line there's nothing left. Assembly line efficiency at its highest level." He made a disgusted face. "Or perhaps I should say 'disassembly line.'"

"Sounds thoroughly sickening," I said. "And can you imagine doing the same thing hundreds—thousands?—of times a day? Every day? I'd shoot myself. But I still don't understand how this idea differs from the Olds model."

"The difference is simple. Each process is broken down to eliminate bottlenecks. Each of the feeder lines is timed out so those parts hit the assembly line at the proper moment. The car never stops moving."

"Sounds like Taylorism."

Edsel laughed. "Don't let my father hear you say that. He already dislikes you enough. We call it *Fordism*." He put a hand on my arm.

"What would you say if I told you we're almost to the point where we can build a complete automobile that never leaves an assembly line? And drive the completed car off at the end?"

I gawped at him. "I'd say you're off your rocker. It's impossible. Unless, perhaps, you're going to build a ten-mile-long assembly line so you can get the paint to dry before the car runs out of belt."

His smile wavered. "That's the only holdup. Here, let's . . ." He motioned toward the rooms enclosing the belt, and we began walking toward them. "Our engineers have tried thousands of different kinds of paint, and so far have found only one that dries fast enough."

"Really?" I said. "I can't believe there'd be even one. But I don't understand. Why isn't one enough?"

He stopped at the entrance to one of the rooms, which I saw now was a paint room, and pulled one of many large pieces of steel off the belt. He held it up so I could see the shiny black finish. "Not just one kind of paint. One kind and one color—Japan black."

CHAPTER THIRTEEN

B lack?" I said. "You've never made an all-black car, have you?"
"No," Edsel replied. "Blue with black trim this year. Otherwise red, gray, and green."

"They'll look nice in black." I nudged his arm and grinned. "Or as nice as a Tin Lizzie can look, anyway. The black might help hide the ugliness."

He gave me a shove. "They're not built for beauty."

"You can say that again."

We spent half an hour wandering up and down the conveyors, discussing the stages of the assembly line. The floors around the paint rooms were littered with steel parts in reds and greens and blues, the colors the buying public expected.

"Too bad about the paint," I said. "I can't imagine how much money you'd save on production."

He shrugged. "Ah, they'll get it. It's only a matter of time."

"You know, you need to put that mind of yours on another problem— traffic. Figure out how to apply assembly line efficiency to the madhouse out there." I gestured toward the street.

He laughed. "Conveyor belts stacked at different heights for different directions—sure, I'll get right on that."

"Something's got to be done, and soon. Unless there's a cop on the corner, it's nothing more than a giant game of chicken."

"I hear they're going to put up a mechanical semaphore at Woodward and Michigan."

"A what?"

He laughed. "It's a most inelegant solution to the problem. A policeman stands next to a big sign and switches it from Stop to Go and back again."

"Perfect. They'll be taking bids—the driver with the biggest bribe gets to cross the street."

Edsel laughed again and clapped me on the shoulder. "Will the cynic."

"Thanks for showing me around. This will give me some good ammunition. Any chance you'll chuck this and finally go to college?"

He ducked his head and toed the floor. "My father thinks it's all poppycock. He wants me here. And, really, he needs me here." He looked up at me. "He needs a counterpoint. Everything to him is price. Make them cheaper, which will sell more, which will make them cheaper, which will sell more, and so on. The Runabout dropped from nine hundred to five-ninety in the last two years—and if we get this done who knows how far down it'll go."

"And your sales are doubling every year. It's working, right?"

"Yes, but what about style? What about speed?"

"Not in an 'everyman's' automobile. You're stuck in the most successful car company in the world. Tough luck."

He grinned. "I know. It's tough all over. But if I could just get him to make something besides flivvers. The opportunity is there." He pulled out his watch and glanced at the face. "Dinnertime. Mother hates it when I'm late."

"Oh, hey, I almost forgot. I want to buy one of those cheap cars from you."

"For yourself?"

I nodded. "I can't deal with the streetcars anymore."

"A Runabout?"

"Torpedoes are faster, right?"

Edsel gave me a sidelong glance. "Say, if you want speed, why don't you buy *my* Torpedo?"

"You want to sell it?"

"I'm working on a new Speedster right now. I could drive the electric for a while, so"—he shrugged—"sure."

"How much?"

His face scrunched up while he thought. "How about five hundred?"

"Sounds like a pretty good deal."

He smiled and wagged his eyebrows. "One owner. Drives like an old lady."

I snorted. I'd never seen anyone drive faster than Edsel. "I'd like to see that old lady."

"You know I made a few modifications, right?"

"I seem to remember a getaway at about a hundred miles an hour," I said with a grin.

"Nah," he scoffed. "We never even hit fifty on that ride. But it'll go a lot faster than that."

"Sold."

"All right. One thing I've learned from my father is when they say yes, stop selling and get the money. When do you want it?"

"How about Friday? I could come by in the evening."

"Deal." He held out his left hand, and I shook it.

"Wait," Edsel said, looking down at my gloved right hand. "The throttle control is on the right. How are you going to run it?"

"I hadn't even thought about that."

He clapped his hands. "I'll move it! Why can't it be on the left? But . . ." He trailed off. I could see the gears turning in his head. Now he spoke slowly, staring off into the distance. "Will you be able to steer well enough with your right hand so you can use your left to adjust the throttle?"

"I'm sure I can."

He rubbed his chin, then grinned and met my gaze. "I'll have it ready by Friday."

When I walked into my apartment the telephone in my den was ringing. I hurried to answer it.

"Will, it's Joe Curtiss. Don't hang up on me."

Joe was the head mechanic at the Detroit Electric garage. "Why would I hang up on you?"

"That's a good question." Joe and I hadn't exactly been close since the first time I was accused of murder, but he sounded downright belligerent now.

"What do you want?"

"We need to meet—tonight."

"Why? What's so important?"

"Listen, my next call is going to be to Tony. You ain't gonna duck me again."

"Tony?"

"Don't even try it, Will."

"Tony Gianolla? Wait, you're the Joe with the Teamsters?"

He blew out a deep breath. "I'm not with the Teamsters, but I'm sure that's how the Gianollas would describe me. Nine o'clock at the Merrill Fountain. Don't be late." He hung up.

I sat at my desk and thought. Could this have something to do with Joe's wife, Gina? She was Italian, but I didn't think she was Sicilian. And what was Joe doing fronting for the Teamsters Union? Beyond the fact that he used to be one of my best friends, he was a mechanic, not a driver. The Teamsters were apparently branching out.

The wall clock showed ten minutes after eight. It couldn't hurt to be early. I went back out and caught a streetcar to the corner of Woodward and Monroe. It was dusk, and the Detroit Opera House, directly across the street, was dark, so I waited in the shadows of the entrance and watched the fountain, a brilliant white archway lit by electric floodlights. Crowds of people passed in front of me on the sidewalk and crossed the street to the fountain and beyond.

At nine, it was fully dark. I lit a cigarette, strolled across the street, and took a seat on the marble railing, my back to the fountain. A few minutes later, Joe stepped out of the billiard parlor across the street and looked around for a moment before crossing to me and standing a few feet away. He was aging, though it could have just been the floodlights. His skin looked like parchment. Lit from below, he was a specter. His normally pink, open face was ghostly white, his thinning hair nearly invisible.

He jammed his fists into the pockets of his jacket and said, "Jesus, Anderson. I'm glad you showed." His eyes darted back and forth. "You alone?"

I stood and held out my left hand. "Hello, Joe. Yes, I'm alone."

He hesitated, then shook my hand awkwardly. "Let's go inside." He nodded toward the billiard parlor.

I followed him back across the street and inside. The room was narrow but deep, with half a dozen green-felt-topped billiard tables, a long bar, and small tables scattered about, everything hazy from a thick glaze of smoke. It was crowded with men from all social strata, from corduroy and denim work clothes to the finery of the city's elite. The click of pool balls, the cursing of men, and the thunk of beer mugs onto tables filled the air.

Joe stopped at the bar for a couple of beers. He handed me a mug and led me past the tables to a booth in back. When he slid into the seat, his beer slopped onto the table. "I'm sorry you had to get involved in this, but listen, Will, I need your help. The Teamsters want in. They want everybody, but I can get them to take just the drivers and mechanics. You have to make it happen."

I eyed the beer in front of me but didn't drink. "How in the world do you expect me to do that?"

He took a gulp of beer and sat back in the hard wooden seat. "You better figure it out fast. You know they're in the AFL?"

"Yeah." I tried to concentrate, but I was distracted by the amber glow of the beer in front of me.

"Well, they're going to call for a general strike. Shut the city down. They can do it too. But that's the least of our troubles. You need to arrange a meeting between your father and Ethan Pinsky." He gave me a piece of paper. "Here's his number."

"Who's Pinsky?"

"A lawyer. He's negotiatin' for the union."

I shook my head. "I don't see how we're going to get this done."

"If you don't, we're gonna be in big trouble."

"You too?"

His face hardened. "These guys aren't messing around. If we don't deliver . . ." He took a quick swallow of beer.

I pushed my mug aside. "Are they going to hurt you?"

"My family." He bit his lip and looked down at the table.

"Is it the Teamsters? Or the Gianollas?"

He shook his head. "Tony Gianolla's the one that threatened me."

"Why are you their spokesman?"

"Because he said I was."

"Does this have something to do with Gina?"

He nodded. "Her dad has been paying off the Gianollas for protection on his flower business. Somehow they connected me with him."

I thought for a moment. "What's your take on this, Joe? Do you want the Teamsters in?"

His head recoiled in surprise. "Hell no. I got no complaints. Your dad's a fair man. But what I want's got nothing to do with anything." He shook his head. "I got kids, Will. We have to do this."

I reached out and laid my good hand on his forearm. "Maybe there's a way out, Joe."

He grunted out a laugh. "You don't know these guys."

We talked for a few minutes, catching up in the awkward fashion of men thrown together after a long history ended by a disagreement—in this case, his belief I was a murderer.

Joe left, saying he needed to get home to say good night to his wife. I looked at the beer in front of me. The head had disappeared, now just a soapy-looking ring around the top of the mug. I picked it up and held it to the light. Half a dozen of these, and I would feel good. A dozen, and I wouldn't feel anything.

I set down the mug and looked around the billiard hall. No one was watching. No one cared in the least if I drank. They were drinking. Most had been drinking heavily. It was what we did.

Once again, the burn clued me in that I was rubbing my hand. I stopped, took a deep breath, and slipped out of the booth.

Time for bed.

I went into the factory the next morning. Mr. Wilkinson directed me to a vacant office on the second floor of the administration building. I needed a strategy. With Edsel taking care of my efficiency project,

I spent my time doodling on a piece of paper, trying to determine how to deal with the Gianollas.

My only lead on the Adamos was the boy who had taken the blackmail money. I was going to have to get him away from the other boys and make him talk. He was a tough little monkey and would be a challenge. But it might be the only way to take care of the Gianollas. Until I could eliminate them, I had to play out the charade. I picked up the telephone's receiver and asked the operator for the number Joe had given me.

After several rings, a woman answered. "Good morning." Her voice was brisk, her tone efficient.

"Yes, could I speak with Mr. Pinsky, please?"

"Mr. Pinsky is not available, sir."

"Oh. This is Will Anderson. I was told to call this number."

"Yes. Mr. Pinsky had been expecting your call earlier this week and was quite disappointed not to hear from you, as was his client. Unfortunately he has business that will keep him out of Detroit until Monday the twenty-third. He insisted he must meet with you and your father the day he returns."

That was a week and a half away. Not calling had bought me some time, at least.

She continued. "You will meet him at the Cadillac Hotel in the boardroom at one P.M. on June twenty-third. Do you understand?"

"Yes, but . . . I don't know if my father will attend."

"His presence is required. Good day." She hung up.

This Pinsky must be a serious man, I thought. And not someone from the Gianollas' social circle. I had expected to talk to a criminal lowlife and instead spoke with a woman who was clearly educated and intelligent. Fooling the Gianollas into believing I was working in their behalf was going to be difficult enough. But this Pinsky—could I fool him too? One more complication in an equation that already had too many variables.

Later that morning, Wilkinson pushed my door open. "Mr. Edison would like to say hello."

"Really? I didn't know he was here."

Wilkinson beamed. "He and your father came to a very important agreement this morning."

I arched my eyebrows and waited.

"I'll let them tell you."

I hurried down the stairs to my father's office. Mr. Edison and a younger man sat in the uncomfortable chairs in front of my father's desk. They both rose. I hadn't seen Mr. Edison for more than three years, since my father and I had visited him at his factory in New Jersey. Though sixty-five years old, he was still in good physical condition and full of energy. His thin gray hair was carelessly pushed across his forehead, his light gray suit rumpled, and his blue striped tie askew, but I had never seen him completely put together—too busy for those kinds of details.

He smiled, and his bright blue eyes crinkled at the corners. "Will, so nice to see you."

I crossed the room with my gloved right hand behind my back. When I reached him, I held out my left hand. After only a brief hesitation, he took it with his. His fingernails were long and rimmed with grease.

"Very nice to see you as well, sir," I said.

"None of this 'sir' stuff, Will. You're not a boy any longer."

"Thank you . . . Mr. Edison."

He introduced me to his secretary, a slight man with a clean-shaven face, pale skin, and small wire-rimmed glasses. We shook hands as well.

My father sat on the edge of his desk and grinned. "Tom's finally agreed to sell that Waverly and get himself a real electric."

"That's good to hear," I said.

"But, more important, we've extended our exclusive arrangement."

Mr. Edison's eyes twinkled. "This father of yours is an old Indian trader. Hoodwinked me right out of my profits."

"Were that only true," my father retorted. "We're paying a premium, but we'll continue to be the only company with the Edison nickel-steel battery."

"And therefore the only electric with an average range of one-hundred-plus miles," Mr. Edison said.

His secretary interrupted. "With the exception of Colonel Bailey, of course."

Mr. Edison waved him off. "A personal commitment, Will, which your father is well aware of. Unlikely to be a hundred vehicles."

My father nodded. "And Tom's guaranteeing the batteries will hold their rated capacity for four years. We're going to extend our battery warranty to five."

"That's wonderful," I said. "The most expensive piece guaranteed to a hundred miles for five years—and exclusive?"

"Nearly exclusive," Edison's secretary fit in.

I clapped my father on the back. "Congratulations. Detroit Electric will continue to dominate the market."

My father put a smile on his face, but it didn't reach his eyes. "This will help."

CHAPTER FOURTEEN

At two thirty I caught a streetcar to Winder Street and walked down to the Bishop Ungraded School. I figured the boys would be heading back toward Gratiot again, so I took a seat on a bench about 150 yards southwest of the school, which gave me a good view of the school yard and would keep me out of their path when they left.

A few minutes after I settled in, the school let out. The craps game commenced about thirty minutes later. Shortly after that, the newsboy traipsed around the corner and met up with the other boys. They gambled for the better part of an hour before the man came to collect the money. Again he shouted at the boy in the derby and shook him by the collar. This time he left without giving him anything.

I followed the boys along the same route they'd taken previously. By the time they neared Gratiot all but three had peeled off from the group—left were the blackmail boy, the newsboy, and the derby-wearing boy I believed to be their older brother. I thought my odds were as good as they were going to get. I hurried to catch up.

"Hey, boys, excuse me?" I called when I was only about twenty feet behind them.

They stopped and turned around slowly. The oldest one, a toothpick stuck in the corner of his mouth, looked at me and cocked a hip. "Help ya?" He hooked his thumbs into his trouser pockets. The top of the pockets sagged from the weight of his hands, and I saw the yellowed bone handle of a straight razor sticking up from the pocket on the right. The blackmail boy started when he saw me but recovered quickly. His face blanked, but he took half a step behind the leader. The newsboy just scowled at me.

"Yes." I caught up to them. "I'm looking for someone, someone your brother knows, and perhaps you do too."

"Who's 'at?" the oldest boy said. He was a little thinner than the others and shorter for what I guessed his age to be, but he shared their thick black hair and a face that could have belonged to the same person at ten, twelve, and fifteen years of age.

"You guys help me, and I'll give you five bucks."

"I'm listenin'."

"And nobody's getting into any trouble."

"Yeah?" he said.

"Ain't worth it," the blackmail boy spat from behind his brother. "Chicken feed."

"Shuddap, Ray," the oldest boy said. He nodded at me. "You're Anderson, right?"

I was surprised he knew. "Yes."

He appraised me for a moment. "Don't look like a killer."

"You don't look like you've got five bucks," I shot back. "But you could in a minute."

"Who you looking for?"

"Vito Adamo."

He laughed. "Five bucks to rat out the White Hand? I look like I was born yesterday?"

I hadn't heard Adamo called that, but I didn't want to slow down enough to ask. "What's it going to take?"

"Why do you think we'd even know?"

"Your brother"—I gestured behind him—"as I'm sure you know, took blackmail money from me. I'm guessing that was arranged by Adamo, which means you know him."

He chewed on the toothpick and said nothing. Finally he said, "If we could find him—if—it would cost you fifty bucks."

It was my turn to laugh. "You're joking, right?"

"Hey, you came up with a grand last year. And we work with the dagos. Can't go pissing in our milk for free, can we?"

"I'll give you ten," I said.

"Forty."

"Twenty."

"Thirty."

"Done."

"And he never knows it was from us, right?" Joey said.

"Sure."

"You got the money?"

"No, I'll have to get it."

"And we gotta figure out where he's at," he said. "Meet me behind the Bishop School Saturday mornin' at ten."

"All right."

"Bring the money."

"I will. But who am I working with?"

"Why do you care?"

"You know who I am. I've got to know who I'm doing business with."

He gave me a dead-eyed stare that put a chill into me. Finally, he said, "Joey."

"Joey what?"

"Bernstein."

"And your brothers?"

He hooked a thumb toward the newsboy. "Izzy." Izzy just looked at me.

"And you've met Ray," Joey said. "Satisfied?"

"Yeah, thanks."

They turned and strolled off down the sidewalk. When they reached Gratiot, Joey Bernstein looked back at me with a sly grin.

I was going to have to be very careful with these boys.

I was walking up the sidewalk to my building when I noticed a beautiful white touring car parked at the curb. I looked closer. It was a Rolls-Royce Silver Ghost. I'd never seen one before, other than in the trade magazines. It was long and stately, with a chrome grille and an engine compartment that seemed to go on forever. I closed my mouth so I wouldn't drool on myself.

Now I noticed a driver sitting in the front. As I got closer, he turned and said something to another man in the backseat. I wrapped my hand around the butt of the pistol stuck in my belt. I wasn't going to be taken by surprise again.

The man in back opened the door, climbed out, and began crossing the patch of lawn to intercept me. His hands were empty. I glanced from him to the driver. Neither looked to be a threat, but I kept my hand where it was. The man walking toward me wore a dark suit and derby, was perhaps thirty years old, and had a handsome, angular face—marred, I saw as he closed on me, by a large pair of buckteeth that strained against his upper lip. He was dark but didn't look Italian. Jewish, perhaps?

"Mr. Anderson?"

"Why?"

He held out his right hand. "My name is Waldman."

I kept my left hand on the gun and did nothing with my right. "And?"

He let his hand drop to his side. "Mr. Pinsky would like to meet with you for lunch tomorrow." He had a strong accent—Russian, I thought.

"Oh." This wasn't good news. "He's back in town?"

"Yes."

"And what is your relationship with Pinsky?"

"I am Mr. Pinsky's personal secretary."

"Then who did I speak with on the phone?"

"Was it a woman?"

I nodded.

"That would have been another of his secretaries. Mr. Pinsky is a very busy man."

"As am I. I'm busy tomorrow, Mr. Waldman. And I'm sure my father already has lunch plans."

"Perhaps you should come alone," he said. "Mr. Pinsky is aware of the . . . delicacy of this matter." He reached inside his coat, and I tensed, but all he did was pull out a piece of paper and offer it to me. "Mr. Pinsky's home address and telephone number. He will be looking for you at twelve o'clock. Please be punctual."

I let go of the gun and took the paper. Waldman tipped his derby and walked back to the car. I looked at the address. It was on Gladstone, not far from the Fords' home.

Even though I was dreading the meeting, I have to admit I was intrigued.

The next morning I stayed home throwing knives rather than going in to work. I was getting pretty good. In fact, the dartboard was shredded—nothing more than a metal ring with a few stray pieces of wood. Dr. Miller's nurse called me to schedule an appointment. I begged off, telling her I'd call back. Finally it was time for my meeting with Ethan Pinsky. I caught a trolley and got off just down the street from Gladstone. The sky was gray and heavy. Rain was coming. Hammers pounded, and saws slashed all around me as I walked the last few blocks. New homes were under construction in all directions.

I stopped in front of a large redbrick colonial, every curtain drawn. The house looked empty, though the landscaping was immaculate. Feeling more than a little nervous, I rang the bell.

Waldman answered the door. "Come in." He held the door open as I entered and then closed it behind me. "Please, sir," he said. "Hold your arms out from your sides."

"Why?"

"I have to search you, sir. No one is allowed to bring weapons into the house."

"I'll spare you the trouble. Here." I reached behind me, pulled the gun from my belt, and gave it to him along with the switchblade. "Give them back when we're finished."

"Certainly, sir. Thank you. But I still have to search you." He set the knife and pistol on a table and looked at me expectantly.

What was one more indignity? I raised my arms, and he patted me down. "Thank you, sir," he said, and led me down a dim hallway. The curtains were drawn, with only a meager light leaking in onto the deep green wallpaper and walnut trim. As my eyes began to adjust, I could see the house was well appointed and meticulously neat. Waldman stopped at the entrance to the dining room.

A man in a tan suit sat across the room at the end of a long table. An auburn-haired woman bent over him from behind, wiping his neck with a towel. His skin was startlingly white, chalky, glowing in the shadows of the room. His round head was as bare as a billiard ball, and he wore a pair of tiny wire-rimmed dark glasses. A large bowl of water sat on the edge of the table, foamy with shaving cream.

"Son of a bitch," I muttered. It was the albino.

He smiled. His teeth looked yellow against the pallor of his skin. "Ah, Mr. Anderson," he wheezed. "Sorry, I'm running a little late. Please come in. Sit."

The woman—Sam Gianolla's girlfriend—meticulously cleaned the blade of the straight razor and set it into a small black satin shaving case. Waldman pulled out the chair at the opposite end of the table and left the room.

I sat. "You're Pinsky?"

"Indeed I am." He smiled again. The woman retreated from the room with the case, towel, and bowl.

"And you work for the Gianollas."

"No, I've been contracted by the Teamsters. The Gianolla brothers have insinuated themselves into the union," he gasped in a breath, "using methods that are best left to the imagination."

"If you don't work for the Gianollas, what was *she*"—I waved toward the hallway—"doing with them?"

"Hmm." His mouth worked like he was trying to get something unstuck from between his teeth. "Oh. Minna. She serves as a liaison between the union and the Gianollas."

"She's doing more than liaising."

He didn't comment, so I changed tacks. "How did you get Esposito to confess?"

"I had nothing to do with that." He took a breath. I could hear the air rattle in his lungs. "I imagine Mr. Esposito was overcome by guilt. . . . I assume he's a Catholic."

"So what exactly is your role in this?"

He worked his mouth around some more. Finally he said, "I arrange things."

"And what of Minna? Does she also arrange things?"

He looked at me from behind the dark glasses. "She assists me."

"I'd like to speak with her."

He looked at me a moment longer. "I will allow you that opportunity."

"In the meantime, perhaps you could tell me what the hell you want of me?"

"I have been tasked with delivering Anderson Electric Car Company to the Teamsters."

"So you're the public face of the Black Hand. Your mother must be proud."

He didn't rise to the bait. Instead, he smiled. "There is no reason for this to become personal. It is simply business."

Minna carried in a silver platter loaded with two steaming bowls of soup and set it on the middle of the table. She wore a simple blue skirt and a white shirtwaist.

"Turtle soup," Pinsky said. "My grandmother's recipe."

She brought a bowl to my end of the table and set it in front of me. I thought about the prostitute I'd seen with Moretti. Before she could leave, I took hold of her wrist. "It was you, wasn't it? At Moretti's?"

She jerked her arm from my grasp and narrowed her eyes. "Do I need to teach you some manners?"

"Please, Mr. Anderson," Pinsky said. "I said you would have an opportunity to speak with her. And you will."

After giving me one last glare, she stalked back to the center of the table and took the other bowl of soup to Pinsky. I saw now that his bowl contained a clear broth rather than the turtle soup. He waited patiently until she had centered it exactly in front of him.

"Bon appétit," he said, and began to slurp his broth.

"Tell me what you want from me."

He smiled and dabbed his lips with his napkin. "In time, Mr. Anderson. . . . I must concentrate on my digestion." He went back to eating and said nothing further. I tasted the soup. It was delicious. After we finished, Minna again appeared with the tray, this time with a plate of fish, caviar, and crackers for me—just crackers for Pinsky—and again with a plate overloaded with beef, potatoes, and bread for me, another with some sort of mush for her employer.

A light rain began to patter against the windowpanes. Pinsky never looked up from his food and didn't say a word.

I picked at the food and waited for Pinsky. When he finished the last of his mush, he sat back and looked at me across the expanse of the table. His dark glasses flashed as they reflected the light of the chandelier. "I appreciate you being patient with what I know to be rather eccentric behavior on my part, Mr. Anderson." He paused and took a deep breath. "I have a particularly difficult time with my physical health . . . being susceptible to all sorts of maladies to the extent . . . that I go outdoors only when absolutely necessary. Nevertheless, when called upon for my services, I deliver as best I can." He steepled his fingers under his chin. "I suppose you should talk to Minna . . . so your mind will be clear for our discussion." He raised his voice. "Minna?"

The young woman appeared from around the corner, carrying an empty platter.

"Sit, please," Pinsky said.

She set the platter on the table before striding down to Pinsky. She pulled out a chair next to him and sat, her posture perfect.

"Mr. Anderson would like to ask you some questions, my dear. Please answer them all as completely as you can."

"Certainly." She turned to me. In the dim light, I could see her in twenty years—and it was a decided change. She was one of those women—one of those people, I suppose—who would enjoy a brief window of attractiveness in her child-bearing years before her appearance turned hard and severe.

"What is your name?"

"Minna."

"Minna what?"

"Pinsky."

I looked at Ethan Pinsky in astonishment. "She's . . . your daughter?"

He pursed his lips. "You find that so unbelievable?"

"No, ah . . ." I realized what I had implied. I was glad I couldn't see his eyes. "I'm sorry." Turning back to the girl, I said, "How long have you been in Detroit?"

"We arrived in May," she said, her diction perfect. "During your trial."

"Were you in Detroit in August of last year?"

"No. I've not had the pleasure before now."

"Do you own a green satin dress?"

"I imagine I do." She gave me a haughty smile. "I have a lot of dresses."

All right, she had a green dress. But I had no evidence she was the woman who had gone with Moretti to his apartment. "Why are you here?" I said.

"To assist my father."

"Assist in what?"

She smiled again. "In whatever he requires."

"Such as murder?"

One side of her mouth turned down in a disgusted frown. "Of course not."

"Mr. Anderson," Pinsky said. "Minna is one of my secretaries, not a criminal."

"Please," I said. "I saw her with her boyfriend."

"Boyfriend?" Pinsky said.

"Sam Gianolla."

His face turned hard, and he glanced at Minna. "We will need to talk."

She gave him a sulky glance, but was quiet.

Pinsky looked back to me. "Was there anything else you required of her?"

I gave her a dismissive wave. "No. She won't tell me anything anyway."

He said something quietly to her, and she got up and left the room, her heels clacking against the hardwood floor. Turning back to me, he said, "You are a most frustrating young man."

"Thank you. I'm pleased I have that effect on you. Now, what do you want?"

He clucked his tongue. "The Teamsters Union would like nothing more than a toehold in your company. . . . How do you suggest we go about facilitating that?"

I stared back at him. "Surely you must know it's not possible."

He allowed me a condescending smile. "Everything is possible, Mr. Anderson. And a union organizing a Detroit automobile company . . . is not only possible, it's inevitable."

"Perhaps someday, Mr. Pinsky, but not while the Employers Association of Detroit exists."

He leaned forward. "What do you know of economics and politics?"

I shrugged. "Little, I suppose."

"Perhaps I could enlighten you a bit, if you don't mind."

"Not at all."

"Millions of immigrants are entering this country every year." His voice took on a professorial air. "Right now they are viewed as nothing more than . . . organisms that consume the goods of this country . . . and supply ready workers that allow the barons to keep wages low. And it works. To a point." He steepled his fingers under his chin. "The barons don't comprehend the danger . . . of allowing European anarchists and socialists into this country. You see, Mr. Anderson," he wheezed, "we could be a few short years away from revolution. The next economic downturn will put millions out on the street." He shifted in his chair. "A million revolutionaries, not programmed by the American educational system to be . . . patriotic automatons to serve the rich. The barons will be washed under in a tidal wave of the poor."

He smiled broadly. "If they let it get that far. Which they won't. Instead, they will give a little here . . . and a little there, and keep the worker pacified." The rain picked up, the drops drumming against the windows. He sucked in another shallow breath. I leaned in to better hear his wheezy voice over the sound of the rain.

"I believe the AFL is prepared to use your company as an example. If they shut down the city . . . the barons will be forced to act. The Employers Association . . . will do as they are told. It won't be immediate, and it won't be easy . . . but the barons will make a concession. By then, dozens will have died, others will be ruined, and everyone will have been inconvenienced. And"—he paused—"by then the Gianollas will have killed your mother, your father, and Elizabeth Hume."

CHAPTER FIFTEEN

I shot up from my chair. It fell back onto the floor with the sound of a rifle shot. "You son of a bitch!"

Waldman raced through the doorway and grabbed me.

"No, Judah," Pinsky called out with alarm. "That will not be necessary. Will it, Mr. Anderson?"

I tried to shake the man's arms off me, but he was too strong. I glared at Pinsky. "How do they know about Elizabeth?"

"Everyone who knows your story knows about Miss Hume. It's not a secret. Now, will you behave?"

I gave him a tight nod.

He gestured to Waldman, who released me and stepped back against the wall. "Please, Mr. Anderson," Pinsky said, holding his hands out in front of him. "I have no more control than you over the Gianollas. . . . My job—our job—is to mitigate the effects of their brutality. Tony Gianolla kept you out of prison. He expects to be repaid."

"He kept me out of prison after setting me up for Moretti's murder. This was all part of the plan."

"I know nothing about that."

"Why is it I don't believe you?"

"Mr. Anderson, as I said, I do not work for the Gianollas. The Teamsters are no more pleased with the intrusion . . . of the Gianollas than you are, I assure you."

"Then get them arrested."

"It does not meet with the needs of the union at this point."

"What? You think you can control the Gianollas? Have you met them?"

"I am very aware of who they are and what they represent. . . . I am doing a job—nothing more, nothing less."

I shook my head. "You're a piece of shit."

He spread his hands in front of him. "Be that as it may."

"You can forget it." I turned and strode toward the doorway. "I'm not helping you."

"Then you pass a death sentence on your loved ones."

I stopped and took a deep breath. Turning back to him, I said, "All right. But when this is over I'm going to come looking for you again."

"That is your prerogative. Now, shall we?" He motioned toward the chair I had knocked over.

I walked back to the end of the table, picked up the chair, and sat. "So talk."

He looked down at the table in front of him for a moment before his pale pink eyes darted up above the rims of the tiny dark glasses. "So . . . I have given you the union's position. But you and I are practical men. And we need a realistic alternative. The union does not completely understand . . . the difficulties of organizing in this city. You have been given a task . . . that is impossible."

"That's what I've been saying."

"If your father were to make a fifty-thousand-dollar gift to the union—in cash—we could bypass all the unpleasantness that may otherwise occur."

I laughed. "So you're not fronting for the Black Hand. You and the Teamsters *are* the Black Hand."

"No, Mr. Anderson, I am trying to help you. I understand the difficulty . . . of achieving what you've been asked to do. And I can convince the union to do the same."

"And what then of the Gianollas?"

"They will get their share. And they will move on."

"So you don't care about getting the union into Detroit Electric. All this bluster about the revolution and the worker is simply lipstick on a pig. What you want is a fifty-thousand-dollar bribe."

He shrugged. "I'd like to end this problem without bloodshed."

My hand burned. I stopped rubbing it. I was going to have to play out this charade until I could get rid of the Gianollas. I stood. "I'll phone you to arrange a meeting with my father."

"Before you leave"—Pinsky shot a glance at the doorway—"tell me what Minna did."

"Oh, you do care about something."

"Please."

"She kissed Sam, but the way she hung on him it was obvious they'd been doing more than kissing."

Pinsky worked his mouth around. "That is most unfortunate."

"Anything else?"

"Yes." He grimaced. "Because of my health . . . I won't be going into the office for a while. Use the home number Waldman gave you. I'll look forward to your call. . . . I hope you won't be too disappointed . . . if I don't show you out."

Without a word, I stood and strode out into the hallway.

"Oh, Mr. Anderson?" Pinsky called.

I stopped, took a deep breath, and walked back into the room.

"The Gianollas are not known to be patient men. I'll need to hear from you in the next few days."

"I won't be able to get an answer by then."

"No more than a week."

"Fine." I walked to the front door, followed by Waldman. He handed me my gun and knife, and I left the house, ducking out into the rain.

The situation was just getting worse. Perhaps if I could discover who really killed Carlo Moretti, I could get Detective Riordan to do something about the Gianollas. But until then, I had to get the Bernstein boys to help me find Vito Adamo. Without him in the mix, I stood little chance of getting out of this with a happy ending.

I stopped at the Peoples State Bank and withdrew my last twelve hundred dollars—all that remained of Wesley's gift to me—in the form of five hundreds to pay Edsel, and seven hundred dollars in fives, tens, and twenties. I was going to need to move quickly, and I was pretty certain people like the Bernstein boys wouldn't take a check. When I got home, I hid most of the small bills under a pile of magazines in my nightstand.

By that evening, the only evidence it had rained were a few dark spots on the cobbles and a wonderful fresh air smell that lifted my spirits a little. I tucked half the money into my wallet and took a streetcar back to Pinsky's neighborhood to pick up my new automobile. Mrs. Ford answered the door. Before I could even finish greeting her, she pointed toward the garage with a smile. I traipsed across the lawn and walked inside. The pair of Detroit Electric coupés, so tall they almost blocked the light from the ceiling fixtures, took up most of the space inside. They shone, blue and brewster green, both with Henry Ford's initials painted in gold on the doors. They really were beautiful cars— curved glass windows, brass headlamps and fixtures, white Motz cushion tires—luxurious opera coaches that not only didn't need horses but were powered by an all-but-silent motor.

In the last stall stood Edsel's Model T Torpedo Runabout—a custom model he'd built with some of the men at the factory. It was an ungainly clatter-trap with a cheap blue paint job, all sharp angles and cheap fixtures, but capable of attaining mind-boggling speeds in a matter of seconds. To be fair, it was more striking than a standard Model T Runabout, though only slightly. It sat lower to the ground, the engine compartment was a bit longer, the fenders were curved so as to be somewhat less ugly, and it was equipped with an oversize eighteen-gallon gasoline tank, 50 percent larger than normal.

And it was Edsel's baby.

He was polishing the hood and looked up when I came around the electrics. "I'll hate to see her go," he said, running a finger along the front fender.

I playfully punched him in the arm. "I'll let you visit her. And if you're good, maybe I'll allow you conjugal rights."

He grinned at me. "I'll sell her to you so long as you promise to race me once I get the Speedster done."

"You tell me the time and place, and I'll be there." I pulled out my wallet and handed him five one-hundred-dollar bills.

He pocketed the cash and gestured toward the cab. "Let me show you what I've done. Hop up there."

I climbed in through the passenger door and slid over on the seat.

"The throttle control is over here now." He pointed to the left side of the steering wheel.

"Perfect."

"The tool kit is in the trunk." Edsel handed me a set of keys. "Now, you do know how to drive a *real* automobile, don't you?"

I waved my hand at him. "Of course I do."

"I could give you a tutorial."

"I'm a professional driver, for God's sake. I can handle it."

"Okay. Still, I'd like to point out that you are a professional driver of sedate electrics, not lightning-fast motorcars. And listen. The throttle is very sensitive. It doesn't take much to throw you back in your seat. Be careful."

"Don't worry about me."

"Would you like me to go on a test drive with you?" He sounded hopeful.

"No, I'm fine. Really."

He looked at the car for a long moment. "Well, I'll get her started for you." After he raised the garage door, he came back, reached inside, and fiddled with the throttle and spark controls. Walking around to the front of the car again, he said, "Set the hand brake." I did, and he gave the handle a crank. It didn't catch, so he tried it again. This time the engine caught. I gave it a little more throttle, and it died. He stood off to the side of the car, glaring at me with his hands on his hips.

"I've got it." I turned back the throttle a bit. "Try it again."

He did, and this time the engine caught and quickly built up to a roar. I nudged the throttle the tiniest bit, let out the hand brake, and slipped the car into gear. It jumped out of the garage and tore down the driveway like a rabbit. I was only just able to turn before I plowed into the neighbor's yard.

"Good luck!" Edsel called out, his words nearly drowned by his laughter. As I drove away, I thought I heard him add, "You'll need it."

A minute and a half later, I was wishing I had taken Edsel up on his offer of a test drive. I stalled the car in the middle of Woodward Avenue and couldn't get it started again. With horns honking and people shouting at me, I adjusted the spark and throttle, ran to the front of the car, and spun the crank again, and again, and yet again. Nothing. I ran back around to the cab and adjusted the levers, though I really had little idea whether I should be moving them up or down. When I spun the crank this time, a strong smell of gasoline wafted out of the engine compartment. Though I'd had little experience with gas automobiles, I knew I'd flooded the engine.

While the commotion continued around me, I turned the throttle lever all the way down and began cranking again. Three boys, perhaps eight years old, leaned against a Peoples Ice truck parked at the curb and sneered at me, making cute observations about my mental capacity. Finally I got it started, jumped back in the cab, and drove like a spastic—fast—slow—fast—slow—nearly run into a wagon—slow again—until finally I reached the Detroit Electric garage downtown. I pulled in with a minimum of humiliation and made arrangements for the car to be housed there when I wasn't using it. My Torpedo was the only internal combustion automobile in the garage, and of course, the men looked down their noses at it. They would never have allowed the car inside the building had I not been the owner's son.

I slept little that night. The joints of my wrist and fingers ached with a deep, dull pain, like that of a toothache. When I got out of bed early the next morning, rain was pounding against the roof and windows of my apartment, driven by a howling wind. Clouds hung low and heavy over the city, and rain poured in sheets, one following another up the road.

After I mixed two grams of aspirin into water and drank it down, I looked out the window at the gray scene. This morning I was meeting with the Bernstein brothers, who were my only hope of finding Vito Adamo. I prayed this meeting was something more than a ruse to try to steal my money. Still, there was nothing to do but to find out.

At eight I phoned the garage and asked them to deliver the car. I wasn't going to get soaked getting down there only to be abused while I tried to get it started. Trying to start it in the rain seemed a better alternative. Fifteen minutes later, one of the Detroit Electric "chasers" pulled my Torpedo up to the curb, jumped out, and sprinted off down Peterboro toward the streetcar stop, holding a hand up near his face to block the rain.

I tucked one of the .32s into my belt and checked my wallet to be sure I had the money, in case the boys actually did come through. Then I grabbed my goggles, put on my waterproof tan duster and a checkered touring cap, and grabbed my umbrella. At the front of the building I paused, watching waves of rain wash over the automobile that now looked so puny against the forces of Mother Nature.

I dashed outside to the car. By the time I got it started, my umbrella had blown inside out and I was soaked to the skin, waterproof duster or not. I started out, my rain-spotted goggles already nearly useless. The Torpedo's leather top blocked some small percentage of the rain. My good luck was that the weather was keeping virtually everyone else off the roads. I managed to complete my journey without stalling the engine or killing anyone.

I parked two blocks away from the Bishop Ungraded School and walked the remaining distance, slogging along the puddled sidewalk with my cap pulled down around my ears. At the school I walked around to the rear entrance, where I stood under the overhang. I reached around behind me and stretched, feeling the pistol tucked into my belt. Water cascaded over the redbrick walls and poured down in front of me like a waterfall.

A few minutes after ten, Izzy, the newsboy, slogged up to me, water splashing around his soaked lace-up shoes and dripping down the bill of his cap. "Come on." He turned and began walking around the building.

I stayed where I was. "Hey, Izzy. Come here."

He stopped and put his hands on his hips in an exaggerated fashion, letting me know he was annoyed. "You wanna know where he is?"

"Of course I do."

"Then follow me." He turned and trudged away. I followed him at a distance, wary of an ambush. Izzy sloshed through the puddles to the front of the school and into the field across the street.

After another block I caught up with him. "Where are we going?"

He plodded along. "Friend of ours place."

"Where?"

"Junkyard."

I hitched up my trousers and ran my hand over the grip of the .32. I hoped I didn't have to use it or even threaten to, but with these boys it was anybody's guess. Izzy cut across the street and marched through an opening in a corrugated sheet metal wall that ran the entire length of the block. The wall varied in height from one section to the next, with panels of faded red and green. The only paint that wasn't peeling was the business's name, FLEISHERS JUNKYARD, scrawled in large black letters on either side of the entrance.

Izzy turned right and walked down a muddy alleyway between piled collections of metal, torn from old machines, trains, and who knows what else. The rain pinged and clanged and thrummed off the junk in a percussive frenzy, surrounding me with noise. I stayed back, more wary now. The piles of junk were easily ten to twelve feet high, the pieces on top perched precariously over the narrow alley. I was beginning to feel claustrophobic. Izzy took a sudden left and then a right, and I lost sight of him.

I pulled the gun from my belt and crept forward. At the end of the row I came to a clearing of sorts. Izzy stood under the roof of half of a Detroit City Railway streetcar, green with white trim, one of the old horse-drawn variety. The car had been cloven in two. All the windows were missing. Two other boys sat inside. I recognized Ray, the blackmail boy, on one of the wooden benches near the back.

"Get your ass in here," Izzy said.

The gun still in my hand, I walked over and hopped up into the car. The rain pounded against the top, like the sound of heavy surf at the ocean. Izzy slipped past me and sat next to Ray. A young man of perhaps seventeen, to all appearances a real tough, sat behind them, one arm flung over the back of the bench seat while he looked at me with amusement. His eyes were brilliant blue.

I nodded toward him. "You the boss?"

"You could say that." He cocked his head to the side, and I spotted a resemblance between him and the Bernstein boys.

"Are you another brother?"

"Yeah. Abe. You got the money?"

"You got the information?"

"Yeah."

"Tell me."

"The dough first."

"Not until I see him."

He gave me a lazy smile. "You don't trust us?"

"Not a bit."

"Then maybe I'll take it."

"Is that so?" I held up the gun.

Abe smiled. "Wouldn't do that if I was you." He tilted his head to his left. "Joey might think you was threatenin' me. You wouldn't want him getting any crazy idears like that now, would ya?"

I glanced off to my right. Joey Bernstein stood outside the car, perhaps fifteen feet away from me, rain dripping off his derby, with a sawed-off shotgun pointed at my head.

"So why don't you put down that peashooter," Abe said with a grin, "and gimme the dough."

I smiled at him, trying to show a lot more confidence than I felt. "Maybe I'll put a bullet in you first."

He barked out a laugh. "Joey wouldn't like that." Still staring at me with that insolent grin, he called out, "If he shoots me, put one in his shoulder. Before he bleeds out, make him hurt—a lot."

Out in the rain, Joey Bernstein snorted. "Lemme kill him, Abe. Let's split up the dough and get outta here."

Abe didn't even look at him. "Shut up, Joey." Speaking to me again, he said, "We do odd jobs for the dagos. Adamo can't know it was us."

I nodded. "No problem."

I could see on his face he'd already made the decision. "All right. Izzy'll show you where Adamo's holin' up."

"One thing," I said to him.

"Yeah?"

"How'd you meet John Cooper?"

Shrugging, Abe said, "Never did."

"Then how did he set up the blackmail drop?"

"Wop set it up."

"Adamo?"

"No."

"One of his men?"

He shrugged again. "I'da know."

I studied him, trying to decide if he was telling me the truth, but I was certain he'd had enough experience telling falsehoods that he'd be pretty good at it. Abe nodded to his littlest brother, who slid over into the aisle, jumped off the end of the trolley, and landed in a puddle with a splash.

I lowered the gun and turned around to follow him.

"Anderson?" Abe said.

I stopped and looked back at him.

"Give him the money when you get there. And—if Adamo hears word one about us helping you, you're dead. One thing you don't wanna learn the hard way is what happens when you make me mad."

CHAPTER SIXTEEN

Izzy and I slogged out of the junkyard and headed south. We crossed Hastings Street to Rivard, and Izzy stopped under the overhang of a building at the corner of Rivard and Mullett.

He nodded toward a saloon on the first floor of a redbrick two-story across the street. "Adamo's been holing up there. A wop name a Mirabile owns the joint. Abe says he's a crook too."

I took out my wallet and gave him a ten and a five. "When I see him I'll give you the other fifteen. I'm good for it."

"That wasn't the deal." For the first time, Izzy looked uncomfortable. "It's thirty bucks."

"Not until I see him."

"Abe said thirty bucks. He's gonna want the dough. Today."

"If you're telling me the truth, I'll pay."

"No!" he shouted. "Thirty bucks!"

"Look," I said, taking him by the arm. "I told you I'd pay if you're telling me the truth. I will."

He shook his head, turned, and gave me a disgusted wave. "Your funeral." He walked off into the pouring rain.

I stood under the overhang for a few minutes, watching the saloon. A sullen-looking man, his head hunched against the rain, hands shoved deep into his pockets, threw open the saloon's door and disappeared inside. With no brilliant plan or confederates to assist me, I reckoned a frontal assault was my best bet. I sloshed across the street and walked inside the saloon.

It was a dark, quiet place, the only sounds murmured conversation in Italian and peanut shells crunching under my shoes. A few men sat at the bar under a thick cloud of cigarette smoke. I found an open spot at the bar and waited for the bartender, a jovial-looking man with thinning hair, to notice me. When he did, he came over and looked at me with a smile and arched eyebrows.

I took off my hat. "I'd like to speak with Mr. Mirabile, please."

His face shut down. "I don' know him."

"How about Vito Adamo?"

He turned away and began wiping a glass with a dishcloth.

"Look, I'm not going to cause them any trouble."

Nothing.

I pulled a five-dollar bill from my wallet, slid it across the bar, and rapped my knuckles on the wood. He turned back to me. "Tell Adamo that Will Anderson wants to talk about a mutual enemy. He'll want to see me."

The bartender slipped the bill into his pocket, but I didn't think I'd actually bought myself anything.

"I'll be back tomorrow. Tell him." Fitting my hat onto my head, I walked out the door. I trudged along in the cold rain that poured down onto the gray city—Mother Nature's vain attempt to clean these streets. I could have told her. The filth was permanent.

I walked to the corner the next morning for a paper, expecting Izzy to harass me for the other fifteen dollars, though I didn't plan to pay until I confirmed he'd been telling the truth. He wasn't there, nor was the redhead, so I headed down the block for a *Free Press*. When I returned home, I sat in the parlor with the paper and a cup of coffee. One of the first articles I saw made me choke.

The headline read, MURDER SUSPECTS TURN SELVES IN. My curiosity turned to amazement as I read the article. Yesterday afternoon, Vito Adamo and Filipo Busolato had walked into police headquarters and given themselves up for the murder of Carlo Callego. According to the writer, Mr. Adamo did not speak English, when in fact I knew him to be more erudite than the majority of American natives. A quote from his interpreter—Ferdinand Palma, the former police detective turned banker turned interpreter for Maria Cansalvo—concluded the article:

Mr. Adamo, a poverty-stricken delivery truck driver

(that made me laugh out loud)

is confused by these charges but wishes to let it be known that he is completely innocent. He wants only to be exonerated and is asking for a speedy trial so that he may return to his wife and children.

It could hardly be a coincidence that Palma was translating for Vito Adamo. It only made sense that the man who had interpreted Maria Cansalvo's damning testimony against me would be helping him. But I didn't see Adamo's angle in turning himself in. The Gianollas must have been getting too close.

Well, I knew where Vito Adamo was now. Today would be as good a day as any to stop by the jail, have a chat, assuming the police agreed to let me talk with him. And I couldn't forget to pay the Bernstein boys. As far as I knew, they delivered on what they said they would.

Now, how to get in the jail? I set the paper down on the coffee table. Murphy. He'd pulled strings before. So long as I paid, he'd do it again.

My father and I were going to the Tigers game at one, which gave me only a couple of hours to get this done. I called the Bethune Street station and, posing as Murphy's brother, asked if he was on duty. My Irish accent was dismal, though apparently passable, as the fourth man to whom I was transferred finally told me that Murphy was out on patrol until 10 A.M. He'd be back then. It was already half past nine. I plunked a derby onto my head and ran out to the streetcar stop. Sunday-morning traffic uptown wasn't heavy, as most of the riders were heading the other direction, to one of the churches on Piety Hill.

I stood outside the station between the driveway and the front entrance until one of the Chalmers police cars pulled up, Murphy in the passenger seat. A lanky middle-aged cop with a sagging face and handlebar mustaches to match unfolded himself from the driving seat and walked inside.

Murphy was still squeezing himself out of the car. "Hey, Murphy," I said, walking toward him.

He forced his left knee out of the car and stepped down off the running board. "Gaddamn midget cars," he muttered. When he noticed me, he said, "Anderson. And just when me pocketbook was getting a mite thin. Whattaya want?"

"I need to see Adamo. Ten minutes, that's all I ask."

"He ain't here. He's down at the First."

Police headquarters downtown, where I had spent many long months. "Fine. But I need you to grease the wheels for me. Make a phone call."

He scratched his chin while he thought. "Twenty bucks."

"Fine." I knew it wouldn't be free. I pulled a twenty from my wallet and handed it to him.

"Wait here." He waddled inside the building and returned about five minutes later. "See O'Toole at the desk. Ten bucks to him."

"Great. Thanks."

Murphy gave me a dismissive wave and walked back into the station. I took a streetcar to Campus Martius, the park at the point from which Woodward, Michigan, Gratiot, and a number of other major streets radiate out like spokes on a wheel. From there I hoofed it a couple of blocks to police headquarters. O'Toole, a thick man with gray hair and dark eyes, forced me to pay him twenty dollars, but finally walked me into the jail and down a pair of long corridors lined with crowded cells. At the end of the second one, Adamo sat on his cot, writing on a notepad.

An image of Wesley popped into my head. This man in front of me, this son of a bitch, was involved in Wesley's murder. My vision went dark, and I felt the heat in my face. I wondered if I could even get the words out of my mouth.

Adamo had dressed down to his role as a poverty-stricken truck driver. He wore a white shirt with a short red tie and pair of gray wool trousers held up by suspenders. His vanity hadn't allowed him to let his grooming go, however. His jet-black hair and waxed mustaches were carefully combed into place.

"Five minutes," O'Toole said, and walked back down the corridor.

Adamo looked up from his pad and gave me a quizzical look. "Mr. Anderson. What brings you out on this fine morning?"

I pushed down my revulsion and said as neutrally as I could, "I think we can help each other."

He set the pad on the cot, rose, and met me by the bars. An amused expression on his face, he said, "And just how are we going to do that?"

"You want the Gianolla brothers dead," I whispered. "So do I."

He chuckled. "So you owe them for providing you with a patsy. And you don't want to pay."

"What—Esposito?"

He just raised his eyebrows.

"I didn't ask them for anything. And I didn't kill your man."

"Please, do not lie to me. I am where you want me to be. Isn't that enough?"

"But Esposito confessed. Why would he confess if he didn't do it?"

"No." The word was short, clipped. "It wasn't him."

"How do you know that?"

"My hands reach into the state prison. I have been assured Esposito was not the killer."

"Well, it wasn't me."

He returned to the cot and picked up his notepad. After a moment, he met my gaze again. "I know you were at Carlo's that night. I know you hold me responsible for the death of your friend. I know you would like nothing better than for me and my men to rot in your miserable prisons. Why would I not also believe that you killed Carlo? Prove to me otherwise, and perhaps I could take you seriously."

"How am I supposed to prove I *didn't* do something?"

He chuckled again. "By proving someone else did."

I tried to persuade him for another couple of minutes to no avail. His position was solid: Prove someone else killed Moretti, and perhaps he'd listen to me.

I walked back to the front desk at the station lobby and asked O'Toole if I could see the Moretti file. He looked around furtively before leaning down and saying, "Fifty bucks."

We dickered, ending up at thirty dollars. He jumped down from his seat and walked me back into a different hallway, where he closed the door and held out his hand. I pried the banknotes from my quickly emptying wallet and gave him the bills. He turned and led me into a large room filled with a dozen desks and rows of filing cabinets against the walls. Other than for us, the room was unoccupied. He walked down the line of cabinets, running a forefinger along the drawers as he wandered along, mouthing letters. "*S . . . R . . . O . . .* there." He pulled a drawer open and flipped through some files before pulling out a thick folder and handing it to me. "You got ten minutes. If I got to come back here for you, I'm gonna introduce you to my billy club."

"Fine." He left. I set the file on top of the cabinet and leafed through half a dozen police reports from the night of the murder and the following days, just skimming the material, looking for names. When I got to Maria Cansalvo's account of the evening, I slowed and really read it. I hadn't thought of her since the trial. Where was she now? On her way back to Sicily, I supposed. The only two people in this whole mess who were completely innocent were Maria Cansalvo and, according to Adamo, Giovanni Esposito, the only two who had been punished.

When I finished her account, I looked through the rest of the file more closely—Esposito's confession, the officers' and detectives' statements, everything. Nothing even hinted at a killer other than Esposito or me. I grabbed a blank piece of paper off the closest desk and wrote down Esposito's home address. If there was a Mrs. Esposito, perhaps I could get some helpful information. Perhaps Esposito was one of the men who had entered the building prior to Moretti coming home. If not, I had to learn the identity of the prostitute. Right now, my only two suspects for the woman playing that role were Elizabeth and Pinsky's daughter. I couldn't quite get myself to believe that either of them would have gone that far.

I walked back to the lobby and headed toward Woodward again. I'd see what I could find at Esposito's address, but I didn't have much hope for help there. Regardless, I'd speak with my father first. He was the key to my only other idea for extracting myself from the situation with the Gianollas—spilling my guts to the Employers Association of Detroit. Their primary function was to eliminate threats against their members, which usually involved one union or another. They responded with fists, knives, clubs, and guns, and used criminals to do their dirty work when necessary. Unfortunately, they wouldn't help me without my father's approval. I had to involve him. Perhaps the power of the EAD could get me out of this.

But I first had to explain it all to my father, a task I eyed with dread.

The man next to me cupped his hands around his mouth and hooted, "Yer a bum, Cobb!"

Ty Cobb glanced our way and gave the man a one-fingered salute before turning back to the action. Others joined in cursing him. Cobb had lost a bit of his popularity this year for beating the hell out of a cripple—a one-handed man—who'd been riding him during a game in New York. I kept quiet. Cobb and the other Tigers' outfielders, Sam Crawford and Bobby Veach, were all they had going for them.

I couldn't get used to the ball field. They'd torn down Bennett Park while I was in jail and replaced it with the gargantuan Navin Field. My father and I sat in the second row behind the right field fence, drinking soda pop and watching the action in the bright sunshine. There wasn't much to cheer about. The Tigers were being whitewashed by Cleveland's ace, Vean Gregg. Nap Lajoie and Shoeless Joe Jackson had each driven in two runs, and the Naps led 4–0 in the ninth inning. Ten minutes later, Gregg put the Tigers out of their misery.

After the game, we stopped at Charlie Churchill's for a drink. We sat at a table in the bar, my father with a brandy, me with a Faygo orange pop.

"Son?"

Startled, I looked at my father. For some time I'd been staring in the direction of the "Brunette Venus" painting behind the bar, lost in my thoughts. I had no idea how to begin this conversation.

"You seem like you're a million miles away. Is that electrotherapy accident still affecting you?"

I shook my head. "I wish it were that simple."

He touched my arm. "What is it? Are you in some sort of trouble again?"

Taking a deep breath, I nodded and began explaining about the Gianollas and the Teamsters, the meeting I had with Ethan Pinsky, and the alternatives he had given us. When I finished, I told him I'd gone to see Detective Riordan but didn't trust any other policemen enough to talk to them. Then I added that I'd spoken with Vito Adamo in jail that morning to ask for his help and was rebuffed.

His face variously registered shock, disbelief, and, at the end of my tale, a fatal acceptance. "This all goes back to Vito Adamo?"

"Yes. The gun battles in Little Italy are Adamo and Gianolla men fighting for turf. But the Teamsters, of course, are a new wrinkle that came with the Gianollas."

My father met my eyes. "I don't have the money. The truth is, I've sunk most of our savings into the company. I couldn't come up with fifty thousand dollars without selling Anderson Electric."

"No. You can't do that. We have to meet them head-on. I want to bring this to the Employers Association."

He nodded. "This is what they were designed for. Well, perhaps not exactly this, but for keeping the unions out. We can get them to help. We'll need to see Finnegan, the security head."

"I asked him about Adamo the other day. He said he wasn't familiar with him."

His forehead wrinkled. "Well, perhaps they don't employ criminals anymore. They changed quite a bit after the Cooper mess."

"The Gianollas might have men inside the EAD as well as the police. Do you trust Finnegan?"

"We haven't had any need for his services for a while. I'll ask around."

"Father, if we do this, you and Mother are going to have to be very careful. If the Gianollas get wind I'm not cooperating, there's no doubt they'll come after you."

His eyes narrowed. "I'd like to see those scum try anything with me. But your mother . . . I'll phone the Pinkertons."

"I'm not sure that's a good idea. They're not exactly invisible. If the Gianollas see them, they'll be gunning for us."

My father thought for a second. "All right. I'll wait. We'll just have to take precautions. Tomorrow morning we'll go see Finnegan. We'll show those Sicilians who runs this city." He leaned toward me and nudged my shoulder. "Dr. Miller wanted me to speak with you about the rest cure again. But I think we can forget about neurasthenia treatments for the time being."

CHAPTER SEVENTEEN

When my father and I left the saloon, I pulled out Esposito's address and took a streetcar up Gratiot into the Russian ghetto, by the open-air Eastern Market, the block-long old-world bazaar filled with stall after stall of goods. Food dominated the offerings, though if someone would pay money for a thing, it was here.

I skirted the market and walked the few blocks out of the ghetto into a section of Little Italy. Esposito's address was on the second floor of a crumbling redbrick apartment building on Wilkins. I pushed open the battered door and climbed the stairs, breathing the stink of fried fish and chamber pots. The smell brought me back to the apartment in which Elizabeth and I had spent a week while she was in withdrawals. Walking into the second-floor hallway, I shook my head. Though we'd been there less than two years earlier, it seemed a lifetime had passed.

I knocked on Esposito's door. A young man opened it and looked at me expectantly. A young woman, presumably his wife, stood inside, a baby in her arms. I asked the man if this was Giovanni Esposito's apartment, to which he responded in heavily accented English that he and his wife had moved in the week before. He did not know Esposito or whether he had a family.

No one was home at the apartment across the hall or to the right of Esposito's apartment, but an old woman in a heavy black dress answered the door on the left.

"Good evening," I said, doffing my hat. "Could you tell me if Giovanni Esposito used to live in the apartment next door?"

She crossed herself and said, "*Sì,*" then reached out and took hold of my forearm. "He is killer, *assassino.*"

I nodded, though I thought I knew otherwise. "Did he have a family?"

"No. Just him," she replied, a scowl on her face.

I thanked her and turned from the doorway, but her expression made me stop and ask her what sort of man he was.

"Bah!" she said. "Bad man. Gambling, up all night. And he kill man!"

"Yes, I've heard that," I said. "Thank you very much." As I returned to the street, I felt somewhat relieved. Even though I was no closer to gaining Adamo's help, at least the man in prison wasn't a saint with eight young children to feed.

My next stop was to see Elizabeth. As much as I missed her, I didn't look forward to delivering this message. But she needed to know the truth. I took a streetcar down to Jefferson and walked the last half mile. Alberts again showed me to the living room, where I waited for Elizabeth, lost in my thoughts.

"Hello, Will." Elizabeth stood only a few feet away from me. I hadn't even heard her enter the room.

"Good evening, Elizabeth. How've you been?"

"I'm fine. You?"

"Oh. Fine."

Biting her lip, she tilted her head to the side. "What's on your mind?"

I didn't know how to start. Finally I said, "Did you see the news about Adamo?"

She nodded, her face grim. "Locked up. Hopefully for the rest of his life."

"Yes." I looked away for a moment before meeting her eyes. "But that's not why I'm here. I'm afraid I've put you in danger again."

"Does this have something to do with Adamo?"

"No. Well, not directly, anyway." I saw no reason to bring up my visit to the jail that morning.

She stared at me. "This is why you haven't called?"

I nodded. "Can we sit?"

Without a word, she walked to the sofa and perched on the edge. I followed and sat back, sinking into the soft cushion. "I've been threatened by a group of Sicilian criminals. If Anderson Electric doesn't either pay them fifty thousand dollars or allow the Teamsters Union to represent their drivers and mechanics, they've threatened to kill my mother and father, and you."

Her face was guarded. I couldn't discern her reaction. "It's not Adamo."

"No. The men threatening me are a different Black Hand gang—the Gianolla brothers. I didn't think they knew about you but found out otherwise. They specifically threatened you."

She shook her head slowly while she gazed at me. "It doesn't end, does it?"

"I'd like you and your mother to leave town again. Just until this is over."

"Did they threaten my mother?"

I thought about lying, but there'd already been too much of that. "No, but I doubt they'll bother to aim too carefully."

"Wait. Didn't you say they threatened us *if* the company didn't take on the Teamsters or give them the money?"

"Yes."

"So you presumably have some time to respond."

"Yes."

"How much?"

"A week."

"So there's no immediate danger."

"Well . . . it's hard to say. If they actually do what they said they would, then no. But these aren't clergymen; they're criminals."

"Tell me if this escalates. Until then I'm not taking my mother away from this house."

"Elizabeth, you've got to go! These men are even worse than the Adamos."

She was quiet for a moment. Finally she looked at me with smoldering eyes and said, "No. She needs to be here."

"Look, the Employers Association is going to help us. We'll get rid of the Gianollas."

"No, you look. My mother is finally acting like herself. The entire time we were in Europe she may as well have been an automaton. I can't take her away again."

I pursed my lips, trying to frame an argument that would change her mind.

"Maybe I could help," she said.

"Lizzie, come on. This is nowhere for a woman to be."

Her eyes widened. "This isn't, but the other places you've led me are?"

In a voice as wretched as I felt, I said, "I don't want you hurt."

Her lower lip quivered. "This isn't about me being hurt. It's about keeping your parents and me from being murdered."

"I won't allow it."

Her face was tight, eyes shining. "Do you know what it's like to have to sleep with the light on every night? Do you know what it's like to be afraid the bogeyman is hiding around every corner?" She looked away. "I never would have come back if I thought Mother could recover anywhere else." Shaking her head, she glanced at me again. "And I *can* help. I'm not who I was."

"How do you mean?"

"No man will ever brutalize me again." Her words carried a threat. "I'll do what's necessary."

"Elizabeth, be realistic. These men are murderers, and you're a society girl."

Her eyes flashed. "First of all, don't call me a girl. I'm a woman. And listen to me with both ears. If I ever again need to defend myself—or a loved one—not only will I have the means, I'll have the fortitude. I will kill before I'll let— Oh, forget it. You'll never understand."

"I know you think you can, but—"

"But nothing. I'm more fit and stronger than I've ever been. I hired a military man in Paris to teach me how to defend myself, and I've been shooting nearly every day."

"Shooting? You?"

"Elizabeth? Are you all right?" Mrs. Hume stood in the doorway. She looked healthy but had aged a great deal since I'd last seen her. She no longer looked like Elizabeth's older sister. "Oh, hello, Will."

I stood. "Good evening, Mrs. Hume. How are you today?"

She smiled, and her face lit up. "I'm fine, thank you. It's nice to see you, Will. My gosh, how long has it been?"

I thought about it. "Nearly a year and a half."

"You look good. How's your hand?"

"It's fine, thank you."

"You should come by more often, Will. We've been back since last July, and this is the first time I see you?"

"Yes, sorry. I've been awfully busy."

"Oh. Right. Sorry." Her face turned gray. "I forgot. I'm glad you're back with us."

"Me too," I said.

"Will and I were just saying good night, Mother. I'll be up in a moment." Elizabeth smiled as her mother walked away. "Unbelievable. She's even happy to see you. That settles it. We're not going anywhere." I could see in her eyes that she'd come to some sort of decision. "You'd better involve me in your planning." She gave me a grim smile. "You and I are going to be partners."

The next morning, I woke with the oddest thought—Mrs. Hume said they had been back since July. If she was right, Elizabeth was in town when Moretti was murdered. It would also mean Elizabeth lied to me, about a subject that should have made little difference to either of us. Why would I care that they got back a month earlier than she claimed they did? If I could rely on her mother's memory, Elizabeth was hiding something. And I was afraid I knew what that something was.

I certainly wasn't going to try to prove to Adamo that Elizabeth killed Moretti. That put me at an apparent dead end with the Adamo gang. But . . . Elizabeth a killer? Yes, she had changed, but I couldn't imagine she'd changed that much. Still, it was just enough of a possibility that I couldn't speak about this with the police or anyone affiliated with Vito Adamo. I had to protect her. This series of events started with my stupidity, and I owed her my life.

But could she be serious that we'd be partners? She seemed it last night. I hoped the dawning of another day had helped her to see what a ridiculous idea that was. I was all for women's suffrage—from my experience, women on the whole were less stupid than men—but when it came to putting a woman in danger, particularly Elizabeth, I had a much less progressive view. Should she continue to try to be involved, I would have to put my foot down.

After two cups of coffee, I went out to the corner of Woodward and Peterboro, looking for Izzy Bernstein. He stood on the corner, bawling out the headlines—Roosevelt may run as an independent, U.S. Marines land in Cuba, eight-hour workday vote in Congress today. It was a Monday-morning blur. Pedestrians hurried across the streets, men and women packed onto streetcars, horns honked, and those with vehicles or horses fought through the overwhelming traffic. Izzy stood there with his bag of papers, an island of hostility.

I walked up behind him. "Hey."

He turned around, a paper in his hand. His right eye was puffy, the skin around it bruised a mottled blue.

"What happened to you?"

He gave me a disgusted look and turned his back on me. "Marines in Cuba! Read it!"

"Izzy, what happened to you?"

He looked back at me and spat, "I told ya Abe wanted the fuckin' money."

"He hit you?"

"Yeah, he hit me. Whattaya think?"

"Shit. Sorry. I've got the money."

"Hang on to it. Abe's gonna collect."

I took the envelope out of my pocket. "Here. You give it to him."

He snorted out a laugh. "Nah, he wants to talk to ya."

"All right. I guess he knows where to find me."

"He'll find ya. Hit the bricks." He turned around and shouted, "Roosevelt running again! Read it!"

"I'm really sorry, Izzy," I said. "I know it was my fault." He ignored me. Shaking my head, I queued up for a southbound streetcar. Abe beat Izzy because of me. I had thought I was being clever holding back half the money, but the Bernstein brothers were growing up in a very different environment than I had. I should have known there would be consequences for Izzy not bringing all the money back. Still, I'd speak to Abe about it.

I was finally able to push my way on board a streetcar. I stuck my nickel in the box and grabbed hold of a railing. The car started up, heading for downtown. I jumped off by the Detroit Electric garage. When I walked in under the red iron archway, I saw Joe Curtiss standing with Mr. Billings, the day manager, next to a maroon Detroit Electric brougham. The fresh air scent of ozone hit me the second I stepped inside. The walls were lined with gleaming Detroit Electrics in blue, green, and maroon, along with a variety of special order colors like midnight black, canary yellow, and fire engine red. The garage buzzed with the sound of stored electricity.

Mr. Billings handed Joe a clipboard, clapped him on the back, and walked toward the office. I caught Joe's eye. He glanced around nervously before nodding toward the back of the garage and strolling in that direction. I followed him.

He stopped at the base of the stairway that led to the second floor and looked around again. "Did you talk to Pinsky?"

I nodded.

"And?"

Joe didn't need to know. "Well," I said, "it's a delicate issue. I've brought it up with my father, and I think I can get him to meet with Pinsky." I shrugged. "You know how tough this is going to be. It's going to take time."

"I don't know how much time we've got." Joe tugged at his collar.

I couldn't meet his eyes. "I'm working on it, Joe. I'm doing the best I can."

"Yeah," he said. "All right. I guess that's all you can do."

"Is there somewhere your family could go until this is over? Relatives, perhaps?"

"I don't know. . . ."

"Figure out somewhere for your family to stay. What about a hotel? I'll pay for it. Have them register under another name. They could even get out of town if you want."

"Yeah?"

"Sure."

"Well . . ." Joe toed the floor in front of him. "I'll talk to Gina. See what she wants to do."

"Okay. Just let me know."

"All right." I turned to walk to the front, but Joe caught my arm. "Will?"

I stopped and looked at him.

"Thanks. I know this isn't your fault, and it shouldn't be your problem. But thanks."

I thought back to Wesley, his selflessness. "What are friends for, Joe? If I can help, I will."

We said our good-byes, and he climbed the stairs while I headed toward the front of the garage. My Torpedo sat between a pair of brewster green extension broughams. Since I hadn't done it before, I pulled the tool kit from the trunk and began inspecting the car. I had no doubt that Edsel had kept it in tip-top condition, but I needed to go through the pre-start routine at least once a week anyway, and I had the time to do it now. I examined the carburetor, inspected the ignition, lubricated the dynamo, pump, and fan, tightened the chains and belts, and finally checked the water and oil. These internal combustion motorcars were certainly complicated, but everything was perfect.

I climbed into the driving seat, set the spark and throttle, and hopped down again. The engine started on the first crank. I pulled my goggles over my eyes and set my touring cap at a jaunty angle before rolling the automobile out of the garage at a snail's pace. Once I was clear, I tore up Woodward toward the factory, obliterating the ten-mile-an-hour city speed limit. The engine roared as I weaved between cars, wagons, carriages, and bicycles, stopping only for the streetcars. The wind blew back my hair and buffeted my cheeks, and I felt an exhilaration I hadn't experienced in a long time. I could see why men preferred gasoline cars—especially fast ones.

When I arrived at the factory, Mr. Wilkinson told me he had set an appointment at two o'clock for my father and me with James Finnegan from the EAD. Prior to that, we'd be having lunch with a few of my father's counterparts in the business. My father was busy all morning, so to keep myself occupied, I wrote down some of Edsel's ideas about efficiency.

At noon I drove my father to the Pontchartrain Hotel, the de facto meeting place for automobile men in Detroit. On the way, I told him about Joe Curtiss.

"They're after Joe too?" he exclaimed. "Lord."

I parked at the curb just down from the hotel. While walking through the dining room, my father greeted a number of men I didn't know—all newer members of the automotive community. We stopped at a table where three men were already seated—Joe Hudson, of both J. L. Hudson Department Store and Hudson Motors; Ransom E. Olds, formerly of Olds Motor Works, now running the REO Motor Car Company; and Bill Durant, who, after being squeezed out of General Motors by bankers, had formed the Chevrolet Motor Company with his former racing driver, Louis Chevrolet.

You needed a program to keep track of the players in this business.

They caught up on each other's families and businesses through lunch. My father waited until we finished eating to bring up the EAD and Finnegan. Hudson and Olds had nothing but good things to say. The Employers Association had been doing a fine job for them in eliminating union threats, and they thought Finnegan a good sort and a solid man. Durant agreed with them, but added nothing to the conversation. After thanking them, my father and I walked out the front door and turned right, heading for my car.

"William?" a man called. Bill Durant cut through the pedestrian traffic in front of the hotel and hurried up to us. He was a small man with a high forehead, kind eyes, and large ears that stuck out from his head. Taking hold of my father's arm, he said, "I didn't want to say anything in there, but I heard some troubling things from the Employers Association about Will."

CHAPTER EIGHTEEN

Troubling how?" my father asked.

"One night after a meeting I had drinks with a few of the EAD men, including Finnegan. He was in his cups already, but after a few more drinks he started up on how it was Will's fault that John Cooper got into the spot he did." He shoved his hands in his pockets and met my eyes. "He seemed to believe you started the chain of events that led to Cooper bribing Judge Hume."

"That's ridiculous," my father said.

"I got the impression Finnegan had looked up to Cooper. He thought Will should be locked up for life. The other men agreed with him." Grimacing, Durant said, "Sorry. Just thought you ought to know."

My father and I shared a glance. He turned back to Durant. "Who else was with Finnegan?"

"Well." He hesitated. Looking out at the street, he said, "Paxton, Whitaker, Bielman, a few others."

My father ran his hand over the top of his head. "Everyone who matters."

Durant nodded.

Son of a bitch. "Anything else?" I said.

"No."

We thanked Mr. Durant and climbed into my car. "It makes sense to me now," I said. "I couldn't understand why he wouldn't acknowledge that the Employers Association works—or at least worked—with criminals. Now I know. He just doesn't want to help *me*."

"Why would Finnegan blame you? You had nothing to do with the bribery or the murders Cooper committed."

"Who knows what Cooper told them about me. He hated me. And I *was* responsible for him meeting Elizabeth and his entry into Judge Hume's confidence." I shook my head. "Maybe you should go by yourself." I pulled out into traffic for the short drive to the Stevens Building.

"No." My father's face was red. "We're doing this together."

He was silent the rest of the way, though I could practically see the steam coming from his ears. I parked across the street from the office. We climbed out and waited for traffic to clear. Before we crossed, he said, "Listen. If we go in angry, we're cutting our own throats. Let's give him the benefit of the doubt, see if he'll work with us. If we can't go to the police, the Employers Association is all we have."

When we reached the EAD office, the receptionist called Finnegan, who met us in the lobby. "Mr. Anderson," he said, holding out his hand to my father. They shook, and I could see my father had a real grip on the security man's hand. Finnegan didn't offer to shake with me this time.

"Can we speak somewhere private?" my father said.

"Of course."

We followed him to his office and took our respective places around his desk. Finnegan leaned forward and folded his hands on the desktop. His face was carefully neutral. "Now, what can I do for you gentlemen?"

"Mr. Finnegan," my father said, "we have a problem."

"All right." Finnegan reached out and pulled a notepad in front of him. "What sort of problem?"

"The Teamsters are making a run at the Anderson Electric Car Company by way of some Sicilian thugs."

Finnegan's eyes darted to me. "Is this that Adamo character you asked about?"

"No," I said. "It's another gang."

"And who might they be?"

I glanced at my father. He nodded. Turning back to Finnegan, I told him about the Gianollas kidnapping me. "I believe they are siphoning off union funds and helping the Teamsters expand. They've threatened my family if I don't get the union into Anderson Electric."

"Hmm," Finnegan said, leaning back. He looked from me to my father. "That's quite a story."

"But listen," I said. "You have to keep this from the police. I'm positive the Gianollas have cops on their payroll. If we don't let the Teamsters in, they say they're going to kill my parents and my—Elizabeth Hume." I'd almost said *fiancée*. "The Gianollas are using a go-between named Ethan Pinsky for the negotiations. And they've told an Anderson employee, Joe Curtiss, that they'd kill his family if we don't get this done."

"I'll try to run down some addresses," Finnegan said. "Anything else?"

"No." I looked at my father, and he shook his head.

"All right." He stood, and we followed suit. "Just so you know," he said. "AFL unions are making runs at companies all across the city, and the Wobblies are filling in the gaps. My men are spread very thin. But this will be a top priority."

My father shook hands again with Finnegan, and we left the office. On the way back to the factory, I said, "I'm not going to be coming in to work for a while. I need to deal with this Gianolla problem."

My father nodded. "What are we going to do about your mother and Elizabeth?"

"I tried to get Elizabeth to take her mother out of town, but she's not budging. Maybe Mother could visit a relative?"

He shook his head. "I'll talk to her, but you know your mother."

"Do you really think Finnegan will help us?"

My father shrugged. "I don't know. I suppose we'll find out."

I spent some time with him in his office at the factory, puzzling through our problem, and then drove back to the garage, where I left the Torpedo and caught a streetcar home. I unlocked my door, walked inside, and was heading for the bathroom when I heard a chair scrape in the kitchen. Whipping the gun out of my belt, I slunk around to the kitchen entrance. There, at the table, sat Tony Gianolla.

———

I saw red. "You son of a—"

A gun barrel pushed against my ear, and the blade of a knife pressed into my throat. "Wouldn' finish that, *paisano*," Sam Gianolla said. "Gimme the piece."

I held my gun up over my shoulder.

He took it with his knife hand. "Siddown."

He shoved me to the kitchen and pushed me into a chair across from his brother, who stared at me with those hooded eyes. "What was ya doin' this afternoon?"

"Just . . . business."

"Yeah?"

"Yes."

He looked over my shoulder and nodded. A fist crashed against the side of my head, knocking me out of the chair. I fell first against the icebox and then to the floor. My head rang like cathedral bells. Sam picked me up, stuck me back in the chair, and stood at my side, uncomfortably close.

Tony smiled. "What was ya talkin' to Finnegan 'bout?"

They knew. I clutched the side of my head and gasped out, "It was routine business."

"Why is it I don' believe you?" Tony said.

"I swear!" I blinked, trying to clear my head. "We're closing down part of the carriage plant." I was making it up as I went. "There's a lot of men to be let go, and we need to coordinate that with the EAD."

After a quick look at Sam, Tony grabbed my face with one big paw. "Listen, shit-sack." He shook my head, rattling my brain. "I know people down there. You fuck with me on this, we're gonna do to you what we did to Sam Buendo. You hear me?"

My face still buried in his hand, I nodded. His palm smelled of garlic.

"You know what we did to him?" Tony said.

He shook my head for me.

"I was like a father to that asshole. The rat tipped the cops on some olive oil that wasn' strictly legal. Sammy took a baseball bat to him for two hours. Break a bone, break another one, break another one. You know how many bones a man's got, shit-sack?"

I shook my head, still clutched in that big mitt.

"More'n two hundred. How many'd you break, Sammy?"

"Most of 'em," Sam grunted.

Tony shoved me back in my chair and let go of my face. "While he could still feel it, Sam cut off his cock. Then we dump him in a field and lit him on fire. So now do you know what we gonna do if you fuck with us?"

I nodded. My head was still ringing.

Tony stood. "I better hear good reports on you, sonny." He walked around the table, fitting his derby onto his head.

"Wait," I said.

He stopped and looked down at me.

"If you want me to cooperate with you, I want the truth out of you on one thing—who killed Carlo Moretti?"

The brothers shared a grin before Tony turned back to me. "You? You want the truth? Why don' you give him some truth, Sammy."

Sam grabbed my right hand and squeezed it. I cried out and tore at his fingers. Agonizing waves of pain crashed over me. He squeezed harder. I fell to my knees, tears streaming down my face. "Stop! Stop!"

His grip slackened just enough that I could speak. "I'll help you," I gasped. "Any way I can."

Sam bent down and looked into my eyes. "That's 'xactly what you gonna do." He gave my hand a tremendous squeeze, grinding the bones back and forth over each other. Lights burst in front of me. When he let go, I fell to the floor.

I heard their footsteps moving away from me, and then my door opened and closed. I tried to stand and made it only to my knees before I threw up.

God damn. God damn, it hurts.

I staggered into the bathroom, trying to hold my hand up as I retched again and again. When I was through, I grabbed the bottle of aspirin. After looking at it for a second, I let it drop to the floor and hurried to the bedroom. I took my remaining pistol from the nightstand, stuffed it in my belt, and wiped the tears from my eyes. My hand burned as if it were still covered with sulfuric acid, eating away at the skin, the flesh, the bone. I would never be able to see this through while dealing with so much pain. I needed something. And the something I needed wasn't aspirin.

I checked my watch. It was 4:48. Stores would be open another twelve minutes. I hurried out to Woodward with my arms crossed, my right hand tucked under my left arm. Pushing past the crowd at the trolley stop, I turned right and staggered the two blocks to Peterson's Pharmacy. The pain in my hand was so agonizing I could hardly breathe.

I pushed open the door. My hand still felt like it was on fire, but I also noticed my mouth was watering. Mr. Peterson, an older man, balding, with his stomach straining against his white tunic, stood behind the counter. "May I help you, sir?" He looked at me expectantly.

I walked up to the counter and took in a shuddering breath. "I need morphine."

"Do you have a prescription?"

"No, and I don't need one. Morphine. Please."

He looked me over. "Sir, I'm afraid that I can't just sell morphine willy-nilly to everyone who comes along."

"God damn it!" I shouted, tugging the glove off my disfigured hand. I stuck it in his face. "See? Now do you understand?"

Averting his eyes, he turned and pulled a one-ounce bottle from the shelf. "That will be a dollar-fifty, sir."

I fumbled the wallet from my pocket and pulled out two dollars. "Keep it."

"No, sir. Dollar-fifty, no more." He gave me two quarters.

I pocketed them along with the morphine. "Thank you," I said. "I appreciate your decency."

"Just so you know," he said, "in the future you will need a prescription. You shouldn't have any trouble getting one."

"Thanks." I stuck my right hand in my coat pocket and practically ran from the shop. I hadn't made it to the corner before I took the first drink. When I got home, I chipped ice from the block, wrapped it in a towel, and carried it into the parlor. I took another good dose of morphine and lay down on the sofa, the ice-filled towel draped over my hand.

The morphine from the first drink I'd taken began to roar through me, and I lay there, luxuriating in the beautiful colors the drug painted in my mind. After not taking morphine for so long, the soaring high was sharp and powerful.

Pain? It was barely there, no more than a minor distraction.

Someone was knocking. Shivering, I blinked and sat up. My trousers were wet. The city lights spilled in through my parlor windows. My mind kicked into gear, and I felt a jolt of fear in my gut. *The Gianollas?*

No, I told myself. They wouldn't knock. Whoever it was would go away. My hand throbbed with pain. *Why are my trousers—? . . . Right. The ice.* I picked up the towel and slid off the wet cushion to the floor, my back propped against the front of the sofa.

When the knocking stopped, I stretched and rolled my neck, trying to get the kinks out. The knocking started up again. I pulled my watch from my waistcoat. Almost nine. Who would be calling at this hour?

When the knocking started for the third time, I decided to see who it was. I stood and walked into the foyer, only wobbling a little. The high had faded to a place in the background, and now my head felt heavy, my mind dull.

I braced myself against the door with my left hand and looked through the peephole. Standing in the hallway staring directly at me was a big man in a black suit, derby, and a thin flowered tie pulled tightly against a winged collar. He looked deranged. I decided to sneak back to the parlor.

"Police!" he called. "I know you're in there. I'll bust it down if I have to."

Shit. I stepped to the side of the door and said, "Who is it?"

"Sergeant Rogers of the Detroit Police," he called back.

"Jesus Christ," I muttered. "Now what?" I raised my voice. "Show me your badge." I looked through the peephole again. He pulled out his badge and held it up so I could see. It looked legitimate. I unlocked the door and opened it.

He took off his derby and held it in his hands. With a piercing stare, he said, "May I come in?"

"Fine." He walked into the foyer, brushing past me as he did, first peeking into the kitchen and then sticking his head into the parlor. He was an odd-looking character, with a bullet-shaped head, a big nose and ears, and a recessed chin.

"Mr. Anderson, I'm not one for wasting time, so I'll get to the point." He spoke in clipped bursts of words. "I'm heading the new Detroit Police Gang Squad, and my object is to eliminate the gangs in this city—starting with the Sicilians. You have an association with the Gianolla brothers, and I mean to find out what it is." He stared at me.

I stared back. I had no idea who this man was. I didn't know if he was in charge of a gang squad or, Detroit policeman or not, if he was actually an associate of the Gianollas. I couldn't talk to him. So I used my standard line when it came to conversations with cops. "I don't know what you're talking about."

He smiled. It simply distracted from the annoyance that filled the rest of his face. "Mmm. That wasn't really the answer I was hoping for." He picked a spot of lint off the lapel of his jacket and looked back up at me. "They were here this afternoon. You met with them. Why?"

"You must have me mistaken with someone else." The pain in my hand was returning with a fury.

His gaze intensified. "I know who you are."

"I'm sorry, you're wrong, Sergeant . . . Rogers, is it?"

He took a step toward me. "This is the only courtesy call you will be afforded, Mr. Anderson. If you do not cease any and all contact with the Gianollas, or if you run afoul of my investigation in any way, you will be very sorry." He marched to the front door. I followed behind.

When he opened the door, he turned back to me. "And just so you know, I don't play fair."

CHAPTER NINETEEN

I slept through the night and woke the next morning with an aching hand and an itch that needed to be scratched. I glanced at the little bottle on the nightstand and looked away just as quickly. I couldn't go through this again. Last night it was medicine I needed. Now it was nothing more than a drug. A drug I wanted more than anything I could think of.

After a good dose of aspirin, a bowl of toasted cornflakes, and a pot of coffee, I phoned my father at the office. "The Gianollas have a spy in the Employers Association. They knew I was there yesterday."

"Damnation!" my father exclaimed. He was quiet for a moment. "Could it be Finnegan?"

I thought about it. "No. They knew we were there, but they seemed to buy it when I told them it was because we're closing down part of the carriage plant. If Finnegan were the rat, they'd have known otherwise."

"I think we're going to have to leave the EAD out of this too. I'm calling the Pinkertons."

"Let me try Riordan again first. From what I hear, the Pinks are as full of holes as the cops. Maybe more so."

"Do you want me to go with you? I don't know how much luck you're going to have."

"No. This is my problem. I'll take care of it."

He sighed heavily. "All right. But you have to convince him. We need help."

"Right. From someone who won't let the Gianollas know what we're doing. It's a short list, I'm afraid."

I stuffed the morphine bottle into the nightstand drawer and got dressed, then phoned the Bethune Street police station. Disguising my voice, I told the man I had information about a crime that I would share only with Detective Riordan. The man argued with me but finally got Riordan on the phone.

"Who is this?" he said.

"It's Will Anderson. Don't hang up."

I heard nothing but ghostly voices in the background. Finally he said, "What do you want?"

"I need to speak with you. I know you don't trust me. And that you think I'm a killer. But you know my parents aren't. Nor is Elizabeth Hume. If you don't help me, all three of them will probably be murdered." That was my best shot.

The silence was longer this time. "Cybulski's saloon in Hamtramck. Four o'clock." The receiver clicked onto the hook.

I loitered around my apartment until shortly after three and then hopped a streetcar, connected twice, and walked the last two blocks. It was nearly four when I pushed open the door and went inside. Cybulski's was a dive near the Dodge Main plant, the lower level of a brick two-story, sawdust on the floor to collect beer and vomit. The stink of the place indicated to me that the sawdust hadn't been changed recently. The windows were small and high on the wall, probably more to discourage wives from prying than to keep out thieves.

Every stool at the bar was occupied, but most of the tables were open. The only sounds were low conversation and glasses clinking on the bar—the murmur of a saloon dedicated to serious drinking. I ordered a Vernor's from the bartender and carried it to a table in the back. Ten minutes later, Detective Riordan walked in, glanced around the place, and strode back to me. He stood next to the table. "What do you want?"

"Would you sit, please?"

He studied me for a moment before taking off his fedora, setting it on the table, and dropping into the chair across from me.

"Thank you. Can I get you a drink?"

He shook his head.

I leaned in and spoke quietly. "The problem with the Gianollas is escalating. They have men inside the Employers Association as well as the police department. They *will* kill my parents and Elizabeth if I don't get the Teamsters in or pay them fifty thousand dollars. Both are impossible." I looked down at the table. "I know you think I'm a rich, spoiled ass. And you're right." I met his gaze again. "But this isn't about me. My parents and Elizabeth need your help. They haven't done anything wrong."

He pulled a cigar from his waistcoat, bit off the end, and spit it on the floor. Stuffing the cigar into the corner of his mouth, he said, "Why am I the lucky one?"

"Because you might be the only honest cop in Detroit. Because if I talk to anyone else, I may be killing the people I love."

He scratched a match over the top of the table and lit his cigar, puffing away with what appeared to be his complete concentration. When he finished, he pursed his lips and looked out one of the windows. Finally he glanced back at me. "Maybe you ought to fill me in. From the start."

Over the next half hour I told him almost everything. I started with the Gianollas kidnapping me and their threats, my concerns about the police and the Employers Association, and finally, my meeting with Ethan Pinsky. The only thing I left out was my backup plan—to use the Adamo gang to deal with the Gianollas. He didn't need to know.

"And that's everything?"

I nodded.

His ice blue eyes appraised me from across the table. He ground out his cigar in the ashtray, picked up his fedora, and fitted it onto his head. I held my breath, expecting him to leave. Instead he said, "What do you want me to do?"

I breathed a sigh of relief. "Ideally, I'd like the Gianollas taken off the street and Ethan Pinsky sent packing. Short of that, I could use any information you can find on any of them, including if Pinsky or his daughter were in Detroit when Moretti was murdered."

"I could look into it."

"And keep it quiet?"

He chewed on the inside of his cheek for a moment before nodding and taking a notepad from his pocket. "Give me names, descriptions. Whatever you think might help."

I did. When I finished, he put away the notepad and said, "Anything else?"

"Yes." I had been wavering on asking him about Moretti's killer, but I had to find out who it was. I would almost certainly need Vito Adamo's help to deal with the Gianollas, and finding out who killed Moretti was the only way I could accomplish that. And anyway, it *couldn't* have been Elizabeth. "Two things," I said. "First, Moretti's murder. I know you think I did it, but I—"

"No," he said. "You don't lie nearly well enough to have kept me wondering this long."

"Well . . . good." I smiled. Detective Riordan actually believed me. It would have been nice for the change to be due to something other than my inability to tell convincing falsehoods, but I'd take it. "Do you think Esposito killed him? I've heard otherwise."

"He could have. Either way, he's where he belongs."

"I trust your instincts," I said. "What do you believe?"

He shook his head. "Tell you the truth, I don't think he did it."

"Did any other names come up in the investigation?" I'd seen nothing in the file, but that didn't mean much.

"No. It was you and then it was him. As I recall it, Moretti came home when he normally did. Some time later, the neighbor saw you outside his door."

"Did anyone say that Moretti brought someone home with him that night?"

"No. Not that I recall."

"Okay." I shook my head. No help.

"You mentioned there were two things?" he said.

"Oh. Right. What can you tell me about Sergeant Rogers and the Detroit Gang Squad?"

"What do you want to know?"

"He says he's going after the Gianollas. Is he straight up? Can I trust him?"

"Let me put it this way: I don't think he's taking money from mobsters. But he'd sell his own mother for a promotion. So do I trust him?" Riordan pushed back his chair and stood. "Not even a little bit."

Around seven I went out to get some dinner at the café around the corner. It was on the first floor of a three-story redbrick building, a small place with a dozen tables, a hardwood floor, and a large window overlooking Woodward Avenue. I ate there often, not because the food was good, but because they cut the meat for me without me asking. I was polishing off the remains of a steak when Abe and Joey Bernstein pulled out the chairs across from me and sat. They hadn't dressed for this part of town—both wore dark wool trousers held up by black suspenders, dirty white shirts, and leather boots.

Abe took a deep drag off the half-smoked cigarette in his hand. Joey pulled the bone-handled straight razor from his pocket and began cleaning his fingernails. He shifted the toothpick in his mouth from one side to the other and looked up at me under half-closed lids.

I got ready to run, even though I thought he was just trying to intimidate me. This was too public a place to attack me and expect to get away with it. But then again, I'd gotten the impression the Bernstein brothers were a bit on the impulsive side. Keeping my eyes on them, I chewed the piece of meat in my mouth and swallowed. Abe just looked at me with those bright blue eyes while I did. "Abe. Joey." I nodded. "You hungry?"

Abe stared at me. "You'd break bread with us?"

"Why not?"

"We got somethin' to talk about, you and me."

"Yeah, we do," I said. "Why'd you hit Izzy?"

He cocked his head. "'Cause you weren't there to hit."

"It wasn't his fault."

"Ain't none of your business. I want my money."

I tapped my jacket over the breast pocket. "I've got it. And I'm buying dinner."

He picked up the napkin in front of him and tucked it into his shirt. "Then let's eat." He nodded at Joey, who slapped the razor closed and slid it into his pocket. When the waitress came over, Abe said, "We'll have what he's havin'." As soon as she left, he leaned toward me. "That wasn't too smart, not payin' us what you owed."

I shrugged. "Like I told Izzy, I wasn't welshing. I tried to pay him the next time I saw him, but he said you'd collect."

"Yeah," he said. He took a puff on the cigarette, sat back in his chair, and leveled his gaze at me. "I don't like playin' bill collector."

I shrugged again. The waitress came back and filled coffee cups for the brothers before warming up mine. When she left, I said, "How'd you know I was here?"

Joey snorted. "You think you can hide from us?"

Abe glared at him. "Shut up, Joey. I told ya." He stubbed out his cigarette, turned back to me, and smiled. "Got friends in low places."

"Yeah? Who?"

"My brothers. My friends. We got a little . . . business group. People don't pay much attention to kids."

"Is that right?" It occurred to me that I could use some unnoticed eyes and ears. "You ever hire yourselves out?"

He didn't bat an eye. "Sure. If the price is right."

I slipped my cigarette case from my pocket and held it out. The brothers each took one. Joey spit his toothpick on the floor. While lighting their cigarettes, I said, "What do you consider the right price?"

Abe took a puff off the cigarette. Eyeing my lighter, he said, "That'd be a good start."

"No, my father gave it to me for my college graduation. But I'll get you one just like it, if that's what it takes."

"I don't know." He shook his head. "There's a lot of guys in the gang— business group." He glanced at Joey before shaking his head sheepishly. He'd inadvertently told the truth, probably not a normal occurrence for him.

"I don't think I'd need all of you."

"All or none," Abe said. "We stick together."

"All right, I'll tell you what. I'll pay you ten bucks a day. You split it up how you'd like."

He guffawed. "We don't cross the street for ten bucks."

I leaned over the table. "Listen, Abe. My father's got money, I don't. The only reason I could pay you the last time is because I inherited some money. It's almost gone. Ten bucks a day or I'll find someone else."

He crossed his arms. A wisp of smoke curled up past his face. "I'll think about it."

"Think fast. I want to hire you to ask around about something."

"What's that?"

"Ten bucks a day?"

He shrugged. "I guess."

"I want to know who really killed Carlo Moretti."

"Who?"

I leaned in toward him again. "I was accused of killing him. Another man confessed, but I'm sure he didn't do it."

He gave me another shrug. "Sure. Why not? Thirty up front."

"Okay. How can I get hold of you?"

"See Izzy. He's gonna be on the corner every mornin' now."

"What happened to the Irish kid?"

"Irish kid?"

"Yeah. He and Izzy got into a fight over the corner."

"Oh, him. Joey convinced him the newspaper business was bad for his health."

Joey's lip curled up on one side in a cruel smile, but he didn't add anything to Abe's explanation.

"Huh." Thinking about the corner put me in mind of another question. I looked at Joey. "Who is it you pay off for the craps game?"

Joey glanced at his brother. A cloud passed over Abe's face. "Why do you want to know?"

"Well, I'm curious if he's one of Adamo's men. Since you've worked together on other things—"

"Ain't your business."

"If it's one of Adamo's men, it is my business."

"We ain't working together on dice, so it ain't your business." Abe's voice was heated. "Tell ya what. You don't ask about my other business, I won't ask about yours."

"Just tell me if it's Adamo."

He sat back and took a deep drag on his cigarette, giving me a smoldering glare over the back of his hand. Finally he said, "It ain't Adamo."

"Fine. Then you're right. It's not my business. Did you hear he turned himself in?"

"Yeah. People sayin' some other wop's after him."

I nodded. "I'd guess that's true. So what does that do to your business with him?"

"Nothin'. Ain't had no business with him for a while now."

I thought of something else that had puzzled me. "Joey called Adamo 'the White Hand.' What does that mean?"

"Well, you got the White Hand Society, which supposably's the honest businessmen fightin' the Black Hand." Abe laughed. "But Adamo's angle is the Black Hand comes around and tells the guy he's gotta pay or else. The guy pays. Then the White Hand comes around and tells him they'll protect him from the Black Hand. He pays them."

"Yeah?"

"Don't you get it? Both of 'em are Adamo's guys." He roared with laughter. I kept myself from looking around to see how badly he was upsetting everyone's dinner. We talked about Adamo for a minute or two and quieted when the waitress brought two more plates. The brothers tucked right into their dinners.

To make conversation, I said, "You're a bright guy, Abe. Why aren't you in school?"

He spoke around the food in his mouth. "School? Ain't been in what, three years? I'm seventeen, for Christ's sake. Gotta help out my ma and pa. 'Sides, when I'm not doin' somethin' more profitable, I schlep stuff around the Ford factory."

"Really?" I laughed. "You work for Ford?"

His fork and knife clanked onto his plate. He leaned in toward me, eyes narrowed, scowl fixed on his face. "What's so funny about that?" His mood had turned stormy in a second.

"Nothing. It's just . . . you don't seem like an autoworker."

After a long moment, his face finally relaxed. "Nah, I'm not. Boostin' parts more'n workin' anyway. Just waitin' for some stuff to come together." He went back to eating.

Inwardly, I breathed a sigh of relief. I had thought he was coming over the table at me. While he and Joey ate, I lit another cigarette and smoked.

Joey finished first. When Abe was done, he pushed away his plate and said, "Now how 'bout the dough?"

I pulled thirty dollars from my wallet and handed him the bills, along with the envelope containing the fifteen dollars I owed him.

He counted the money, tucked it into his pocket, and gestured toward my right hand. "What's the story with the glove?"

"I had an accident. My hand doesn't look too pretty."

"Doesn't seem to work too well, either."

"No, it doesn't."

Joey stood. The yellow handle of the razor stuck up from his pocket. Abe pushed back his chair, but before he got to his feet, he said, "Don't forget what I said about the dagos. If Adamo finds out we ratted him, I'm gonna kill ya."

CHAPTER TWENTY

The doorbell rang. I tiptoed into the foyer, hoping it was Detective Riordan. I looked through the peephole and wasn't disappointed to see Elizabeth. Opening the door, I said, "What a pleasant surprise," and stepped aside. She walked into the foyer and set her purse on the table. She wore a robin's-egg-blue coat and a matching wide-brimmed hat with a plume of egret feathers, and looked wonderful, as always.

Right hand behind my back, I held out my left for her hat and coat. When she gave me the coat, I saw she was wearing a burgundy shirtwaist and tan knee breeches.

I looked her over. "Are you going riding?"

"At night?"

"Well, I'm glad it's night. That outfit would cause car accidents in the daytime."

She smiled. "Why can't women be comfortable too? All this spending hours getting primped and perfumed—just to be seen by men? It's silly." She pulled out her hatpin, lifted her chapeau from her head, and removed a strategically placed comb. Her hair fell in an auburn cascade around her head. She looked fetching, dangerous.

"Would you like something to drink?" I said.

"Do you have soda pop?"

"Ginger ale. Why don't you sit in the parlor, and I'll get it."

She headed in. A second later, she exclaimed, "What happened to your wall?"

"What? Oh." I followed her in. The wall was pocked with dozens of holes, most of them inside of or surrounding the paltry remains of the dartboard. Some of the holes were only chinks, while others were inches across. I hadn't really thought about it for a while. I shrugged. "Knife-throwing."

"At your wall?"

"Have to practice somewhere."

She eyed me for a moment. "You know, I have to say you're looking fit. It can't be this." She waved toward the wall.

"No, I've been exercising too."

"Really? Will Anderson exercising? Stop the presses."

"Well, I can't trade on my rugged good looks my whole life, now, can I? At some point, I may actually have to do something."

She raised her eyebrows at the "rugged good looks" remark but also gave me the hint of a smile.

"I'll be right back." I headed to the kitchen and chipped off some ice, then poured us each a glass of Vernor's and set them on a tray. When I walked into the parlor, Elizabeth was standing with her arms folded across her chest, looking out the back window toward downtown. The electric lights of the city lit the horizon to a soft white glow, and the spotlights at the top of the downtown skyscrapers emphasized their grandeur. I stood next to her and took in the view.

The lights represented the Detroit I had loved. I was born into the modern age, growing up alongside electricity. When I was a child, electric lights were barely more than a novelty. Electric service was just beginning to spread outside of downtown. The only electric streetlamps were the 125-foot-tall monstrosities Mr. Edison had sold the city. Otherwise, all the outside lights, and the vast majority of inside ones, were lit by gas. There were no electrical contraptions—toasters, mixers, and the like.

Detroit was prosperous and desperately competing to be one of the titans of the United States, next to New York, Philadelphia, Boston, and Chicago. But the last few years had taught me that this prosperity was nothing more than gilding, a thin layer of gold over rusting pig iron, hiding what the city really was. What all cities were.

I nudged Elizabeth's arm, and she took one of the glasses. "Thank you." After taking a sip, she turned toward me. "Are you all right?"

"I'm fine." I set the tray on the coffee table and took the other glass. "Why?"

She pointed at the wall. "This might indicate a psychological problem."

"No." I took a sip. "I'm just practicing. It's safe. There's no one here but me."

She turned me toward her. "Look at your wall. What would your landlord think? What would anyone think?"

I chuckled at that. "And why exactly would I care? Is this why you came here? To discuss my mental health?"

She took a deep breath. I could see she was trying to control her temper. "No. I'm here because you haven't called."

"About?"

"We're partners, remember?"

"Elizabeth, we talked two days ago. I don't have any information yet."

"Bullshit."

I cocked my head at her. "That's quite a vocabulary you developed in France."

"How else am I going to get your attention? Anyway, it's only a word. Words hold no power of their own, and, contrary to what you might think, curse words are not the exclusive property of men. Now, tell me what you've been up to."

I sighed. She wasn't going to give up. "To be truthful, it isn't much so far. I have to set up a meeting between my father and a man named Ethan Pinsky, who's negotiating for the Teamsters and the Gianollas."

"And what am I going to be doing to help?"

"Elizabeth." Our eyes locked. I'd seen this look before. She wasn't going to let this be.

"And no secrets, either," she said. "I'm in all the way, or I'll do this on my own."

I took a deep breath and exhaled slowly. I was going to have to string her along and hope she didn't see it. "Okay. Partners?"

She held out her right hand. "Partners."

I shook it with my left. "All right then."

"Tell me everything," Elizabeth said.

It seemed I was at a crossroads. My choices were to let her go out on her own looking for revenge or to work with her. Working with her, I at least had a chance to protect her, so I nodded toward the sofa, and we sat. And, once again, I laid out the story of my trials with the Gianollas and Ethan Pinsky.

When I finished, she was studying me intently. "You didn't kill Carlo Moretti?"

"No. I was there, but I didn't kill him."

She stared off into the distance. "I can't imagine what it would feel like to kill someone."

The image of the auburn-haired woman with Moretti crossed my mind, but I banished the thought and said, "I hope you never have to find out."

She pursed her lips.

"What?" I said.

"I think I could kill Vito Adamo—and Big Boy." She shook her head. "I feel ridiculous calling him that. You never found out what his real name is, did you?"

"No, but it's probably something like Myron Featherbottom."

She laughed and took a sip of ginger ale. "Could I have a cigarette, please?"

"Of course." I pulled the case from my pocket and held it out to her. It was time to broach a subject I didn't think she'd be happy about. "If Detective Riordan can't help me get rid of the Gianollas, I'm going to try to get the Adamo gang to help."

She looked up at me in shock, her hand still hovering over the case. "What? Why?"

"We can't get help from the EAD or the police. The Gianollas represent much more of a threat to us than do the Adamos. If I set up the Gianollas *for* the Adamos, instead of vice versa, they can take care of our problem."

She took a cigarette, and I lit it for her. "The Gianollas may be the bigger problem, but they didn't help kill my father and Wesley. Vito Adamo did." She took a deep drag on the cigarette.

"I know that, and I'm sorry. But if you want to work with me on this, you have to agree to put your feelings about Adamo aside."

"Why do you think they would work with *us*, anyway?"

I hesitated. "I don't know if they would. I already talked with him—Vito."

Elizabeth gave me a dark look. I held my hands up in front of me. "I know. I don't like it any more than you do. Anyway, he said I had to prove to him that I didn't kill Moretti. I've investigated. I even talked to Detective Riordan. I don't see how I'll be able to prove anything to Adamo, but I think he'd work with us if it was in their best interest. The Gianollas obviously have more power than the Adamos. If Vito wasn't afraid of them, would he have turned himself in? He needs help, and he's smart enough to know it."

Elizabeth shook her head. "You're forgetting one thing. He's in *jail.* He can't do anything. Is Salvatore capable of something like this?"

"I don't know. He's no Vito, that's for certain." I lit a cigarette for myself. "Listen, if you have a better idea, I'm all ears. I can't think of any other way to get rid of the Gianollas."

She bit her lip. "Work with the Adamos?" She was quiet for a few moments before looking into my eyes. "I'll do what I have to. We need to end this."

I nodded. "Why don't we drive out to Ford City tomorrow, see if we can figure out where they're holing up."

"Ford City?"

"The Gianollas gave me an address where we might find the Adamo gang."

"All right. Do you want me to drive?"

"No." I grinned. "I'll drive."

"You bought a car?"

"A special car."

She looked at me with raised eyebrows, but I waved her off. "It's better that you experience it first. If we find Salvatore, we can propose a truce. I'll pick you up. Say, nine o'clock?"

She handed me her glass. "Then I'll see you in the morning."

I followed her to the front door and helped her into her coat, as best as I could with one hand. She piled her hair up on her head and fixed it in place with the comb before putting on her hat and running it through with the hatpin.

"Would you like me to see you home?" I said. "It's no trouble."

"That won't be necessary." She opened her bag and pulled out a Browning pistol.

I looked at her in surprise.

She popped out the magazine, checked the load, and tucked the gun back into her purse. Glancing up at me, she allowed herself a little smile. "It was my father's. I've helped myself to his gun cabinet. And I've got the Baker. I'll be safe."

Elizabeth's father bought a Baker Electric shortly after she broke off our engagement—much more, I'm sure, to bother me than because he thought it was the right automobile for his family. (Not that there was anything wrong with a Baker. It just wasn't a Detroit.)

I opened the door for her. "Drive carefully."

"I will. Good night." She stepped out into the hallway but stopped and turned back to me. "Thank you for trusting me. I'll be of great help to you. You'll see."

She headed off down the hall. Rubbing my hand, I watched her go. I'd be seeing a lot more of Elizabeth, but she'd be right in the line of fire.

At 9:05 I pulled the Torpedo to the curb just down the block from Elizabeth's house. She was waiting in the swing on the porch. My heart ached. The swing was our spot, one of the few places we could get out from under the spying eyes of her father when we were courting. She saw me coming up the sidewalk and skipped down the stairway, turned out perfectly in an emerald day dress with a matching purse and long coat, and a straw boater on her head cocked at a jaunty angle. "My, aren't you the swell?" she said. "You look like an advertising model in *Horseless Age*."

"Thank you. Wait, is that a compliment?"

Her eyebrows rose. "Yes."

Today was the first time in a very long while I'd actually put some thought into my clothing. I'd gone with a tan tweed Norfolk jacket with matching knickerbockers, knee-length stockings, and a pair of sturdy brown shoes with leather gaiters—the perfect outfit for a rugged outdoorsman. These days, no ensemble of mine was complete without a gun, so of course I had a pistol tucked into my belt at the small of my back.

"You look very nice this morning as well," I said.

She gave me a curtsy and smiled. "Thank you, sir."

My. She was in a good mood.

She gestured toward the Torpedo. "Is that a Model T?"

"Yes," I said. "It was Edsel's. He modified it with some of the men at Ford."

"Modified?"

I grinned. "I'll show you." I escorted her to the car and helped her up into the passenger seat, then set the spark and throttle and walked around front to start it. I got it going on the second crank and climbed into the car, squeezing past Elizabeth into the driving seat. I gave it some throttle, and the engine went from a purr to a roar.

Her eyes widened. "This is no ordinary flivver."

Handing her a set of driving goggles, I smiled and said, "Here. You'll need these." I drew the throttle back down and got ready to pull out. "Oh. Did you bring a gun?"

She raised her purse. "You?"

I nodded and started out down Jefferson, heading west toward downtown. It was a perfect morning. A few clouds drifted across the sky, the temperature was already in the mid-sixties, and explosions of green filled the trees and garden beds. Elizabeth was affecting me more than I knew.

I sneaked a glance at her. The wind riffled through her hair. Her classic Helen of Troy profile was marred only by her forehead, which was creased in concentration.

"What are you thinking about?" I asked.

"What? Nothing." She forced out a laugh. "Just thinking."

When I stopped for traffic at McDougall, I said, "Oh, some interesting news this morning." I dug out the front section of the newspaper from under the seat and handed it to her, folded over to an article. The headline read, ADAMO MURDER TRIAL TO BEGIN MONDAY.

I'd been surprised it would start so soon. Both the State and the defense had called for a speedy trial. Ferdinand Palma again assured the public of Vito Adamo's innocence, while District Attorney Higgins vowed to put him behind bars. The entire article filled a mere quarter column. Adamo had done a good job of staying out of the limelight. He had no more significance to the newspapers or the general public than any other man accused of a crime.

I nudged my way through traffic at the corner and continued down the street with a glance at the speedometer Edsel had installed. With the Detroit Electric I normally drove, changing from first to second moved the car from five to eight miles per hour. Gasoline automobiles weren't so predictable.

After perusing the article, Elizabeth looked up at me and said, "Might be an interesting way to spend some time."

"Going to the trial?"

She nodded. "I'd like to see him squirm. And I especially want to be there for the sentencing."

"I'm sure we can find time to stop by."

We passed through the city to the shacks and coal yards at the outskirts and then burst into the surrounding countryside. The cobbles ended abruptly, and we splashed down into a puddle on the pitted dirt road running parallel to the Detroit River. I was watching a barge pass, three huge pyramids of dusty black coal on its flat deck, when Elizabeth said, "Open it up."

"What?"

She leaned over to look at the speedometer. "This automobile will go faster than twelve miles per hour, won't it?"

"Certainly."

"Then open it up. Let's see what this thing can do."

I looked ahead. The road was clear. "Goggles?" I pulled mine down over my eyes, and Elizabeth did likewise. "Okay, hold on!" I jerked the throttle lever down, and the car leaped forward. We raced down the road, laughing and shouting like children, the wind buffeting our faces and blowing back our hair, as we jounced through puddles and potholes. I saw puffs of smoke on the horizon, and before I knew it, we had caught up to an interurban train, five cars behind the locomotive on the tracks alongside the road, chugging toward Wyandotte.

"Faster!" Elizabeth shouted.

I glanced at the speedometer. We were already going thirty. "Are you sure?"

"Come on, Grandpa!" she said as we were both thrown forward by a pothole. "Punch it!"

I pulled the throttle lever nearly to full speed. We blew past the train and flew down the road—literally at times. Elizabeth gripped her door and the top of the dashboard in front of her, grinning with delight, her hair spilling out from under her hat. "Faster!"

I risked a glance at the speedometer again—forty-five miles per hour. I'd never driven this fast. Few people had. A hill was coming up ahead. I nudged the throttle agan, hoping to catch some air at the top. We both whooped as we roared up the hill. At the peak, the tires left the ground. We sailed for ten feet before rattling back to earth.

The rear of the car slid left. I was losing control. I jerked the wheel left, and we fishtailed back and forth, barreling into the field before I was able to get control. We slid to a stop in a cloud of dust. My hand burned as if on fire. I'd grabbed the wheel with both hands. I grimaced but kept the cry from escaping my lips. When I thought I could control my voice, I took a deep breath and looked at Elizabeth. "I'll take it a little slower now, if you don't mind."

She smiled. "That seems to be a reasonable idea."

I pulled the throttle lever down and kept our speed at fifteen miles per hour, which now felt like a crawl.

Elizabeth sat back and pulled out her hatpin, then swept her hair out of her face and back up under her hat. Replacing the pin, she nodded. "Wow, that was fun. Our Baker won't do that."

We passed the Michigan Alkali Company's huge factory and pulled into the little village of Ford City. The address Tony Gianolla had given me was on Antoine. It was a small commercial area with shops and of-fices, and many of the signs on the buildings were in Italian. We both peered into the building in question as we passed at five miles per hour. It was a small grocery.

Elizabeth turned to me with a question on her face. "Are you sure about the address? I've never taken the Adamos for grocers."

I shrugged, then circled around and pulled to the curb across the street from the store. "Let's take a look. Is your gun loaded?"

She nodded. "Yours?"

"Yep. And listen. Be ready for trouble. If we come across Salvatore, I don't think he's going to be happy to see us." We hopped out and crossed the street to the market. It was well stocked and clean. The back wall was lined with beer kegs. The two men working in the store looked Italian, but I didn't recognize them. We took a lap through the aisles and stopped at the counter. "Excuse me," I said to the back of one of the men. He turned and looked at me expectantly.

"I need to get a message to Salvatore Adamo."

He looked wary but shrugged and said something to me in Italian, finishing with the word *"Inglese."*

I pulled out my wallet and laid a five-dollar bill on the counter. "I'm Will Anderson. I need to talk to him."

He pushed the bill back toward me and shrugged again, his hands spread in front of him. I left the bill. I thought he had shown recognition of the Adamo name, but there was no way to know for sure. I hoped he spoke the universal language of money. When I turned around, I saw Elizabeth trying to talk to the other man, who didn't seem to speak English either.

I caught her eye and nodded toward the front of the store. We walked out to the boardwalk. "What do you think?" I said.

Elizabeth was staring across the street. I followed her eyes. The sign on the building directly opposite us read, DROGHERIA GIANOLLA.

CHAPTER TWENTY-ONE

It was another small market—similar size, red brick, the first floor of a two-story building. "Let's go see if I recognize anyone," I said.

We crossed the street and walked inside. Three older men in dark suits sat at a small table by the front window, sipping espresso from tiny cups. A tall shelf filled with liquor bottles stood behind them, the bottles glittering in the sun. I pulled my eyes away, walked past, and looked around the store. The only thing I thought unusual was the large quantity of liquor in front and the stacks of beer kegs towering against the rear wall.

A young man in a crisp white apron stood behind the counter. I sauntered up to him. "Do you speak English?"

"*Sì,*" he said, holding his thumb and forefinger half an inch apart.

"Who owns this store?"

"*Non so.*"

"I don't understand," I said.

"He said he doesn't know," Elizabeth said. "Do you know who owns the market across the street?"

His eyes became wary. "No."

"Have you ever heard of Salvatore Adamo?"

"No. *Scusa,*" he said, turning away. He began rearranging tins of coffee on the shelf.

We looked around for a while, but I didn't see either of the Gianolla brothers. With nothing better to do, we sat in the Torpedo watching the stores. "I don't know," Elizabeth said. She shifted and put her arm up on the back of the seat. "Do you really believe Vito Adamo and Tony Gianolla are grocers?"

I shrugged.

"I wonder, though. If they are, did their dispute start over a thumb on the meat scale or a price war on lettuce? It's just so bizarre that they would have these stores across the street from each other."

"In Ford City, yet. The two most feared names in the Detroit underworld belong to a pair of grocers. From Ford City. Unbelievable."

"So what have we gained?"

"Not very much. I'll tell Detective Riordan about this, though. Maybe he can sniff them out." I put my hand on hers. "What do you say we get some lunch and then take a drive around the area? Maybe I can spot the house the kidnappers took me to."

Elizabeth agreed, and we had lunch in a small Italian restaurant. When we finished, we drove around the village, looking for a needle in a haystack—the white clapboard house with a fruit tree between the house and the stable. I saw nothing familiar. After an hour, we decided to go back to Detroit.

Fifteen minutes outside of Ford City, the Torpedo's engine began sputtering. Elizabeth looked at me, alarmed. "What is it?"

"I don't . . ." The engine sputtered one last time and quit. We drifted around a corner, and I pulled the car under an oak tree on the side of the road. *Son of a bitch.* "I forgot to check the gasoline."

She laughed and clapped her hands. "Will Anderson, renowned endurance driver and former world-record holder, runs out of gasoline on a trip to the country. Wait until the press hears about this."

"Ha ha. Very funny. Although I *am* flattered you think the press would be interested in something other than my criminal activities." I motioned for her to exit the car so I could do the same. "If you please." Elizabeth, still snickering, climbed down from the car. With both eyes fixed on the pleasant sight of her behind, I followed her out. Fortunately, Edsel had left a small gasoline can in the trunk. Unfortunately, it was empty. I grabbed it and said, "Would you care to join me in a lovely stroll through the countryside, or would you prefer to wait under the tree?"

She looked up toward the sky and cupped her chin in her hand, enjoying dragging this out. "Well, it is a lovely day. Perhaps I will join you."

We had no sooner started back up the road toward Ford City when the sound of a motorcar bubbled up in the distance. When we reached the straightaway, I saw an automobile racing toward us. "Well, maybe it's our lucky day," I said. "Surely they'll help a fellow motorist."

We stood at the side of the road and watched the car approach. As it got closer, I could see it was a blue Hudson touring car, with two men in front. When they were perhaps fifty yards away, the passenger gave a start and twisted away from us, showing us his back. The driver, a big brute in a black pin-striped suit and straw boater, stood on the brakes, and the Hudson threw up a cloud of dust as it slid to a stop. He threw it into reverse, and the car jerked backwards, partway into the field next to the road, and then roared off again in the opposite direction.

I held up the gasoline can and shouted, "Hey! We need help!"

"What was that about?" Elizabeth asked as we watched the car disappear from sight.

I shook my head. "I don't know, but the man in the passenger seat didn't want us to see who he was."

"Did you recognize the other man?"

"No."

"Do you think they might have been following us?" she asked.

"Could be."

"Who do you think it was?"

I grunted out a laugh. There were so many possibilities.

We were lucky enough to find a farmer only a few minutes down the road who siphoned enough gasoline out of his tractor to get us back to Ford City. There, we were directed to a lumberyard, where a man filled our tank from a fifty-five-gallon barrel they had set up in front—but at twenty-four cents a gallon it was no bargain.

We set out for Detroit, and this time I kept the speed down. I drove Elizabeth home and left her with a promise that I'd call her before doing anything else. Then I drove over to Hastings Street and parked six blocks from the Bucket—as close as I thought I could get and have my car still there when I came back. One way or another I had to speak with Salvatore.

It was a surprisingly uneventful visit. The saloon was nearly empty, Big Boy was absent, and the bartender was certain he'd never heard of Salvatore Adamo—or anyone at all named Adamo—even after I tried to jog his memory with a five-dollar bill. I could have brought Elizabeth after all.

I passed the evening hurling various knives in the parlor. I had accumulated a jackknife with a four-inch blade, a six-inch switchblade, and a pair of daggers, both with eight-inch blades, one thin and lightweight, the other heavy with a thick handle. For fun, I also grabbed the butcher knife from the kitchen. The more I practiced, the better I got, though it took dozens of throws to adjust from one to the other. The butcher knife was the easiest to stick in the wall, followed by the daggers, which I attributed to their balance. The jackknife was challenging, but the switchblade was the hardest by far. The haft and spring mechanism were virtually all the weight of the knife, which caused an uneven spin and gave me no margin for error.

I found that throwing straight overhand worked best, but the amount of wrist action and the distance from the board varied greatly from knife to knife. It was actually relaxing. I'd found that concentrating on the problems of knife-throwing blocked out my other thoughts. Each knife needed to be thrown from a different distance in order for the blade to stick in the wall, their length and my wrist action determining the rate of spin. My switchblade stuck most often from about fifteen feet away, while throwing my butcher knife required me to be in the hallway. By the time my neighbors started pounding on the walls, I thought I was getting pretty good. Perhaps if I had to go on the run I could find a job with the circus.

At eight o'clock the next morning, I was reading the paper in the parlor when Wilkinson phoned me to come down to see my father. When

I got to the outer office, Wilkinson was sitting at his desk with a grimace on his face. I caught his eye and arched my eyebrows, but he just shook his head and told me to go right in.

Detective Riordan was sitting in front of my father's desk in what looked like Wilkinson's chair. One of the uncomfortable chairs was missing. Unfortunately, that left one for me.

My father cleared his throat. "Detective Riordan thought he ought to speak with me directly."

Riordan half turned in his seat. An unlit cigar was clenched in his teeth. "I wanted to see if your father's understanding of the situation squared with what you told me."

"And it does," my father said.

Riordan nodded at me. "Pinsky's a lawyer, Jewish by way of Russia, no criminal record. He's worked with both the IWW and AFL. He's based in New York, but the New York police wouldn't say a word about him, which means he's connected. I couldn't find a record of a Detroit address for him."

I took my wallet from my coat, pulled out the piece of paper Waldman had given me, and handed it to Detective Riordan. "Here's his address and telephone number."

"Good." He copied them into his notebook.

"Any idea where Pinsky was when Moretti was killed?" I said.

"He appears to have been in New York last August. Now, the Gianollas." He chewed on the cigar. "I didn't find anything. Not in Detroit or Ford City. No records, nothing. As far as the U.S. government's concerned, these guys don't exist." He shifted in his chair so that he was facing me. "Your father's never seen them, and he's only heard about them from you. I have to ask. Do they really exist? Because if you're sending me on a wild-goose chase—"

"Yes, they exist. And thanks for reminding me." I dug another scrap of paper out of my coat pocket and handed it to him. "These are addresses of groceries in Ford City that I believe to be owned by the Adamos and the Gianollas. And feel free to ask your Sergeant Rogers if I made them up. I told you he was investigating them."

"I couldn't confirm that."

"Really?" I said. "Why would he lie to me?"

Riordan hesitated. "Well . . . he may be investigating them. Like I said, I couldn't confirm it." He sat back and glanced at each of us. "Gentlemen, I am on the outside these days."

"I'm sorry to hear that, Detective," my father said.

"It's not your fault," Riordan replied to my father. "And, as much as I'd like to blame him, it's not your son's either. I did it to myself. But that is neither here nor there." He picked up his fedora from my father's desk and twirled it on a finger. "You're in a fix." He shook his head. "You'll have to meet with Pinsky, and he has to think you're serious. I need you to buy us some time while I figure this out."

My head drew back in surprise. *"Us?"*

Detective Riordan turned back to me, his face a blank page. "I suppose I owe you something. And the Lord knows someone needs to show you how to get *out* of trouble."

Detective Riordan joking? I didn't say anything, afraid to burst the bubble.

He took the cigar from his mouth, contemplated it for a moment, and said, "Three things, nonnegotiable. Number one—we do everything legally. Are we clear on that?"

My father and I agreed, though I wasn't sure I'd be able to live up to the commitment.

"Number two—my bosses wouldn't look kindly on me running an investigation without approval. I'm already on thin ice. No one else can know I'm helping you."

We agreed.

"And three—I have a job and a family. I'm not going to be able to devote a lot of time to this."

"We're grateful for any assistance you can lend us, Detective," my father said.

"What should I do about Joe Curtiss?" I said. "I told him to get his wife and children out of town until this is over. He's scared to death."

"I wouldn't recommend that," Riordan said. "If the Gianollas are who you say they are, when they find out they'll know he's turned."

"Couldn't his family just be on vacation or something?"

Riordan shrugged. "Maybe. Maybe not."

"I think he's going to do it," I said.

He spread his hands in front of him. "Everything's a risk, gentlemen. If they stay, they may get killed. If they leave, Joe might. You might."

"I know that's a risk he'd take," I said. "And I would too."

"How much time did Pinsky give you to arrange a meeting with your father?" Riordan said.

"A week."

"From when?"

"Last Friday."

"Before we do this," Riordan said, "I want to be sure you don't want to pay him off."

My father shook his head. "I've got everything in the business. I can't come up with fifty thousand dollars."

"And there's no guarantee that the Gianollas won't just keep coming back to the well," Riordan said. "In fact, I'd be shocked if they didn't. Easy money." He looked at me. "What do you say we surprise Pinsky and call a day early?"

I looked at my father and then back at Riordan. "And tell him what?"

"That your father refuses to meet with any representative of a union."

"What?" my father and I both exclaimed.

"If you give in too easily, he'll know something's up. When he pushes you, ask him to give you more time. But not until he pushes you."

I made the call. Waldman answered the phone and asked if I could wait a moment.

"Mr. Anderson?" Pinsky's wheezy voice struggled through the telephone line.

"Yes, Mr. Pinsky. I wanted you to know that I've spoken to my father, and . . . well, he said he won't meet with you."

"That is most disappointing," Pinsky said. "You do know the consequences of his inaction?"

"Yes, but . . . I don't know how I could convince him."

"I have a few ideas," Pinsky said. "But they all involve someone"—he gasped in a breath—"being badly hurt."

"Give me some time. I'll figure it out."

"I hope so, for the sake of your loved ones." He paused. "If I have not met with your father"—he took a breath—"within the next five days, I will pass on the news"—he took another breath—"that you are uncooperative."

"I'll work on him, Mr. Pinsky."

"Very well, Mr. Anderson. I'll wait to hear from you. I would suggest he bring the money with him." He hung up.

I replaced the receiver on the candlestick and recounted the conversation to my father and Detective Riordan.

"Good," he said. "We've got until the twenty-fourth. Now, we can't be seen talking to each other. We need a go-between. Any ideas?"

"I'm sure Edsel Ford would help," I said. "How much risk do you suppose there is?"

"That's hard to say. Do you see him socially?"

"He and I talk all the time. And I just bought a car from him."

Riordan glanced at my father. "Is that okay with you?"

Though he looked worried, my father nodded.

Riordan pulled a notepad from his inside coat pocket, wrote something, and handed the paper to my father. "Here's my telephone number. If you have an emergency, you can catch me there most nights after eight. Tell Edsel that too."

When Riordan left, I called Edsel and filled him in on the situation. After I gave him the telephone number, I copied it and tucked the sheet of paper into my wallet. It seemed a reasonable bet that, sometime, I'd need to get hold of Detective Riordan in the middle of the night.

CHAPTER TWENTY-TWO

Edsel phoned me at home that night. "Just wanted to let you know that I talked to our mutual friend. And of course I'll help you with your car in any way I can."

Now we're speaking in code. As they say, being paranoid doesn't mean everyone really *isn't* out to get you. "Great. Thanks, Edsel." I picked up the candlestick and sat back in my chair. "I just want to be sure you don't get hurt."

"I'll be fine. It'll make my life interesting. Who wouldn't want that?"

"Me, for one," I said. "I've had enough of it. Did our friend give you any details?"

"He essentially repeated what you already told me, though I didn't let him know that. And I'd like to extend you an invitation. F. W. Taylor is going to be speaking about scientific management at Detroit College next Monday night. Would you like to go with me?"

"Certainly." I was sure there was more than Taylorism to be discussed that night. "I'll look forward to it."

"Will?" His voice took on a plaintive note.

"Yes, Edsel?"

"Be careful. . . . That car's got a lot of power."

"I will. And you be careful in that Speedster. Good night, Edsel."

"Good night, Will."

I hung up the receiver and set the candlestick back on the desk. Edsel was nineteen now, a man, and he was smart. He'd be okay.

On Friday I checked with Izzy to see if they had found out anything about Moretti's killer. He said they hadn't, but Abe told him to let me know they'd keep searching if I paid for another three days. I told him to forget it. I was going to run out of money if I kept paying the Bernsteins for what I suspected was absolutely nothing.

The weekend passed with no contact from Riordan, the Gianollas, or Ethan Pinsky. Elizabeth and I spent some time in the office at the factory but stayed away from Ford City and the Bucket. Given that I was meeting Edsel Monday night, I hadn't expected to hear from Riordan, but I couldn't help thinking we were cutting it too close. I didn't let Elizabeth go anywhere without me, and I always had my gun handy.

Monday morning I rolled over onto my right hand and woke, shouting in pain. I held the abomination up in front of my face and looked at it. This hand was a curse—a scarred, ragged, burgundy curse with which I would be saddled for the rest of my life.

The rest of my life.

As that sank in, I thought, *Maybe I should quit complaining and get on with it.*

Repressing the thought of the morphine in the nightstand, I went into the bathroom and mixed three grams of aspirin into a glass of water. I drank that before dressing for the day and putting on my glove. At seven o'clock, Elizabeth rang my bell. I asked her in for coffee, and we sat at the kitchen table. Steam rose in a slender wisp in front of her face.

"Any developments?" she asked, tipping some cream into her cup.

"Nothing."

"Then let's go to the trial today."

"All right. I need to do something to take my mind off Pinsky. I sure hope Riordan gave Edsel some answers."

She took a sip of coffee. "You're worried about Detective Riordan delivering on something he said he'd do?"

"Of course I am. He's not God, you know."

"There's nothing you can do about it, is there?" In a matter-of-fact voice, she added, "Worry about things you can change, not the things outside your control. You'll be much happier."

"I suppose that's good advice," I said, frostier than I intended.

"Perhaps you *should* listen to a little advice."

I sat back. Why was I getting angry with her? Was it simply that a woman was trying to tell me how to live my life? "Lizzie, I'm sorry. You're right. I'm just nervous."

She smiled. "I know that, Will. Say, to take your mind off your problems, why don't you fry me up some bacon and eggs?"

"I don't have any bacon."

She jumped up and opened the door of the icebox. "But you have eggs." Thrusting the box of eggs at me, she said, "Over-hard, please. And some toast. Don't burn it."

I got up and began making breakfast. I had to work harder than I might have, given my useless right hand, but I tried to make the entire operation look effortless. Being a cripple had already meant losing my dignity in enough ways. After we ate, I left the dishes in the sink. Washing them meant taking off my glove, something I wasn't prepared to do in front of Elizabeth.

We took a trolley to the courthouse and queued up half an hour before the doors opened. Only a few other people, none of whom I recognized, had beaten us there. We sat in the front row on the left-hand side, where we would be just behind the defendant. I hoped I'd have a chance to speak with him.

The courtroom filled quickly. I turned around and looked through the crowd, hoping to see Salvatore Adamo, but he was nowhere in sight. In the back row on the far side, I spotted Angelo, the young man who had guarded Wesley and me at the Bucket on a night that seemed so long ago. He looked emaciated, with sunken eyes and a ragged pair of black mustaches. I caught his gaze. He tore his eyes away and began studying the floor in front of him.

Just before nine o'clock District Attorney Higgins and an assistant sat at the prosecution's table. A few minutes later, a bailiff brought out Vito Adamo, Ferdinand Palma, and two other men from behind a closed door. One of them was a rough-looking Italian I presumed to be Adamo's accomplice, Filipo Busolato. The other was a swell in a fancy suit with broad pinstripes. The lawyer, no doubt.

Adamo looked good as he always did, though he still wore the poor truck driver outfit he'd been in when I saw him in jail. His disguise didn't go as far as his face, however. His expression was just this side of a smirk. He was allowing this trial, his face said.

The bailiff led him to the table in front of us. He looked around, and his eyes caught mine. One corner of his mouth turned up in an amused smile. He looked at Elizabeth, and his smile grew larger. He bowed toward her, though just with his head. "Enjoy yourselves," he whispered.

"We need to talk to your brother," I said.

He shot a glance behind him before whispering back, "Why?"

"The Gianollas."

He narrowed his eyes. Before he could speak, he was joined by his codefendant and lawyer. His gaze lingered on me a moment longer before he turned and sat at the table.

The trial began with Higgins's opening statement. He paced in front of the jury for half an hour, droning on about how they would prove this, and they would establish that. The only thing he proved was that he was going to bore the jury to death.

When he finished, Adamo's lawyer jumped up and explained that Mr. Adamo and Mr. Busolato were actually at church when Carlo Callego was murdered, and five witnesses—five, he repeated, holding up a hand with all five fingers extended—including a priest, would swear to that. This trial was a sham and nothing more than the persecution of a pair of poor immigrants trying only to provide a good life for their families. They were being railroaded for a crime they did not commit, would never commit.

When the court adjourned for lunch, I looked for Angelo, but he had disappeared, so I drove Elizabeth home, telling her I'd pick her up for the speech at six thirty. We didn't speak much on the drive. The trial had depressed both of us.

I was certain Adamo would be acquitted. I was conflicted. On the one hand, I wanted him dead or at least spending the rest of his life behind bars. On the other, he could help me get the Gianollas out of my life.

I wasn't sure which was the better hand.

That evening I dressed in tie and tails, grabbed my umbrella, and caught a streetcar downtown. I stood in the aisle and stared out the window, wondering what the evening would bring. Raindrops sprinkled against the windows of the trolley, gathering and running down in rivulets onto the wooden window frame.

I hopped out a block away from the Detroit Electric garage, popped the umbrella, and trotted down the sidewalk. I was just opening the front door when Joe Curtiss ran out, almost knocking me over. "Oh, shit, Will," he said. "What the hell?" He looked around before pulling me down the sidewalk to the alley next to the building. Shoving me against the wall, he said, "You told me you met with Pinsky."

"I did."

"Sam said you were supposed to meet Pinsky today. You didn't show. What the hell is wrong with you?"

"Oh." Now I understood—the meeting we'd originally set up. "Pinsky and I rescheduled that. I've already met with him once. And I'm going to phone him tomorrow."

His relief was palpable. "Good. I hope to hell he tells the Gianollas that."

"Why? What happened?"

"So far, just a phone call. But Sam said I'd better have some answers tomorrow. I was just heading to your place."

I shook my head, thinking about Sam Gianolla. "I'll make sure Pinsky tells them, Joe."

"Okay."

"Did you get Gina and the kids out of town?"

"No. I just . . ." He shrugged. "I don't have the dough."

"I told you I'd pay for it." I pulled my wallet from my coat and handed him five twenties. "Here. That will get them somewhere nice."

He stared at the bills in amazement. "Shit no, Will." He handed three of the twenties back to me. "They can go to Gina's sister's place in

Kalamazoo. Thanks. A lot." He put a hand on my shoulder. "I'll pay you back."

"Just get them out tonight. And I'll phone Pinsky right away."

He nodded, and we said our good-byes, heading in opposite directions—him for the trolley stop, me for the garage. I tried phoning Pinsky from Mr. Billings's office, but no one answered. I'd try again after the speech. I got my car and picked up Elizabeth, and we headed up Woodward to get Edsel.

I rang the Fords' bell shortly before seven. Edsel answered the door, dressed in black tie and tails—with a football helmet on his head.

I cocked an eye at him. "What's that about?"

He grinned. "Just thought I might need a little protection if you're going to drive."

Elizabeth laughed. I rolled my eyes. Edsel took off the helmet and glanced at the hallway mirror to fix his hair. "Well, if Elizabeth lived through the drive over here, I suppose I'll just have to buck up." Picking up an umbrella, he said, "We can't live forever, can we now, Elizabeth?"

Smiling, she took his arm. He turned and shouted out, "We're going to the lecture now, Mother. I'll be late." Turning back to me, he said in a low voice, "We'll talk in the car."

He opened his umbrella, and we walked to my car through a fine mist of drizzle. Edsel helped Elizabeth into the Torpedo, and she maneuvered herself into the backseat. I climbed into the driving seat with Edsel next to me. Craning my neck to see behind us, I began backing down the driveway.

"Looks like you've gotten a bit of control over the throttle," Edsel said.

"Thanks for noticing," I replied, pulling onto Edison Street. "So what did Detective Riordan say?"

"He wants you to call Pinsky tomorrow morning. Set up a meeting with you and your father for tomorrow at three o'clock."

"That's a good idea. I wouldn't want my father to go there alone." I reached out and turned the handle of the windshield wiper back and forth.

"Detective Riordan will be surveilling Pinsky's home for the meeting."

"Good," I said. "I don't know that I can sneak any weapons past Pinsky's man."

"At noon tomorrow," Edsel said, "he wants three reliable Anderson security men to meet him at the telephone company's office on Lafayette. One will monitor Pinsky's phone calls. The others will accompany Detective Riordan. He's quite certain there will be no danger to either of you. Pinsky needs cooperation to achieve his ends, not compulsion."

I turned right on Woodward. Elizabeth leaned forward. "Let me come. As a secretary. His man won't search me."

"His daughter will probably be there," I said.

"She won't find anything," Elizabeth said.

I thought about it. If Riordan thought it would be safe . . . "Fine. So long as my father agrees, you can go—as our bodyguard." I spun the wiper handle again.

"Bodyguard," she said. I could hear the smile in her voice. "That sounds about right."

I was coming up quickly on an opera coach pulled by a pair of horses. I let up on the throttle and hit the brake. A streetcar was crawling through the intersection. I slowed and stopped behind the coach. "What are we supposed to accomplish at this meeting?" I wiped the windshield again.

"Detective Riordan wants your father to start out hard-nosed, then at the end leave the door cracked just a bit. Riordan wants to stir things up. Pinsky will either make phone calls, which will be monitored, or send messages to his confederates, which will be intercepted before going on to their intended recipient. Once Detective Riordan determines the location of the Gianollas, he'll have them apprehended. In effect, you're flushing out your game."

While Edsel was talking, the trolley cleared, and the coach started up again. I swung around it, tires spinning on the wet pavement as we rocketed past. I parked just down the street from Detroit College. We checked our coats in the lecture hall's lobby and were heading toward some open seats near the front when I caught a flash of white skin from the corner of my eye. I turned and looked. The crowd in the aisle parted, and my gut twisted.

Ethan Pinsky strutted down the aisle in a black silk tuxedo and top hat, a big yellow smile on his face, wearing Minna on his arm like jewelry. Her pink silk evening dress plunged into her cleavage and rippled in her wake; her diamond necklace, bracelets, and rings sparkled dollar signs in everyone's eyes. Her auburn hair was pinned into tight ringlets under a narrow-brimmed pink chapeau.

They hadn't noticed me yet, and I wanted to keep it that way. I turned to head up the aisle and almost ran over Waldman, who stood with his feet planted, blocking the aisle. "Mr. Pinsky would like to speak with you."

CHAPTER TWENTY-THREE

I tried to push past Waldman. "I don't want to speak with him."

He grabbed my arm. "I must insist. Don't make a scene."

"Ah, Mr. Anderson," Pinsky wheezed from behind me.

I glanced down the aisle. Edsel and Elizabeth were heading toward the front, not having noticed that I'd stopped. Good. I took a deep breath and turned around. "Why are you following me?"

"Following you?" He smiled and raised a well-worn copy of Taylor's *The Principles of Scientific Management*. "I'm here to learn. All businesses need to think scientifically."

I leaned in toward him. "Why didn't you tell the Gianollas we're cooperating?"

His forehead furrowed, and he frowned. "I have done so."

"That's not what Sam told Joe Curtiss. He's afraid for his life."

Pinsky pursed his lips and shook his head. "He has nothing to worry about. I will phone them. This evening, in fact."

"Now."

Minna gave an impatient sigh and rolled her eyes.

"Certainly," Pinsky said. "There is no need for Mr. Curtiss to be concerned."

"Will?" Edsel appeared at my side, hands on his hips. "Everything okay?"

"Yes," I said, putting a smile on my face. "I was just discussing Taylorism with these folks."

"Hello, Mr. Ford." Pinsky held a gloved hand out to Edsel. "It's a pleasure."

Edsel shook his hand. "I'm afraid you have me at a loss, Mr. . . . ."

"Pinsky, Ethan Pinsky. This is my associate, Mr. Waldman."

Edsel gave a start of recognition at Pinsky's name, but quickly blanked his face and shook Waldman's hand.

"And my daughter, Minna," Pinsky said.

She flashed a big smile at Edsel and held out her hand, palm down. "It's a pleasure."

He took her hand and gave it an awkward shake. "Mine, I'm sure."

Pinsky got his attention again. "Mr. Anderson and I have been"—he took a rattling breath—"discussing doing business together. In fact I believe I'll be meeting tomorrow with his father. Isn't that right, Mr. Anderson?"

I gritted my teeth and nodded. "Three o'clock?"

"That will be satisfactory. At my home?"

I nodded again.

"Ah, Miss Hume, is it?" Pinsky said, looking to the other side of me, where, I now saw, Elizabeth stood. "You're quite a lovely young lady."

She said nothing, just gave him a cold stare.

"I'm Ethan Pinsky. This is my associate, Mr. Waldman, and my daughter, Minna."

Again, Elizabeth said nothing.

Minna put on an exaggerated smile. "The proper response would be 'How do you do?'" She spoke as if she were talking to a small child. "Or perhaps 'It's nice to meet you.'" She turned to Pinsky. "Do you think we could find a governess for Miss Hume to teach her how to—?"

"That's enough, dear," Pinsky said, taking her hand. "Enjoy the speech, gentlemen, miss." He motioned toward the front of the auditorium. "After you."

"Go on, Edsel, Elizabeth," I said, gesturing for them to leave. "I'll be right there."

For the first time ever, they both actually obeyed me. When they had gotten far enough away, I said, "I need one thing before I'll continue to cooperate. Tell me who killed Carlo Moretti."

An amused smile played on Pinsky's mouth. "Haven't we already discussed this?"

I looked at Minna. "Was it Sam?"

She arched her eyebrows at me. "Of course not. Weren't you arrested for it?"

"We don't know who did it," Pinsky wheezed. "Now, we'd better find our seats. It's nearly time for the lecture."

"You'll call Tony?" I said. "Tonight?"

Pinsky grinned, showing off yellow teeth against pale lips. "This instant."

I spotted Edsel and Elizabeth in the fifth row, an open seat between them and a pair of old men who sat on the aisle. I slipped past them and sat. Elizabeth's face was red. She looked at me, and I could see fire in her eyes. "That nasty bitch," she whispered. "What is he doing here, anyway?"

I shrugged and sat back, thinking. Could he really be here just for the speech? He had the book, which meant he had been prepared to come tonight. To know we were going to be here, he would have had to listen in on my telephone call with Edsel. Not outside the realm of possibility, but given the condition of the book I thought this might well be a coincidence—that he actually was here to see Taylor. Either way, I was shutting Edsel out of this mess once and for all. It was bad enough that I couldn't shake Elizabeth. I wouldn't get Edsel killed.

The hall was soon packed with businessmen in suits and tuxedos, who talked loudly to one another, filling the hall with a deep hum. Edsel and Elizabeth talked quietly with each other. I was lost in thought.

"Say, have you read either of Taylor's books on management?" Edsel said.

No one answered. I glanced at him. He was leaning in front of Elizabeth, looking at me.

"Oh, sorry," I said. "I haven't read his books, but I'm conversant—

improve productivity by measuring everything, breaking down each task to its component parts, and so on. I studied it at university."

"Well, pay attention tonight. You'll learn enough to satisfy whatever curiosity your father has regarding efficiency."

"I don't know how concerned he is with the topic at the moment."

"Still," Edsel said.

Frederick Winslow Taylor strode to the podium, and the crowd quieted. He was a severe-looking man in his mid-fifties, with thin gray hair and a neatly trimmed gray mustache. He adjusted the lapel of his black tuxedo and announced, "No one will be let in or out of this room once my lecture has commenced. I will be speaking for two hours. No one is to interrupt me. If you need to leave, please do so at once."

He spent the next two hours (virtually to the second) lecturing about the stupidity of the worker and the best methods to get a ridiculous amount of work from him. He did make a few good points regarding the use of time-and-motion studies to determine the most efficient means of production and that sort of thing, but I stopped listening about thirty minutes in.

He was discussing his work at Bethlehem Steel—how he'd gotten four times the production from a group of pig iron handlers. When he was concluding the topic, he said, "One of the first requirements for a man who is fit to handle pig iron as a regular occupation is that he shall be so stupid and so phlegmatic that he more nearly resembles in his mental makeup the ox than any other type. Therefore, the workman who is best suited to handling pig iron is unable to understand the real science of doing this class of work. He is so stupid that the word 'percentage' has no meaning to him, and he must consequently be trained by a man more intelligent than himself into working in accordance of the laws of this science before he can be successful."

I sat in my seat, fuming. The goal of scientific management is to create automatons out of stupid people? But it made me think. Was there an application for Detroit Electric? It didn't take me long to decide it would be very limited. We employed hundreds of skilled craftsmen—machinists, carpenters, upholsterers, painters, mechanics—and only a handful of laborers. And those laborers did a variety of jobs, not one single mind-numbing act day in and day out.

Ford, on the other hand . . . Taylorism was just the thing for their new assembly line. An automated line assembling interchangeable parts held no room for craftsmen and lent itself perfectly to Taylor's methods. If Ford was able to duplicate Taylor's results and get four times as much work out of men as they were getting now, their profitability would soar, and they could become even more aggressive with their pricing.

It seemed a sea change was at hand. And it was a change that would be entirely at the expense of the worker.

Taylor yammered on for another hour, finally finishing with, "In the past the man has been first; in the future the system must be first. . . . The first object of any good system must be that of developing first-class men. Thank you."

He bowed, and the men in the audience leaped to their feet, raucous in their applause.

I watched for Pinsky on the way out of the auditorium but didn't see him. The air was cold and wet, though the rain had stopped. As soon as I started the car and climbed back in, I said, "Edsel, you need to listen to me. As of now you are out of this. I am not going to involve you in—"

"So long as I stay away from the gangsters I'll be fine."

I cleaned the windshield and pulled away from the curb, edging out into traffic. "We're not talking about this," I said.

"Will—"

"No." I turned up Woodward, heading toward Edsel's house. The cobbles glistened in the electric light from the streetlamps. An uncomfortable silence fell over us. The only sound was the Torpedo's tires whizzing over the wet pavement.

Elizabeth leaned forward. "Can you believe that nonsense Taylor was spewing?"

"Nonsense?" Edsel said. "I thought he made a number of good points."

"Now, wait, Edsel," I said. "Treating employees like beasts of burden?"

"You're referring to the pig iron handlers?"

"Yes."

Edsel turned sideways in his seat so he could look at both of us. "I think he went overboard when he said a trained gorilla could handle the job, but still. How much time have you spent with men who do these sorts of jobs?"

"Not much," I said.

"More like none?"

"Well . . . yes," I admitted.

"Elizabeth, how about you?"

"Servants, I suppose."

"Believe me," he said, "when I say that your servants have little in common with these men. Listen, you two. Not everyone is meant for the manor house. Some men are fit for that sort of work."

"But 'beasts of burden,' Edsel?" Elizabeth said.

"No, you're right." He turned toward her. "That's too harsh. But those men couldn't thrive in most settings. It makes good business sense to put the right men into the right jobs. And no matter what you think of Taylor or his methods, is it really the better option to have these men set their own schedule of work? Any men, for that matter? There needs to be proper training, expectations, and constant supervision to get a good day's work out of most employees."

"Well, it's no wonder the unions hate the man," I said. "He's just turning workers into another part of the machine."

"And thereby creating a more consistent product at a lower price, which will benefit everyone," Edsel shot back.

"I'll be honest, Edsel," I said. "It worries me. One thing Pinsky said to me has stuck. And that's that millions of workers with no allegiance to this country will be ready for revolution if the worker isn't accounted for. It's hard to imagine there could be more strain between management and employees than there is now, but this is going to make things worse. Much worse."

"It's interesting to me," he said, "that Pinsky was there. Could Taylorism improve the Gianollas' business?"

"Pinsky told me all businesses needed to think scientifically," I said. "It scares the bejesus out of me that those animals could apply the scientific method to their organization."

I pulled into his driveway. Before climbing out, Edsel said, "Will, I want to help you. Just think about it."

"No. I appreciate the offer, Edsel, I do. But I'm not risking your life."

"That's what you said last time, Will. If you'll recall, Wesley and I saved your bacon."

I felt my face flush. "That's right, Edsel!" I shouted at him. "And it got Wesley killed." I turned to face him. "Now listen to me, God damn it. You stay the hell away from me, and stay the hell away from this mess. I don't even know what I was thinking. You're still a kid. Jesus!"

"Will!" Elizabeth said. I threw her a warning glance.

Edsel didn't say anything. He just looked at me for a long moment, those big dark eyes shining, then threw open the door, pulled himself out of the car, and began striding up to the house.

"Are you really that coldhearted?" Elizabeth said.

I didn't answer. I wanted to say something to make Edsel feel better, but it would only encourage him to help us. With tears in my eyes, I backed down the driveway and tore away up the street.

"Well?" Elizabeth demanded.

"Do you want to see Edsel killed?" I said, my voice cracking.

"No, of course not."

"So do you think he'd really have stopped?"

She was quiet for a moment. "No. You're right. I'm sorry."

With a heavy heart, I drove Elizabeth home. Edsel was my best friend. But when it came right down to it, I'd rather lose his friendship than get him killed.

Driving from Elizabeth's house to the garage, I realized how much of a complication it was to own a car. Not only was there constant maintenance—adjusting this, greasing that, and tightening the other thing—but picking up and dropping off the car often took as much time as the trip itself. Unless I wanted to pay a chaser to deliver the car (which I didn't), I had to catch a trolley to the garage to pick it up, then go wherever I was going, then drive back to the garage and take another trolley home. A carriage house or one of these new "home garages" would be a real timesaver, but it wasn't to be. As it was, if I left the Torpedo on the street it would be stripped or stolen. I might be able to get away with it if I owned a coupé or brougham that could be locked up, but there was no way to keep someone out of an open-bodied road-ster.

I turned right on Woodward and a few blocks later swung into the Detroit Electric garage, where I dropped off the car and hopped a trolley for the ride back home. It was late enough that I managed to get a seat. The cobbles shone in the reflection of the streetlamps, casting a reddish glow, as if a translucent red veil had been dropped over the city. It was beautiful but surreal, dreamlike. The past year had been surreal, though it was anything but beautiful.

Where did we stand?

Ethan Pinsky and the Gianollas wanted fifty thousand dollars that my father didn't have, or to get the Teamsters Union into Detroit Electric, something my father couldn't do. When we didn't deliver, they would do their best to wipe us out. And their best was pretty good.

We couldn't ask the Employers Association or the police for help. Sergeant Rogers and the gang squad wanted the Gianollas, but Detective Riordan said I couldn't trust them. The Adamos hated the Gianollas, but Vito Adamo still believed that I killed Carlo Moretti. That left us with me, Elizabeth, a few Anderson security guards whose most difficult assignment had been staying awake at night, and a police detective who could help us a few hours a day.

Not exactly a hotshot lineup.

I phoned my father when I got home, telling him about Riordan's request for security men and our three o'clock appointment with Pinsky. He asked me to drive to the meeting, given that my car could go about three times the speed of his, and who knew if we would need a quick getaway. I'd pick him up at two forty-five, since his office was only a mile from Pinsky's house.

I didn't sleep well, and I stayed home the next morning, fretting about the meeting. Finally at one thirty I dressed and prepared to pick up my car. I was on my way to the door at two o'clock when my phone rang.

It was Waldman. "There is a change in plans," he said. "Mr. Pinsky will meet you at 4300 Dubois Street in Hamtramck. Three o'clock sharp."

"Why?"

He hung up. I threw on my duster and touring cap, and hurried out of the apartment to pick up Elizabeth. We were going to need some extra time. I was locking the door when I heard footsteps coming up the front stairway. Thinking nothing of it, I headed down the hall toward the steps.

I was almost at the stairway when a pair of rough-looking men in straw boaters turned the corner. I didn't recognize one of them, but the other was the big brute who had been driving the car that followed Elizabeth and me from Ford City. They gave a start when they saw me. I spun and bolted away from them, down the hall toward the back steps.

"Anderson!" one of them barked. "Stop!" Their footsteps pounded down the hall after me.

I hurtled down the back stairs, the men right on my heels, and ran for the door. I hadn't even twisted the knob when one of them ran headlong into me, smashing me into the wooden door. I bounced off and fell to the floor, dazed, a stabbing pain in my hand. The men grabbed my gun, cuffed my hands behind my back, and dragged me out to the blue Hudson. After throwing me in back, one of the men sat beside me. I twisted to the side, trying to take the pressure off my burning hand. The other man climbed in the front, pushed a button, and stepped on the clutch. The car started up.

I leaned against the door and struggled to sit up. "Who are you?" I could hear the pain in my voice.

"We're cops," the man next to me said. "Now shut up."

"Cops? What did I do now?"

"Why don't *you* tell *us* why you was running."

"Because I didn't know who you were."

He laughed. "You always run away when you see strangers?"

"Strangers who have been following me around? Yes, I suppose I do. Now you tell me—what is this about? I haven't done anything."

"Sergeant Rogers needs to talk to you."

"Listen, I've got somewhere I have to be. I'll come in and talk to Rogers later, I promise."

He ignored me.

"Listen to me. I'm serious. This is life and death. If I don't get to a meeting, my family's lives will be in danger. You've got to let me go."

He gave me a warning glance. "Shut your mouth."

"You've got to listen. I can't—"

He threw an elbow into my gut, doubling me over. "I said, shut up."

I stayed quiet, trying to think.

I had to get Rogers to listen to me.

CHAPTER TWENTY-FOUR

I slammed my fist against the door of the interrogation room for the thousandth time. "Let me out of here! God damn it!" I pounded on the door with the flat of my hand, looking at my bloody knuckles. Sweat poured down my face. I grabbed the knob and shook it with all my might.

Neither Elizabeth nor my father knew the meeting location. It was almost six o'clock.

Slamming my fist on the door, I screamed, "Rogers! Rogers! Open this door!" My voice was a raw croak.

A key rattled in the lock, and the door swung inward. Sergeant Rogers stood silhouetted in the doorway—ramrod straight, big shoulders, derby pulled down low over his eyes. I grabbed him by the front of his shirt. "You son of a—"

He threw me over the table in the middle of the room. I tried to brace my landing with my hands, but one of the chairs went down with me, and I landed on it, ribs against the front of the seat, right hand pinned underneath. I howled and rolled off the chair, sharp pains cutting into my side, waves of searing agony shooting up from my hand. I cradled the hand in my left and rolled on the floor, trying to stifle the groans that forced themselves from my lips.

When I could, I got to my feet, wincing, and stalked back toward Rogers, who stood where he had, watching me with a scowl on that stupid face. "God damn you!" I shouted. "You've killed my parents!"

He held up one big forefinger. "Stop."

I stopped a foot away and stared coldly into his eyes. "You son of a bitch. You don't even know what you've done. Let me out of here."

"Sit." He pointed at the table.

"You've got to let me leave," I pleaded. "They're going to kill my parents."

He pushed me toward the chair I'd knocked over. "I said, sit down." I stared at him a moment longer before stalking around the table, picking up the chair, and dropping into the seat. Rogers took off his derby and ran a hand through his wiry brown hair. "The Gianollas?"

"Yes."

He fit the derby back onto his head and leaned over the table. "Tell me about it."

The pain in my hand made it hard to concentrate. I tried to focus. "They want to get the Teamsters into Detroit Electric, and if we don't do it, they're going to kill my parents and Elizabeth Hume." I used my handkerchief to wipe the sweat from my face and neck. "Look, I'll come back and tell you everything. But you've got to let me out of here."

"You're not going anywhere until you answer some questions. And I better like the answers."

The pain in my hand had me rocking back and forth on the chair. I didn't have time for this. But I wasn't going anywhere until he was satisfied. "All right. A man named Ethan Pinsky is negotiating for the Teamsters. We were supposed to meet with him this afternoon and would have if not for your gorillas. Pinsky moved the meeting location, and I'm the only one who knew it."

"Pinsky, huh?" He patted his pockets until he found a pad and a pencil. "How do you spell that?"

I spelled it for him.

"Where's he live?"

"He's on Gladstone. Can I go now? I'll come back tomorrow and tell you everything."

One corner of his mouth twisted up in what apparently, for Sergeant Rogers, passed as a grin. "Why would I let you go now that you're finally answering my questions?"

I just gave him the dead-eye look.

"Tell me everything."

I hurried through the story of the Gianollas' threats, the Teamsters, and Pinsky. I left out everything else, including Detective Riordan's involvement.

He took notes, and when I finished, he sat back and gave me another of those twisted grins. "There now. That wasn't so hard, was it?"

"Can I go?"

Nodding toward the door, he said, "Get lost."

I stopped only long enough to retrieve my gun from the desk sergeant before running out of the station and down Bethune to Brush Street. It would take forever waiting on a trolley, so instead I ran, thankful for all the exercising I'd done. Even so, I was exhausted when I finally turned onto Rowena.

The feeling of dread I'd had since Rogers's men grabbed me intensified when I caught the first glimpse of my parents' three-story shingle-style Victorian. I ran up the sidewalk and took the steps two at a time.

At the top of the stairway I froze. A cold slug dropped in my stomach. The front door was open a few inches. I pulled the gun from my belt and approached the house cautiously. Using my fingertips, I pushed the door open the rest of the way and sneaked in, sliding to the right, listening for voices, movement.

The house was still. I moved on, walking heel to toe, trying to be silent. I stuck my head into the parlor. Nothing. Down the hall to the kitchen. *Oh, shit.* A pile of dirty dishes sat beside the sink. My mother would never leave the house without washing the dishes. But nothing else. I tiptoed around the rest of the first floor, seeing no sign of anyone or clues as to where they might be.

I climbed the steps, afraid of what I would find in my parents' bedroom. It was empty, as was the rest of the floor. All that was left was the basement. I took a deep breath as I crept down the steps. My senses were sharp. The musty odor seemed more powerful than usual. I inched across the floor, seeing the shadowy shapes of the boiler, stacks of crates, my father's golf clubs.

Nothing.

I climbed the stairs and hurried to my father's den, thinking to call the factory. But it was after hours. No one would be there.

Wilkinson. He would know. I phoned him at home, but he didn't answer. I cursed and walked out of the house, using my key to lock the door behind me. My parents weren't here. That could be good. It was, at least, better than finding them here, victims of the Gianollas. Now, for the Humes' house.

Running again, I made it to the Humes' yellow and white Queen Anne in about fifteen minutes. Their door was closed and locked. I rang the bell several times, but no one stirred inside.

I talked to servants at the houses on either side of theirs. No one had seen or heard anything. A Jefferson Line streetcar rolled past, heading toward downtown. I sprinted out to it and jumped up on the step, riding all the way to Woodward, where I started running again, this time to the Detroit Electric garage. I picked up the Torpedo and raced out to Hamtramck, to the house at which we were supposed to meet Pinsky. It was dark, empty.

I sped to Gladstone, nearly causing a pair of accidents before I stopped in front of Pinsky's house. Seeing no lights on in the front, I crept around to the back. No lights, no sounds, nothing. No one was home.

"Son of a bitch!" I shouted, slamming my hand against the kitchen door.

My parents, Elizabeth, and her mother were all missing, and the only man who could tell me where they were had disappeared like a wisp of smoke.

I drove home and started phoning the area hospitals. No one matching my parents' or the Humes' descriptions had been admitted. I took a deep breath and called the city morgue. Again, no matches. I tried Riordan's home number.

"Hello?" a woman answered.

"Is Detective Riordan in?"

"Who's calling?" She had a British accent, which surprised me.

"Will Anderson."

"Oh, Will. He's talked about you. I'm afraid he's not here at the moment. I haven't heard from him since he left for work this morning."

I thanked her and asked her to have him phone me when he came home. She said she would. I sat back in my chair and racked my mind for ideas. Where could everyone be? Could my parents and the Humes have left of their own volition? Unlikely. More likely was what I didn't want to acknowledge—that the Gianollas had done exactly what they said they would.

Which would mean they were dead.

Elizabeth.

My mother.

My father.

Because of me. Because I didn't deliver.

I was dizzy. I couldn't catch my breath. My thoughts were fractured, broken. Images raced through my mind, horrific images of Elizabeth, my parents. My hand tortured me.

I had to get control. I had to be able to think.

The little bottle. It was still in the nightstand.

I hurried into my bedroom, pulled open the drawer, and rooted around for the morphine. When I felt the bottle, I pulled it out and unscrewed the cap.

Just a capful.

I tipped enough morphine into the cap to fill it and drank it down. Then I lay back on the bed and wished it to happen. And it did. The numbing warmth in the throat . . . the ripples of peace lapping against my mind . . . the waves of contentment . . .

I smiled. I could think again. I would find them. And the Gianollas would pay.

I decided to go back to my parents' house. Perhaps all this was a mistake. I couldn't just assume the worst. I didn't know if it was the morphine giving me hope, but I also didn't want to examine it too closely.

I took four hundred dollars from the nightstand and tucked it in my wallet. The bottle of morphine went into my trouser pocket. I drove to my parents' house and wandered around, looking for clues. All signs pointed to them leaving the house quickly, but there were no signs of violence, so I was hoping they'd gotten out when I didn't make it to the meeting.

I broke into my father's gun cabinet and took a double-barreled twelve-gauge shotgun. After loading it and filling my pockets with shells, I locked up the house again and cruised slowly around Little Italy. It was senseless, I know. The odds of finding my parents and the Humes were one in a million, but I couldn't sit home and do nothing. I considered driving out to Ford City, but it made no more sense than what I was already doing. I had no idea where the Gianollas would hole up.

I smacked the steering wheel. Rogers had ruined everything. My parents, Elizabeth, and Mrs. Hume could already be dead. Or worse, considering what Sam Gianolla did to the man who betrayed them.

After a few hours of useless trolling, I drove back to my parents' house and phoned the Humes. No answer. I tried Mrs. Riordan again. She still hadn't heard from her husband. I gave her my parents' number and asked her to have him phone me as soon as he got home.

Returning to the foyer, I flipped on a single light and sat on the stairway, the twelve-gauge lying across my thighs. I had a clear view of the front door, but someone there would have to look hard to see me. If my parents or the Gianollas came back, I'd know it.

I sat forward, my elbows on my thighs, and fingered the shotgun. I had to do something, but what was there to do? Of one thing I was certain: Regardless of whether my parents and the Humes were safe, I was going to have to kill the Gianollas.

After another swallow of morphine, I settled in to wait for them to return. I don't know how long I stayed awake, but finally unable to hold up my head, I leaned against the wall and fell asleep.

I was perhaps five years old. We were vacationing in South Haven, staying in a resort hotel on Lake Michigan. My sisters had gone off for a walk down the beach, to meet boys, no doubt. I was playing with a shovel in the wet sand near the lake. My mother and father sat on a blanket behind me. A soft breeze blew in, carrying a faint odor of rotting fish.

I looked out at the lake. A small boat with a crimson sail bobbed perhaps a hundred feet offshore. It was unoccupied. A single rope, tied to the front, angled out into the water. I stood, turned, and called, "Father! I want to ride in that boat!"

He looked away from my mother, and glanced first at me, then at the boat. With a smile, he stood and strode past me in his woolen bathing costume, tousling my hair as he went by. "You stay on the beach, boy." He waded into the freezing water and, when he was almost up to his waist, dived in and began swimming straight out, bobbing up and down in the waves as he cut through the water with strong, sure strokes. The sailboat seemed to be farther away now, but he kept swimming.

Then I was sitting on the blanket near my mother. We watched my father swim out far past the pier, so far that his head was nothing more than a pinpoint bobbing in and out of view, but he was no closer to the sailboat.

My mother gripped my shoulders and pulled me to her. I could feel her heart racing. A warm droplet of water fell onto my head. And another. I looked up at my mother's face. Her mouth was stretched open in a silent sob. I looked out again at the lake.

My father was gone. The boat was gone. I turned to look at my mother. She was gone. The wind picked up, the smell of death stronger now. Waves crashed against the shore like thunder.

Without another thought, I ran to the water and plunged in. Instantly an undertow pulled me away from shore. I tumbled across the bottom, my back scraping against sand, my head hitting a rock, all the while being pulled deeper and deeper into the endless lake. I held my breath and fought to reach the surface. My lungs ached.

"Thank God," a woman's voice said from far away. "Will?" Now she was closer. She grabbed me from behind and stopped my tumbling, but still I was underwater. I looked up toward the surface. A hundred feet above me, waves rolled by one after another.

"Will?" she said again.

I tried to pull away, to swim to the surface, but strong hands held me in place. I craned my neck around and saw Elizabeth smiling at me. Her auburn hair undulated in the current. She held me like a baby. I knew it was all right to give up. I took a deep draught of water into my lungs.

"Will? Wake up."

I blinked and squinted into the sunlit room. I was lying on the staircase, propped up against Elizabeth, who sat behind me with one hand on my shoulder, the twelve-gauge gripped in the other. I sat up, my mind still half in the dream. She leaned in and hugged me hard. "Thank God," she said again before letting go and standing. "Will, come on, we've got to go." I saw dark smudges under her eyes. She wore a rumpled indigo day dress that looked as if it had been slept in, with a red ribbon tied sailor-style around her neck. She wasn't wearing a hat, and her wavy auburn hair spilled down over her shoulders.

I rubbed my eyes. "Are my mother and father all right?"

"They're fine."

Relief flooded through me. "And your mother?"

"Fine too. But we might not be if we don't get moving."

I pushed myself up off the step.

Elizabeth touched my arm. "What happened to you?"

"The cops happened to me. That's why I didn't pick you up."

"Thank God it wasn't the Gianollas."

"What's going on?"

"We can catch up after we get out of here." She held up the shotgun. "Do you want to take this?"

Nodding, I grabbed the cold barrel and hefted the gun. "Just a minute. I need one more thing." I ran down to my father's shop and grabbed a hacksaw from the wall.

The shotgun needed some work if I wanted to carry it around with me. And I definitely wanted to carry it around with me.

CHAPTER TWENTY-FIVE

I pulled on my duster as we hurried outside into the early dawn. The sun was peeking out above the buildings downtown, bathing the city in its red glow. My father's Detroit Electric roadster stood by the curb. "Did he—is he here?" I said.

"No." Elizabeth walked around the car to the driving side and climbed in. "He's at the Pontchartrain with our mothers."

"Okay," I said. "I'll follow you there."

I started the Torpedo, hopped in, and stayed close behind her on the short drive to the hotel, feeling dazed. They were all alive and outside the Gianollas' reach. After the previous night, it seemed too good to be true. Yet the evidence was in the car in front of me. It was still early enough that virtually no one was on the street. Still, Elizabeth drove carefully, keeping her speed below ten miles per hour. She pulled up to the curb just down the block from the hotel, and I was able to park behind her.

I shoved the shotgun farther under the seat and joined her as she was pulling a flowered ivory valise from the backseat. "You packed?" I said.

"Some of my father's guns and a couple of knives."

"Do you mind if I take a look?"

She set the bag back down on the seat. "Go ahead."

I opened it and looked inside. Pushing aside boxes of bullets, I saw a pair of switchblades and a Browning .32, like the one Elizabeth had been carrying in her purse, lying atop a Marlin rifle case. "What, no land mines? No hand grenades?"

She made a sour face at me. "No, but I'm also *carrying* a couple of guns."

I closed the bag and lifted it out of the car. "A couple? I saw the one in your purse the other night." I eyed her. "Where's the other one?"

"Gentleman don't ask questions like that."

"What's that got to do with me?"

"Oh, you're right, I'm sorry. It's none of your business where my guns may or may not be." We were both giddy with relief.

"So what happened yesterday?" I asked.

"When you didn't pick me up I called your father's office. He had Mr. Wilkinson come get my mother and me and bring us to the factory. After he talked with Detective Riordan, we all came here."

We started walking toward the Pontch. "Why did you leave?" I said.

"I needed to find you." After a brief hesitation, she added, "We're partners, right?"

"My father wouldn't have let you take his car and go out by yourself."

A shy smile worked its way onto her face. "No. I had to wait until everyone had fallen asleep to swipe the valet ticket for his car and get out of the room. It was three o'clock by then."

"Is someone guarding them?"

"Yes. Your father has two security men inside. They're armed."

"What's Riordan doing?"

"Last I knew he was out trying to track down Pinsky and the Gianollas. He stopped in at the hotel around eleven but hadn't had any luck. He left shortly thereafter to run down some leads."

We walked up to the hotel. The doorman held the door for us, and we hurried inside, taking the elevator to the fourth floor.

When we turned the corner in the hallway, we saw two men wearing the Anderson Electric Car Company's blue security uniforms standing in front of a room with their hands inside their coats—shoulder holsters, no doubt. They looked twitchy, but when they saw it was us, they relaxed. Both were men in their late fifties or early sixties, and had worked for my father for years. Their normal responsibility was guarding the factory from generally nonexistent thieves, not protecting people from murderers. I was embarrassed that I didn't know either of their names.

"Didn't sign up for this type of work, did you?" I said.

They both let out a nervous laugh. "No, sir." One of them knocked on the door.

When my mother opened it, she nearly fainted. She gave me a long embrace, complete with hard kisses on the cheek. "I thought you were dead," she whispered.

I hugged her awkwardly with one arm. "I'm all right, Mother."

Elizabeth and her mother stood face-to-face, talking quietly, their arms around each other.

I glanced at my father. "I borrowed a shotgun. You probably won't get it back."

He shook my hand. "That's fine. I'm just glad you're here." I could see the relief on his face. "Why didn't you pick us up for the meeting?"

I started telling my parents what had happened to me.

"No," Mrs. Hume said, "you can't."

I looked over at Elizabeth and her mother. They had separated, now standing a few feet apart. Mrs. Hume looked stricken. "Mother—" Elizabeth began.

"I won't lose you too." Her fears were etched into her face, deep lines between her eyebrows, on her forehead, around her mouth. Her eyes pooled with tears. "I can't lose you, dear." Her voice was wet, heartbroken.

"Here." Elizabeth took her hand and led her to the bed, where they sat down and began again to speak quietly.

I told my parents about my day. By the time I finished, Elizabeth and her mother had rejoined us and stood side by side with their arms around each other, Elizabeth with a grim expression, Mrs. Hume with red, teary eyes.

Biting his lip, my father nodded. "When you didn't show up, I consulted with Detective Riordan. He and I went to Pinsky's house, but no one was there. I had to assume the worst and get the women to safety, so I brought them here." Turning to Elizabeth, he said, "And at some point we'll have to speak about automobile theft."

"What else have you heard from Riordan?" I said.

He shrugged. "I talked to him a few hours ago. He hadn't made any progress."

"Mr. Anderson," Elizabeth said, "you need to take our mothers somewhere—out of town—and let Will and me handle this."

His eyes widened. "You can't be serious. You've got to get out of the city."

Elizabeth shook her head. "I'm not leaving."

"The same goes for me," I said.

My father put his hands on his hips. "I've got a business to run. I can't just leave."

"You've been meaning to get down to the Cleveland plant," my mother said. "This might be a good time."

My father looked conflicted. Finally he said, "If all of you will join us, we could spend some time in Cleveland."

"Mr. Anderson," Elizabeth said, her chin quivering. "With all due respect, I'm not going anywhere, but I'd like you to take my mother."

I took half a step toward her. "I'm not leaving. This is my fight."

My father folded his arms over his chest and glared at me.

"Father, take Mother and Mrs. Hume to Cleveland. Let us look into this. Anyway, we'll be working with Detective Riordan. He'll keep us out of trouble."

My father snorted. "Like anyone could do that." He just stood there, shaking his head. Finally, he sighed. "All right. I'll take the women. But, Will"—he stood and walked over to me—"if you bring Elizabeth in on this, you're going to be responsible for her life."

I looked into his eyes. "I know that, Father. I'll protect her."

"Wait just one moment." Elizabeth's face was red. "I am not a child."

"Elizabeth," her mother said. "Mr. Anderson only wants you to be safe."

"I know that. But I'm as capable as Will. More so."

More capable than me? I felt real anger but decided to swallow it for now. We needed to present a united front.

After a moment, my father nodded and crossed the floor to her. "You're right. I apologize."

So he agrees. Perfect.

He held his arms open. Her frown melted and she hugged him.

"I think it would be a crackerjack day for a drive down to Monroe," I said, trying to keep my voice even. "They've got a very nice train station. That would be a good place to start."

My father got my drift and nodded. The Gianollas might be watching the Detroit train stations. "All right, ladies," he said, putting some enthusiasm in his voice. "Let's go on vacation! What a lucky man I am to be able to escort two such lovely women."

He didn't get a smile out of either one. Elizabeth grabbed her valise, and we all walked out into the hallway. My father stopped in front of the security men. "Do either of you know how to drive an automobile?"

"Yes, sir," one of them said. "I can."

"Could you take a drive with us down to Monroe and bring the car back?"

"Of course, sir."

My father turned to me. "Why don't you take a little protection?" He nodded toward the other security man.

"No. We're working alone."

He tried again but soon shook his head and allowed us to walk them down to the lobby. Elizabeth gave my father a sheepish grin while handing the ticket to the valet. While he retrieved the car, we went through our tearful family good-byes.

We waved as they drove away. Turning to me, Elizabeth said, "What now?"

"Thanks for the vote of confidence." My voice was just as cold as I intended it to be.

"What?"

"You're 'more capable' than I am. Thanks. I'm sure it filled my father with pride to know his son is a complete Nancy."

"That's not what I said."

"No, but it's what you implied."

"Oh, Will," she said, waving a hand at me. "You're too—" She stopped abruptly. Her face softened, and she grasped my arm. "You're right. That was insensitive . . . and wrong. I know you're better able than

I to deal with these people. I'm sorry. I just didn't want to go, and I feel terrible having my mother leave. I hope she doesn't regress."

I folded my arms across my chest. "So you don't think you're more capable?"

"Well . . . it depends on what you're talking about. For man-things, of course I'm not."

I didn't think it would be productive to explore her meaning of "man-things," so I just said, "Fine."

She gave me a tentative smile. "So now what?"

"We go see Izzy Bernstein."

"What do you want with him?"

"I'm going to have the Bernstein boys find the Gianollas for us."

"Why?"

"It's time to go on the offensive."

I parked two blocks from Peterboro on the other side of the street. With the likelihood that the Gianollas were after us, I didn't want to get any closer to my apartment than necessary.

Izzy Bernstein stood on the corner, newspaper bag slung over his shoulder, bawling out his headlines. "Murder suspects not guilty! Getcher paper! Wright brothers fly into fairgrounds today! Read about it!"

"Hey, Izzy," I called, standing just outside the crowd. He looked at me. "Come here," I said.

"Come here yourself." He turned back to his customers. "Murderers freed! Paper, paper!"

I walked over to him. "I need a favor, and I'm paying."

"Why didn't ya say so?" He cut through the crowd to us and squinted up at Elizabeth. With a grin, he said, "Hey there, beautiful. How'd you like the ride of your life?"

Elizabeth could only stare at him.

"Keep it in your trousers, Bernstein," I said. "She'd probably take you more seriously if you'd already hit puberty."

He glanced at me in confusion. I'd introduced him to a new word. It was probably better that he didn't understand it.

Elizabeth recovered enough to say, "How old *are* you?"

He looked offended. "Old enough." He muttered something in Yiddish before shaking his head and turning to me. "Ya hear about Adamo?"

"What about him?"

"Him and the other wop got off."

"He what?" Elizabeth said, her voice strident.

"What happened?" I said.

I think he smiled, though it looked more a sneer. "Buy a paper and find out."

I flipped him a nickel. He gave me a newspaper but kept the change. Elizabeth grabbed the paper away from me and started reading. I turned back to Izzy. "I need to talk to Abe. There's real money in this for you guys."

"What kind of real money?"

"Don't worry. It'll get Abe's attention."

"Yeah?" He looked curious.

"I need to talk to him today. You arrange that, and I'll give *you* five bucks. And it's just between us. Abe doesn't need to know about it."

He hesitated. "Yeah, all right. The Saint Petersburg Restaurant on Gratiot. Eight o'clock. He'll be there. Now gimme the dough."

"You promise?"

With a grin, he said, "Hey, how we gonna do business if ya doesn't trust me?"

I pulled a five from my wallet. "Tonight," I said, hanging on to the bill. "He better be there."

Izzy sneered. "Or what?"

"Or I'm going to come looking for you, that's what."

"Hah," he barked. "He's a reg'lar comedian."

I let go of the bill, and he stuck it in his pocket. "Just get him there, all right?" I said.

"Said I would. Now shove off."

Elizabeth still had her face buried in the newspaper as we walked back toward the car. "I can't believe this." She looked up at me. "The only eyewitness never made it to court. Adamo was acquitted and released. He's out."

Right then I felt an icy jab in my gut. "Oh, shit! Joe! Come on!" I began running toward the car.

"What's wrong?" Elizabeth said, trying to keep up with me.

I raced across the street. "Joe Curtiss! The Gianollas were holding him responsible for putting this deal together. Son of a bitch! I can't believe I forgot about him."

I ran through the first floor, shouting, "Joe! Joe!"

Elizabeth was right behind me. Plenty of other men were working, but Joe was nowhere to be seen. I took the stairs two at a time to the second floor, where mechanics were at work on a dozen or so automobiles. I shouted out his name again. All the mechanics looked my way to see what the panic was. No Joe. We skipped down the stairs again.

The day manager, Mr. Billings, a heavyset, balding man of about forty, stood at the foot of the stairs. "What's going on?"

"Where's Joe Curtiss?"

He frowned. "That's what I'd like to know. We've been behind all day."

"He didn't come in?"

"No."

"Did you try phoning him?"

"Yeah. No one answered."

"Let's try him again." Squeezing past Mr. Billings, I ran into his office, grabbed the phone, and asked the operator to ring Joe's number. The phone rang. And again. "Come on, Joe," I muttered. The phone rang ten more times. No answer. "Let's go, Elizabeth," I said, heading for the door.

We ran for the Torpedo. I started the car, pulled out onto Woodward, and raced up to Highland Park. I turned onto Church Street and stopped in front of Joe's house, a small red-brick two-story on a street of similar houses, some brick and some wood, all quite close together.

"You're still armed?" I asked Elizabeth as I climbed out of the car. She nodded, and we headed up the walk. The house was dark. I peered through one of the small panes of glass in the door and then leaned over and looked through the window at the edge of the parlor. Nothing. To all appearances, the house was empty. I rang the doorbell and waited a minute before taking hold of the doorknob and trying it—locked. "Let's go around back."

I glanced at Elizabeth as we walked behind the house. Her mouth was tight, her forehead furrowed. My stomach sank when I saw a broken pane in the kitchen door. I turned the knob and pushed. The door swung open. I looked back at Elizabeth, put my finger against my lips, and nodded toward the inside. "Stay behind me," I whispered, and pulled the pistol from my belt. I saw she already had a gun in her hand. We walked in and crept silently from room to room.

The house looked as I expected it would on a normal day—the oak floor clean, a few dishes in the drying rack next to the sink, a stack of folded towels, edges squared, on the coffee table in the parlor. Seeing nothing on the first floor, we climbed the stairway, shoes scuffling softly on the wooden steps. I first looked in the bedroom on the right—the children's room—empty. Giving only a cursory glance to the bathroom as I passed, I hurried to Joe and Gina's bedroom—also empty. A clacking sound came from behind me, somewhere beyond the hallway. I walked back out of the room.

"Will," Elizabeth said. It came out a croak, reverberating in such a way that I knew she was in the bathroom. Something metal clattered onto the tile floor. I hurried down the hall and stopped in the doorway.

"Will." This time, her voice caught in her throat.

Elizabeth stood motionless before the tub, her hand on the bath curtain, her eyes cast down in front of her, her gun lying on the floor.

CHAPTER TWENTY-SIX

I stepped forward and caught a glimpse of crimson on ivory skin. I grabbed hold of Elizabeth's shoulder and turned her away. Taking her arm, I led her to the first bedroom, sat her on the bed, and bent down to look into her eyes. "Wait here."

Eyes wide, she nodded. I took a deep breath and went back into the bathroom.

Joe lay in the tub, naked, brown eyes staring at nothing. He was partially turned away, knees up toward his chest as if in modesty. Other than his head, which was a gray white, he was painted in blood. The limbs that were visible, his right arm and leg, were shattered, white bone splinters sticking through the skin. The blood was heavier around his midsection. What I could see of his groin was nothing more than blood and tissue. A crimson curl ringed the drain.

Joe. *God damn it.* If I had only . . . Could I have saved him?

I realized I was holding the morphine bottle in my left hand. I didn't remember tucking my gun into my belt or taking out the bottle. I spun off the cap and took a pull, then recapped the bottle and shoved it into my pocket before rejoining Elizabeth in the bedroom. Her eyes begged me to tell her it wasn't real, that she didn't see Joe like that.

A calming weight began to settle around my mind. The drug cut through my horror and fear. I sat next to her and took her hand. "Sam Gianolla did it." My voice was thick.

Her head slowly turned toward me, and she looked into my eyes. Her bottom lip trembled, but she remained silent.

"We have to get out of here." I stood. "But first we need to wipe down everything we touched. The cops will be lifting fingerprints everywhere."

"Okay." She didn't move.

"Elizabeth."

She looked up at me.

"We need to wipe everything down. Now. We have to get out of here."

"Yes," she said. "Yes, you're right." She seemed to be coming to her senses.

"Go downstairs. Wipe down the banister, all the doorknobs, anything else you might have touched. I'll take care of this floor."

"I . . ." She faltered.

"What, Elizabeth?" If the police caught us here, we'd both be going to prison. I was beginning to lose my patience, but shouting at her wouldn't help.

"I touched the curtain." She waved vaguely toward the bathroom.

"I know. Now go downstairs." I helped her to her feet and led her out of the room. "And be sure to get the banister."

"Yes."

She began down the steps, using her dress to wipe the wooden railing. I hurried back into the bathroom, picked up her gun and stuck it in my belt, then used a towel to wipe her fingerprints off the curtain. I gave quick service to the front of the sink, in case she touched it as well, then got each of the doorknobs. I threw the towel on the bathroom floor and ran down the stairs. Elizabeth stood near the kitchen door, trembling.

"Did you get all the doorknobs?"

Her eyes still staring off into the distance, she nodded.

I took hold of her arm and turned her toward me. "Are you sure?"

"Yes." She shook her head and glowered at me. "Of course I'm sure."

"Okay. Let's go." I took a look into the backyard. Seeing no one, I gave her a gentle push out, closed the door, and wiped down the knob with my shirt before leading her to the front of the house. "Wait here for a minute."

She nodded. I slipped past a hedgerow and, as casually as I could muster, went back to the front door and wiped down the knob. I thought we had gotten everything. Taking a surreptitious glance around us, I hurried back to Elizabeth and led her to the car. After helping her up onto the seat, I started the car, climbed on, and slowly pulled away from the curb, my brain operating on automatic.

Tears spilled from Elizabeth's eyes. "I can't do this, Will," she whispered. "I can't."

"That's all right, Lizzie. No one would expect you to."

"I thought I could. But . . ."

"It's okay." I was certain that, without the morphine, I would be every bit the wreck Elizabeth was. So long as I could stay sharp, the drug would help me.

So long as I could stay sharp.

Neither of us spoke while I drove away. My mind was still coated with the soft shine of morphine, and her mind—well, I didn't want to think about what was in there. I drove through Hamtramck to give us some distance from Joe's house, and then down West Grand to Belle Isle.

I pulled the Torpedo into a gap in one of the island's stands of trees and shut off the car. "I'm going to cut down the barrel of the shotgun and then drive you up to your aunt's in Flint. You can stay with her until this is over. Perhaps you can get your mother to join you."

Looking exhausted, she shrugged and climbed out of the car. She wandered off and leaned against a tree about thirty feet away, looking out at the river and Windsor beyond.

Keeping one eye on her, I wedged the shotgun barrel in the door to hold it in place and cut it down to a foot long. Now the gun would destroy anything within ten feet of me. I wanted to be that close when I killed Sam Gianolla. I fit the shotgun into the lower left inside pocket of my duster. It sagged but not so much that I thought it would be a problem.

I walked over to Elizabeth and touched her shoulder. "Come on. We should go."

She turned and looked at me. "Could we . . . sit for a minute?"

"Sure."

We walked over by the pond and sat on a park bench in the shade of half a dozen dense elm trees. Elizabeth wiped her eyes and looked at me. "Lord . . . Joe." A freshening breeze riffled through her hair. Her hat lay on the bench next to her, hatpin atop the brim. Her hair had spilled down around her shoulders.

I put my arm around her. "Don't think about it." Canoes floated past on the island's small pond, young ladies facing their beaux, who idly paddled while they looked for an advantage. It wasn't so long ago that that was us, but the memory was vague, like something I'd read in a book when I was a child.

Elizabeth pressed closer to me and laid her head against my chest. "What do we do now?" Her voice was muffled by my duster.

We? "I'm driving you to Flint, remember?"

"I don't know." Her voice was quiet, barely a whisper.

"Elizabeth, this is too much for you. You said it yourself." I stroked her head. "And there's no shame in that. This is too much for anyone. You need to get away from all this—permanently."

"Yes, but—"

"Elizabeth, please. Let me do what's best for you for a change."

Her head rose, and her emerald eyes met mine. "No. I can't. I have to see this through."

Bending over, I propped my elbows on my knees and held my head in my hands, ignoring the pain in the right one. I was exhausted. How had my life gone so wrong? Could it all have been that one moment, the moment in a drunken stupor I decided to make love to Elizabeth whether she wanted me to or not? Could a single idiotic decision lead to the deaths of so many and the ruination of so many more?

God damn it. I sat up and turned to her. "You're going to stay?"

She looked away and nodded.

I took a deep breath. "All right. I'll call in Joe's . . . I'll call Detective Riordan."

"He has to help us," Elizabeth murmured. "We have to kill them."

"He won't do that. He's not going to break the law."

She glanced up at me again. "Then who *is* going to help us?"

I grimaced. "There's the Adamos—maybe. But when it comes right down to it, it's you and me now, Elizabeth." I took her hand. "Can you do it? Can you help me kill the Gianollas?"

She sat up and wiped her nose with her handkerchief. With her mouth set in a grim line, she said, "It doesn't matter if I can. I have to."

I left Elizabeth on the bench and walked over to the Casino, where I used a pay telephone in the lobby to call the Bethune Street police station. Again using a disguised voice, I asked for Detective Riordan. He wasn't available. I hung up and tried his home number.

Mrs. Riordan answered. "Good afternoon."

"It's Will Anderson. Is Detective Riordan in, please?"

"He's not here," she said quietly. "He said if you called to tell you to phone back after eight tonight."

"All right. But . . . I need some help now. A friend of mine was—" My throat constricted. My eyes burned. I burst out sobbing, unable to speak, tears streaming down my face. It was as if a dam had burst inside me.

"Shh," she said over and over. "What's the matter?"

"God," I was finally able to choke out in a strangled voice. "I'm sorry." I wiped off my face with my sleeves. "A friend of mine was murdered. I don't want the police to just go in and make their standard mess of things. I was hoping your husband could—"

"Tell me the name and address," she said. "I'll get word to him."

I gave her the information.

"Phone back tonight," she said.

"I will."

After I hung up I phoned the Detroit Electric garage and asked them to send a chaser to pick up the car. I didn't want to drive it back to the garage myself, nor could I leave it where it was—or virtually anywhere in the city, for that matter. I was fortunate it hadn't disappeared from in front of my parents' house. This was Detroit, after all, the automobile-theft capital of America.

Before I returned to Elizabeth, I checked the contents of the morphine bottle—less than a quarter full. A trip to the pharmacy had to be in my near future. Elizabeth and I walked back to the car. I put my shotgun into her valise, hefted it, and made one more attempt to talk her out of continuing this quest. "It's not too late," I said. "Let me take you to your aunt's."

She shook her head and began walking toward the road. We caught a trolley down to Jefferson and stopped at the Western Union office just down the block to send my father a telegram. It read:

> JOE CURTISS WAS MURDERED STOP DO NOT COME
> BACK TO DETROIT STOP TELL WILKINSON WHERE
> YOU ARE STOP I WILL BE IN TOUCH
>
> WILL

We exited the building and walked down the sidewalk toward the trolley stop on the corner. "All right, Elizabeth. What do you say we find a place to stay?"

With her eyes glued to the concrete in front of her, she nodded.

"Do you have any ideas?" I had some of my own, but I had to draw her out of her head, get her thinking about something other than Joe.

She brushed her hair away from her eyes and glanced up at me. "How about somewhere around Eastern Market? It's close to Little Italy, but everyone there is Russian, so we don't have to worry about someone telling the Gianollas—or Adamos, for that matter—that we're there."

"Good idea." Good. I had her talking, at least a little. She still looked terrible—not like her heroin days, but pale and sad and tired. Very tired.

We climbed on the first trolley, changed cars once, and hopped off on Riopelle, just down from the Eastern Market. The sidewalks were packed with pushcart vendors, their sales pitches blending one over the top of another:

"Roasted sweet potaaatoooes!"

"Jewelry for the missus, cheaper'n stealin'."

"Getcher veg! Beans! Peppers! Carrots!"

A three-story grayish clapboard hotel, dubiously named the Cosmopolitan, sat on a corner a block up the road. I shouldered through the crowd on the sidewalk into the dimly lit lobby and walked past three rickety wooden chairs to the counter. Behind it, a little man sat slumped on a stool, his belly like a medicine ball under his shirt.

"We'd like two rooms, please," I said, setting Elizabeth's valise on the floor.

He eyed me suspiciously, then looked at Elizabeth before turning the register around to me. I wrote in *Edward Smith* and *Esther James,* the first two names I thought of.

"Fifty cent a night a room. Two day in advance," the man said in barely understandable English.

I handed him five dollars. "Keep it. I'm not sure how long we'll be here."

He gave me a pair of keys but continued looking at me under a furrowed brow. We didn't belong here.

As we walked to the stairs, I noted a pay telephone screwed into the wall on the other side of the lobby. We climbed to the second floor, where I unlocked Elizabeth's door and opened it for her. She wandered in and sat on the bed. After closing the door, I sat next to her. I thought I'd give it one more try. "I could still take you to Flint. Your mother could join you. She needs your help anyway."

Elizabeth looked at the floor. "I can't. I can't leave." She turned back to me. "Give me an hour. I'll be ready to go."

"All right. Rest."

She didn't reply.

I left her room and closed the door softly before heading back down the stairway to the first floor. The Empire pharmacy was only a few blocks away.

Mick's prices had gone up slightly. He charged me five dollars for two bottles of morphine. I didn't complain. The first thing I did when I got back to my room was cut a small hole in the side of the mattress and tuck the bottles inside. I didn't want to carry them around, nor did I want them discovered by anyone else, not that I expected maid service at the Cosmopolitan. I drank another capful of morphine and settled in.

After a few minutes, I gazed out the window. The ubiquitous coal dust painting the redbrick buildings shone softly with rainbow coronas. Where I had seen age, now I saw a quiet majesty. Where I had seen neglect and disrepair, now I saw beauty in the sacrifices these buildings had made for their inhabitants. I took a deep breath and exhaled slowly, marveling at the sight.

When the hour had passed, I climbed out of bed, walked down to Elizabeth's room, and knocked. The door swung open. My jaw dropped. "E—Elizabeth?" Her hair had been sawed off to only a few inches long. Her beautiful auburn tresses lay in a pile on the floor behind her.

She looked away. "I need some new clothes." Her voice was quiet, barely more than a whisper.

I glanced up and down the hall. "Can I come in for a minute?"

She stepped back out of the doorway, and I slipped inside, studying her face. "Are you all right?"

"I'm fine. I just . . . I just don't want anyone to know I'm me. I want to dress as a man."

"That's a good idea," I said in a soothing voice. "You already look different. Once we get you some clothes, no one will suspect."

Brushing the hair from her forehead, she said, "I need some pomade, and we both need clothing. We have to pass as men who belong here."

"Sure. I'll go down to the market."

"Boots, trousers, shirts, underwear, the works. Used is better than new." She paused, frowning. "Except the underwear. Definitely new underwear."

I nodded. "No argument from me."

"Could you get me a corset? If I'm going to pass as a man, I've got to tone down my figure."

I arched my eyebrows. "I didn't *think* you were wearing one." That prompted a ghost of a smile from her. Then I thought about what she'd said. "Wait. Me? Buy a corset?"

Her face brightened a bit at the thought. "What? Are you afraid people are going to think it's for you?"

"Well, I wouldn't be the first. But, all right, fine. What else do you need?"

"A duster with lots of inside pockets."

"Okay. But you're all right?"

"I'm fine, Will." She tried to put on a smile, but it was nothing more than a grimace. "Go on."

"Okay. But I'm worried about you."

"Don't be."

I looked at her a moment longer. "Stay here. Lock your door."

She nodded. I left her room and descended the stairs, walking out into the sunshine, heading for the Eastern Market. It seemed every pushcart vendor in town was here restocking his cart. Voices rose and fell— Russian, Italian, Greek, with heavily accented English as the middle ground.

No one seemed to pay me any attention as I purchased a small tin of pomade and a pile of used clothing— two pairs of black wool work trousers, a pair of white shirts, stockings, garters, and boots, and a corset and a black oilskin duster for Elizabeth. I added a beat-up black derby for myself and a black snap-brim fedora for her. It would shade her face better than a derby. No one who saw her clearly could possibly believe she was a man. As promised, the underwear I bought was new (purportedly, anyway). All this for less than five dollars.

When I returned to the hotel, I gave Elizabeth her new clothing, and she set to cutting down the corset so it would cover only her chest. I wished I hadn't left the hacksaw in the car. It would have come in handy. We took turns sawing away at the fabric with our knives, ripping out the whalebone supports, and generally stripping the garment of most of its purpose. When we finished, she asked me to leave, saying she'd come get me when she was ready. I retreated to my room to change. About twenty minutes later, a quiet knock sounded against my door. I opened it to find a reasonable approximation of a short, slight, very young man with a five o'clock shadow, dressed in immigrant garb with a black duster and fedora. The young man held Elizabeth's valise in his hand.

I stared at "him" for a moment before nodding. "Pretty good. If I didn't know you . . ." I ran a finger across her jawline and glanced at the faint gray smudge.

"Coal black." She slipped past me into the room, set the valise on the bed, and opened it up. Turning back to me, she said, "You have the thirty-two, right?"

I nodded.

She pulled the sawed-off shotgun, a box of shotgun shells, and a box of bullets from the bag and handed them all to me. "Fill up an outside pocket with ammo."

I dumped half a dozen shells and at least twice that many bullets into the left-hand pocket of my duster.

"Do you have a knife? Or anything else?"

"Jackknife," I said. "That's it."

She pulled one of the switchblades from the bag and handed it to me. I pressed the blade-release button on the knife, and a four-inch blade zipped out from the haft. The balance felt good—for a switchblade. I flipped it up into the air and caught it. "Nice."

Elizabeth sat on the edge of the bed and stared at the floor in silence. Finally, shaking her head, she looked up at me. Her eyes were the green of a stormy sea. "If we can get Detective Riordan coming from one side and the Adamo gang coming from another, we can do this. We can send the Gianolla brothers back to Hell."

CHAPTER TWENTY-SEVEN

We walked to the Saint Petersburg Restaurant, a small storefront in a three-story redbrick apartment building. It held perhaps fifteen tables, sturdy oak with no tablecloths, and smelled sour and musty. It was crowded with families, everyone speaking Yiddish. Elizabeth and I headed for an open table in the back.

I took a seat against the back wall, expecting Elizabeth to sit on the other side of the table. Instead, she pulled out the chair next to me and sat. I believe I smiled, because she gave me a look. "You don't expect me to sit with my back to the door, do you?"

"No."

"So I can sit next to you even though I'm a 'man'?"

I laughed. "I'm not too worried about people thinking I'm a homosexual."

"Because you're so manly?"

"No. Because I don't care." Whatever concern I had left after befriending Wesley was erased by the morphine. I looked up to see a few men staring at us. I smiled back at them.

I nudged Elizabeth and whispered, "We can't let the Bernsteins know what our plans are. They've worked with the Adamos. They may have an affiliation with the Gianollas too."

Elizabeth nodded.

An older man with a white apron tied at his waist bustled out the kitchen door behind us. He had wisps of white hair around the sides of his head and was probably in his seventies, but he looked as strong as a bull. "Can I help you?" He had a heavy accent, and the *h* sound was strong and percussive, like he was clearing his throat.

"Coffee," Elizabeth said. I nodded for the same.

He walked back through the door, which opened again almost immediately. I looked back. Joey Bernstein leaned against the wall behind us, silent, his eyes scanning the room. He knocked twice on the kitchen door. A few seconds later, Abe walked out. "So, Anderson, you wanted to see me?"

"Have a seat," I said, motioning toward the chair across from me.

He walked around to the other side of the table and stood for a moment, looking back and forth between Elizabeth and me. "Who's your friend?"

"Just a friend," I said. Elizabeth stayed quiet.

Abe stared at her for at least ten seconds before he began to smile. "Wait a minute. Is this one of them she-shes?"

"What?"

"One of them dames that likes other dames."

I laughed out loud. Elizabeth stared at him with a stony silence. Abe spun a chair around and straddled it, his forearms resting on the chair back.

"Never mind him, Abe. I need something. And I'll pay well."

He pantomimed smoking a cigarette. "Got a smoke?"

"Sure." I pulled out my case, and he took one. Elizabeth declined. I held the case over my shoulder, and Joey took one as well. It made me nervous to have him standing behind us, but I was determined not to show it.

"Light?" Abe said.

I slipped the lighter out of my coat pocket, flicked it open, and lit it. He leaned forward with his cigarette in the flame, held his hands around mine, and inhaled deeply. The cigarette flared. When I snapped the lighter shut, Abe's hand closed around it. I looked up at him, surprised.

"Can I see it?"

"Yeah, okay." I let him take it from my hand.

He examined the engraving on the sides and held it up, turning it back and forth to reflect the light. "To Will on his grad . . . gradua . . ."

"Graduation day," I said.

His eyes flickered to mine, showing his annoyance. "I know. I was figurin' it out." He looked at the lighter again. "From his proud parents. Nice." He handed it back to me. "Now, whattaya want?"

The old man returned with four cups and a pot of coffee. He poured, and Abe said, "Thanks, Mr. Markovitz. My friend here"—he gestured toward me—"is payin'."

The man nodded and hurried back into the kitchen. I flicked the lighter again and held it up over my shoulder. Fabric rustled as Joey bent down; then I heard the inhalation right next to my ear, the fire and smoke being sucked into the tube, the popping of tobacco seeds. I flipped the lighter closed and tucked it into my coat pocket, my eyes on Abe all the while. "I need you to find some people for me."

"Who?"

I leaned in closer to him. "The Gianollas."

He looked around before whispering, "The *Black* Hand this time? Anderson, you play in the wrong side of the sandbox."

"So you know them?"

"Heard of 'em."

"Can you find them?"

Holding the top of the chair with both hands, he bounced back and forth. He hit the chair of the man behind him, who did nothing more than squeeze himself closer to his table. "If they're in the city, I can find 'em. Gonna be expensive, though."

"How expensive?"

"Fifty bucks—half now, half when I find them."

"That's a little steep, don't you think, Abe?"

"That's what it costs. Take it or leave it." His bright blue eyes glinted at me from under his heavy lids.

"I'll pay it if you also arrange a meeting for me with Vito Adamo."

"You're just spoilin' for a fight, ain't ya?"

"No. I just need to talk with these guys. I think the Adamos will want to meet, but I doubt the Gianollas will, so I just need to know where they'll be at a particular time."

"Extra twenty bucks for Adamo," Abe said.

I nodded.

"Awright. I'll even throw in a little information for free."

"What's that?"

He held out his hand. "Thirty-five up front."

He may not have had a lot of education, but his math skills were fine. I eyed him for a moment before pulling my wallet from my coat and handing over the money.

He tucked it into his pocket. "What you wanted me to look into before?"

"Moretti's killer?" I said.

He nodded. "Heard it was a pro."

"Pro?"

"Assassin." He seemed to relish saying the word. "Expensive one."

"Did you get a name or description?"

"Nah. People don't talk much about these guys."

"Who paid?"

Abe shrugged. "Don' know." He stood and walked around the side of the table. "I'll call when I find them guys."

"No, that won't work. Tell you what. Why don't you leave a message for me at the Cosmopolitan Hotel—Rivard and Wilkins."

He cocked his head and gave me a puzzled grin. "Little ratty for the likes of you, ain't it?"

I shrugged. "Just convenient. Now, how do I get hold of you?"

Pointing toward the kitchen door, he said, "If you're gonna be slummin' down here, leave a message with Markovitz."

I looked him in the eyes. "What if you don't find the Gianollas? What about my money?"

He laughed. "That ain't what you should be worryin' about. You should worry about what you're gonna do when I *do* find 'em."

When we returned to the Cosmopolitan, we stopped in the lobby to use the pay phone. I dropped a nickel into the coin slot and the metal clamp over the receiver sprang open. Detective Riordan answered on the first ring. "Hello?"

"It's Will," I said, my hand cupped over the bell of the telephone.

"Good. You're all right?"

"Yes."

"Elizabeth too?"

"Yes." My hand throbbed. I tried not to think about it.

"I talked to your father. You and Elizabeth need to get out of town, right—"

"Forget it. You can't do this by yourself. You've never even seen these people."

"Will." He sounded like he was trying to hold his temper. "Elizabeth doesn't belong in this."

"Would you like to try talking her out of it?"

He grunted. "No. Your father said she wouldn't listen. But you have to keep her safe."

I glanced back at Elizabeth. From behind, her small stature made her look like a boy playing grown-up in a suit and hat. "I will," I said.

"I had warrants sworn out for Pinsky and Sam Gianolla," Riordan said. "You gave the testimony, by the way. I'm sure I botched your signature, but it was good enough to get the ball rolling."

"Good."

"You two stay out of sight while I figure this out."

"I'm not making any promises. I want the Gianollas."

"Let me find them. You are in so far over your head you can't see the surface."

I thought about my dream. "I'm used to it."

He sighed. "All right. Call me tomorrow night."

"Sure."

"Is there a number I can get you?"

"I'm not sure where we'll be." I didn't want to tell him where we were, in case he thought he ought to lock us up for our own good.

"Okay. But, Will?"

"Yeah?"

"Be careful."

"You too." I hung up the telephone and turned to Elizabeth. "It's early yet. Would you like to take a walk?"

"Sure," she said.

My hand had begun to really hurt. I excused myself to urinate, though what I did instead was duck into the bathroom for a sip of morphine. I wasn't sure I'd gotten enough, so I finished the bottle. We walked outside, and I looked up at the cerulean sky. Sunset was near. I filled her in on my conversation with Detective Riordan while we wandered down to Jefferson and along the riverbank.

The delicious fuzziness began to envelop me. We sat on a bench overlooking the river and just looked out at the water. As more of the morphine worked its way into my bloodstream, my mind began to soar, over the river, into the sky. My eyes closed.

"What's wrong with you?"

I opened my eyes and was surprised to see a young man sitting next to me. He wore a dark fedora and a black duster. *Oh, shit,* the little voice in the back of my mind said. *That's Elizabeth. I took too much.* The voice that so often hounded me was afraid, but it was barely a whisper in the roar of the freight train running through my head.

"Well . . ." My tongue felt too large for my mouth. I thought about that.

"Are you all right?"

I sat up straighter, tried to look alert. "Oh, yeah, just . . . thinking."

"About what?"

"You know. This af-afternoon." My tongue kept getting in the way.

"Are you on drugs?"

"No." I tried to summon some indignation, but it was all I could do to speak intelligibly. "Of course not. I'm just . . . in shock." I shivered and wrapped my arms around myself. "Aren't you?"

She looked at me a bit longer before turning back to the river. "If you say so."

The next time I turned my head to say something to her, she was gone.

I was lying fully clothed in my bed at the Cosmopolitan when a knock on the door awakened me.

"Will?" Elizabeth called quietly.

"Mmph." I cleared my throat and tried again. "Just a minute." Remembering the night before, I felt a moment of sheer terror. *She knows.* "I'm not decent. Give me a few minutes."

"All right," she said. "I'll wait in the lobby."

She walked off down the hallway, and I lay back with my hands over my eyes. Elizabeth knew I'd been taking drugs. I was going to lose her again. I pushed myself up in the bed, my back against the wall, and looked out the window to see a light rain falling. It was frightening how easily I'd fallen again into the morphine habit. It was natural, almost instinctive, at this point. But I was done. I had to be.

I pulled up the bedclothes and rooted around in the hole I'd cut in the mattress. Nothing. I dug deeper. Still no bottles. I struggled to remember returning to the room last night. Had I thrown them away then, or had someone found the bottles and stolen them? I sat on the edge of the bed and thought. It didn't matter. They were gone. Now I could get on with it.

Trying to ignore the throbbing in my hand, I put on my immigrant clothing. Even with the rain, the morning was hot and humid, so I left my duster in the room when I headed out. An old woman now sat behind the desk in the lobby, assembling corsages of silk flowers—no doubt how she paid the bills left unpaid by her hotel wages. She looked up at me when I passed, and I saw she was toothless, her mouth sunken in on itself.

I smiled at her and tipped my derby. "Good morning."

She didn't reply, just bent once again over her materials, her jaw working back and forth as she sucked on her lower lip while fitting a needle into tiny stems.

I continued on to Elizabeth, who stood by the door. "Good morning, sir."

She turned and appraised me. "You sound a bit better than you did last night."

"Yes, I—I don't know what was wrong with me. Maybe yesterday hit me harder than I thought."

Her eyes gave me nothing. "Okay."

I looked away. "How about some breakfast?"

She nodded and ducked out into the rain. I followed her to a little restaurant across the street from the Eastern Market. While we ate, I glanced at her, trying to see her as a man. She would have been maybe sixteen, a short, slight young man, perhaps an artist or a teacher. No, she was too damn pretty for that. I gave up. "What should we do today?"

She swallowed the scrambled eggs in her mouth and said, "You should check with Mr. Wilkinson to see if your father has been in touch."

"Right. What else?"

"I don't know. I thought you were the criminal mastermind."

I thought about it. "Do you want to look around Little Italy? See if we can scare up the Gianollas?"

"Makes as much sense as anything else," she said. "Until we hear from Abe I don't know what we can do."

After we ate, I called my father's office from the Cosmopolitan's lobby and got Mr. Wilkinson on the phone. "This is Will. Have you heard from my father?"

"Yes. He sent a telegram." He was quiet for a moment while papers rustled. " 'Tell Will to get out of Detroit, stop. We are on our way to safe place, stop.' Does that make any sense to you?"

"Yes. Excellent." I thanked him and hung up.

We spent most of the day waiting at the hotel for word from Abe Bernstein, and the rest slogging around Little Italy in the rain, ostensibly to look for Gianollas, but in reality doing nothing but killing time. The rain had finally stopped when we returned to the hotel for good just after eight o'clock.

The little fat man was back on duty. He opened his eyes long enough to say, "Message," and pushed a folded piece of paper across the counter to me. I picked it up and read it.

Tawked to both. Mich Coal Co docks 2 AM Bring my 35 AB

CHAPTER TWENTY-EIGHT

A tingling sensation spread through my body. Tonight we'd meet with Abe and presumably at least one of the gangs. If it was both, we could end this. The Adamos wouldn't bypass an opportunity to kill the Gianolla brothers, regardless of who was providing the intelligence. I tucked the paper into my pocket and nodded toward the stairs. We hurried up to Elizabeth's room, and I handed her the message.

She glanced at it and looked up at me. "Can we trust him? Who's to say they don't just kill us?"

"Abe likes my money. I don't think he'd sell us out. Assuming he's arranged for both gangs to be there, this could be our chance to rid ourselves of the Gianollas once and for all. Can you . . . that is, are you sure you can do this?"

"I'll be fine. It's you I'm worried about."

I didn't meet her eyes. "I'm fine."

"You're not taking anything, are you?"

I didn't have to think too long to know what she was talking about. "No." I met her eyes again.

She studied me for a long moment before turning away. "All right. I'm going to get some rest. Should we phone Detective Riordan first?"

"Maybe we should wait until tomorrow to talk with him. It's possible our problem will be solved tonight, and he won't need to get involved at all. And he certainly doesn't need to know what we're doing tonight."

She looked doubtful but finally nodded. "Okay. I'll come get you at midnight. We should get there early."

"Good. We'll pick up my car at the garage."

She smiled and reached over, squeezing my good hand. "We can do this."

Trying to look confident, I nodded and squeezed back. "I'll see you in a bit." I returned to my room and sat on the edge of the bed, checking the load on my pistol and shotgun. I was ready, but I was afraid. Even if the Adamos helped us, this would be a dangerous mission. The Gianollas would be armed to the teeth and ready for trouble. We would be facing one of the most dangerous gangs in Detroit. I was putting Elizabeth squarely in the crosshairs.

Still. Killing Sam Gianolla after what he did to Joe . . . I was game to try it. I'd see if Elizabeth was.

She knocked on my door a few minutes later. Her fedora was pulled low over her forehead, and her black duster hung nearly to the floor. Even though she made a very small man, tonight she looked like a tough.

I slung on my duster and fit the shotgun into the lower inside pocket. Without a word, we descended the stairs and walked out of the hotel into the dark, heading toward Woodward. Clouds obscured the moon and stars. Few people were on the street. The area was quiet, little noise other than distant automobile motors, the faint sound of a crowd, a piano player banging out ragtime.

I stopped Elizabeth a block away from the Detroit Electric garage. "Wait here while I get the car."

She nodded. I hurried to the garage and knocked on the door underneath the red metal archway. Perhaps half a minute later, Ben Carr's elfin face appeared at the bottom of the window in the door, looking up at me. I hadn't seen him for how long—two years? It didn't seem possible. But I imagined that, after I nearly got him sent to prison, he avoided me as much as my guilt made me avoid him. To his credit, his expression remained neutral when he saw me.

He unlocked and opened the door. "Mr. Anderson?" His tone was wary.

"Just picking up my car, Ben."

"Sure." He didn't meet my eyes.

"Could you get the door for me?"

"Sure." He walked toward the overhead door, and I grabbed my key from the board. I scanned the room, looking for my Torpedo among the automobiles arrayed against the walls. It wasn't hard to find, being the only ugly car among the hundred or so shiny Detroit Electrics. While I started it, Ben raised the door. He gave me a halfhearted wave as I drove past him, turning up Woodward toward Elizabeth.

Before she got in, she slipped one arm out of her duster and slid the strap of the Marlin rifle off her shoulder. She placed the gun in the backseat and climbed in. We drove in silence down to Jefferson and west, past Zug Island and its massive foundry. The blast furnace threw a hellish white light over the shoreline. After we crossed the River Rouge Bridge, I took a left on Pleasant Street, and we headed down toward the docks. I switched off the Torpedo and let it glide to a stop two blocks over and three blocks back from the coal yard. When my motor shut down, a low rumble became apparent—the foundry. Once we were out near the water, the noise from the blast furnace would obscure small sounds. We'd have to be very alert.

Elizabeth pulled the .32 from the pocket of her duster and popped out the magazine. "Have you checked your weapons?" Her voice was higher than normal, tight.

"Elizabeth, you don't have to do this. Here." I pulled the car key from the ignition and handed it to her. "Go back to the hotel. I'll see you there."

She was quiet.

"I won't think any less of you."

"No." Turning to me, she said, "I have to. I have to do this."

"Please. Go back."

"No." This time she sounded certain. "Do me a favor, though. Check your ammo."

She popped the magazine out of her pistol and looked at it. I dug into my pocket, feeling bullets and shotgun shells . . . and something else. My hand froze in place. Two little bottles. I must have hidden them there last night while under the spell of the opiate. When I had a chance, I'd dump them. I pulled my hand from my pocket, stepped out of the car, and reached back for my shotgun. Elizabeth grabbed her rifle and hid it under her coat again. "Let's go."

"All right. But if anything goes wrong tonight, let's meet at the car as quickly as possible."

She nodded.

I climbed out. Flood lamps on the corners of a few buildings provided the only illumination. Staying in the shadows of the redbrick warehouses lining the road, we walked down to the coal yard. The street dead-ended at the Michigan Coal Company's office, a squat cement-block building with a few flood lamps around it. Jutting out from both sides was an eight-foot-tall wooden fence topped with barbed wire, dozens of coal pyramids backlit behind it.

We stopped in front of the building. "Why don't you go down that way," I whispered, pointing to my left. "See if there's a way in. I'll look on this side. We'll meet back here."

"Okay."

"Be careful. They could have somebody here already."

She nodded. We separated, and I hurried around the perimeter of the fence. It ran down into the river and out perhaps fifty feet into what I assumed would be deep water. But if we couldn't get in any other way, we could swim it. I returned to the front of the building. Elizabeth appeared a few seconds later. "It looked to me like we could swim around the fence," I whispered. "Anything else on your side?"

"No."

"Let's go back to the warehouse and wait for Abe."

We walked across the street and sat on the warehouse's stoop, hidden in the shadows. I listened to the faint rumble from Zug Island, remembering my journey through the snow with Elizabeth's father's body and my fall into the icy water.

My memories, it seemed, were virtually all of bad things—tragedies, lost love, foolish blunders, missed opportunities. Surely good things had happened to me once upon a time. But I couldn't think of any without the pull of their resolution. My father believed I would be the man to carry on the family business, building it to even greater heights. I rewarded him with drunkenness, open disregard, and dereliction of duty. Elizabeth gave me her heart. I rewarded her with my stupidity and brutality, and her love for me resulted in the ruination of her life. And it indirectly caused the death of both her father and my best friend.

Elizabeth nudged me and whispered, "Someone's coming."

I looked up the street and saw no one. Then a quick movement caught my eye as a shadow flitted into the gap between buildings. Taking care to be quiet, I stood, pulled my pistol, and scanned the area for perhaps five minutes. Elizabeth stood next to me doing the same.

"Hey, Anderson." The whisper came from the edge of the stoop, only a few feet away. I must have leaped three feet into the air. Elizabeth whirled around, pointing her gun at the unseen man.

She grunted as it was torn from her hand. "Settle down there, sport," Abe said with a smile, the glint of his teeth reflecting a far-off light. "It's only me. Got my thirty-five bucks, Anderson?"

"Are they both going to be here?"

"No. Gianollas."

"What about Adamo?"

He shook his head. "Ain't gonna meet with ya."

"Shit!"

I glanced at Elizabeth. Her eyes were hidden by the fedora. "Give me my gun," she growled at Abe.

"Sure, sport," Abe said. "Just didn't want you shooting an innocent man." He handed the gun back to her. "Now, about my dough?"

Even though he hadn't gotten us a meeting with Vito Adamo, I pulled the full thirty-five dollars from my wallet and gave it to him. Without even looking at them, he slipped the bills into his pocket and said, "Come on."

He trusted me. He lived in a world in which trust was dangerous, yet he trusted *me*? Must be because I posed no threat to him. He could make me disappear just as easily as the Gianollas or Adamos could. Abe was an intelligent boy with the wiles, charisma, and morals of a politician. He was going to be a formidable man.

He led us around the left side of the fence. About halfway down, he pried off a board and turned back to us. "Nobody else needs to know about this," he whispered. "Once't in a while we need some coal."

"No problem," I said. "We'll keep it quiet."

"Awright." He rested the board against the fence. "They oughtta be here soon. From what I hear, the shipment's comin' in at two."

"Shipment of what?"

He shrugged. "Booze? Wops? Drugs? How should I know? And what does it matter, anyway?"

"You're right. It doesn't."

"They'll bring the truck to the docks through the gate in the middle." He pointed over the fence toward the river.

I extended my left hand to Abe. "Thanks."

"Don't mention it." He took my hand and pulled me a little closer. "And I mean that."

"Not a problem. I understand."

"Okay then." He let go of my hand and sauntered off, not a worry in the world.

"Will," Elizabeth whispered. "What are we going to do?"

"I was thinking we could watch them, assess the situation. If it's only the Gianolla brothers, or we get a good chance to kill them, we should do it. Otherwise, we can just watch. Maybe we'll come up with something we can use against them."

She didn't say anything for a moment. Finally she nodded. "You're right. Who knows if we'll get another chance."

"Let's go in. See how the place is laid out."

Elizabeth nodded and slipped through the hole in the fence. I grabbed the loose board and squeezed through backwards, then propped the board into the hole. Elizabeth stood about ten feet away, surveying the landscape. We skirted a few coal piles and walked toward the river. Another fence ran parallel to the shoreline, blocking off the coal yard from entry via the river. A pair of ten-foot-wide gates stood at the center, secured in place by iron rods set into metal sleeves in the concrete. I pulled up one of the rods and swung the door out far enough for us to slip through. The hinges creaked. Three long docks, each about fifteen feet wide, cut out into the river. Empty barges sat at the two outside docks. A cement path the width of a road ran from the end of each and converged in front of the gates.

"Okay," I said. "They'll almost certainly open both of these gates. With my weapons, I'm going to have to be close. But you can stay farther back, use the rifle. We'll catch them in the cross fire." The farther I could keep her from the action, the better.

"There's no cover here besides the fence," she said, gesturing around us. The coal piles were all at least fifty feet from the gate, far outside the range of the sawed-off.

"What if . . . What if I got down underneath the center dock? They won't be looking for anyone there. If the situation's right, I'll blow the Gianollas to pieces with the shotgun. Otherwise, I'll sit tight. You do the same."

"You'll only shoot if the odds are with us?"

"Of course." But that wasn't what I was thinking. This might be the only chance I got to kill the Gianollas. With them dead, my loved ones were safe. If I had to, I'd die to make that happen. We walked back into the coal yard, and I pointed toward a towering pyramid, a triangle of void, darker than the night. It just happened to be the coal pile closest to the loose board in the fence. "Use that pile for cover. If they search the yard, you'll be able to sneak out. If not, you can pick them off with the rifle."

"Okay." She sounded breathless.

"Listen, Elizabeth." I took hold of her elbow. "Don't shoot until I do."

"How will I know it's you?"

I hefted the shotgun. "You'll know."

"Okay," she said again.

"We'd better get into place."

She reached out and touched my arm. "Be careful."

"You too." I stepped back outside the gate. Elizabeth swung it shut and rammed the iron rod back into place. I could hear her footsteps crunch on the coal dust as she moved away from me.

I caught the flash of headlamps near the office building and heard the low rumble of a gasoline engine. The Gianollas. I ran down to the river, lay down, and slipped under the center dock. My heels and the backs of my ankles were in the water, my forehead only six inches below the wooden slats. I hoped Elizabeth was well hidden.

The sound of the engine grew louder, and light from headlamps squeezed through cracks in the fence. Half a minute later, hinges creaked, and the engine revved.

They were driving out to the docks.

CHAPTER TWENTY-NINE

The sound of the engine got louder, and headlamps lit the river-front.

It was then that I saw the spiders—hundreds of fat spiders on the underside of the dock, some within inches of my face. The activity and light had stirred them into a frenzy. One dropped onto my forehead. I swatted at it, hitting the dock as I did, rousting even more of its friends.

The engine was very close now, and the lights fixed on the dock. I froze. A pair of boots clomped onto the wooden slats, directly over me. Another spider and then another dropped onto my face and proceeded to crawl over my eyes, past my mouth, down my neck. It felt as if thousands of them were crawling over my body. The Gianollas' men walked only inches above me, but it was all I could do not to run screaming into the water. I screwed my eyes shut and tried not to move.

The men were talking, though I didn't understand a word of it. One of the voices sounded familiar, and finally I placed it—the three-fingered man who drove when they kidnapped me. With panic only seconds away, I pushed myself a little farther into the river. The cold water filled my boots and lapped at my calves. The spiders still danced their dance on my face, down into my shirt, who knew where else. I tried not to think of where else. I pushed myself down a few feet more into the river. The water was nearly at my waist now.

The kidnapper stopped directly above me. I froze again. He lit a cigarette and dropped the match into the water. It hit with a sizzle, which startled me, and I jerked my head toward the sound. A sharp pain flared in my cheek, and, without thinking, I slapped at it, spattering a juicy spider over the side of my face.

"*Silenzio!*" the man above me shouted.

I froze again, as did everyone else. They seemed to listen for a moment; then the kidnapper barked out a command and they all began moving again. He walked down the dock. I pulled the shotgun from the pocket of my duster, held it out of the water, and slid farther into the river. The bullets in the pistol were watertight, so I didn't think I'd have a problem with that, but I had to keep the shotgun shells dry.

More spiders scurried up my neck and onto my face, looking for dry ground. Chills ran through me. I slid deeper into the river, while my mind screamed at me to get underwater, get the spiders off. Perhaps a dozen of them now congregated on my face, scuttling back and forth. I wasn't stopping, no matter who heard me. I took a deep breath through my nose and slipped the rest of the way underwater. The spiders floated away.

Keeping the shotgun out of the river, I pushed myself out a little farther and then crouched in three feet of water, my head a foot under the dock. My cheek throbbed, and the skin felt tight. It was swelling. I hoped the spider hadn't been poisonous.

Another voice rose above the others, a voice I immediately recognized—Tony Gianolla. He walked onto the edge of the dock, joining the kidnapper. I tracked him with the shotgun. Tony and the other man walked over my position and stopped a little way past me, then turned and walked back off the dock. Tony called out to Sam, who answered. In a spirited conversation, the three men began moving toward me.

I stuck the shotgun under my arm, pulled the pistol from my belt, and held it upside down, making sure all the water was emptied from the barrel. I'd heard that so long as the barrel was clear, pistols that had been immersed would still fire. This wasn't the best time to experiment, but there was nothing to be done for it. It would work or it wouldn't. I stuck the gun into the highest pocket in my duster and took hold of the shotgun again.

Two of the men walked onto the dock. The other stayed back. I wasn't sure both men above me were Gianollas, but at least one of them was. The other was near. I'd shoot these men from down here, then come up on the side of the dock with the pistol and shoot the other. The two men on the dock stood close together, only two feet in front of me. I braced the shotgun against my shoulder, trying to steady it with my bad hand. Taking a deep breath, I aimed between the slats at the silhouettes and pulled both triggers.

The gun slammed into my shoulder. The roar of the twelve-gauge, so near my ear, deafened me, but the dock shook when the men fell. One pitched into the water. I dropped the shotgun, pulled the pistol from my pocket, and swept up from the side, looking for another Gianolla.

Gunshots fired from all around, bright flashes in the dark, muffled explosions in my damaged ears. A bullet thudded into the wood next to me. Another whizzed over my head. I shot at everything man-shaped I could see. A muzzle flashed beside a coal pile on the other side of the yard, and then another and another. Elizabeth had opened fire.

Something hit me from behind, spinning me around. A man ran at me from the end of the dock. Fire leaped from the end of his gun. I dived into the water and swam underneath the dock to the other side, toward one of the barges. My right arm didn't seem to work. Now sharp pains arced through my shoulder. I came up for a breath and ducked into the water again, swimming for the last dock. The pain sharpened, was overwhelming. Trying not to gasp in water, I dug with my left arm and my legs, trying to get as far away as I could.

When I came up again, I was ten feet from the front of one of the barges. Sporadic gunfire came from the coal yard. Two men walked up and down the middle dock, scanning the water. A number of others hustled a big body toward the truck.

I swam one-armed to the front of the barge and underneath the dock to the far side, Elizabeth's side. Sharp pains, like the stab of an ice pick, pulsated in my shoulder. Hidden in the dark, I pushed myself as close to the shore as I could before trying to stand. My head spun. It was all I could do not to cry out from the pain. *The morphine.* I crouched down, steadied myself, and fished one of the bottles from my pocket.

I took a long drink and hurried around the outside of the fence. It was getting hard to focus. I felt weak and tired. The truck started up and roared away, the headlamps careening over the coal piles. In seconds, it was gone. I hurried to the loose board and saw that it lay on the ground outside.

I hoped that meant Elizabeth had escaped. She hadn't cried out. There had been no triumphant shouts from Gianolla's men. I climbed through the hole in the fence and took a quick look inside, then propped up the board as quietly as I could with one hand and hurried down the shoreline.

Holding my right arm in my left, I ran up the road toward the car. I was on the right side of the street and then the left and then I was back again on the right. I tried to straighten out but couldn't quite seem to do it. Finally I saw the car and the silhouette of a small person crouching near it in the dark. I slowed and called out quietly, "Elizabeth?" My voice was thick, my tone dull.

"Will," she said. "Come on."

I lurched up the street to her. "Are you all right?"

She steered me toward the Torpedo. "I'm fine. Let's get out of here."

"I'm fine." *Wait. She didn't ask.* I was so tired. I adjusted the throttle and spark and felt my way around to the front to start the car. Elizabeth was already there, spinning the crank. The engine caught. When I turned, my head spun again, and I nearly fell over. I steadied myself against the car until it passed.

"Come on," Elizabeth said, her voice urgent. "We've got to get out of here."

"I'm coming." I stumbled around to the side and climbed in the car, veering into the back door before squeezing past. She followed behind, pushing me in. "Did you shoot any of them?" I said, putting the car into gear.

"One, I think."

I pulled out, trying for quiet. Instead the engine revved and the tires squealed. I nearly ran into the curb on the other side of the road.

"Let me drive, Will."

"I'm okay." I straightened out the car and drove up the street, keeping my speed down. "Did you hit either of the . . ." I forgot their names. "Brothers?"

"I don't think so, but I'm pretty certain you did."

Now out to Jefferson, I opened it up and roared away. The streetlamps whizzed past on the sides of the empty street. My head felt like it was going to float up into the clouds. "I've got to make a stop," I said, my voice thicker now, set in molasses.

"Where?"

"Dr. Miller's."

"Why? What happened?"

"I got hit."

"Hit? By a bullet?"

"Yeah."

She leaned forward and looked at me. As we passed under a streetlamp, I heard a sharp intake of breath. "Oh, my God. You're really bleeding."

"I'm not feeling so good," I mumbled.

"Let me drive."

"No, I'm . . ."

She grabbed the wheel, reached over, and pulled the throttle lever all the way up while maneuvering the car to the curb. Pulling back on the hand brake, she said, "All right, now move." She helped me out and into the backseat, then climbed in again and pulled the car onto the road.

When I woke I was alone. I smelled chloroform and disinfectant. My right arm was in a sling taped to my chest. Using my left hand, I propped myself up on the bed and looked around at the understated blue wallpaper, the oil paintings of the countryside, the white cabinets full of medical supplies, and the vegetable garden through the window— Dr. Miller's office.

I was exhausted. My right shoulder hurt like a son of a bitch. My hand throbbed with the burning to which I'd become so accustomed. I looked at it, nestled into the white cloth of the sling. Someone had taken off my glove. The skin was mottled, burgundy and white. My fingers touched at the tips. I needed a smoke. I thought I would get up, find the doctor, but instead I lay back and slept again.

Some time later, Dr. Miller bustled into the room. "Will, my boy. How are you feeling?"

"Fine. Is Elizabeth all right?"

"Yes." He worked the sling over my head and began peeling a layer of bandages off the front of my shoulder. "She's sleeping now. She's been staying here all along."

"Oh." It took a moment to register. "All along? What do you mean?"

"You've been here three days."

"You're not serious."

He stood up straight and looked me full in the face. "I nearly killed you with morphine before I operated. Elizabeth didn't know you'd already taken some. Almost enough to kill you, in fact."

"Oh, right. I just happened to . . ." When I saw the look on the doctor's face, I trailed off.

He shook his head slowly. "I've seen no evidence of withdrawal symptoms, so obviously you're not as far gone as you were before. It's your call as to what you do. You can be a coward and continue to drug yourself. Or you can face your pain like a man."

"Yes . . . well . . ." I looked away from him. I didn't know what to say.

"Morphine will kill you, you know."

"I know. It's not what you think."

He studied my face for a moment before saying, "She loves you."

"What? She said that?"

He nodded. He finished changing the bandage on the front of my shoulder and began doing the same to the one on the back.

Could it be? Elizabeth loves me?

"You got hit pretty good, by the way," Dr. Miller said. "The bullet nicked an artery. Had Elizabeth gotten you here ten minutes later, I don't think you'd have pulled through."

"Will I have any long-term damage?"

"No. It should heal well. In a month or so you'll be able to use the arm again."

"Do the police know about any of this?"

"Of course not. Elizabeth explained to me what you're dealing with. No one knows but me and my nurse. And she's discreet. Here now." He worked the sling over my head and put one hand below my shoulder blades, the other on my chest, and gently pushed me back onto the bed. "Rest. I'll check on you in a while."

"Could I have a cigarette?"

"Ah, you'll have to take that up with Elizabeth."

"What? Why?"

Patting my arm, he said, "Talk to Elizabeth." He left the room.

I lay back and thought. Could it possibly be true? Elizabeth still loved me? It was so unlikely. Certainly she had once, but that was long ago. An awful lot had occurred since, none of which I could remember with pride. It was ludicrous. Dr. Miller was raving.

Elizabeth walked into the room a few hours later, wearing a simple burgundy skirt and a white shirtwaist. I pulled the sheet over my hand.

She stood next to the bed, arms folded across her chest. "How are you?"

"Fine. Good. How are you?"

"I'm fine." Her voice was frosty.

"Have you got a cigarette?"

"We've quit."

"What?"

"We've quit," she said. "It's bad for you. You haven't had any tobacco for three days now, so you've slept through the hard part. Now, have you got any other surprises you've forgotten to tell me? Or any more lies you'd like to retract?"

"No."

"Are you sure? Get them out now, because the next time you lie to me will be the last. And from this moment forward, if I ever believe you're on drugs, we're finished. Forever. I walked into a gun battle with you—my only ally—on drugs." She glared at me.

"I took the morphine *after* I got shot."

She crossed her arms over her chest. "You had two bottles in your pocket."

"I'd . . . you were right the other night. I was taking morphine. It seemed to help. But the night at the coal yard, I didn't even realize I had it until we got there. I only took it after I got shot. You have to believe me."

"I don't know why I should."

"I don't either. But you have my word. I'll never lie to you again. And I'll never take drugs."

"What about smoking?"

If I was going to be miserable anyway, what's the difference? "Sure. I'll quit that too."

"Good." Her face relaxed, but she didn't smile. "Your father escorted our mothers to Cape Cod and is on his way back."

"Thank God they're safe. But my father's coming back?"

She nodded. "He told Dr. Miller he's not going to let a bunch of criminals dictate his life."

"Damn." I shook my head. "I wish he would stay away."

"It might be all right. I don't think the Gianollas can afford to devote too much attention to us."

"How do you mean?"

She gave me a grim smile. "The Adamos and Gianollas are in an all-out war. Every day the newspapers give the account of more shootings in Little Italy. Three men have been killed since our gunfight, and I don't know how many wounded. The Gianollas must have thought the Adamos shot Tony."

I lowered my voice. "Tony? Is that who I shot?"

"He's *one* of the men you shot. The other was Vicente Scarpella, otherwise known as Three-Finger Vinnie. They fished him out of the river the next morning."

The kidnapper. I killed him. "I didn't hit Sam?"

She shook her head.

"Shit. Tell me at least that I killed Tony."

"I don't know what happened to him," she said. "The only reason I know it was Tony is I heard them say it. He was moving when they carried him back to the truck." She smiled. "And cursing. He sounded like he was in a lot of pain. Hopefully you hit something critical. But Dr. Miller checked with all the hospitals within an hour of the city, and he hasn't been to any of them."

"Has anyone been arrested for Joe's murder?"

"No."

"God *damn* it. What's Riordan doing?"

"Riordan," a man said, an Irish accent coloring the name, "is doing everything he can to help you."

I looked toward the door. Detective Riordan stood framed in the doorway, his scar a purple slash. "And I don't appreciate you taking the Lord's name in vain."

"Sorry," I said.

He walked up to us. "The doc said you were awake. Thought I'd come by and tell you what an imbecile you are."

"Thanks."

"You and Elizabeth taking on the Gianollas? Are you out of your mind, boy?"

My head pounded. "You could make a case for it, sure."

"You—need—help." He punctuated each word with a jab of his finger into my good shoulder.

"Okay, you're right. So what have you come up with?"

Elizabeth sat on the bed at my feet. Detective Riordan leaned against the wall at the head of the bed, pulled out a cigar, and stuffed it into his mouth. "First of all, the situation: It's clear that everyone in Little Italy knows who the Gianollas are—and because of that, no one will say a word, not even in places controlled by the Adamos or Pietro Mirabile. Nobody wants what happened to your friend happening to them."

"Do you know if they're looking for us?" I asked.

"No way to know that. Some good news though—Pinsky's been arrested and extradited to Boston. We won't see him any time soon."

"Boston? I thought you said he lived in New York."

"An extortion beef with the Teamsters. Their headquarters is in Boston."

"Well, that's a relief anyway."

Riordan pulled the cigar from his mouth and looked at the soggy end. "I don't know how much more information I'll be privy to. I'm an eyelash away from suspension. The chief raked me over the coals for horning in on Rogers's investigation of the Gianollas. I'm on deskwork for the foreseeable future." He took a deep breath. "However, Elizabeth and I talked about the possibility of trying the Adamos again."

I looked at Elizabeth. "What's the sense? They told Abe they wouldn't meet with me."

"Right," she said. "They won't meet with *you*. Abe didn't say anything about me."

I cocked an eye at Detective Riordan. "Assuming they cooperate, you'd work with Vito Adamo?"

He gave me a sad smile. "If the two of you can bury your feelings for the bastard, I guess I can overlook a statute or two."

"All right," I said. "I guess it's worth a try."

"Good." He pushed himself off the wall and turned for the door. "Glad you're feeling better," he said on his way out of the room.

Elizabeth stood and stepped up to me. "Dr. Miller said you're going to need to rest for at least a few more days. They'll keep until then. So rest."

I studied her face. The softness of her features had hardened—the lines of her brow, the cut of her mouth. She was suffering. I took her hand. "Thanks. For everything."

She looked down at me, biting her lip. "You're welcome. But listen to me, Will. You better heed my warning. I've already given you a second chance. And a third. There won't be another."

CHAPTER THIRTY

I was awakened the next morning by the door opening. My father peeked around the corner. When he saw my eyes open, he smiled and walked in. "How are you feeling?"

"Better."

"Good." He pulled up a chair and sat next to the bed. "Your mother and Mrs. Hume are fine."

"Yes, thank goodness. Elizabeth told me."

"I've made arrangements for you to join them in Cape Cod. The train—"

"No. I'm still going after the Gianollas."

His eyes widened. "They almost killed you. You can't be serious."

I looked away. "I am."

"You're done with the drugs?"

"Yes." The word didn't come out nearly as boldly as I thought it would.

"If it's the Teamsters you're worried about," my father said, "you needn't be. Whatever reticence the EAD may have had, they're throwing us their full support now. The factory and our home are practically fortresses. I won't lie to you, though. Labor tensions are high all around the city. It feels like something is going to break." He was quiet for a moment. "Let me bring in some Pinkertons to do the dirty work."

"No. This is personal. They killed Joe and threatened to kill you and Mother."

"You're as stubborn as Elizabeth. I tried talking her out of it, but she didn't listen either. You both seem bent on suicide. That's all this is, you know."

"No, it's not. They're going to pay for killing Joe. It's as simple as that."

"Lord." Shaking his head, he stood. "I never knew I had raised such a complete idiot." He turned and strode to the door before turning back to me. "You're actually going to do this?"

"I have to."

He looked down at the floor and then met my eyes again. "Do you really want to die?"

"No. But what would you have me say to Gina Curtiss? Gosh, I'm sorry Joe's dead, but I'm afraid to do anything about it? They might hurt me?"

He looked into my eyes a moment longer, then gave the slightest of nods and walked out the door.

I wasn't sure if that nod was one of approval, or at least acceptance, but I decided to believe it was. They killed Joe. Surely my father understood. I had to stop them.

That evening, Dr. Miller took off my sling and began working my arm through a range of motion. It hurt, but I gritted my teeth and took it. I had to get better. When he finished I settled in for the night. Left alone with my thoughts, I felt a hunger deep within me that reminded me of my time in the Detroit City Jail. I craved the peace of morphine, but I was determined to stay sober. Against all odds, Elizabeth was giving me another chance, and I wasn't blowing it this time.

After two more days Dr. Miller declared me fit to leave so long as I took an extended rest. He offered to make a reservation for me at the Glen Springs Hotel, but I told him I'd take care of it myself. It wasn't completely a lie. Perhaps someday I'd have the time to experience their healing mineral springs.

I phoned Elizabeth with the news. When she showed up at Dr. Miller's, she was wearing a simple navy blue skirt and white shirtwaist, with a large blue handbag slung over her shoulder and a wide-brimmed blue hat—an outfit that would be inconspicuous in most places. After a surreptitious wink at me, she told Dr. Miller she'd keep an eye on me while I recuperated.

I tugged the glove onto my hand and got dressed. Elizabeth had bought me a suit while I was laid up, made of dark gray cloth in coarse fiber that fit tighter than was fashionable—more in keeping with the immigrant populations in which we'd be trafficking. I put that on with a white shirt that had an attached collar, which took a little getting used to, a blue-and-white striped tie, and a black derby. I left the sling on the bed. Looking at myself in the mirror, I thought I could fit in.

Dr. Miller asked me to join him in an examination room. The minute he saw me, he said, "Where's the sling?"

"I feel okay now. I don't need it."

He put his hands on his hips. "Do you want to recover?"

"Yes." There didn't seem to be any other answer.

He left the room and came back a few seconds later with the sling. While he was putting it on me, he said, "Don't take it off, except when you change clothes or sleep. Come back and see me in a week." Giving me a bottle of aspirin, he said, "It's up to you now, Will."

Even though the thought of aspirin gave me little comfort, I nodded and stuffed the bottle in my pocket. After Elizabeth and I thanked him repeatedly, he wished us luck and excused himself. Elizabeth pulled a .32-caliber Browning pistol from her duster and handed it to me butt first. "It's loaded, and the safety's on."

"Is this the one I had?"

"No, I bought you another one. When we got here the only weapon you had was the switchblade. Which reminds me." She pulled the knife from her duster and gave it to me. I slipped it into my pocket. "By the time I went back to the hotel, my bag was gone. Not surprising, since I didn't think of it until two days after we left."

Tucking the gun into my belt, I said, "Thanks."

"I talked to Mr. Markovitz. He said he'd get Abe to meet with us tonight at eight. Detective Riordan's going to meet us there."

"Great." I fished in the left-hand pockets of my trousers and duster for my car key. "Where's the car?"

"Out front." She held up the key. "I'm driving."

"So, back to the Cosmopolitan?" I asked as we walked outside. Only a few puffy clouds drifted across the bright blue sky, and I guessed the temperature to be in the low eighties. I actually felt pretty good—much more energetic than I expected. I breathed deeply. The breeze smelled of freshly mown grass.

"I suppose we could stay there again," Elizabeth said. "It would be worth stopping there at least. Abe might have left us a message."

She helped me into the Torpedo, then started it up and pulled away from the curb with perfect control. It was as if she had broken a wild palomino. She was a much better driver than I had ever been, even before my hand was damaged. That was a difficult realization, since driving was the only claim I could make to possessing a skill.

Along the way, people were hanging red, white, and blue bunting from the windows of a number of the buildings. I looked at Elizabeth, the wind riffling her short hair under the hat. "Is it July already?"

We were coming up on a long line of cars. She slowed the Torpedo and glanced over at me. "Tomorrow's the Fourth."

I kept staring at her. She was so beautiful that, even after all these years, she still took my breath away.

Three blocks from Jefferson, traffic stopped dead. Horns blared, drivers shouted, and pedestrians cut between the automobiles. The traffic jam wasn't an unusual occurrence, but after ten minutes of sitting still, I got the attention of a man walking past, bent over from the weight of a canvas bag on his back. "Has there been an accident?" I shouted.

"Accident? It's the same all over town. Didn't you hear? The DUR's shut down—strike."

I groaned. When the streetcars *were* running, traffic in Detroit was ridiculous. Now it would be impossible to get around. Every vehicle in the city would be on the streets, not to mention a hundred thousand angry pedestrians.

I looked at Elizabeth. "I'm going to grab a newspaper." I eased out of the car and walked down to the corner, where I bought a *Free Press* from a newsboy. Front page center—DUR MOTORMEN AND CONDUCTORS ON STRIKE!

I skimmed the article while walking back to the car. When I climbed in, Elizabeth said, "What's going on?"

With my head buried in the paper, I said, "Division twenty-six of the Amalgamated Association of Street and Electric Railway Employees has gone out on strike. The DUR fired a motorman for 'careless operation.' He just happened to be on the union's executive committee."

I read further. "Shit." Looking up at Elizabeth, I said, "The Teamsters and the Hotel and Restaurant Employees Unions have already gone out in support of the DUR employees. Another half-dozen AFL unions are voting on it. This is what Pinsky was talking about. The Gianollas are making their move just in time for the Fourth of July. They're trying to shut down the city."

"All right." Elizabeth looked over her shoulder. "I'm turning around. We'll take the side streets." She jockeyed the car back and forth until she was able to swing around to the other side of the street. "What should we do with the car?"

"I think we'll have to leave it at the garage. Assuming we can get there."

She looked at me. "Can you handle the walk from the garage to the hotel?"

"If I can't walk for fifteen minutes, I'm certainly not going to be able to take on the Gianollas. What do you say we find out?"

Elizabeth drove past the cemetery before turning left on Charlevoix and zigzagging toward downtown. She forced the car through the intersections, squeezing around the myriad automobiles, trucks, wagons, carriages, coaches, horses, bicycles, and pedestrians all jockeying for position. My head pounded from the blaring horns and motorcar exhaust. It took an hour to make a ten-minute drive, but we finally arrived at the Detroit Electric garage. Elizabeth waited in the car while I walked inside to have someone open the overhead door.

Not a single person was in sight. Most of the charging bays were filled with Detroit Electrics, but there was none of the normal activity—chasers running cars in and out, chargers hooking them to the charging stations, prep men washing and waxing, cleaning the interiors. Even the grind of the air compressor had been silenced.

I opened the door, and Elizabeth drove in. She pulled the car off to the side, climbed out, and we exchanged a mystified look. I could just make out a voice in the back of the garage. Elizabeth and I began walking toward it.

"No, sir." A pause. "I understand, sir. We're doing everything we can to locate it. We'll have it to you in no time." It was Mr. Billings. We turned the corner to see him holding the telephone's candlestick to his mouth and the receiver to his ear. "Yes, sir. I'm sorry, sir." He hung up the telephone and sighed.

"What's going on?" I said.

"Lord. 'What isn't?' might be a better question. Most of my chasers disappeared right off the street—leaving the automobiles. I've got everybody else trying to find the cars and get them to their owners." He glanced at my arm in the sling. "What'd you do?"

"Oh, sprained my shoulder. Nothing serious."

He nodded. The telephone rang, and he gestured toward it. "Since the streetcars aren't running, every one of our customers wants their car—right now."

"I wish I could help, but . . ."

"Don't worry about it," he said. "Unless, of course, you've got fifty friends looking for something to do tonight." He glanced back at the telephone—still ringing.

I thought about the Bernsteins and their network. "I could probably come up with fifty, but you'd never get the cars back."

"Thanks, but no." He picked up the telephone again. "Detroit Electric garage, Mr. Billings speaking."

We walked up front, listening to Billings try to assuage the concerns of another customer. Elizabeth hung the Torpedo's key on the board, and we walked outside. This time she carried her bag. We headed up Woodward, crossing the street in the middle of hundreds of stalled vehicles.

"Look!" Elizabeth shouted to be heard over the cacophony of blaring car horns. She pointed at an ice truck and a coal wagon parked side by side in the middle of the street. "There's no driver in either one. Pretty soon nobody's going to get anywhere."

Fortunately, once we got off Woodward the cars quieted. The streets were congested, but traffic was moving. It took us only about ten minutes to make it to the Cosmopolitan. I was a bit winded but hid it from

Elizabeth. I didn't want to provide her with any excuse for going out on her own.

When we walked in, the old man behind the counter straightened. "Oh, my friend, come in, come in." He bustled out from behind the counter and waddled up to me. "You Mr. Anderson, yes?"

"What? Why?" We had used aliases when we checked in before.

"Why you no tell me you friend of Abe?"

I stared at him.

"Here. I have something." He hurried back to the counter and pulled out Elizabeth's valise.

She scowled at him. "You told me you hadn't seen it."

He gave her a sheepish look. "I didn' know you with boys. Sorry. Something else." He rang up a sale on the cash register. When the drawer opened, he pulled out a piece of paper and gave it to me.

Somebody wants to talk to you. See Mr. M at St. P. AB

I handed it to Elizabeth. She read it and said, "Seems Abe was a step ahead of us."

I shook my head. "When hasn't he been?"

Elizabeth came to get me at six thirty. I opened the window to check the temperature. It was still quite warm—mid-seventies perhaps—so I decided to leave the duster in the room. I pulled out the aspirin bottle and saw it contained one-gram tablets rather than powder. I chewed up four of the foul-tasting pills, made sure I had the switchblade, and checked the load in the .32. After I tucked it in my belt and pulled out my shirt to cover it, I worked the sling over my head and tossed it on the bed.

"Will," Elizabeth said, "you need the sling."

"No. I don't want to show Abe any more weakness than necessary. I'll put it on when we get back."

I fit my derby onto my head, and we headed out to grab some dinner. Whenever my arm moved, my shoulder hurt, but I tried not to show Elizabeth. At seven thirty, hoping to rendezvous with Detective Riordan prior to our meeting, we started our trek to Russell, heading toward the river among the throngs of forced pedestrians. We stopped when we reached Gratiot and looked through the crowd for Riordan. He was nowhere in sight.

"You go in," Elizabeth said. "I'll wait for Detective Riordan."

"Why don't I wait?" I said.

"Abe is going to be looking for you. He won't recognize me as a woman. Once Detective Riordan gets here, we'll come inside and sit elsewhere—just in case Abe is thinking of trying something."

"Why would he try anything?"

"Someone's meeting you tonight. It could be Vito Adamo, and he still thinks you killed his man. I'd guess Abe's alliance with Adamo will trump any arrangement you have with him."

"Good point. All right." I took her hand. "Just be careful."

She nodded and gave me a little push toward the restaurant. I walked the last fifty feet to the Saint Petersburg with my head on a swivel, but I saw no sign of Riordan. A pair of men were standing in the restaurant's little entryway, chatting away in Yiddish. Squeezing past them, I walked into the restaurant, hung my hat on the rack by the door, and sat in back at one of the few open tables.

The restaurant was full of families eating dinner, laughing, and talking in Yiddish. I inhaled as much of the other diners' cigarette smoke as I could and had a cup of coffee while I waited. Elizabeth walked in at five minutes after eight, gave me a mystified shrug, and took a seat at a tiny table near the front.

Riordan hadn't come?

I had two more cups of coffee before Abe and Joey Bernstein slid into chairs across from me. They looked agitated. "'Bout time you came around," Abe said. Joey chewed on a toothpick and gave me his normal stony stare.

"Sorry," I said. "I've been busy."

Abe leaned in close to me. "You heard about the war?"

"The Sicilians?"

"No, the Austro-Hungarians." He sneered. "A course the wops. Geez, Anderson."

"Yes. I've heard."

"I got somebody here wants to talk to ya."

"Who?"

"Need your gun first."

I sat back. "Why?"

"He's just bein' careful."

I thought for a moment before pulling out the .32 and handing it under the table to him.

A mellifluous voice with a strong Italian accent rang out behind me. "Hello, Mr. Anderson."

I turned. Ferdinand Palma stood by the kitchen door in a white suit and fedora, red handkerchief in his breast pocket and a matching carnation on his lapel. I wondered if he ever wore anything else. As one of Vito Adamo's lackeys, he made me a bit nervous, but even Adamo wouldn't dare try anything in a crowded restaurant. Palma nodded for the Bernsteins to get out of their chairs. They looked annoyed but did it. That told me a lot about their relationship with Palma. He kept looking at Abe. "You may go."

Abe looked like he was going to say something back but apparently thought better of it. "Markovitz'll have your gun," he said to me, and strode through the kitchen door, Joey right behind him.

Palma sat and leaned forward, hands clasped on the table. His hair practically dripped with pomade. "Signore Adamo wants to help you."

I needed his help more than he needed mine, but I wasn't going to cede all the power to Adamo. I laughed. "Sure. And the Tigers are going to win the World Series this year."

"I would suggest you no laugh. He wants to help you kill the Gianollas."

I sat back and hooked my good arm over the chair next to me. "He said he wouldn't work with me."

"Yes," Palma said. "He believed you killed Carlo Moretti. He now believes otherwise."

I sat up. "Why?"

"Thomas Riordan stopped by and gave me his thoughts." Palma must have seen the surprise on my face, because he added, "At one time I was a fellow detective. Thomas and I are not friends, but I know him to be a truthful man. Now, will you let Signore Adamo help you?"

"Why doesn't he do it himself?"

Palma looked uncomfortable. "He is having . . ." He thought for a moment. "There are complications."

"In other words, he needs *my* help."

He looked away. "*Sì.*"

"What does he want me to do?"

"He needs you to set a meeting with the Gianollas and tell him the time and place. That is all."

"The Gianollas will kill me when they see me."

Palma smiled. "You must only get them the message. You will not need to go to this meeting, only tell Signore Adamo the time and place."

"All right. How should I get in touch with him?"

Palma reached inside his coat and pulled out a folded piece of paper. "Call this number when you have set the meeting. The man who answers will put you in touch with Signore Adamo."

I tucked the paper into my shirt pocket and nodded. Without another word, Palma stood and walked to the front. He opened the door and took a quick glance in both directions before turning right and striding away.

Where the hell is Detective Riordan? I took a last gulp of coffee, pushed my chair back, and stood. Digging a quarter out of my pocket, I caught Elizabeth's eye and nodded toward the door.

Outside, a shot rang out. And then another. A man shouted, and a stream of people bolted past the front of the restaurant.

I ran to the door, shouting to Elizabeth, "Stay here!"

When I burst outside, people were scattering, running in all directions. On the street corner to my right, fifty feet away, lay Palma, half on the sidewalk, half in the street. His white fedora lay upside down on the pavement. A man and woman were ducking down behind a Model T roadster near him.

Detective Riordan ran across the street toward Palma, a pistol in hand.

What? I ran toward Palma. Riordan and I converged on the corner at the same time. "Why the hell did you shoot him?" I demanded.

Riordan's cold eyes met mine. He raised his gun and pointed it at my face.

CHAPTER THIRTY-ONE

Duck!" Riordan shouted.

I dropped to the pavement as he fired off three quick shots. A bullet coming from the other direction punched into a car behind me. Another whanged off the metal lamppost. I scrambled for cover while Riordan crouched and kept firing. When I'd gotten behind the building, I saw Elizabeth running down the sidewalk toward us. "No!" I yelled. "Get out of here!"

Riordan grabbed me and pulled me down the sidewalk toward the restaurant. "Go! I'm out of ammo!"

Ahead of us, Elizabeth turned and ran the other way. We'd gotten only thirty feet when a gun fired behind us. The bullet ricocheted off the sidewalk in front of me, kicking up a chip of cement. The gun fired again. A bullet whizzed over my shoulder. We caught up to Elizabeth just before the restaurant's entryway, and Riordan threw open the door and pushed her inside. The patrons were diving under tables. Slamming the door again, Riordan pressed me back against the bricks of the recessed entryway. It was just deep enough for us to stand by the side of the door without being seen. Flattening himself against the wall, Riordan pulled a big jackknife from his pocket and flipped out the blade. With his head turned toward the sidewalk, he held the knife in his fist, up near his shoulder.

A big man rushed around the corner, and Riordan plunged the knife into his throat, hitting him hard enough that his feet slipped out from underneath him. He slammed into the door, smashing the glass, and fell to the sidewalk, gurgling and clawing at his throat. I felt a jolt of recognition. He was the hulking man who had kidnapped me for the Gianollas.

Riordan grabbed the man's revolver from the pavement. He glanced around the corner of the entryway and stepped out, firing the gun again and again. I peeked out and saw a man clutch his shoulder and stagger.

When I turned back the big man was pulling a revolver from a shoulder holster, even with the knife lodged in his throat, blood pumping out around it. I dived for the gun as he swung it toward me, and it went off in a smoky explosion. I wrapped both hands around his and tried to wrench the gun away. It fired again. The bullet cracked into the doorjamb.

Though I pushed the gun away with all my strength, he kept twisting the barrel toward me. It was pointed at my arm and tracking to the center of my chest when I swung my elbow back as hard as I could against the haft of the knife, driving it deeper into his throat.

A gun fired. I stared at the end of his pistol as it tipped out of his hand and clattered to the pavement. Startled, I looked at his face. His right eye was gone, the socket pooling with blood. Bone shards and pieces of brain were sprayed on the bloody sidewalk to the left of his head. Elizabeth stepped through the broken door, her trembling gun still pointed at the dead man.

Pain overwhelmed me. Searing fire burned my hand and waves of pain stabbed into my shoulder. I fell back against the wall and rolled out onto the pavement, cradling my hand and cursing. I'd grabbed hold of the gun with my right hand. The pain was incredible.

Riordan rushed over and knelt down next to me. "Where are you hit?"

"I wasn't," I gasped.

"Elizabeth," he said. I looked at her. Her eyes were fixed on the big man's body. "Elizabeth," he said again. "Are you all right?"

She nodded but didn't take her eyes off the man she'd killed.

Riordan pulled me to my feet. "Get out of here. Both of you." He pushed me away.

I took Elizabeth's elbow and tried to get her to move, but she was frozen.

"Go, I said!" Riordan grabbed Elizabeth's arm, pulled her out of the entryway, and pushed her down the sidewalk. I took her arm again. After a step or two, she began running. We passed the body of Gianolla's other man, who lay sprawled across the sidewalk. A neat little hole was punched into his forehead, leaking blood into a pool on the pavement.

"I'm a policeman!" Riordan shouted to someone behind us.

We hurried past Palma's body on the corner. His mouth was slack, a thin line of saliva stretching between his lips. The red carnation on his lapel was torn, surrounded by a larger crimson bloom, like the flower had exploded. His leg twitched, but his eyes remained shut.

We ran up Russell, crossed the street, and cut down the first alley. Between the pain and the shadows, it was hard to see anything. I careened from a garbage can into a pile of wooden crates but kept my feet, kept my grip on Elizabeth. At the end of the alley, we stopped, and I peered around the corner before bolting across the street and down another darkened alleyway. I tried to elevate my right hand, but it hurt my shoulder too much. My shirt was sticking to my back. My heartbeat pounded in my hand. My fingers felt like they were going to explode.

We zigzagged through alleys, putting as much space between us and the Saint Petersburg as possible. Finally, perhaps ten blocks away, I spotted a wooden frame stairway leading to a rear entrance. We crawled underneath it and slid back into the shadows.

I put my arm around Elizabeth's shoulders. Her whole body was trembling. "We need to think, honey," I whispered. "What should we do?"

"I . . . I don't know." She sounded small, breathless. "How did they know we were going to be there?"

"I don't think they did. They must have followed Palma. If they knew we were here they would have killed us at the same time."

A shiver went through her.

"We'll be okay," I said. "Detective Riordan will keep us out of it." I remembered my derby on the hat rack, but there was nothing to tie it to me. "So long as we're not identified by witnesses, the Gianollas won't know we . . ."

"Killed their man," Elizabeth finished in a wooden voice.

"We've got to get off the streets," I whispered. "But we can't go home or back to the hotel. It's not safe." Every beat of my heart set a new wave of fire burning up my arm. I swallowed the groans that wanted to force themselves from my mouth.

"The mission," Elizabeth said. "We can stay there."

"But that's for men. What will you do?"

"The sisters will let me in. I'll stay with one of them."

The McGregor Mission sounded like a good idea to me. It was close, and it was full of men who looked at least as bad as I did. And nobody was going to look for us there. Tonight we'd be safe, and tomorrow we'd call Vito Adamo and work up a plan.

I remembered the aspirin and swallowed half a dozen; then we crawled out from under the stairs and stood in the light of the streetlamp, looking each other over. Her dress was rumpled, but other than that she looked fine, so long as you stayed away from her eyes. She thought I looked enough of a bum to fit in at the mission. I wasn't sure if it was her sense of humor coming back or if she was serious, but I left it.

Few people were on the streets, but we struggled to look like a couple out for a stroll. As much as my hand and shoulder hurt, I don't think I pulled it off very well, but no one stopped us. We threaded through back alleys for fifteen minutes before turning a corner and seeing the Mc-Gregor Mission, a narrow three-story red-brick building. A line of perhaps twenty men stood outside, shuffling forward as another of their ilk was either allowed in for the night or sent away with a stern admonition.

Elizabeth put a hand on my arm. "I'll wait until you get inside and then go around back. If the father doesn't let you in we'll have to figure out something else."

"Why wouldn't he let me in?"

She shrugged. "He's not always the most rational sort. Now go." She gave me a little push.

"When will we meet up?"

"They roust everyone at six for breakfast. We'll talk then."

I held my arms out and took a step toward her, ignoring the flare in my shoulder. She let me hug her and returned it, though her grip was tentative. "I'll see you in the morning," I said. "If you need anything, you know where to find me."

"No offense, Will, but the sisters might be better company for me tonight."

I nodded and walked to the end of the line. Father McGregor's booming Scottish brogue cut through the murmured conversation around me. "Paddy! Good to see you again, lad. How's the missus?" A minute later, "No, sir, not drunk! Be gone with you!" An old man walked past me, away from the mission, muttering curses. McGregor kept up the patter as I moved forward one step at a time, staring at the pavement. I peeked up when he started talking to the man in front of me. The priest's long gray hair bobbed in rhythm with his speech. He didn't quite have a John the Baptist look, but he was tall and thin with wide eyes, a bony face, and a somewhat fevered countenance—the kind of man who might cause you to think about moving to the other side of the street if you saw him approaching.

The man in front of me walked inside the mission with McGregor's blessing, and the father cast his gaze on me. "Yeh've been here before, haven't you?"

I shook my head. "No, sir." I did my best to sound like a poor man. My accent struck me as somewhere between Black Irish and Black Death.

He cupped his chin in his hand, studying me. "How do I know ya then?"

I looked at the pavement. "Don't know, Father. I been around."

"Yer not drunk?"

"No."

"What happened to your arm?"

I realized I was cradling my right arm in my left. "Hurt my shoulder workin'."

"What kind of work you do?"

"Ice." It just popped into my head. "Ice delivery."

"Can't do that with a bum shoulder, now, can you?"

"No, sir."

"Let me guess. They fired you after you got hurt."

"Yes, Father."

"What's that on yer neck?" He gestured toward the right side of my throat. "Don't look like dirt."

I ran a hand over my neck and looked at my palm. It was streaked with blood.

A lead weight dropped in my gut. "Oh." I pushed down my revulsion, forced out a laugh, and started babbling. "My shoulder. One of the big tongs at the factory got me. Can't get it to stop."

He reached out and touched the left elbow of my jacket. His finger came away tacky with blood. "Yer really bleedin'. Look at me, son."

I raised my eyes. He appraised me for perhaps a quarter of a minute before nodding toward the doorway. "See one of the sisters for bandages. No smokin', no drinkin', and if you can help it, no fartin' either. Go on in. I think there may be some soup left if you're hungry."

"Thank you, Father."

In any other setting, McGregor would likely have recognized me. But no one expected Will Anderson to be sleeping at a charity mission. I was so out of context as to be almost invisible. I climbed the final steps into the first room, a large dining hall with long tables running front to back and a serving window at the far end. A few men sat at the tables with bowls in front of them.

I climbed the stairway toward the second floor, and a mass of noise filtered down to me—men talking, laughing, shouting. When I reached the top of the steps, I turned the corner into a huge room with perhaps four hundred cots lined up in tidy rows. Men lay or sat on about two-thirds of the beds while a few of them milled about, talking to one another.

My pulse was pounding so hard in my hand I thought it would rip the glove open. I headed for the bathroom. The smell was horrid. The toilet arrangement was that of a long trough covered by a stained board with six holes cut through it—similar, actually, to the toilets in the Anderson Electric factory. I shrugged off my coat and washed the big man's blood off my neck. Then I peeled off my shirt and did my best to wash off the blood, both the big man's and mine that had leaked out around the bandages on my shoulder.

Other men came in and used the facilities, but I hid my hand from them, and they all left me alone. I washed the blood off myself, my shirt, and my coat. Finally I set my jaw and worked the glove off my hand. My thumb and first two fingers were purple and swollen, like sausages ready to burst. The other two, though nothing but gnarled scar tissue, had turned a darker shade of red. I looked at myself in the mirror. My eyes were sunken. My face looked bony, nearly skeletal. I made a pact with myself to avoid mirrors for a while. There was no getting the glove back on. I'd have to keep my hand in my pocket and hope I'd be able to keep it hidden well enough to avoid notice.

I took a cot near the back wall and watched the activity for a while, trying to take my mind off my pain. The men were unshaved and dirty, smelling of body odor and stale tobacco, some with whiskey working its way through their pores. They spoke in a polyglot of languages, none really distinguishable over the drone. Four nuns in black habits worked the room, getting men into beds, taking away cigarettes, scolding recalcitrants. Eventually all the men climbed onto cots, and the father came up and said a prayer before shutting off the lights.

I lay awake a long while. My hand and shoulder throbbed, and my mind raced. I got little sleep. Awake was better than asleep. When I did manage to fall off, my dreams were haunted by gushing fountains of blood.

Something exploded into my kidney. My body arched back, my hand reaching to ward off the blow. Again, something smashed into my lower back. I fell off the cot and landed on my right shoulder, crying out from the pain.

"Is 'at him?" a voice growled.

"Yes, it is," Father McGregor said.

"Get up, ya jackass," the first man said. There was just enough light to see McGregor and a policeman standing over me.

"What?" I held up my left hand in front of me. My eyes watered from the pain.

The policeman was a thin man with long handlebar mustaches. Raising the club over his head, he said again, "Get up."

"All right, all right." I struggled to my feet. "What do you want?"

He grabbed my arm and shoved me forward.

"Hey, let 'im alone," a voice called. Another man yelled at the cop to leave me be.

He just shoved me again and shouted, "I'll bring the whole lot of you in if you don't shut your holes!"

The men grumbled, but no one made an issue of it. He pushed me to the stairs, down to the first floor, and outside, where a fat policeman stood in the light of a streetlamp with his back to us, hand resting on his holstered pistol.

The other cop pulled me down the stairs. "Murphy, we got our man."

"Zat right, Scotty? Let's have a look."

Murphy? I began to turn toward him. The first cop rammed the truncheon into my stomach, doubling me over, and then shoved me to the ground. I struggled to catch my breath. Through the tears, I saw the two of them standing over me.

"Don't look like much, does he now, Scott?" Murphy said. "Whattaya think? Shoot him and toss him in the river, or bring him in?"

"Murphy," I gasped, "it's me, Will Anderson."

He stared at me, dumbfounded. "Anderson? *Jaysus* Christ . . ."

"I can explain. Just let me talk to you for a minute."

The thin cop looked at Murphy. "You know this asshole?"

Murphy met his partner's gaze. "Take a hike, Scotty. Lemme talk to him a minute."

The other man frowned at him, shook his head, and walked away. Murphy helped me to my feet. "Christ, Anderson, look at ya."

I was still bent over from the blow to the stomach. "It's a disguise, Murphy, and it's a long story."

"Well, ya better start the tellin'. We got a couple'a dead bodies over on Gratiot, and you're the guy stinkin'a blood down at the mission."

"Listen, Murphy, I need a favor. Let me walk. I'll make it worth your while."

He scratched his head with his billy club. "Don't know about that. They're sayin' Tommy Riordan and a pair of accomplices murdered those guys and put Ferdinand Palma into a coma."

A shock went through me. "What?"

"You and Riordan are old buddies."

"Riordan wouldn't murder anyone. If he killed somebody it would be in the line of duty."

Murphy gave me a big smile. "Ain't what the witnesses are sayin'. Him and some Annie Oakley turned Gratiot into a shootin' gallery." He rubbed his chin. "Sergeant Rogers has been lookin' for ya anyway. If I hand ya over to him, it's prob'ly worth a promotion for me. They might even make me a dick. What's he want you for, anyway?"

"How much?" I was already pulling my wallet from my coat.

He snatched it away from me and pulled out all the bills with a pudgy fist. Handing the wallet back, he riffled through the money. "Hundred, two, hmm." He pursed his lips, pushing his bottlebrush mustache up against his nose, then shot a glance down the street in the direction his partner had gone. "Tell ya what. Make this a down payment, I'll let ya off."

"Done." I didn't know where I'd get any more money, but that was the least of my concerns.

"Ah, don't know why I got a soft spot for you, Willy, my boy, but awright. Enjoy your holiday."

I didn't wait for him to tell me twice. Holding my stomach, I trotted off down the street, in the opposite direction his partner had gone.

CHAPTER THIRTY-TWO

I hid in an alley six or seven blocks away, behind a dozen overflowing garbage bins. I'd go back for Elizabeth at six. I wrapped a rag around my right hand and tried to fall asleep again, but the pain was too great. I swallowed another handful of aspirin.

While I lay there, I tried to decide what to do. The cops were after me—or rather the gang squad was looking specifically for *me*, while the rest of them were after the people who helped Detective Riordan kill the men outside the Saint Petersburg last night, particularly the female accomplice. If this didn't end soon, we'd have no chance of getting the Gianollas out of our lives. I had to get Vito Adamo to help us now. I hoped he was serious about working together.

Near six I crept over to an alley near the mission and watched the front door. A few minutes later, Elizabeth ran around from the back, her eyes scanning the street. When she looked my way I waved and caught her attention.

She hurried over to me and grabbed my arm. "I heard about the police. I can't believe I slept through it. I thought you . . . I'm so glad you're still here."

"I knew one of the cops. He let me go."

"That was lucky."

"Maybe our luck is changing."

She nodded and gave me a tentative smile. "It probably can't change for the worse. Say, why don't we find a place for you to hole up for a little while. I'll get us some breakfast and find a place we can make that call."

"Sounds good. About twenty cups of coffee would be a good start." I nudged her arm. "How are you doing?"

She stared at the brick wall opposite us. "I had to do it. He was going to kill you."

I nodded. "I know it's not enough, but thank you."

"It feels . . . cold. Inside. At the pit of my stomach. I took someone's life."

"Like you said, he was going to kill me. You did what you had to do."

She nodded and glanced at me. "I know. I keep telling myself that. It's just going to take a while."

We headed over to the alley in which I'd spent the rest of the night, and I tucked myself back in behind the trash cans. "I'll be back soon," Elizabeth said. She bent down and gave me a kiss on the cheek before turning and leaving the alley.

She returned about fifteen minutes later with a pair of coffee mugs in one hand and a heaping plate of scrambled eggs and toast in the other. She handed me the mugs and sat next to me. "They charged me a dollar for the plate and mugs, but I thought it a worthwhile investment," she said. "I wouldn't give them the two dollars they wanted for silverware, so dig in."

I gave her one of the mugs, took a piece of toast, and loaded a pile of eggs on top. I wolfed it down and sat back, savoring the coffee. "Thank you. I can't tell you how good this all tastes."

"Funny, isn't it?" she said. "If you'd have gotten a meal like this in a normal circumstance you'd probably have complained about it. But now it's like eating at Delmonico's."

I swallowed another precious sip of coffee. "I wouldn't know about Delmonico's, but I take your point. Our appreciation of things is relative to our circumstances."

"Good," she said with a smile. "Now you need to figure out how to appreciate things regardless of your circumstances."

I wasn't in the mood for a lecture, but I just shrugged. "Did you find a phone?"

She nodded. "There's one at a store just down the block."

"I'm going to see if I can get hold of Detective Riordan too. I hope he hasn't been arrested. We need his help."

We lapsed into silence. When we finished eating, we left the plate and mugs out where someone would find them, and headed over to a general store. The pay telephone was screwed into the wall, like at the Cosmopolitan. I checked my pockets and came up with thirty-seven cents. I dropped a nickel into the coin slot, and the arm over the receiver released. A few seconds after I gave the operator the number, Mrs. Riordan answered the phone.

"Hello?" This time her voice was cautious from the first word.

"Mrs. Riordan, this is Will. Can you talk?"

"No, Mrs. Callaghan," she said in an overly cheery voice. "I'm afraid I'm not up to a trip downtown at four o'clock. My little ones haven't even broken in their old shoes yet."

Obviously, someone was listening. "How can I get in touch with your husband?" I whispered.

"Why, you'd think those children of yours were horses, Mrs. Callaghan, the way they go through shoes. You enjoy your shopping trip this evening. Bye now." She hung up.

I set the receiver on the hook and gave Elizabeth a puzzled look. "Someone was there. Almost certainly the cops. She gave me a message, but I don't have any idea what it was."

"What did she say?"

"She called me Mrs. Callaghan and said she couldn't go shoe shopping downtown at four o'clock."

"Four o'clock must be when Detective Riordan can meet you. Callaghan—is there a Callaghan's shoe store downtown?"

"I've never heard of it." Then it hit me. Callaghan—shoes—horses—downtown. "She said my children must be horses to go through so many shoes. Callaghan's Livery on Fort Street. My father used to keep Comet there. Detective Riordan will be there at four."

"Thank God he didn't get arrested."

I nodded and dropped another nickel into the slot. I gave the operator Adamo's number this time. An Italian man answered the phone. *"Pronto."*

"I need to speak with Vito Adamo. This is Will Anderson."

"Uno momento." The receiver clanked against a hard surface.

Perhaps a minute later, Vito Adamo came on the line. His normally deep voice was thin, strident. "What was your involvement in Palma's shooting?"

"What? He gave me this number, he left, and Gianolla's men shot him." I cupped my hand over the bell of the telephone. "We killed *them*. In self-defense."

Adamo let off a string of Italian curses ending with the word *Gianolla.* Then he said, "If you are lying to me—"

"I'm not lying. Why would I shoot Palma?"

"Because he works with me."

"I've been trying to get you to work with *me*, remember? Last night Palma asked me to help you kill the Gianollas. I agreed to call you. He left and was shot down."

He blew out an explosive breath. "You want the Gianollas dead, yes?"

"Yes."

"Where are you?"

"Why?"

"We have some planning to do. I will send a car to pick you up."

I hesitated. He had thought I was involved in Palma's shooting. But at this point what did I have to lose? With both the Gianollas and Adamos after me, I was already as good as dead. "Bagley and Third," I said.

"Excellent." The receiver clicked, and the line went dead.

We left the store and walked into the nearest alley. "Okay," I said. "Where are you going to go? I'll come for you after this meeting."

She laughed and shook her head. "No. I'm going with you."

"Elizabeth, it's too—"

"—dangerous, I know," she said, folding her arms over her chest. "I'm going, and that's that."

I decided not to waste my time arguing. We waited in the nearest alley and kept our eyes peeled. Half an hour later a dark blue E-M-F touring car edged up to the corner. I took a surreptitious glance at the inside. The top was up, the driver hidden in the shadows. I thought it was likely one of Adamo's men, but there was no way to be sure.

"Wait here a minute," I told Elizabeth, and stepped out into the sunshine, wandering out near the road. I watched the car from the corner of my eye for a few minutes, still not sure if I should approach it. People were starting to get out into the streets, and they streamed past, heading for some holiday amusement.

"Signore Anderson," a voice said. I turned around. Vito Adamo's brother Salvatore stood before me. I hadn't laid eyes on him in nearly two years. He was still a young man, perhaps thirty, but looked at least ten years older. Dark circles painted the undersides of his eyes, and he was thin, sickly-looking. His ragged mustaches hung over his upper lip. He looked like a man on the run. "Open your coat," he said.

I held my coat open with my left hand. He pulled out the right side, looking for a weapon.

"Turn around."

I did. He pulled up my coattail.

"We should go," he said. "It's not safe."

I nodded Elizabeth over. She ran to us, and we hurried to the E-M-F. Angelo was in the driving seat. The rest of us piled into the back. No sooner had we gotten in than the car sped away from the curb. Angelo turned down the first alley and raced into Little Italy, finally stopping in front of a warehouse. He jumped out and opened an overhead door. When he climbed back in, we bumped over the threshold into the darkened building. Angelo shut off the car and ran back to close the door.

Salvatore hopped out and flipped a switch, turning on the lights. Elizabeth and I stepped down onto the concrete floor, and Angelo gave me a thorough search. He relieved me of my switchblade and then held out his hand for Elizabeth's purse. She glanced at me. I nodded. We had to cooperate.

"That way," Salvatore said, motioning toward the back of the building. He walked us to a wooden door, opened it, and said, "Wait here."

I looked inside to see a small room with no furniture, probably an office when the warehouse was in use. "Why?"

"Make sure no one follow," he said.

We walked in, and he closed the door behind us. Elizabeth crouched down and used her palm to sweep dust off a spot on the floor before sitting down. I walked over to her, put my back against the wall, and slid down to the floor.

"Don't mention anything about Riordan to the Adamos," I whispered. "We need an ace in the hole."

She nodded. A few moments later, she said, "My Lord, Will. Did you ever think . . ."

I grunted out a laugh. "Hard to imagine that only a few years ago we were a couple of rich kids without a worry in the world."

She nodded, and after a few moments her right hand searched out my left. When she found it, she gripped it tightly. After a few minutes, I let go and wrapped my arm around her shoulders. I believe it was the first time I'd ever touched her without it being sexual. In the past, regardless of the situation, whatever touch I'd been allowed made me crazy with lust. Now it was different. Compassion? Friendship?

Salvatore and Angelo came for us perhaps half an hour later and led us to an open-bed delivery truck stacked with beer kegs. Salvatore gestured at the truck. "We will drive to my brother. Get in back." We climbed onto the bed and sat in the center, in an open space surrounded by kegs. Salvatore climbed up after us. "You got to be blindfold." Elizabeth and I traded a glance before we both nodded. He tied handkerchiefs around our heads.

The engine started, the overhead door screeched, and the truck pulled onto the road. From the sound of the engine echoing off the tall brick walls, I could tell we spent more time in alleys than we did on roads. After a number of turns, the truck finally stopped. I pulled off the blindfold. We were in an alleyway between a pair of three-story redbrick buildings. We could have been anywhere.

We climbed down and walked into the back entrance of the building to the left of the truck. After climbing two flights of stairs in silence, we walked about thirty feet down a hallway. Salvatore knocked on a door— three fast knocks, two slow.

Filipo Busolato cracked open the door and peered out. A moment later, Vito Adamo stood in front of us, holding his derby with both hands like a man asking for a handout. "I apologize, Mr. Anderson, Miss Hume, for the inconveniences. It is an unfortunate but necessary part of my life at the moment."

He stepped back and held out his arm toward a kitchen table. I looked around as I took the two steps necessary to reach it. We were in a small one-room apartment with four cots in the back, a large shelf along a side wall filled with supplies, and a single table in the front of the room with a chair on each side. I glanced out the window. A red-brick wall stood perhaps thirty feet away. We were in a Detroit apartment building, almost certainly in Little Italy, perhaps the same one Carlo Moretti had lived in. It was almost funny that Vito Adamo had been forced to live like this. I turned back to him, unable to resist a jab. "Nice place."

He smiled a weary smile. "Believe me that I would prefer to be with my wife and children."

He still looked good. The skin on his handsome face was perfect, his mustaches were firmly waxed in place, and not a single strand was awry in his thick shock of black hair. He wore a stylish gray suit with an ivory silk waistcoat. Dark curls spilled over the open neck of his shirt. This was the first time I'd seen him without a tie. His eyes looked haunted. I could see that his edges were beginning to fray.

He turned to his men and said something in Italian. Angelo and Busolato left. Salvatore stood near the door, watching us.

Elizabeth and I sat at the table. A notepad lay atop it, open to an amateurish pencil drawing of a stiletto plunging into someone's back. An Italian caption had been written in underneath. Adamo sat across from us, flipped the notepad shut, and gave us a sheepish smile. "At times I fancy myself to be a writer. I am trying my hand at the dime novel."

"Really," I said. "What's it about?"

"Oh"—he waved at me, embarrassed—"it's only childish nonsense."

"No, really. I'm interested."

He shook his head slightly but said, "It's the story of a boy who is imprisoned for a crime he did not commit, and the revenge he takes on the men who wronged him."

I looked at him through narrowed eyes. "The story sounds familiar."

A hint of a smile played around his mouth. "Well, I suppose I have to get my inspiration somewhere."

I looked at him for a moment before saying, "So now you believe I didn't kill Moretti?"

"Yes. Though if Ferdinand was wrong I will kill you myself." He tossed off the sentence as casually as if he were commenting on the weather. "But that is not why we are here. I would like to apologize to you, Miss Hume, and you, Mr. Anderson, for the problems I have caused you. Miss Hume, I truly liked your father and, believe it or not, considered him a friend. I had no idea who killed him until after the . . . rest of your ordeal."

She didn't respond.

He turned to me. "And Mr. Anderson. If I could take back the history between us, I would. But, of course, that is not possible. So here we are, all targeted for murder by those *contadinos*."

My face must have shown my confusion because he added, "Peasants. The Gianollas"—he feigned spitting on the floor—"are nothing but peasants, brutal and stupid." He looked at me again. "Mr. Anderson, I am a bit confused about your involvement in this matter. I believe the Gianollas had Esposito confess to Carlo's murder, thereby making you beholden to them. But what did they have to gain?"

"The Gianollas wanted me to get the Teamsters Union into Detroit Electric. And they wanted me to help them kill you."

He smiled once more. "And how were you supposed to do that?"

"They were going to offer you a piece of the Teamsters. When you got comfortable, they'd kill you and wipe out your operation."

Nodding, he said, "You must help me rid the world of their stink." His eyes shone. "We will kill them together."

"How?" I asked.

He sat back in his chair, looking down at the table. A few seconds later, he glanced up at me again. "You are going to give them exactly what they want."

Mystified, I shook my head and shrugged.

"There is one thing they want most." Vito Adamo smiled again. "Me."

CHAPTER THIRTY-THREE

Adamo looked out the corner of his eye at Elizabeth. I followed his gaze. She was looking at him with a grim expression.

"Do you have a problem with this, Miss Hume?"

"Before I answer that, I'd like the truth from you on one thing: What happened to the eyewitness at your murder trial?"

"Oh." He shook his head. "There was no eyewitness. Filipo and I were innocent. No doubt the Gianollas paid someone to testify, and this person decided"—he looked at me with a question in his eyes—"that the better part of valor is discretion? Do I have that right?"

I nodded. "Straight out of Shakespeare."

Elizabeth didn't look convinced. She glared at him but finally said, "I'm willing to do what we must to get the Gianollas out of our lives, but you can't seriously think I would forgive you for what you did."

"The . . . drugs?"

"No. That was my fault. But whether you directly assisted John or not, you helped kill my father. You used me as bait to lure Will almost to his death. Your man helped John kill Will's friend and nearly kill both of us." She sat back and folded her arms across her chest. "Is that enough to hate you for?"

His expression didn't change. "For what it is worth, it was business."

"I am willing to put it behind me for the good of Will's family," she said. "But don't expect me to like you."

"Fine," Adamo said. "Now, shall we decide how to kill the Gianollas?"

We both nodded. I realized with surprise that my hatred of this man was slipping. I had to remember Wes.

"They will say they will trade your lives for those of the Adamo brothers. Of course they will kill you, but not until we are gone. You need to set up the meeting they were asking for."

"I agree," I said. "The way I see it, they'll still want to pretend to offer you a piece of the Teamsters. They won't tell you the meeting site until the last moment and will ambush you, and probably me, at the meeting."

"Yes," he said. "Therefore, we must move the meeting to a place more of our liking."

"They won't go for it. If the odds aren't on their side, they won't meet with you."

"We must even the odds," he said. "I am willing to face them man to man, but I will not help them kill me."

I snapped my fingers. "The Bernsteins. You know the Bernstein boys, don't you?"

"They work for us occasionally."

"They have a big network of kids around Detroit. We could spread them out around the Gianollas' territory to keep an eye on what they do."

"I do not know," Adamo said. "Do you trust the boys?"

I thought about it. "Abe's come through for me. He could have handed me over to the Gianollas, but he helped us. I think so long as there's money in it, they'll do their job."

He absently twirled the end of one of his waxed mustaches. "With enough advance knowledge, we could still hold the meeting at their chosen location. The Gianollas will be overconfident. Our men could ambush *them*."

"Exactly."

"Make the arrangements with the boys. Until we have rid ourselves of the peasants, I am taking no chances." Adamo pushed back his chair and stood. "Contact the Gianollas. Set up the meeting."

Elizabeth and I got up from our chairs.

Adamo took me by the arm and led me to the door. "Do you still have the telephone number Palma gave you?"

"Yes."

"When they set the meeting time, call that number. Do not talk to the boys until you absolutely need to." He glanced at Salvatore before looking at Elizabeth with a grimace. "I am afraid we will need to blindfold you again for the drive. They will bring you wherever you would like."

Salvatore opened the door. Busolato walked in, and we joined Angelo in the hall. We had taken only a few steps when Vito Adamo called out from behind us. "Miss Hume? I *am* sorry. When this is over, perhaps I can find a way to make amends."

As we continued toward the steps, I marveled at the man's charisma. A phrase went through my head: *The enemy of my enemy is my friend.*

But Vito Adamo was not my friend. I needed to remember that.

I had them drop us off in front of the Western Union office on Grand Boulevard just up the street from Electric Park. Salvatore gave me my switchblade and handed Elizabeth her purse, and the car sped away. Elizabeth opened the purse and rooted around inside. Satisfied, she latched it shut.

"Do you still have the thirty-two?" I said.

She nodded.

"Could I borrow it?"

We walked to the nearest alley, where she pulled out the gun and gave it to me. I tucked it in my belt at the small of my back. Walking into the Western Union office, I could hear girls screaming from atop one of Electric Park's roller coasters. It made me long for those simple days of youth, when my biggest concerns were my grade in mathematics and whichever girl I had the vapors over at the time.

We sent a telegram to my father, telling him we were still all right. After that I had Elizabeth change a dollar, and I used the pay phone in the lobby to call the Gianollas' grocery in Ford City. I felt exposed and had to keep myself from constantly looking around for them here. The operator began the process. I waited a few minutes while the connection was established. A man answered in Italian. At first he denied any connection with the Gianollas, but when I said I could deliver the Adamo brothers he told me to phone back in two hours. Then he hung up.

We left the office and, after Elizabeth paid the twenty-five-cent admission fee for each of us, walked through Electric Park. It was packed with holiday revelers enjoying a rare Friday off from work. Miles of red, white, and blue bunting hung from the coaster supports, ribbons of the same colors fluttered from the roofs of buildings, and banners proclaiming HAPPY INDEPENDENCE DAY! hung in great arcs over the midway.

Negotiating the crowded walkways was difficult, particularly as we weren't paying much attention. Elizabeth was quiet and moody, and I was nervous. I used all but a nickel of my remaining change at a concession stand to buy her some pink fairy floss and myself a bag of popcorn. She plucked small dabs of the sugary candy and popped them into her mouth while we wandered. The only amusement we allowed ourselves was the scale model re-creation of the Johnstown Flood, which we watched several times. It was a long two hours before we returned to the Western Union office.

Elizabeth changed another dollar to make the phone call. The same man answered. "They will meet you. Michigan Central station on Jefferson. Thirty minutes."

"That's not what—"

"If you don' show, they will know you are lying." The phone clicked.

I set the receiver back onto the hook and told Elizabeth what he said.

"We need someone to back us up," she said. "It's insane to just walk into their trap. What if they *do* know we're responsible for the deaths of their men?"

"Give me an alternative. They're not going to stop until we're all dead. How long are we going to be able to avoid that?" I thought for a moment. "And if we get the chance, we're going to kill the Gianollas and end this."

Jefferson was jammed with traffic, so we joined a few thousand pedestrians heading for the big parade on Woodward. Most had on festive hats and some sort of patriotic garb. I stood out in the crowd with my smelly and wrinkled immigrant outfit. We hurried down the street.

"We shoot," I said, "only if we can get both of them. They'll keep coming if we only kill one."

Elizabeth nodded. "Assuming Tony is still alive."

"Right."

Bang! Bang! Bang! Explosions, like gunfire, came from my immediate right. I jumped and almost threw Elizabeth to the ground before seeing it was children blowing off firecrackers. Hundreds of people milled about the ferry landing, pushing into the queues for the dozen steamers taking holiday revelers to Tashmoo Park, Bob-Lo Island, or perhaps just a jaunt out on the river. A huge crowd lined Woodward just inland from the ferry landing, waiting for the parade to begin. Between the two was a huge knot of people we needed to pass through.

I looked at my watch. Ten more minutes to get through this crowd wasn't enough. I began shouldering and pushing my way through. Now the explosions began in earnest as firecrackers, roman candles, and homemade fireworks boomed and whistled and cracked.

We made it to the train station almost exactly thirty minutes after the telephone call. I had the pistol in my left-hand coat pocket, ready to shoot if I saw the brothers. Elizabeth hung back with a hand inside her purse. People hurried in all directions, cutting through the mob for one track or another, or heading out into downtown Detroit. The tile floor, high plaster ceiling, and brick walls made the large room an echo chamber. The sounds of shoes striking tile, shouted conversations, and train whistles created a booming cacophony. I was surprised the train engineers and conductors hadn't gone out in a sympathy strike, but the trains looked to be running as usual.

I felt a gun barrel in the middle of my back. I turned to see Sam Gianolla staring at me with those killer's eyes.

"Bang, bang, ya dead," he said with a nasty smile.

I reached behind me. My hand was closing on the butt of my pistol when he jabbed his gun barrel into my back and said, "Gimme your piece. Slow."

I pulled Elizabeth's gun from my belt and handed it to him. All around us, people hurried past, paying us no notice. It was bizarre.

"That way," Sam said, jabbing me in the back with his gun. I waded through the crowd, hoping Elizabeth wasn't too far behind. Sam steered me toward platform 3, where a large crowd was boarding a green Michigan Central passenger train, its smokestack billowing oily smoke into the blue sky. We climbed up the steps into the nearly full car, and he nodded toward the back. I walked down the aisle to a pair of open seats and glanced at Sam. He shook his head and nudged me along, stopping me at the end of the car by the steps.

I turned and stared into his eyes. "You're going to pay for killing Joe."

"Fuck you talkin' 'bout?"

"Don't even try."

He smiled at me. "I killed a lot a guys name Joe. Anyone in pa'ticlar?"

I shook my head, smoldering. "You better watch your back."

Across from us, a train was beginning to pull away from platform 4. Only four cars were connected to the engine, three passenger cars in front of the caboose.

Sam grabbed me and shoved me off the train. "Move."

I nearly fell on my face but just caught my balance before I did. He grabbed my arm and pulled me along with him to the other platform. We hopped up on the step of the last passenger car as the train pulled away from the station, heading west toward Ford City. I glanced back to see if Elizabeth had spotted us, but she was nowhere to be found.

I was on my own. Sam pushed me up the steps into the car. When I turned the corner, three guns were pointed at me, one by a thug in front, another by a thug in the back, and the third held by Tony Gianolla, who sat in one of the upholstered blue seats in the middle.

He was alive after all.

"Frisk him," Tony said.

The man in front searched me and took my knife. Sam gave him my gun and pushed me forward, grabbed me by both shoulders, and shoved me down into the seat across from his brother. Tony's right leg stuck out straight in front of him. He didn't have a cast, but I took some small satisfaction in knowing I had at least hurt him.

I gestured toward his gun. "Didn't think you guys were that scared of me."

He pulled back the left side of his coat and stuck his gun into a shoulder holster. "This is your goddamn fault, shithead. Why didn' you meet with Pinsky?"

"My father and I both would have been there, but the cops picked me up."

"So why wasn' *he* there?"

"Because he didn't know where the meeting was."

"Why didn' you tell him, shithead?"

"I should have, but I didn't think I had enough time."

He looked over my shoulder, then back at me. "You had what, two fuckin' weeks? That ain't enough time?"

"No, Pinsky moved the meeting at the last minute."

Eying me, Tony sat back. "He didn' tell me nothin' 'bout that."

"I can't help what he told you. His secretary called and told me to go to a house in Hamtramck."

"Hamtramck? Why the fuck would he be in Hamtramck?"

"I don't know. Maybe you should ask him." How these idiots could be successful criminals was beyond me. They didn't even communicate with one another.

Tony stared at me for a long moment. Shaking his head, he said, "Don' matter now, anyway. D'ja find the Adamos?"

I nodded.

"Good. You gotta set up a meetin' with 'em."

"So you can kill them?"

"Things have changed." He looked down at the floor in front of him. "We're losin' too many men. It's costin' us money. We'll let you off the hook—no Teamsters, no nothin'—if you get Adamo to meet with us so we can make peace."

"You're actually going to meet with them."

His heavy-lidded eyes never wavered from mine. "Yeah. We need to end the killin'."

I almost laughed in his face. I controlled that but couldn't keep the beginnings of a smile from appearing.

He leaned forward and spoke in a somber tone. "There's enough action for them *and* us. If we kill each other off, the Yids or Micks'll get the business. We'll meet 'em at eleven o'clock tonight at Giuseppe's on

Rivard. Their friend, Pietro Mirabile, owns that restaurant, so Adamo ought to be okay with it. It's just us, the Adamo brothers, and you and Miss Hume. It'll be safe. Mirabile'll make sure there's no weapons."

"There's no sense in Elizabeth being there."

"Yeah, there is," Tony said. "It might keep your dumb ass from doin' somethin' stupid." He sat back. "When we're done here, go home. We'll call you before the meetin', make sure you got it set up."

Time to play the suspicious partner. "How do I know you'll leave us alone if I help you with this?"

Tony reached across the space between us and patted my cheek with a meaty hand. "You do your job, ever'body will be fine. We'll be done wit'cha."

I was fully convinced he meant to kill us along with the Adamos. Still, I needed to sell him that I was going along with it—that I would willingly stroll into my own execution. I pushed his hand away. "Give me your word."

From behind, Sam grabbed me by the throat and hauled me over the top of the seat. "He said everybody'd be fine," he growled into my ear. "So *fuck* you."

I couldn't breathe. I tried to pry one of his hands off my neck, but his grip was like a vise.

"Hey," Tony said. "Gentle with him."

"Sure, Tony." Sam gave one last squeeze and let go. "Ya done?"

Tony nodded and looked over my shoulder. "Give him back his gun." The thug handed me the .32 and the magazine separately, and Sam gave me a push me up the aisle. "Not until the train stops, Sammy," Tony called.

"Sure thing," Sam replied. "Too bad," he added under his breath.

The train was slowing. He herded me to the front of the car and down the steps. I put my left hand on the doorframe to brace myself and leaned out the open door to see a station just ahead. The train was nearly to the platform and down to perhaps ten miles per hour when Sam put his hands into the small of my back and shoved me out the door.

CHAPTER THIRTY-FOUR

I flew off the train, windmilling my arms, and managed to land on my feet, taking two huge strides through the stones bordering the track before I lost my balance and somersaulted into a stand of tall grass. I rolled to a stop and lay there, trying to catch my breath. When I was able, I took stock of myself. My shoulder stabbed at me. Blood seeped through the torn fabric of my trousers at the knees. My right hand hurt badly again, and the palm bled onto the rag. But other than that, I was in fine shape.

I levered myself to my feet and spent ten minutes hunting for Elizabeth's pistol and the magazine, finally finding them in the grass. Then I remembered the thug hadn't given me back my knife.

Fortunately, I still had the nickel necessary to buy a ticket for the short ride back to the Jefferson station. During the twenty-minute wait for the train, I thought about the best method of killing Sam Gianolla. It had to be something that hurt—a lot—and lasted a long time. I considered a number of alternatives but decided his personal method of murder would serve as well as anything else. I just had to get control of him long enough to start in with the baseball bat. The train arrived before I determined how best to do that.

When I hopped off downtown, I wandered through the station looking for Elizabeth. Harried people rushed past me, pushing to and from the platforms. I finally found her sitting on a bench in the lobby, looking forlorn and defeated—until she saw me walking toward her. With a huge smile, she jumped up, ran to me, and threw her arms around me. "Thank God," she said. Her voice broke, and she turned her face away.

At that moment, I realized this nightmare was worth the pain. She did love me.

"I'm okay," I said. "A little worse for wear."

After a moment, she stepped back and looked me up and down. She appeared to have regained her equilibrium. "A little worse," she agreed.

"The Gianollas are going to make their play tonight. They want me to get the Adamo brothers to a restaurant in Little Italy at eleven o'clock—ostensibly for a meeting. I'm sure the Gianollas plan to kill them." I looked at my watch. It was almost three thirty. "We've got a lot to do. I've got to call Vito and get a message to Abe. Then we need to rendezvous with Detective Riordan."

We pushed through the crowd to the phone booths and waited a few minutes until one was available. Elizabeth stood outside while I called Adamo. I filled Vito in on the details of the Gianollas' plan and where I thought it would lead.

"Giuseppe's?" he said.

"Right."

"Pietro Mirabile owns that restaurant. Don Mirabile is my friend. . . . What are they thinking?"

"I don't know."

He was quiet for a moment. "Do they want you at the meeting?"

"Yes. Both Elizabeth and me."

"Have you talked to the Bernstein boy yet?"

"No. That's my next stop."

"I will dispatch men to Giuseppe's and around the area immediately. If Gianolla's men are in hiding there, we will kill as many as possible and go back to our war. If not, we will withdraw and watch. However, since they have given us notice of the location, it's unlikely they will attack us there. My guess is they will move the meeting place at the last moment or try to ambush us on the way. Our plans will need to be fluid."

"Check the buildings around the restaurant," I said. "There are probably some good spots for snipers."

"The Gianollas are not the first to try to assassinate me, Mr. Anderson."

"Listen, I'm not trying to insult you, but do you have the men to pull this off?"

"Don't worry about my part. You do yours."

I gave him my home telephone number should he need to get hold of me.

"After you talk to them again," he said, "phone me at this number. We'll make final preparations."

We rang off, and I told Elizabeth about our conversation. She suggested I detour to the restroom to wash out my cuts and scrapes before we continued our odyssey. I did so; then we walked to the Saint Petersburg Restaurant. Markovitz agreed to have Abe phone me as soon as possible. He also gave me the .32 Abe had taken from me when I met up with Palma. I'd forgotten all about it. I tucked that one into the front of my trousers to match the other I had in the back.

Our next stop was Callaghan's Livery, a throwback to an earlier time, one of the few large stables left in the city. The smell of horses and manure, only a few years ago so prevalent I never noticed it, hit my nostrils when we were half a block away. The barn was freshly painted a bright red with *Callaghan's* in script written bold over the wide doors.

I wasn't sure how to play it, so at first we just waited outside. After ten minutes and no contact, I decided to find Callaghan. We were directed to a fireplug of a man in a dirty white shirt and a pair of bright red suspenders holding up a pair of brown trousers, who sat reading a book in the tiny office.

I knocked on the doorjamb. "Mr. Callaghan?"

He didn't look up. "Hmmpf?"

"I'm Will Anderson."

His eyes stayed on the book. "Last stall on the right."

We walked to the other end of the barn. I peeked over the rail into the stall but didn't see anything. "Detective?" I whispered.

Hay rustled inside the stall, and the door swung open. Elizabeth and I walked in. She closed the door behind us. Detective Riordan stood in the shadows, wearing a rumpled dark suit and his fedora. "Have a seat," he said to me. "You look like you could use one."

"Thanks." I lowered myself onto a hay bale in the corner.

"I can't believe they're saying you murdered those men," Elizabeth whispered.

Riordan shrugged.

"What are you going to do?" I said.

"Eventually I'm going to have to give myself up. But I need to help you through this first."

"No," I said. "You'll just end up getting shot or something. I'll testify for you, and I'll bet Markovitz, the owner of the restaurant, would do the same."

"You'll have to pardon me when I say your testimony isn't worth a bucket of warm spit. Keep an eye out for the police. They might be after you too. So tell me. D'ja get run over by a streetcar?"

"You almost got it," I said. "Sam Gianolla shoved me off a train, though he did have the decency to wait until it slowed down. But tonight they're meeting with the Adamos. Tony Gianolla claims he really wants peace, but I still think he's going to try to wipe them—and us—out."

Riordan nodded. "What time?"

"Eleven at a restaurant called Giuseppe's in Little Italy."

"I know the place. That's Mirabile's territory."

"Right."

He rubbed his chin. "Last I knew, Mirabile was aligned with Adamo."

"As far as the Adamos know, he still is," I said. "We met with them. Vito claims he'll work with us."

"Do you think he really will?"

I shrugged, and paid for it with a sharp pain in the shoulder. "If we had a choice in allies, we'd probably choose the alternative, but we don't have a choice. We're throwing in with Vito Adamo."

Riordan's head shook slowly. Finally he sighed. "I'll go with you. You're going to need my help."

"We have to go to Will's apartment," Elizabeth said. "The Gianollas said they'd call there to give us final instructions."

"All right," Riordan said. "I'll meet you there. I've got some reconnaissance to do first. I'll come by later, seven o'clock or so, in case they move up the timetable."

We both nodded, and Elizabeth stepped up to him and gave him a hug. "Take care," she said.

"I will." Riordan smiled at her. "See if you can keep this baboon alive until I get there."

We were lucky enough to flag down a cab just outside Callaghan's. We talked little on the ride, even though the drive that normally took twenty minutes took almost an hour. The cabbie squeezed through every alley and side street he could, but so many vehicles were on the roads it was nearly impossible to get through. There looked to be fewer abandoned vehicles, which gave me hope that the roads would clear soon, streetcars or no.

I had the cabbie drop us off on Second Street, two blocks away from my building, in case the police had decided we were Detective Riordan's accomplices. Elizabeth paid again. I was discovering it was nice to have a wealthy girlfriend.

We sneaked to the back of my building and scouted around a bit. There was no sign of the cops. Elizabeth suggested she go up first, just to be certain the police weren't waiting to ambush me there. A minute later, she waved me in through the parlor window.

When I got inside, she led me through the apartment to the bedroom. "Do you still keep your first aid supplies in the medicine cabinet?"

I nodded.

"Sit tight. I'll be right back."

I sat on the bed, thinking about what we might expect tonight, until Elizabeth returned with bandages and wet washcloths. She set the supplies on the bed next to me and said, "Take off your shirt."

I obliged her. She removed the soiled dressings from my shoulder, washed the wounds, and taped on new bandages. Her touch was cool and soft, fingertips brushing over my skin. We said nothing. I was so aware of her, the heat from her body, her breath grazing the back of my neck, the gentle way she rested her hand on my good shoulder.

"Now your trousers."

I looked up at her.

"Your knees," she explained.

I took off my shoes, then stood, unbuckled my belt, and let my trousers drop to the floor. When I sat again, she knelt down in front of me and cleaned the cuts and scrapes. I watched her—her eyes studying my wounds, her hand moving in slow passes over the bloody parts so as not to hurt me any more than necessary. I filled with love for her.

She sat on the bed next to me and said, "Give me your hand."

"No, it's fine."

"It's all right, Will." Her voice was soft, caring. "Let me have your hand."

I took a deep breath and held it out to her. She pulled off the rag. My hand was naked in front of Elizabeth—the pits, the scar tissue, the gnarled endings of my fourth and fifth fingers. I turned my head away.

She cradled my hand in her arm and stroked the palm with the washcloth. Then she gently bandaged it. When she finished, I began to pull away, but she held on. I watched in astonishment as she raised my thumb to her lips and kissed it, followed by my forefinger, middle finger, and the stumps of my fourth and fifth fingers. She pressed the back of my hand against her mouth for a moment before lowering it and turning to face me.

"I love you, Will." She cupped my cheek in her hand, leaned in, and kissed me. Resting her forehead against mine, she said, "I may never get the chance to tell you again. I love you."

I felt my face flush. "You know I love you, Lizzie. I always have. I always will."

She kissed me, and again, this time with urgency. After a minute, she pulled back, stood, and took off her hat and jacket. Then she unbuttoned her shoes and took them off—along with a short-bladed dagger tucked into the right one. Looking into my eyes, she stood, unbuttoned her shirtwaist, and let it slide off her shoulders. All she wore underneath was a silky white chemise, which she slipped over her head and dropped to the floor. I watched her, entranced, letting my eyes take in the glory that was Elizabeth—her auburn hair, angel's face, brilliant green eyes, and slim, athletic body.

I couldn't breathe. "My God, Elizabeth, you are so beautiful."

She unhooked her skirt. It soon lay on the floor with her shirtwaist and chemise. A holster was strapped to her thigh, with a small pistol on the front of her leg. She unbuckled it and set it on the floor, then peeled down her underwear and stepped out of it. I thought my heart would explode. She leaned down and kissed me again before gently pushing me back on the bed and removing my stockings and underwear. Her face deadly serious, she climbed on top of me and we made love, slowly at first and then like animals, years of anger and frustration fueling our fire.

Afterwards, we lay side by side under the covers, the fingers of her left hand intertwined with the mangled fingers of my right. Even though I hurt all that much more, I remember thinking, just before I drifted off to sleep, that this was so much better than morphine.

The bell on my telephone trilled. Elizabeth and I sat bolt upright. I jumped out of bed and ran to the den. "Hello?"

"Anderson?" It was Abe.

I cleared my throat. "Yeah." I felt logy and dull, that is until Elizabeth appeared in the doorway, draped in my sheet. I smiled at her, realizing I was standing naked in front of her and didn't care.

"What'cha need?" Abe sounded impatient.

I glanced up at the wall clock. It was almost eight. "I need your network," I said. "Right away and maybe all night. I'll pay you fifty dollars."

"Tonight? Fireworks are tonight."

"I'll make it a hundred."

He let out a low whistle. "A hundred, huh? Sounds dangerous."

"Maybe. But I need all the eyes and ears I can get." I explained to him what the Gianollas had planned. "I need your boys to spread out around their territory as well as Mirabile's, particularly around the restaurant. I'll be going to the meeting, and we need to know where the Gianollas are going to ambush us. You coordinate this with your boys and call me if they find anything. If we actually make it all the way to the restaurant, meet me there so you can fill me in on what they've seen."

"I can get that done. I'll send Izzy over for the money. Just in case you screw this up, I want it all in advance."

"That's fine. He should go to the back door. Tell him to jerk up on the handle while he's turning it, and it'll pop open."

"Ya oughta get that lock fixed, Anderson. There's a lot a criminals in this town."

"So I've noticed."

Abe laughed. "Once he gets the money, I'll get the boys on the streets. It'll take about an hour."

"Hurry." As an afterthought, I added, "Thanks."

"Just remember this when I ask *you* for a favor."

I knew it would be costly, but what I was asking him to do wasn't without a price. "I'll remember. Tell the kids to be careful. By the end of the night there's going to be only one gang left."

I hung up the phone.

"Detective Riordan should have been here an hour ago," Elizabeth said.

"I just hope he wasn't picked up."

She murmured her agreement. Though neither of us wanted to be the one to say it, we'd been counting on him to get us through the night. If he didn't come, well, I didn't want to think about it.

We dressed, and after I filled Elizabeth in on my conversation with Abe, we walked into the den. She sat in one of the chairs in front of my desk. I stood near the window, adjusting the gun in my belt while I looked through the blinds at the street in front of the building. Bursts of firecrackers shot out, some near, some far.

Without turning around, I said, "May I ask you a question?"

"Yes." She sounded amused.

"You don't have to answer it," I said, "and either way I won't hold it against you."

"What is it?" She didn't sound amused anymore.

Still looking out the window, I said, "Your mother told me you got back in July. Moretti was killed in August. Were you here?"

She hesitated only a second. "Yes. I've been meaning to tell you, but it never seemed like the right time. I had nothing to do with—"

"Son of a bitch!"

"Will, let me explain."

"No, not that," I said. "Out there." The blue Hudson, with two big men in the front, pulled to the curb across the street. The driver wore a straw boater, the passenger a derby. I couldn't tell if he was Sergeant Rogers, though that didn't much matter. It would have been a fine time to exit via the back door, but we couldn't leave the apartment. If they broke in, they had us.

Elizabeth walked over and spread the blinds with her fingers. "That's the car that followed us from Ford City."

"Yeah. The Gang Squad."

Both men turned and looked up at my apartment. Rogers was the man in the passenger seat. Elizabeth let go of the blinds, and we stepped back.

"What do we do?" she said.

"If they come up here, I'm not opening the door."

Elizabeth took half a step closer to the window. "I guess we're going to see how they react to that."

I looked. Both men were crossing the street. Rogers had his pistol out, checking the load.

CHAPTER THIRTY-FIVE

I ran to the door and turned the key in the lock, then hurried to the parlor and opened the window over the fire escape. "Watch the back," I whispered to Elizabeth. "One of them might come around. If not, that's our escape route."

She nodded but a second later pushed me farther away from the window. "The driver just came around the corner."

Footsteps pounded up the stairs and then knocks sounded against my door.

I pulled the .32 from my belt and whispered to Elizabeth, "Have you got that gun handy?"

She nodded.

"You might need it."

She took hold of my arm and led me back into my den—the farthest corner away from the door. "You want me to shoot a policeman?"

"No, but I'm not letting them stop us."

She shook her head. "All right. Turn around." She reached down and started to pull up her skirt. I watched as the fabric rose above her ankle to the curve of her calf, but when I arched an eyebrow she punched me in the arm. I grudgingly turned around until I no longer heard the sound of fabric rustling. I turned back to see that she had a little Mauser pistol, smaller than her hand.

The knocks got louder. Rogers called out, "Anderson! Don't make me break down the door!"

Elizabeth's forehead creased in concentration. She looked at the window. "Could we get up to the roof from here?"

"I don't know. I've never tried."

Glancing out the front, she raised the blinds and threw open the window, then stuck her head out and twisted around. "The gutter is only a couple of feet above the top of the window," she whispered. "Do you think you could pull yourself up?"

"With one arm?"

Something crashed against my front door. It held.

"I'll go up first and help you," she said. "It's our only way out. Here." She handed me her purse, then with no ceremony at all, she hiked up her skirt and slid the gun back into the holster. I put her purse inside the file drawer in my desk while Elizabeth climbed out on the windowsill and worked her feet onto the ledge, a chunk of stone that stuck out perhaps five inches.

"I don't know about this," I said.

"Shh. Hold on to me."

The door shuddered a second time. I held Elizabeth's arm as she eased up against the window.

"Give me a boost," she whispered. I used my left arm to thrust her upward. Her feet dangled in front of the window for a moment, swaying back and forth, and then lowered back to the ledge. I wrapped my left arm around her thighs to hold her there. "Damn it," she said. "I'm not strong enough."

Another smash against the door. This time, it sounded like wood splintered.

"I'll help you," I said. "Move over."

Elizabeth slid to the end of the ledge, about a foot past the window. I climbed out, trying not to look down. Rogers hit the door again, and it crashed open, followed by another crash, this one brittle and sharp— something from my china cabinet hitting the floor. I eased myself to my feet, reaching up with my left hand for the gutter. "Quickly," I said, edging across the ledge to Elizabeth.

I bent down to grasp her around her thighs. Quiet footsteps, heel to toe, were just audible. Rogers was close.

"Get away from the window," I whispered, and slid back to the other side just as a shadow fell across the windowsill. We flattened ourselves against the bricks, trying to keep our weight back as our shoes hung over the edge.

The footsteps started up again, moving away, but returned perhaps thirty seconds later, stopping at the window. I held my breath. Then Rogers stepped away, his footsteps quieting as he moved from the den. A minute later, he yelled, "Seen anything?" It sounded like he was in the parlor.

"Nothing!" the other detective shouted back.

"All right. Stay back there and keep an eye out. I'm going to see if I can figure out what he's up to." He started walking again, his shoes clomping across the floor this time, louder and louder. A chair—my desk chair—creaked. A drawer slid open, objects rattled around, and the drawer slammed shut. A few streets over, a string of firecrackers blew off, fifteen or twenty little bangs.

I glanced over at Elizabeth. Her eyes were closed, and the fingers of both her hands gripped the gutter.

Another drawer opened. "Huh," Rogers said. A few seconds later, a number of objects clattered onto a hard surface.

My weight shifted the slightest bit forward, and I swayed out over the edge. I was just able to get my balance before taking a three-story drop. Something slapped onto the desk, and Rogers began riffling through papers.

From the corner of my eye, I caught a movement to our left. The detective in the straw boater was walking across the lawn, heading for the Hudson. I looked at Elizabeth again. Her eyes were still screwed shut, and she looked like she was trying to meld into the wall. The detective skipped onto the cobbles and crossed the street to the car.

My heart hammered. As soon as he turned around he would see us. Rogers sat at my desk, five feet from the window. We had nowhere to go.

The detective leaned over into the Hudson, grabbed something, and began to turn around.

"Harmon!" a man yelled. The detective's head jerked back, and he looked at the side of the house opposite my building. I followed his eyes.

Detective Riordan walked out from between the houses, both hands high in the air. "I'm giving myself up."

What? An instant later I understood. He was surrendering to keep Elizabeth and me from being caught.

The detective pulled his gun and leveled it at Riordan, who kept walking toward him. "Sergeant!" the cop called out, his eyes never leaving Riordan's form.

My desk chair creaked again. Rogers's shadow slid across the windowsill and stopped. "Riordan," he muttered. "Will wonders never cease?" He walked briskly from the den, his footsteps pounding away.

"Elizabeth," I hissed. "Inside. Now."

She nodded. Her eyes were wide. We both grabbed hold of the underside of the window. She must have lost her balance because the window jerked down, pulling me into her. We both began falling off the ledge.

As I fell, I hooked my left arm over the sill and grabbed Elizabeth's shirtwaist with my right hand. She clawed for the ledge but missed. Bolts of pain shot up from my hand and shoulder, but I clamped my left arm against the inside wall and clenched my teeth, fighting through the pain, desperate to hold on to Elizabeth. She reached up, legs kicking, took hold of my belt, and began trying to climb up my body.

Three floors below, the front door opened, and Sergeant Rogers walked out, cutting across the lawn toward the two detectives standing in the street, one holding a gun on the other.

Elizabeth pulled herself up, one hand at a time. When she was finally able to take hold of the windowsill, I reached down with my right hand and helped boost her up. She fell inside, then jumped up and grabbed my shirt. We both pulled. I got a leg up on the ledge and then we tumbled onto the floor of the den.

Finally able to relax my muscles, I collapsed. Tidal waves of pain crashed onto me. The next thing I knew, Elizabeth was leaning over me, lightly slapping my face. "Will, wake up. Will."

The pain came back, so intense I was sick to my stomach. I took a shuddering breath, and another, trying to push down the agony in my hand and shoulder.

Elizabeth peeked out the window. "They're coming back," she whispered.

I fought my way to my knees. "Inside my wardrobe. He won't search the place again."

She helped me to my feet, and we hurried to my bedroom and climbed inside the wardrobe, pushing back into the soft folds of clothing. Elizabeth pulled the door closed behind us, and the light extinguished. I thought I was going to be sick. "What'd they do," I panted, "with Riordan?"

"The other detective cuffed him," Elizabeth whispered. "I don't—"

Leather shoes slapped against the wooden floor, getting louder. They stopped. A moment later, muffled voices began talking. Rogers. And Riordan. I pushed the door open an inch.

"—should just take me in," Riordan said. "Let the chief sort it out."

"What's your story, anyway?" Rogers said. "I mean, I understand the whole 'last cop with integrity' shtick, I appreciate that. But why always against the grain? Why can't you get along?"

Riordan barked out a laugh. "Tell me what grain I should be going with? The cops with their hands in everybody else's pockets? Or cops with their heads so far up the chief's ass they can smell his breath? Like you, for example. Now take me in or let me go."

"All right," Rogers said. "I'll be happy to have you brought in."

"Then let's go."

"I'm not going anywhere," Rogers said, with a sneer in his voice. "Why'd you show up here, Riordan? Coincidence? I don't think so. I think you were meeting your buddy Anderson."

"Why are you here, anyway?" Riordan said. "Why aren't you after the gangsters you're supposed to be catching?"

"Which one is he working with, Adamo or Gianolla?"

Riordan laughed again. "Rogers, you're not stupid enough to believe he's a gangster, are you?"

"Don't matter what I believe, Tommy." One set of footsteps pounded across the wood floor and stopped abruptly. Rogers began talking a few moments later. He gave my address, asked for a patrol wagon, and hung up. Footsteps again. "Let's go outside," he said. "Don't want to scare away your pal. I'd expect he's coming home soon."

The door slammed after them and rebounded against the wall. I pushed the wardrobe door the rest of the way open, and we climbed out and crept into the den. Staying in the shadows, we looked out the window.

Rogers and the other detective stuffed Riordan into the back of the Hudson. They conferred for a minute before the other detective cut around to the back of my building again.

"I'll see where he's going," Elizabeth whispered. "Watch Rogers." She tiptoed out of the den, heading up the hall to the parlor. Keeping my eyes focused on the detective, I sat in my desk chair. Elizabeth's purse lay upside down on the desk, the contents strewn across the top.

Rogers climbed into the Hudson, started it up, and drove down Peterboro to Third, pulling around the corner. After he got the car turned around, he parked where he had a full view of the front of the building but wouldn't be conspicuous.

Elizabeth tiptoed back into the den with the bottle of aspirin and a cup from my bathroom. "He's hiding behind the shed in back." She unscrewed the top of the aspirin bottle and gave it to me.

I shook out five or six tablets and popped them in my mouth, then took the glass and washed them down. "Thanks." I looked at the wall clock. It was eight thirty now. Two and a half hours until we had to be at the restaurant. Some time between now and then, one of the Gianolla brothers would call with instructions.

I hoped Rogers had somewhere to go tonight.

My front door creaked. I pulled the .32 out of my belt and stood by the den's doorway, listening. Shoes clomped across the wood. I tightened my grip on the pistol. Then a child's voice whispered, "Anderson. Anderson. You here?"

I looked around the corner. It was Izzy. He looked younger than his ten years. His black hair stuck out underneath his floppy newsboy cap, and his clothes were about two sizes too large. Smiling, I tucked the gun into my belt and waved him down the hall.

Elizabeth tiptoed out of the parlor and followed him. He turned to her. "Hey, doll." I could hear the smile in his voice.

"Hello, Izzy." She was smiling too. His obnoxiousness was endearing to her as well.

"Aw, why'd ya cut off the locks?" he said to her.

She shrugged. "Had to."

"Well, I'd still take ya out on the town, sweetheart," Izzy said as they walked up the hall. He nodded at me. "What was the circus act about?"

"Oh, out there?" I hooked my thumb toward the den.

Rolling his eyes, he said, "No, the elephant parade." The Bernstein boys didn't suffer fools gladly.

"Just trying to stay out of sight."

"Hanging out the fuckin' window prolly ain't the best way to do that, college boy."

Elizabeth snickered.

"I'll try to remember that." I could hear a siren now.

Izzy looked off toward the front door. "The bulls do the remodelin'?"

"Yep. How'd you get in without them seeing you?"

"Ya got some neighbors downstairs ain't too careful about latchin' their windows. Came in the side."

Elizabeth whispered, "I'll keep an eye out," and padded into the den.

Izzy held out his hand. "Abe says you got a hundred for me."

"Oh, right. Wait here." I crept into my bedroom and pulled half my remaining inheritance—five twenty-dollar bills—from the nightstand. When I turned around, Izzy was peering through the bedroom door. The siren kept getting louder.

"No use looking for valuables," I said. He didn't even have the manners to look sheepish. I gave him the money. "Tell him to hurry."

The siren was deafening. It shut off abruptly. Brakes squealed and springs creaked in front of the building. Seconds later the engine revved, and the vehicle pulled away.

Elizabeth stuck her head out of the den. "They took him. Rogers is sitting in the car."

Izzy started down the hall before stopping in his tracks and turning back to me. "You gotta get out a here, right? What'cha gonna do about the cops?"

"I figured we'd sneak out after dark."

His lips pursed, and he moved them back and forth while he thought. Looking up at me again, he said, "I could keep 'em from follering ya. Cost ya 'nother one a these." He held up the twenties.

"And you would do what?"

"Got some taters?"

"Yeah." He followed me into the kitchen, and I pulled a canvas bag of potatoes from the pantry.

He grabbed as many as he could fit into his pockets. "These oughtta do the job." Holding out his hand, he said, "Awright. Hand it over."

I went back to my bedroom for another twenty and gave it to him. He gestured toward the front of the building and grinned. "Just watch the buggy."

"Get word to Abe right away that I paid you."

"Yeah, this'll take two shakes. Turd'll never know I was there." He headed for the foyer.

"Hey, Izzy," Elizabeth said.

He stopped and turned around.

"Be careful."

Wagging his eyebrows at her, he said, "I knew you'd come around. Come see me when you're ready for a real man." He glanced at me. "No offense." He walked out into the hallway without a good-bye.

Elizabeth and I shared a smile before we tiptoed to the den and took our places on either side of the window. Dusk was approaching. The street was bathed in a golden hue with elongated shadows cutting across the lawns, stealing the daylight. Rogers was slumped down in the seat.

Perhaps a minute later, Elizabeth nudged me and pointed down Third Street. Izzy was peeking around the corner of the house behind Rogers's car. He was just the depth of the front yard, perhaps forty feet, away from the Hudson. He moved stealthily across the lawn, staying in the shadows. When he reached the sidewalk he eased himself to the ground and crawled, soldier style, to the street behind the car. Rogers never moved.

Izzy pulled the potatoes out of his pockets and laid them on the cobbles. He selected one and pushed it into the tailpipe. It slipped right in. The next one took a little more work to fit in, and the last couple of them were much too large to fit easily. It was hard to see clearly from the third floor, but it looked like he was screwing the larger potatoes into the tailpipe.

I realized I'd been holding my breath. "You've done this before, haven't you, Izzy?" I whispered.

When he finished, he peeked out at Rogers from under the car and began crawling up toward the sidewalk, where he stood, sneaked back to the house, and disappeared behind it.

Sergeant Rogers never saw or felt a thing. He just sat there, staring idly at my building.

CHAPTER THIRTY-SIX

Elizabeth returned to the parlor, and I kept an eye on Rogers. The burning in my hand had turned into a deep bone ache, like an infected tooth. The aspirin was doing nothing to cut through it. The phone rang. I picked up the receiver and whispered, "Hello?"

"Sorry for what Sam did." Tony Gianolla's gruff voice sounded almost kind. "He ain't much for controllin' his temper."

"So I've noticed."

"Yeah, I'm workin' on him. Anyways, just like we said, bring both Adamos to Giuseppe's at eleven o'clock. Pietro Mirabile will be there in case Vito thinks I'm tryin' to pull somethin'. Mirabile's guaranteein' their safety. His men are gonna frisk ever'body. Once you all are inside, my brothers and me'll come in. We'll get frisked too."

Elizabeth stuck her head into the den.

"No," I said. "You go in first. Better yet, I'll look the place over, then you come in, and *then* the Adamos come in."

"Yeah, okay. Now listen to me, Anderson. This ain't no bullshit. We're both losin' too many men. Pretty soon neither side's gonna have any shooters, and somebody else'll step in. I'm tryin' to keep that from happenin'. Detroit's plenty big enough for both of us."

"Okay." If his nose grew when he lied, it would be about eighteen feet long by now.

"You tell him that. No tricks. We're comin' unarmed, and he better too."

"I'll tell him."

"And listen. Your ma and pa got nothin' to worry about from us. That was all a mistake."

"Elizabeth as well?"

"Yeah. I'm tellin' ya. We just want this shit to stop so's we can get back to business."

We rang off. I stared at the phone for a few moments after he hung up.

"What did he say?" Elizabeth whispered.

I recounted our conversation and added, "Tony acted conciliatory on the train, though I have to say the impact was lessened a bit when Sam threw me off. But this time he really sounded like he was trying to make peace."

"Maybe they're hurting worse than we thought," she said. "They've lost a lot of men. Could he be sincere?"

"Well, we certainly can't trust him. I hope the Adamos are prepared for the worst."

The bangs and booms and whistles of firecrackers and fireworks sounded from all across the city. I glanced up at the wall clock. It was almost nine. "And speaking of the Adamos." I picked up the telephone's receiver and asked the operator to connect me. Vito was there, and I filled him in on what Tony had said.

"So it is still Giuseppe's, eh?" Vito asked.

"So he says."

"Hmm. Reports are that it is clean. I have spoken with Pietro as well. He told me the Gianollas have asked him to broker peace between us. I believe I can trust Don Mirabile."

"Are you sure?"

"There is no 'sure' in this life. As I said, I believe I can trust him. Let's meet fifteen minutes early."

"At the restaurant?"

"No. Where my men picked you up yesterday." He was quiet for a moment. "By the way, I discovered that Carlo Moretti was killed by someone known as 'the Razor.'"

"The razor?"

"For his choice of weapons."

I immediately thought of the two men who entered Moretti's apartment building ahead of him. One was medium height, medium build, the other short and thinner. I knew a pair of brothers who fit that description, and one of them always carried a straight razor. But . . . they were kids. At fifteen years old, could Joey already be known for his method of murder? It seemed unlikely but, given his temperament, not impossible.

"Mr. Anderson?"

I brought my attention back to Adamo. "Yes, I'm still here."

"Do you know who that might be?"

"No . . . no, I don't." I was not going to share my suspicion with him.

"Listen to me," he said. "If they start shooting, cover Miss Hume with your body. They will be gunning for the Adamos, but I don't think they will be discriminating." He laughed. "Do you like that? Now I can say words like 'discriminating' without a stumble."

I laughed with him. "You're becoming an American."

"Oh, I don't think I can go that far, Mr. Anderson. But I am, what's the word? Assimilating?"

"That's the word." The guy amazed me.

"I must go make preparations. Be careful. And tell Miss Hume the same. Good luck to you."

"You too." God help me, I meant it.

I hung up the receiver and sat back in my chair. After I thought for a moment, I called the Detroit Electric garage and told them to deliver the Torpedo to the corner of Charlotte and Cass as soon as possible. The man I talked to said it might take an hour, but they'd get it there.

I looked at Elizabeth. "Adamo says Moretti's killer was someone known as the Razor. You haven't spent a lot of time around Joey Bernstein, but he always carries a straight razor."

She thought about it and shook her head. "No. It couldn't be him. That would mean Abe has been working with the Gianollas from the start. If that were the case, he never would have set us up to ambush them."

"You're right. And Joey's fifteen, for crying out loud. Never mind." I leaned forward. "Okay. Assuming Izzy's little trick works, we ought to be able to get out of here. But I don't know how much we can count on Adamo. We need an angle."

She patted her leg. "I've got the twenty-five. And the knife in my shoe."

"It's a start."

"Why not leave a note for Detective Rogers?"

"What?"

Elizabeth crouched down next to me. "It will take the police a while to get to Giuseppe's. If we cut it close on the timing, maybe they could catch both the Adamos and the Gianollas—and get us out of there alive."

"Good thinking. What else?"

Her forehead creased. After a few moments, she shook her head.

I stared at the desk in front of me. The contents of Elizabeth's purse were scattered across the surface from Rogers's search. The sight of the switchblade gave me an idea. I looked at my glove. "Maybe . . ." I pulled off the glove and reached inside, trying to work the cotton out of the fifth finger, but I couldn't hold on to the outside with my right hand. Elizabeth saw what I was trying to do and reached over, took the glove, and pulled out the cotton. She looked up at me.

I handed her the switchblade. "Fit that in there."

"What are you going to do with your pinkie?"

"I'll just push it into the fourth hole."

She took the switchblade and stuffed it inside. It wasn't exactly finger shaped, but the size was reasonably close—a little wider, and of course flat rather than rounded, but I thought inside the black glove it might pass.

Now for my fingers. I set my jaw and pulled the glove back on, with the stub of my little finger jammed into the fourth finger slot. The pain was about what I expected. When I'd gotten the glove all the way on, I held it up in front of me. Not bad. The knife wouldn't pass close scrutiny, but the Gianollas had seen me wearing the glove often enough that they might just overlook it.

When I finished, I removed the glove, a burst of air forcing from my mouth. While I did, Elizabeth pulled a notepad from my desk and wrote:

Sergeant Rogers: Giuseppe's on Rivard. 11:00 PM. Adamos AND Gianollas. Hurry!

She showed it to me. I nodded.

We had a chance. If Rogers found the note in time, he could upset the Gianollas' plan. I had to keep us alive until then. I set the note on the kitchen table before putting the glove back on and changing into a black shirt and trousers. We settled on the sofa in the parlor to wait.

I nudged her. "So you were saying before we were so rudely interrupted?"

"What?"

"You came back in July?"

"Oh." She laughed and immediately clapped her hand over her mouth. "Sorry," she whispered. "My uncle Peter—my mother's brother—was trying to get her money. He had her committed. She was locked up at Eloise asylum for almost a month before I could get her out."

"Oh. Gosh, I'm sorry."

"I didn't have anything to do with the murder, if that's what you were thinking."

"I didn't think so, but . . ."

"You couldn't help but wonder."

I nodded.

She took my hand. "Don't worry about it. I understand."

Homemade fireworks began to explode in the sky, lighting the night green and white and red. In the distance, I could just hear the city's fireworks booming out over the river a mile and a half away. I wondered about the Gianollas' timing. The official fireworks would be finished before eleven, but there would be plenty of people shooting off fireworks and firecrackers well into the morning.

It would be an ideal time to shoot people.

From this far away the fireworks downtown were nothing more than a distant thud and a glow on the horizon. Occasionally the bursts rose far enough that they peeked out above the skyscrapers as they exploded.

Elizabeth sat next to me on the sofa in the parlor, nestled in under my left arm, one of her arms around my waist, the other hand resting on my stomach. Her hair smelled of vanilla. She was no more than a vague black form, yet I could picture her exactly. I traced the outline of her cheek with my left hand and then leaned down and kissed the top of her head through her short curls.

"Elizabeth," I whispered. "Thank you for giving me another chance." A string of firecrackers blew off down the street. I waited until the explosions stopped. "Being with you like this is worth a thousand beatings. It's worth my life."

She reached up and caressed my cheek. "Mine as well. I never thought I could be happy again."

I took hold of her hand. "I want you to stay here tonight. Let me go alone."

She sat up slowly, not the angry response I expected. "No, Will. Neither of us will be happy again without the other. I've faced that." She laughed quietly. "We're both ruined for anyone else anyway. So if either of us has to die tonight, let it be both."

I started to protest, but she pressed a finger against my lips, then leaned in and kissed me. It was a soft kiss, but her lips lingered. I knew she was memorizing this moment, just as I was—her smell, the feel of her soft, full lips pressed against mine, the love that passed between us. It was only a moment, but it was perfect, the most perfect moment of my life.

She wrapped her arms around me and laid her head against my chest. We sat like that until the downtown fireworks stopped. The next part would be tricky. We needed to get away, but we also needed to alert the detectives to our departure.

I nudged Elizabeth. "Are you ready?"

She sat up. "Yes. Let's go."

"You've got your gun and knife? And they're hidden?"

"Yes. Nobody's going to find the gun, but I've got a bruise that's killing me."

"I noticed." My arched eyebrow was a waste in the dark. She didn't say anything, and I wondered if she was smiling. "Okay, let's go out the back. We'll sneak to get past him, but I'm going to shout for you to run once we get far enough away."

After I ducked my head into the hall to see if it was clear, we tiptoed to the stairs and padded down to the first floor. I eased the back door open and slipped outside into the dark, Elizabeth right behind me. We crept alongside the building, ducking under windows so as not to be framed by the light.

From somewhere behind Third Street, a shrill whistle split the silence, followed by a bright white burst in the sky.

"Hey!" the detective yelled. "Get back here!"

"Run!" I shouted. We raced across the lawn. I looked back over my shoulder to see the cop lumbering along, much nearer to us than I'd hoped he'd be. Given that I had to get the Torpedo started, it was going to be close. No one ever wished they had a self-starter more than I did right now.

"Stop, or I'll shoot!"

"Keep running, Elizabeth!" I called over my shoulder. I turned the corner onto Charlotte and sprinted to the car, which sat just outside the cone of light from a streetlamp. I jammed the key into the ignition, flipped the spark and throttle levers to a quick approximation of starting positions, and ran around the front. Elizabeth reached the car and jumped up in the seat as I started spinning the crank. The engine didn't catch. I spun it again. Still nothing.

"Elizabeth, check the spark and throttle!" I yelled.

I looked out at the street. The cop was perhaps a hundred feet away now, running toward us with his gun hand extended. His hat flew off his head. "Stop, asshole!" he shouted.

"Turn the crank, Will!" Elizabeth yelled.

I spun it again. The engine caught.

I ran around, jumped into the car, and jerked down on the throttle lever. The tires spun and the car fishtailed away from the curb. The back end caught the cop in the hip, knocking him to the pavement. I hurtled around the corner, just able to squeeze between a pair of cars on Woodward.

Elizabeth was still turned in her seat, looking out the back. "That's not going to be good, Will."

"Really?" I demanded. "Running over a cop isn't going to be good? Any more important information you'd like to share?"

We glared at each other until Elizabeth started to giggle. And then we both broke out laughing. When she caught her breath, she said, "I don't think you really hurt him, but you should have seen his face."

I glanced over at her. "What did he look like?"

She made a face, her eyes wide and her mouth in a big O. "Somewhere between surprise and sheer terror."

"Well, thank heaven for small favors. I'd hate to add cop-killer to my résumé."

Once Rogers discovered his car wouldn't start, he would go back inside my apartment looking for clues as to where we'd gone. I hoped all would be forgiven between us when he found the note and caught the Gianollas. It would take the police a while to get to Giuseppe's. If the timing didn't work out, we were in a lot of trouble.

I drove through alleys where I could, otherwise staying on side streets. It was ten minutes of eleven when we arrived in front of the mission. I didn't see Adamo. I hadn't expected to. He would be at least as suspicious of my motives as he would of Pietro Mirabile's. For him to wait like a sitting duck would have been stupid. And Vito Adamo was anything but.

I pulled to the curb, fished the switchblade out of my pocket, and set it on my lap while taking off my glove. After Elizabeth shoved the knife into the finger hole, I pulled the glove back onto my hand. I tried to hide the pain when I jammed the stub of my pinkie in with my ring finger, but her sympathetic frown showed I didn't do so well.

When I thought I could keep the pain out of my voice, I held my hand up in front of her. "Not too bad, huh?"

Nodding, she said, "It might pass. If they don't look too closely."

"I may need your help with that."

"I know just the thing."

I looked at her with a question on my face, but she just shook her head and smiled. Half a minute later, the blue E-M-F pulled up alongside us, Angelo the only occupant. "Follow," he said, and the car shot forward. I drew down the throttle and trailed behind.

"Where do you suppose the Adamos are?" Elizabeth asked.

"I don't know. But they're not taking any chances. That's good." I looked over at her. "We're going to need them to keep us alive tonight."

CHAPTER THIRTY-SEVEN

Along the way, we passed four or five children I thought were likely members of Abe's "business group." When Angelo pulled the E-M-F to the curb in front of Giuseppe's Restaurant, I parked just behind him, almost directly under a streetlamp. Ray Bernstein sat on a stoop across the street. When I caught his eye, he shrugged and held his hands out to his sides.

He hadn't seen anyone? That seemed unlikely. I leaned toward him and made the same gesture back, pantomiming, *Nobody?*

He shrugged again and shook his head.

Angelo climbed out of the car, unholstering a pistol as he did. Filipo Busolato came from around the side of the restaurant and walked up to him. They spoke for a few moments. Angelo nodded and pulled a sawed-off shotgun from the backseat. He turned to me and nodded toward Ray. "Gianollas?"

"He says no." I bit my lip. "But we better be sure."

"My man say the same. But we will be sure." He turned toward the restaurant. "Come with me."

He walked to the door, shotgun in one hand, pistol in the other, followed by Busolato. Elizabeth and I fell in step behind them. When Angelo opened the door, a pair of toughs who were just inside let us in. The interior was well lit, but the walnut paneling made it seem dim. Streetlights shone through a pair of small windows in the front wall.

Starched white tablecloths covered every table, which otherwise were empty. Behind the dining area was a corridor that I assumed led to a back door. I thought it looked like a relatively safe place to meet. Or as safe as a place could be with the Gianolla brothers present.

An older man in a dark suit stood in the center of the dining area, his silvery hair shining in the restaurant's lights. He said something in Italian, and the men stepped back and let us pass. I squeezed Elizabeth's hand, and we walked in behind Adamo's men. The pressure on my pinkie finger was incredible. I tried to move it, hoping to relieve the pain, and was rewarded with even more.

The old man was short and squat, and had three deep scars on his left cheek that fanned out like a cat's whiskers. "*Buona sera,* gentlemen, miss," he said, in a deep, gravelly voice.

Angelo bowed to him. "Don Mirabile."

They talked in Italian for a minute. I discerned from the tone of the conversation and Angelo's hand motions that he wanted to search the restaurant before handing over his weapons, a sentiment with which I wholeheartedly agreed. Mirabile gave his approval, and called two of his men from the kitchen to join Adamo's men in their search.

Mirabile turned to us. "Mr. Anderson, Miss Hume, we gotta search you. No weapons at this meetin'."

"Fine," I said. "But they'd better be careful with her." I nodded toward Elizabeth.

"*Sì,*" he said. "My men will show respect."

He called one of the men from the door to search us. I gave him the .32, held my hands out to the side, and tried not to look nervous. He started at my ankles and worked his way up.

When he began patting down my arms, Elizabeth lifted her skirt above her shoes, showing her ankles, and said, "Say, I have a knife." His hands stopped at my wrists. She took a step toward us and turned to show off the knife sticking out of her shoe, giving us a lovely flash of her right calf. The man searching me stopped immediately, his eyes glued to her legs. She plucked the knife from her shoe and handed it to him.

"*Grazie,*" the man said, and forgot me completely. I started breathing again. After apologizing to Elizabeth, the man searched her, beginning with her hat. He confiscated her hatpin and started moving downward.

He didn't touch her breasts but looked carefully enough. I held my breath when he politely asked her to spread her legs. She moved her right leg over about a foot. He began at her ankles, patting the outside of her skirt, higher than I thought he would. And sure enough, his hand touched the pistol.

His eyes darted up to her face. "She got a gun."

Mirabile folded his arms across his chest. "Miss Hume."

Elizabeth, her face flushed, reached up under her dress and pulled out the little pistol. I tugged at my glove, desperate to ease the pain in my hand. I tried to hide the movement, but at this moment, I could have carried in a Gatling gun. Not a man in the room had his eyes anywhere other than Elizabeth's legs. She handed the pistol to the man who'd searched her. "I want that back."

When he took the gun he made a mock-grimace and passed it from hand to hand, like it was a hot potato. Every man in the place except for me burst out laughing.

"Hey," I said. "What about respect?"

"What about respect?" Mirabile said with scorn. "Your girlfrien' brings a gun to a meetin' with no weapons, and you ask me about respect?"

I didn't have an answer for that.

We were down to my switchblade. Our margin was getting thinner.

Adamo's men soon returned with a pair of waiters in black trousers with white shirts, and searched them. No weapons were found. Still, I was certain this was a trap. I pulled Angelo aside. "Do you know these men?"

"No, but Don Mirabile say they work for him for years. He trust them."

I looked over at Mirabile. "So once again we have to trust *him*."

"Don Adamo trust him. That is enough."

"All right. But don't let Vito come until the Gianollas are here and unarmed."

He nodded and said something to Busolato, who walked outside. Angelo stopped in the doorway with Mirabile's men and handed over the shotgun and pistol, another pistol tucked inside a shoulder holster, and a stiletto.

When he came back, I pulled him aside. "You have more men here, don't you?"

His eyes cut to me and then away. Finally he said, "Don' worry 'bout it."

"You're not serious. It's just you, Busolato, and the Adamo brothers?" I remembered seeing only four cots at the apartment.

"I said, don' worry 'bout it." He stepped away from me.

Mirabile pointed at a table in the center of the restaurant that had four chairs facing the door and three facing away—Elizabeth and me and the Adamo brothers on one side, the Gianolla brothers and Mirabile on the other? If so, the Gianollas would be sitting with their backs to the door. I wondered if that meant they truly were not expecting trouble. I pointed Elizabeth to the seat on the end, with me next to her. I wanted her as far away from the gangsters as possible.

Mirabile stood opposite us and forced a smile. "I'm sorry for all this." He waved vaguely around us. "But the trouble's gotta stop." He grunted. "It's bad for business."

We didn't have long to wait, but with the searing pain in my hand, the five minutes felt like an eternity. One of the thugs from the train came in first and looked around for a few minutes before calling out the door to the brothers, who filed in a few seconds later. Sam was followed by Tony, who limped in stiff-legged, swinging his right leg out to the side.

Mirabile's men locked the door. The Gianolla brothers and their man walked up to Don Mirabile and opened their suit coats. While Angelo looked on, one side of his mouth drawn back in a snarl, Mirabile's men frisked them and came up with nothing. The Gianollas continued back to us, sitting at the table—Sam directly across from me, Tony in the middle, their thug on the other side. Mirabile moved away from the table and stood perhaps ten feet from us, facing the front door.

Tony smiled at me. The tips of his canines creased his lower lip. "I hope you done your job."

"I did my job," I said, mopping my forehead with my handkerchief. "They'll be here. And when this is over, you are going to leave us—and our families—alone?"

His mouth flickered with just a hint of irritation. "Said so, didn't I?"

"Yes. And I'd like you to say it again."

Tony laughed. "Sure. If the Adamos show, when we finish tonight we ain't gonna have nothin' against any of ya." He turned partway in his seat and rested his forearm on the back of his chair. His dark eyes took in Elizabeth. With a nod, he smiled his predator's smile and said, "Miss Hume, it's a pleasure."

Her revulsion was so strong I could almost see her shudder. "Meeting you is certainly no pleasure, Mr. Gianolla."

He grinned. "Oh, now, that ain't very nice."

Sam glared at me. "Maybe you oughta put a muzzle on your girl-frien'."

"Maybe you ought to mind your own business," I shot back at him.

I could see in his eyes he wanted to come over the table at me, but he just sat there, his mouth set in a grim line.

"Boys," Tony said. "Play nice. This here's a peace meetin'."

"Yeah." Sam's eyes never left mine. "Sure, Tony."

One of the waiters came to the table. "Would you like something to drink?"

Tony looked at Elizabeth. "Miss Hume?"

"Nothing."

He glanced at me. "Coffee," I said.

Tony ordered espresso. For Sam, it was whiskey. While we waited, Tony and Sam talked in Italian. I had no idea what they were saying, but since they seemed relaxed and Mirabile was within earshot, I decided to ignore it. The waiter brought our drinks and set them in front of us. Sam snatched up his glass, threw back the whiskey, and said, "*Un'altra.*" The waiter nodded and scurried off to the kitchen, returning a few seconds later with another whiskey. This one Sam left on the table.

Somewhere close, a string of firecrackers blew off. *Bang! Bang! Bang! Bang! Bang!*

For the first time, it occurred to me that Vito and Salvatore might not come. I took a sip of my coffee. When I put the cup down, it rattled against the saucer. Elizabeth glanced at me. I gave her what I hoped was a reassuring look, but she didn't appear convinced.

A voice called out from the back of the restaurant. "Don Mirabile?"

Mirabile looked up, said, *"Scusi,"* and walked around the table, heading for the back.

When he disappeared down the corridor, Sam laughed. "They comin' in the back 'cause nobody lets their kind in the front."

"Sam." Tony was staring daggers at him. "Shut it." He got a dark look in return.

Mirabile called from behind us, "Angelo, Anderson. Come here."

I glanced at Elizabeth.

"Go ahead, Will," she said. "I'll be fine." Her voice was steady.

I pushed back my chair and followed Angelo down the dark paneled hallway. Vito and Salvatore Adamo stood just inside the door, with Mirabile next to them.

Vito said something to Angelo in Italian, and he replied in kind. Vito nodded and turned to me. "How does it look to you?" His dark eyes held mine with great intensity, like he was trying to read my mind.

"Near as I can tell, none of the Gianollas have weapons." I nodded toward Mirabile. "The only people here with guns are his guys. It seems safe. That is, if you trust him."

Vito nodded.

I wondered what he was up to. Surely he wasn't coming in here without a backup plan. I looked at Mirabile. "May I speak with Signore Adamo privately?"

He appraised me for a moment before nodding and walking up the corridor. I leaned in close to Vito. "You've got something up your sleeve, don't you?"

He glanced at the sleeves of his jacket and gave me a mystified look.

"Do you have a plan?" I whispered.

He gave me a sad smile. "I have nothing left. Most of my men—the ones who are still alive—have fled. And who could blame them? I can't protect them anymore. Nor can they protect me." He put a hand on my shoulder. "I am here to bluff. If that fails, to bargain for the lives of my men and my family."

"Jesus," I whispered.

"Yes," Vito said. "We could use his help."

I threw his hand off me. "Why didn't you tell me? I never would have brought Elizabeth here. You said you would turn the tables on them." I looked at Salvatore and then Angelo. "Is it just you three and Busolato? Four men?"

He shrugged, and in that moment I realized I had misjudged him. His penitence may have had some basis in reality, but he was just using us. We were pawns in his last-chance gambit.

I stared into his eyes. "I should have killed you."

"Let us pray you have another chance to try." He looked up the hallway. "Don Mirabile, if you please?"

Mirabile hurried back to us. Adamo might be willing to cede his fate to the Gianollas, but I wasn't. "Don Mirabile, what are the security arrangements?"

"I have two men on both doors, and they'll be locked. The only people inside will be you and two waiters, both loyal to me."

"You're sure about that," I said.

Mirabile scowled. "These boys—"

"It is not necessary for you to explain, my friend," Adamo said. "I accept your word."

In an apologetic tone, Mirabile said, "*Mi scusi,* Don Adamo, but my men gotta search you in front of the Gianollas. If ya got anythin', I should take it now. Might be embarrassin'."

"We are unarmed."

Mirabile locked the door and gestured toward the front. "Awright. Whattaya say we start?"

I pushed against the door, which stayed shut, and gave Mirabile a smile before following Vito, Salvatore, and Angelo down the corridor. Two of Mirabile's men shadowed us, pistols held by their sides. The Gianolla brothers watched us approach with phony smiles on their faces.

I sat again next to Elizabeth, leaned over, and whispered in her ear, "Be ready to run."

She glanced at Sam, whose eyes were locked on the Adamo brothers, and looked at me with a question in her eyes.

I gave a slight shake of my head and mouthed, *Be ready.* I took a nervous gulp of coffee.

She nodded and shifted her weight forward on the chair.

Mirabile's men frisked the Adamos, who were unarmed as agreed.

When the search was complete, the Gianollas and their man stood and greeted the Adamos, who returned the greetings with much less enthusiasm.

Mirabile waited until everyone was seated before he stood at the end of the table and started speaking in Italian.

I interrupted him. "How about English so *we* know what's going on?"

He looked at the two sets of brothers. Vito and Tony both nodded.

"Awright," Mirabile said, "you're here to fix the problems between ya. Nobody's got weapons. Ain't even no silverware. It's up to you." He said something to his men in Italian and looked at Vito, who nodded to Angelo.

Mirabile escorted Angelo and the Gianollas' other man, along with all his men, to the door. He held it as they filed out, then turned back to us. *"Buona fortuna."* He stepped out of the restaurant and locked the door behind him. Both of the windows went red as fireworks burst somewhere in the distance. The light pulsed and then faded.

It was down to the Gianollas, the Adamos, and us.

Tony spoke first. "Let's have some drinks." He looked at Vito and laughed. "A war like this gives ya a thirst, am I right?" Vito's head raised a fraction, but he said nothing. Tony looked over the Adamos' heads and waved a waiter over. "'Nother espresso for me. How's 'bout you, Adamo?"

"Nothing."

"I'll have some more coffee." With my hands under the table, I began pulling off the glove. I steeled myself against the pain and set my jaw, trying to keep a neutral expression on my face.

"What you doin'?" Sam leaned over the table, trying to see my hands.

"Nothing." I stopped.

"Get your hands on the table," he demanded.

I raised my hands and set them on the edge of the table, keeping the knife in the pinkie finger of the glove tucked underneath my hand.

It was quiet until the waiter returned. He set Tony's espresso in front of him and refilled my coffee. Tony stood. Salvatore flinched but managed to stay seated.

Spreading his hands in front of him, Tony said, "My thanks to Don Mirabile for settin' up this meetin' today."

I slipped my hands under the table again, but Sam glared at me. "Get 'em up." He knew I was up to something. He just couldn't figure out what. Unfortunately, it didn't matter. I wasn't going to be able to get at the knife with him watching me.

"Adamo," Tony continued, "I know we got bad blood. But we're both losin' too many men. This war has to stop."

I glanced at Sam to gauge his reaction just as his eyes flickered over Vito's head.

Turning, I saw the waiters sneaking up behind the Adamo brothers. The one nearest me had a bead of sweat on his forehead. His right arm was held close to his body, his hand grasping something he was trying to hide. As he moved forward, a sharp point caught a light and glinted into my eyes.

I picked up my coffee cup and flung it into the waiter's face just as he was raising the dagger. He screamed, and the knife fell from his hand, clattering to the floor. Everyone leaped up from the table. Vito grabbed the dagger from the floor and slashed it across the waiter's throat just as the Gianollas' thug dived over the table and knocked him down. The other waiter stabbed Salvatore in the back as he was twisting out of his chair.

I grabbed Elizabeth and pushed her away from the table, shouting, "Go! Hide!"

Sam Gianolla threw the table aside and tackled me. Vito and Salvatore wrestled with Tony Gianolla and his thug. Chairs and tables crashed to the floor.

Explosions like gunfire erupted outside the building.

Sam held my left arm down and reared back to punch me in the face, but I slipped my head to the side, and his fist smashed into the wooden floor. He howled in pain. Holding the fingers of my mangled right hand stiff, I jabbed him in the eyes just as Elizabeth hit him in the head with a chair, knocking him off me.

I looked at her, startled. "Elizabeth, why—?"

Someone kicked in the front door. Gunshots rang out. I looked toward the sound and saw Gianolla's men running in.

Elizabeth grabbed my hand and wrenched me to my feet. One of the waiters' daggers lay on the floor. I scooped it up as we ran for the back hall. Bullets ripped into the wall in front of us. I tipped over a table, and we dived behind it. The air was hazy with smoke, and my ears rang with the cracking of guns coming from all around us.

Between gunshots, police sirens became audible, but they were a long way off. *Rogers*, I thought. *Finally.*

"Adamo! Adamo!" a familiar voice shouted from the back of the restaurant. I turned and saw Abe Bernstein at the entrance to the rear corridor. He saw me looking at him. "Get Adamo!" he shouted, pointing to my right.

I looked. Vito and Salvatore were crouching behind a table, Angelo's twisted body next to them. Salvatore's white shirt was stained red. Bullets thwacked into the table in front of them. Sirens blared, close now. Tony Gianolla shouted something in Italian, and his men began to fall back, sliding one by one through the doorway. While they did, they kept a steady barrage of bullets going at the Adamo brothers. No one was firing back. Filipo Busolato lay slumped just inside the door.

"Adamo!" Abe yelled. "This way!"

I took hold of Elizabeth's hand and ran for Abe. Vito must have noticed him about the same time, because he and Salvatore almost ran into Elizabeth and me as we ran down the hallway.

Abe shoved the back door open and ran out into the alley. We followed him, jumping over two men's bodies lying on the dirt, their eyes staring sightlessly at the sky. The sirens were suddenly louder.

Joey Bernstein leaned against the redbrick wall of the building opposite Giuseppe's, his derby tipped low over his forehead, a toothpick in the corner of his mouth, a sawed-off shotgun in his hand. Without a word, he raised the gun and shot Salvatore Adamo in the face. His head exploded in a mass of bone, brain, and blood. He fell over backwards, dead before he hit the ground.

Elizabeth screamed.

Vito stopped in his tracks, staring at Abe with a look of disbelief.

Now I saw the pistol in Abe's hand. "Sorry," he said, and shot Vito in the chest. Vito staggered but took a step toward Abe.

"Abe!" I shouted. "No!"

Abe shot him again. Vito fell to his knees and pitched over onto his face. But he pushed himself up and began crawling toward Abe.

"We gotta go," Joey said, and blew out the back of Vito Adamo's head with the shotgun.

CHAPTER THIRTY-EIGHT

Elizabeth fell to her knees. Palming the dagger, I knelt down and took her in my arms, shielding her from the Bernsteins. Her face was blank, eyes staring off at some vision in the distance, like a soldier I saw years ago who'd just come back from the war in the Philippines.

The sirens began to fade into the distance. I looked off toward the sound as the police cars raced away down Rivard. Rogers wasn't going to save us.

Abe's footsteps crunched on the dirt behind me, moving closer. My shoulders hunched in anticipation of the shot to the back of the head. I twisted around so Abe couldn't see the dagger. I had to wait until he was close enough. I'd stab him, grab his gun, and shoot Joey.

"Let's go," Abe said.

I half turned and looked at him, my hand still hidden. He was ten feet away, holding the gun loosely at his side. "Go?" I said. "Go where?"

"We got a appointment."

I kept looking at Abe. "Why the hell did you kill them?" A string of firecrackers went off a street or two away.

He squinted down at us. "You gotta know which way the wind's blowin'. It wasn't blowin' their way."

"But, my God, Abe," I said. "Joey's what? Fifteen? You've got him killing men?"

"Stop bein' such a pussy. Let's go."

"I thought I knew you."

"Yeah, well, you thought wrong."

"If you're going to kill us," Elizabeth said in a shaky voice, "do it here."

The sirens were getting louder again. Joey slid two more shells into the breech of the shotgun and snapped it shut. "Abe, they ain't gonna cooperate." He pronounced it *coop-erate*. "We gotta get out of here. I don't mind shootin' 'em if you want."

"Shut up, Joey. We need 'em." Abe released the hammer on his pistol. "Let's go," he said to me. "Nobody's gonna shoot ya. We're getting paid for killin' the Adamos, not you."

The sirens were still probably half a mile away, but they were getting closer. Maybe we had a chance. "Paid?" I said.

"Five hundred big ones," Abe crowed. "Two-fifty apiece. This is gonna keep us in smokes for a long time. Might even finance somethin' big. You're my witness." He looked off toward the sound of the sirens and then gestured down the alley with the gun. "Now move."

He said they wouldn't kill us. I didn't know if that was true, but it was unlikely I could kill both of them before we got shot. The police were no more than a minute away. If we were here when they got back, someone was going to get killed. Probably more than one. And Joey wasn't going to wait all day.

I stood and held my hand out to Elizabeth. "Come on, honey." She took my hand, and I helped her to her feet.

"Gimme the pigsticker," Abe said.

I looked at him.

"Come on." He raised the pistol and gave me a *hand it over* motion. "I seen it."

I gave him the dagger.

"Go. Double time." Abe pointed down the alley with his gun. I put my good arm around Elizabeth, and we began trotting, skirting the bodies of the Adamo brothers. Abe and Joey followed behind us. Tires squealed in front of the restaurant, and the sirens shut off.

We had just turned down a dark lane, perhaps ten feet wide with three-story buildings on either side, when behind us a man called out, "Will! Elizabeth!" It was Detective Riordan. He'd gotten out.

Abe shoved me forward and directed us on a zigzag path down dark alleys and unpaved lanes. Farther up the road, a pair of roman candles fired almost simultaneously.

"So, Joey," I said. "I thought you preferred the razor. Isn't that what you're known for?"

"What do you mean?" he said.

"Isn't that what they call you? The Razor?"

"Shut up," Abe growled. "Keep movin'."

As we walked, the brothers talked quietly. Certain they were discussing our fate, I strained to listen in. Joey was agitated, but the only words I could make out were "He better not hit me again. That's all I'm sayin'."

Abe's response was too quiet to hear. Moments later, he pushed me up the walk toward a big white two-story home and knocked on the door.

Waldman answered.

Waldman? Elizabeth and I exchanged a startled glance. "What the hell?" I muttered.

"Come in," he said. "All weapons stay here."

Joey pushed me in the back with the shotgun, and I stepped up into the house, Elizabeth beside me. The Bernsteins followed. The foyer was dimly lit by electric sconces on the dark paneled walls.

"They're clean," Abe said, waving toward Elizabeth and me.

Waldman glowered at him. "You don't tell me anything. I tell you." He closed the door and began giving me a pat-down but stopped and glanced at Joey. "What are you looking at?"

Joey shifted the toothpick to the other side of his mouth and gave him a lazy grin. "Nothin'. Just want my money."

Waldman barked something at Joey in Yiddish, then added, "Every time you see me you get paid."

"Seems like you get paid a lot more," Joey said.

"You think you're a big shot now? Huh?"

Joey started to say something, but Waldman turned to Abe. "Are you going to shut him up, or am I?"

Abe nudged Joey and shot him a warning glance. The grin didn't leave Joey's face, but he shut up. Without getting anywhere near my hands, Waldman finished with me and began searching Elizabeth.

It finally hit me. "The craps game." I pointed at Waldman. "That was you." I turned to Abe and stared into his eyes. "You've been playing me from the start."

He just gave me a shake of the head, clearly disgusted with my stupidity.

Finished with Elizabeth, Waldman held out his hand toward the main hallway. "Mr. Anderson and Miss Hume, dining room. Second door on the right."

"Why?"

Joey pushed me in the back. "Go," he said.

Elizabeth looked at me, and I nodded. We walked down to the doorway and stepped into the dining room.

At the end of a twenty-foot table, with Minna on his lap, sat Ethan Pinsky.

Minna had one arm draped over his shoulders, running her fingers along his lapel. In her other hand, she held a semiautomatic pistol. It was pointed at me.

Pinsky said something quietly to her. She stood and slipped into the chair next to him. "Please." He waved us in. "Sit."

I stood in the doorway. "You were arrested. You're supposed to be in Boston."

He chuckled, his breath rattling, and started laughing harder before breaking into a coughing fit. When he finished gasping, he smiled at me again and said, "No. *Ethan Pinsky* was arrested."

"What?"

"Think, Mr. Anderson. My Lord, you are dim at times. Now sit."

I stood there openmouthed. Minna used the gun to motion us to the table. I took Elizabeth's elbow, and we sat. I shrugged at him. "I don't understand."

"You made an appointment with Ethan Pinsky," he said. "Waldman went to your apartment and changed the meeting date." He gasped in a breath. "He gave you a new telephone number . . . with which to call Ethan Pinsky. Except it wasn't Ethan Pinsky." He grinned, pleased with himself. "It was me. The real Pinsky wanted you to facilitate . . . getting the Teamsters into Detroit Electric. I simply want the money."

I stared at him until my mind caught up. Joe and the Gianollas asked me why I hadn't met with Pinsky—the real Pinsky. "You son of a bitch. Who are you?"

"To keep things simple, why don't you just think of me . . . as Ethan Pinsky the Second."

"You weren't working with the Gianollas."

He gave a faux shudder. "Of course not. I never associate with Sicilians."

"But . . ." I glanced at Minna. "Wait. She was feeding you the information from them. She was your spy."

"Congratulations," the albino said.

I glared at him. "What do you want?"

"Are the Adamo brothers dead?" he wheezed.

I nodded.

"And who is responsible?"

I nodded toward the hallway. "Butch and Sundance back there."

"The Gianolla brothers? Are they dead?"

"Not as far as I know."

"Mm." He worked his mouth around for a few moments.

"What's your angle?" I said.

He sat back in the chair and smiled at me. I wanted to plant my fist in the middle of those yellow teeth. "Did I not tell you I arrange things?"

Under the table, I began pulling off my glove, one finger at a time. "You did."

"Well, then . . ."

Was it really this simple? "You provoked a gang war. Why?"

"The Sicilians have taken over virtually all the . . . Detroit rackets," he gasped. "I needed them out of the way. Unfortunately, we are still only halfway there."

The picture was falling into place. "It wasn't the Gianollas. *You* set me up. *You* had Moretti killed."

He did nothing other than to look at me from behind the dark glasses.

I got the glove off and worked the switchblade out. "You had it done while I was there so the Gianollas would have leverage over me."

"Good. Now you're thinking," the albino said.

Pushing the blade end against the seat of my chair, I pressed the release button on the knife and eased it up so the blade would extend quietly. Hooking a thumb over my shoulder, I said, "The Bernsteins killed Moretti too, didn't they?"

"Please. You insult me. Tonight they got lucky. Do you really think I would send boys . . . to do that sort of work?"

"But you sent your daughter to be used by Sam Gianolla, didn't you?"

"She's not his daughter," Elizabeth said.

I glanced at her and then at Minna. She stared back at Elizabeth, a cool smile on her face. Both her hands were on the table. The gun was pointed at my chest.

Elizabeth stood. "Besides confirming your thugs killed the Adamos, was there anything else you wanted with us?"

He looked from her to me and smiled his yellow-toothed smile. "There is still the matter of my fifty thousand dollars."

"You can't be serious," I said.

"It's only a matter of time until the Gianolla brothers are out of my way. Fifty thousand dollars will buy me enough men to take over the city."

"Joe Curtiss died so you could take over the rackets?" It hit me then that Sam Gianolla hadn't killed Joe. "Oh, Christ. You had Joe killed so it would look like the Gianollas did it. Did you send boys to do that?"

He shook his head, amused. "Do you really think they could have tortured a man that way?"

"If they didn't do it, then how do you know he was tortured?"

"Believe me when I say work like that requires a specialist."

"Oh," Minna said. "I'm blushing."

My jaw dropped. "You?"

She gave me a coquettish smile. "You'd be surprised what a woman is capable of, Will. For example . . ." She opened her purse with one hand and pulled out a black satin case—the shaving kit. After flipping it open, she took out the straight razor and angled it so the blade would shine into my eyes. "Nearly cutting off a man's head, for example. I so wanted to do you and your girlfriend, but my sweetheart said no."

The albino had ordered Joe's death, and Minna killed him. And she killed Moretti. A cold rage burned through me. They were responsible for all of this. They had to die. I did a quick reckoning. The doorway split the table exactly. I estimated the distance between the albino's chest and me—twelve feet. Minna—nine feet. I needed fifteen. She had the gun.

Three steps. Kill her. Take the gun. Kill him.

I palmed the knife and stood. Minna's gun barrel tracked me. I turned and walked toward the end of the table with my head in my hands, then turned back to the albino, anguish on my face. "How could you?" I sobbed. Now I was fifteen feet from Minna. I'd wait for my chance.

Elizabeth leaned over the table. "So now what do we do?" she demanded. "What about the Teamsters? And the Gianollas?"

"If"—Pinsky held a gloved index finger in front of him—"if Mr. Anderson pays me my money, I will end the Gianollas' threat."

"You son of a bitch," I said. "Why would we believe you?"

"He just wants his money," Minna said in a honey-laced tone. She kept her eyes and the gun trained on me.

Elizabeth cocked her head at Minna. "Just like *you* want his money. Why else would you be here?"

Giving Elizabeth a languid smile, she reached under the table, massaging the albino's groin. "Besides his brains, you mean?" She was leaning forward, her left arm on the table, her heart about two inches above her forearm. Her gun was still trained on me.

My eyes focused on the gap between Minna's ribs. I'd never tried such a difficult shot. Miss and she gets nothing more than a flesh wound. And we both get killed.

"Whore," Elizabeth spat.

The albino clamped his hand down on Minna's wrist. "Not now."

Glancing over at him, she winced and let go.

I took hold of the blade and whipped the knife at her. It hit her chest with a thud and buried to the hilt. She made a sound like a little hiccup, and the gun fired, punching a hole in the wall behind me. I dived over the table and crashed into her, wrenching the gun from her hand. Her chair went over, and I fell on top of her. I rolled and pointed the gun at the albino's chair. It was empty.

I heard the unmistakable sound of shells being racked into a shotgun.

"Put it down, Mr. Anderson," the albino said.

I looked over the table. He stood now, holding a shotgun on Elizabeth.

Where the hell did that come from?

Waldman ran in, tracking the room with a pistol. The barrel lighted on me about the same time I aimed Minna's gun at the albino's midsection from under the table.

"Don't shoot him, Judah," the albino said. "It won't be necessary. Will it, Mr. Anderson?"

Minna coughed up a bubble of blood.

God damn it. I was so close. "Let Elizabeth go."

"That is the plan," the albino said.

"Then do it. Elizabeth, leave."

"As soon as you give Waldman your gun," the albino wheezed. "You may both leave."

Minna groaned, and more blood gurgled up from her mouth.

"Your girlfriend is dying while we talk," I said. "Let Elizabeth go."

"Minna is no longer useful to me. She consorted with that *animal*. . . . I'm afraid I can't allow Miss Hume to leave . . . until you give us the gun. Because once she's gone you will shoot me . . . regardless of the danger to you. I understand you, Mr. Anderson. Put down the gun, and you both may leave. You have my word."

My gun wavered, but I kept it aimed at the albino. A soft creak came from the wooden floor of the hallway. I glanced at Waldman. He was leaning over the table, his gun pointed at my head. The albino kept the shotgun trained on Elizabeth's torso. It would blow a very big hole through her.

If I gave them the gun, Elizabeth would probably die.

If I didn't, she would certainly die.

I set the gun on the floor and began to stand, my hands spread in front of me.

A shotgun roared, and sparks lit the room. I dived to the floor to grab

Minna's pistol. Another gun fired. The shotgun thundered again, and something crashed onto the table. I snatched the gun from the floor, rolled, and aimed at the albino.

Except now he was lying on his back, still. A body slid off the table and crumpled to the floor. Waldman. Elizabeth crouched where she had stood, hands over her ears.

I looked up at the doorway. Abe and Joey stood there, smoke still rising from Joey's shotgun. He racked in two more shells and spit onto Waldman's prostrate body. Looking down at him, Joey said, "Guess I *am* a big shot, huh?"

I stood. Abe looked at me and held his hands out in front of him, keeping his gun pointed at the ceiling. "Remember, I said we ain't gonna hurt ya, but you gotta put the gun down." Joey swung the shotgun over toward me. Abe batted it away and gave him a dark look.

My odds had improved only slightly. The minute I raised the gun, one of them would shoot me. Or Elizabeth. And I didn't really think Abe wanted to kill us. I set the gun on the table and hurried over to Elizabeth, keeping my eyes on the boys. Abe knelt down next to the albino's body and reached inside his coat. "Aw, goddamn it, Joey." He looked back at his brother and raised the bloody corner of a hundred-dollar bill. "Ya had to shoot him in the fuckin' wallet, didn't ya? Ya dumb sonuvabitch, we ain't getting' nothin' outta this."

I glanced at Waldman's body. The top of his head was gone, his skull a bloody crater. Shuddering, I looked away quickly. "Let's go," I whispered to Elizabeth, pulling her toward the hallway.

"Not yet," Abe said. He nodded to Joey. "Bring 'em out the back and wait for me."

A cold look on his face, Joey pointed the sawed-off at my head. We walked up the hallway to the kitchen and out the back door. I kept my arm around Elizabeth. She was shaking. My mind was reeling.

A minute later, Abe came out, shaking his head at Joey. "Ya fuckin' goop. Waldman had two goddamn bucks on him." He shook two banknotes in Joey's face. "Two goddamn bucks on a five-hundred-dollar score." As he walked past us onto the lawn, he said, "Let's get outta here. I got one more thing for ya."

Joey pushed the barrel of the shotgun against my back. "Move."

We cut through the lawn of the house behind and turned right at the street. Elizabeth wrapped her arm around my waist and pulled me close. Firecrackers popped down the street, answered by others all around. It was easy to imagine the fusillades coming from guns and cannon.

"Where are we going, Abe?" I said.

"Just gotta go up here a minute. Then you can leave."

"Why'd you kill them?"

"Who?" He gestured back toward the house. "Whitey and his boy?"

"Yeah."

"You don't got respect, you got nothin'. We weren't gonna get nothin' else out of him anyway." He looked over his shoulder at me and laughed. "Plus, you're the craziest sonuvabitch I ever met. I wanna see what you do next."

"Were you working for the albino all along?"

"Workin' *with* him, you mean?"

"Sure."

"Yeah." He grinned at me. "Unless we was workin' with Gianolla. Or Adamo." He stopped and turned around. "See, what we do is work for ourselfs. Got to where we come from, right?"

"I suppose so."

He started walking again and turned down an alleyway. We followed, and Joey brought up the rear. Light leaked out from a few windows above us, casting a muddy glow over the alley. Two figures sat in the shadows about a hundred feet in, on the stoop of a rear entrance— Ray and Izzy.

They stood when we got close. "D'ja get it?" Izzy asked.

Abe shook his head.

"Why not?"

Abe hooked a thumb over his shoulder toward Joey. "Ask Quick Draw." He turned back to me. "You owe me. You know that, right?"

I nodded. It was hard to argue with him on that score.

"I'm gonna need the wheels greased now and then. You got connections, so that's your job now."

"We'll see. Depends on what you want."

He stared into my eyes for a moment before reaching inside my coat. He pulled out my gold lighter and flipped it up in the air. "Here's a start." He caught the lighter, tossed it into the air again, and nodded his brothers toward the alley's entrance.

Sobbing, Elizabeth threw her arms around me. I held her tightly. Over her shoulder, I watched the Bernsteins walk away. Joey and Ray fell in behind their oldest brother, but Izzy ran to him and leaped to try to catch the lighter on his next toss. Abe reached up and grabbed it just before it would have fallen into Izzy's hand.

"Hey!" Izzy shouted.

Startled, Elizabeth turned and looked at them. I kept my arms wrapped around her, and we watched the brothers walk down the alley. A tracer shot up from behind the building across the street, a white flare rising in a gentle arc.

Again, Abe flipped up the lighter. Izzy pushed him, just enough to get him off balance, and snatched it out of the air. The firework exploded in a blinding burst of white sparks.

The boys stopped and stared up at the embers showering down toward the street. When the last one burned out, Izzy began dancing around his brothers, cackling, flicking the lighter at them. Abe feinted at him and laughed when Izzy bolted away. The boys continued down the alley, their silhouettes getting smaller. Finally they turned the corner, and Abe led his brothers out of the dark alleyway and into the bright lights of Detroit.

Author's Note

Writing a historical novel requires walking a fine line—giving the history as you know it while dramatizing events that didn't really happen. So it is with this book. I spent a lot of time perusing the Detroit newspapers of the day and then imagining how those events might have played out with Will and Elizabeth in the mix.

Although most of it was fought in 1913, the Adamo-Gianolla war actually occurred, and the Gianollas were victorious. Along the way, Tony Gianolla was wounded, as was Ferdinand Palma, former Detroit Police detective-turned-banker-turned-interpreter at Vito Adamo's murder trial. The last mention I found of Palma during this time period came immediately after the Adamo brothers were shotgunned. He stated, from his hospital bed, his desire to get out of Detroit as quickly as possible. However, he must have reached an accommodation with the Gianollas, as he returned to Detroit and continued to run a very successful business.

Vito Adamo did turn himself in to the police and was exonerated for the killing of Carlo Callego, a move that may have signaled to the Gianollas once and for all that they had the upper hand. The murder of the Adamo brothers actually happened in November, during the day, just down the street from Vito's house. Inside, the police found a notepad with writing in Italian and crude pictures of stilettos plunging into men's backs. They thought this would give them insight into the gang war until they had it interpreted and discovered that Vito Adamo was writing a dime novel starring himself as the wrongly persecuted boy.

Strangest of all—for me, anyway—is that the Adamos and Gianollas did have groceries across the street from each other in Ford City, a village that has since been swallowed by the city of Wyandotte. Did the war start because of "a thumb on the meat scale or a price war on lettuce"? Probably not. More likely it was the old story of greed and ambition.

As for Detroit Electric, the Fords, F. W. Taylor, and the labor movement, most of the events depicted in this book did take place, though I have moved things around a bit to serve the story. Contrary to popular belief, the Model T was made in a variety of colors prior to Ford's "perfecting" of the assembly line, which required the change to black in order for the paint to dry in time.

A note for Detroiters who may think I'm geographically challenged—the Merrill Fountain originally stood at the corner of Woodward and Monroe, in front of the old Detroit Opera House. It was moved to Palmer Park in 1926.

Finally, a plea for the legacy of Edsel Ford. The man was smart. He was kind. He was generous. Above all, he was loyal, working his whole life for his father, who berated and humiliated him time and again until he put Edsel in an early grave from stomach cancer caused by ulcers. It's bad enough they named that car after him. (Although, to be fair, it was meant to be a tribute.)

Let's remember Edsel Ford as he was—a hell of a guy.

Acknowledgments

I'd like to thank my early readers, and they are many: my lovely wife, Shelly Johnson; my daughters Nicole, Grace, and Hannah; Yvonne Cooper; and a pack of voracious writers known as the West Michigan Writers Workshop, including, but not limited to, Steve Beckwith, Albert Bell, Patrick Cook, Greg Dunn, Vic Foerster, Jane Griffioen, Fred Johnson, Norma Lewis, Karen Lubbers, Roger Meyer, Paul Robinson, Dawn Schout, and Nathan TerMolen.

Once again, a shout-out to the amazing research facilities around the Detroit area, particularly the Benson Ford Research Center and its wonderful director, Judy Endelman, and the Detroit Public Library and its National Automotive History Collection. Thanks to Tony Barnes for help with the legal aspects of the story, to Yvonne Cooper and Emilie Savas for their medical knowledge, to Galen Handy for his assistance with Detroit Electric history, and to Jack Beatty for allowing me to ride in his beautifully restored 1916 Detroit Electric coupé and helping me in other ways.

Thanks to Cherry Weiner for gaining me the opportunity, and to Daniela Rapp for her patience, kindness, and encouragement while trying to wrench this book out of my mind.

Finally, I'd like to thank Richard Bak, a fine writer who gave me great insight into Detroit history and helped me appreciate Edsel Ford.